PAWFECT CHRISTMAS HEARTS

JOSIE RIVIERA

INTRODUCTION

To keep up on newly released ebooks, paperbacks, Large Print Paperbacks, audiobooks, as well as exclusive sales, sign up for Josie's Newsletter today.

As a thank you, I'll send you a Free PDF ... The Beauty Of ...

Josie's Newsletter

Did you know that according to a Yale University study, people who read books live longer?

5 STAR READER REVIEWS

"A nice combination of characters....Max, Sarah and also the message of Christmas. Loving nature, the environment was perfect with the birds and the others of the forest. Toss in a harmonica and a puppy....(who doesn't love a little puppy?) and the scene is set.

Truly a wonderful positive story for this upcoming season. Most highly recommended…" - Amazon Reviewer (*A Christmas Puppy To Cherish*)

InD'Tale Magazine Review:
Inspirational Romance
"If one is looking for a sweet, Christian story, Josie Riviera is a go-to. The sweet and innocent chemistry between the protagonists will make the reader smile. A feel-good story from beginning to end!"

"Josie has written another awesome book about owning a toy store, being a pediatrician, flying in an airplane, raising a son, and of course, falling in love. I recommend this and all of

Josie's books to everyone." - Amazon Reviewer *(Christmas in the Air)*

This book is dedicated to all my wonderful readers who have supported me every inch of the way.
THANK YOU!

CONTENTS

COCOA'S CHRISTMAS LOVE

PRAISE AND AWARDS

USA TODAY bestselling author

DEAR READER

Welcome to my "Puppies For Christmas" collection:
A Heartwarming Holiday Romance Series

Get ready to be transported to the coziest corners of small-town charm, where love blooms like winter flowers, and the magic of Christmas is accompanied by the pitter-patter of tiny paws. In the "Puppies for Christmas" series, enjoy a heartwarming journey filled with sweet, clean, inspirational, and wholesome romance that will leave you inspired and smiling.

Each book in this series is a delightful gift wrapped in the spirit of the season, tied with a bow of adorable puppies. These stories are more than holiday romances; they highlight the power of love, second chances, and the enduring warmth of small-town communities.

In *A Christmas Puppy To Cherish*, discover that love knows no boundaries, not even those of communication, as an open heart leads to a heartwarming connection.

Christmas in the Air takes you on a journey where secrets

shared on an airplane come to light under the twinkling holiday stars.

And in *Cocoa's Christmas Love*, the magic of the season is reignited through the gentle touch of a florist's Wishing Blooms, a rescued pup's unconditional love, and the transformative power of Christmas itself.

These are stories to savor by the fireplace, to read with a cup of hot cocoa in hand, and to share with loved ones. *The Puppies for Christmas* collection promises romance that will warm your heart, puppies that will melt it, and the kind of holiday cheer that leaves a lasting glow.

This collection contains 3 books. Available in ebook, paperback, and Large Print paperback.

Each book and audiobook also sold separately.

A Christmas Puppy To Cherish

You don't need ears to hear God's plan. All you need is an open heart...

Music of both birds and harmonicas fills Max's life, but it's the near-silent forest guide he meets in Cherish, SC, who captures his attention. Small and slim, pretty Sarah's smiles and graceful hands speak louder than her voice. In fact, she's so quiet, he's not sure he's made much of an impression. But with her, he can imagine making this temporary stopover into something permanent.

Sarah has found a comfortable niche in Cherish, working miracles with plants, arranging flowers for church, and taking in stray animals. In fact, her house is so full, she's not sure she can say yes to the Sheriff's plea to take in one more puppy for Christmas.

Max has definitely captured her interest, and he shares her love of nature. But maybe she should take in that puppy after all, because a ball of fur that needs her will fill the empty space in her heart when Max's research sends him off looking for bluer skies.

Christmas In The Air

What if you told your innermost secrets to a guy you assumed you'd never see again?

Penelope Reid, a single mother in her late 40s with a challenging twelve-year-old son, crosses paths with an intriguing stranger during a plane trip to Hilton Head Island. She pours out her life's ups and downs, unaware that the man, Jacob Williams, retains every detail.

Two months later, Jacob emerges as the town's new pediatrician, and secrets unravel. As their connection deepens, they exchange stories of their pasts, dreams, and ambitions. Penelope finds herself inspired by Jacob's selflessness and determination.

Their budding romance faces opposition from her critical son and a curious community. With Christmas approaching, her son yearns for a puppy, but can he handle the responsibility? Can Penelope juggle a new romance and an adorable puppy in her life?

Cocoa's Christmas Love

A florist's Wishing Blooms rekindles the faded Christmas spirit of a disillusioned hometown photographer, but can her cheer, a rescued pup, and the magic of the season revive his holiday hope and love?

Ivy Bennett's flower shop is the heart of Evergreen Valley, but a critical article threatens her success. Blake Shepherd, a disillusioned photographer, returns to his hometown with a newfound passion for capturing nature's beauty. When their paths cross at Ivy's Wishing Blooms ceremony, Blake's cynicism begins to melt.

As Ivy rescues an abandoned puppy named Cocoa, Blake joins the journey, rediscovering the joy of Christmas. Their connection deepens through playful puppy antics, enchanting Christmas markets, and Blake's captivating photos.

But a tempting job offer tests their bond. Can the magic of the season and Ivy's Wishing Blooms bring them back together for a picture-perfect Christmas and a guaranteed Happily-Ever-After?

JOSIE RIVIERA

PUPPIES
CHRISTMAS

A Christmas
PUPPY
TO Cherish

PRAISE AND AWARDS

USA TODAY bestselling author

Top 35 Amazon Bestseller Animal Fiction

CHAPTER 1

*M*axwell Archer gave up. The harmonica wasn't there.

He might as well walk the short distance from his rental home in Cherish, South Carolina, to Musically Yours, the local music store. The store was reputed to be the finest in town. Likewise, it was also the only music store in the small town.

Open suitcases lay on the floor in the compact, plain living room of his rental. Further cluttering the room was a confusion of chirping budgies, oversized birdcages, and a stack of research notes piled beside his computer. He definitely needed some air.

Momentarily diverted by Angel, a silvery green budgie who chattered, "God bless us, every one," over and over, Max shrugged on his olive-green twill jacket, uttered a brief good-bye, and headed out the door.

He'd recited numerous words to his parakeets. The key to teaching a parakeet to talk was repetition, but "God bless us, every one," was the only phrase Angel repeated. She was a rescue bird, and her previous owner had been an elderly woman who apparently had watched Charles Dickens's, *A Christmas Carol*, on television many times.

The other two parakeets—one timid, the other bolder—squawked, chirped, and carried on between themselves.

As Max strolled, a brisk December breeze invigorated him, and he paused to regard the poignantly familiar mom and pop shops. Whitney's, the ice cream store, and Big Brothers Big Sisters, where he'd spent many afternoons after school finishing his homework. The brick building looked the same.

At twelve years old, Max had delivered the *Sunday Sentinel* to all the businesses along Main Street, accompanied by a racing dog his foster family, the Monroes, had owned. He remembered that dog. He loved that dog. A Labrador husky named Tinsel.

He couldn't contain his smile as he reminisced.

The calendar showed December fifth, and downtown was in the process of being transformed into a Yuletide fairyland. Numerous workers scurried past him, draping tiny white lights on bushes and sprinkling artificial snow over miniature pine trees.

Through the years, he'd indulged in visions of settling here in Cherish. He had envisioned a prestigious house on the prosperous outskirts and living out his days wealthy and respected.

Three decades had passed, and he hadn't accumulated wealth in any sense of the word. In fact, his last year's research project had been stalled because of insufficient funding.

And respected? In academic circles, perhaps. He fingered the bow tie beneath his chin—his acknowledgement to the realm of academic nerds, in which he was a charter member.

In any event, his appointment to the ornithology department of a large university in Jacksonville, Florida, began January first.

As he stepped inside the music store, a slim woman with dark hair and striking green eyes greeted him.

"May I help you?" she asked.

He nodded toward the frosted-glass front window decorated with treble clef signs, animated polar bears, and a model train weaving around an ice-covered mountain scene. "Nice." He made a comical face. "The motifs enhance the window with a …"

She raised an eyebrow. "Festive touch?"

"Complete with tiny icicles." He moved inside, toward a shelf crammed with key holders and picked up a key holder shaped like an amplifier. Clever. However, he doubted he was allowed to hammer nails into his temporary rental house.

He sighed and surveyed the tidy store. "Do you sell harmonicas?" he asked.

"Yes. A wide assortment." The woman nodded toward a side wall. "Is this for a Christmas gift?"

"For myself. I lost my harmonica during my move." He rubbed his shoulders and unzipped his jacket. Though his rental was furnished, his limbs ached from lifting heavy bird cages and suitcases. He was an academic, not a body-builder.

In addition, his brain was flooded with information. He'd been embedded in research the entire morning when he should have been unpacking. The hours flew by whenever he examined data and he frequently lost track of time.

"Any particular brand or style?" she was asking.

"Fenders. Key of C."

"I'll show you our bestseller, which comes with a vented plastic case." She wended around numerous aisles, located a gold-edged case on a display shelf, and handed it to him.

"Here's our most popular model. A twenty-tone diatonic harmonica in the key of C."

"An exact replacement for the one I lost." He ran his fingers along the case. "Thanks."

A sudden, booming symphony burst through the speakers, and they both jumped.

"Sorry," the woman said. "The background music in the store constantly needs adjustment." With a self-conscious grin, she dashed to the counter and lowered the volume. "Beethoven will do that."

"Do what?"

"Startle customers with crashing chords." She darted him a sideways glance. "I haven't seen you before, by the way."

Well, that didn't take long, he thought. A stranger in a small town called for questions from the local shop owner.

"I lived here for a brief spell when I attended junior high school," he said. "I arrived yesterday after an almost three-decade absence."

She didn't press for additional information, and he didn't elaborate.

"Are you here permanently?" she asked.

"Only for December. Then I'm off to my dream job in Florida." Again, he massaged his nape. Was it from the move or stress? "My name is Max, by the way. Maxwell Archer."

"Hi, Max. I'm Dorothy Edwards. My husband, Ryan, and I own this store and we sell music, instruments, and fun novelties. We also offer lessons if you're ever interested."

"Which instruments?"

"Harp, voice, guitar and piano." She hailed an entering customer with a warm smile. "Joanna, are you here for your harp lesson with Ms. Emmanuelle?"

The little girl nodded.

"She's waiting in her studio."

8

"Thanks. Is the puppy here? Ms. Emmanuelle mentioned that he might be."

"He's in the back."

"Yay!" The girl's face brightened. "Sorry, I'm late." She clutched her music to her chest and hurried past them.

"Joanna attends Big Brothers Big Sisters," Dorothy said. "Are you familiar with the organization?"

"Yes."

Uncertain where the conversation might be leading, Max looked away. The last subject he cared to discuss was the Big Brothers program. He remembered it well. Fond memories surfaced. Some not so fond as well, but those weren't because of the excellent program.

"Scarlett, who is married to Joseph Slater, is heavily involved," Dorothy went on. "Emmanuelle is providing Joanna with free instruction and a harp. Joseph is a well-known worship singer and songwriter. He's also on our staff when he isn't touring."

"I've never heard of him," Max said.

"Do you listen to contemporary Christian music?"

"Never." Max dismissed her inquiry with a wave. "Does anyone teach harmonica? I play for fun, not professionally, but always appreciate any tips."

"Sorry, we don't. Try YouTube," she joked.

He had. He did. On a shoe-string academic budget, self-taught lessons suited Max perfectly. Learning had little to do with musicality, and more to do with determination, goal-setting, and an appreciation for music.

Dorothy set the harmonica on the counter. "What brings you here, Max?"

"I study budgies and how they mimic birdsongs and music." He smiled and handed her his credit card.

She rang up the order. "The two are related?"

9

"Absolutely. To quote a noted philosopher, 'birds vocalize conventional scales.'"

"Interesting."

Interesting? The fact was more than interesting.

"You studied birds in college?" she asked.

"Yes. I earned a master's degree from a New York City university affiliated with the Audubon Society."

"Is New York City home for you?"

"I don't have a permanent home. I drove down from New York to Cherish yesterday."

"A ten-hour trip," she commiserated. "My husband travels to Atlanta for opera rehearsals, and the four hours back and forth is exhausting."

"My trip was quite an adventure—to put it mildly, especially with three parakeets, all my possessions stuffed into two suitcases and a canvas backpack." He grimaced as he recalled the harrowing journey through the icy Virginia mountains.

"The birds stayed in their cages?"

"I can't imagine them flying around my van while I drive. I secured their cages with seat belts." Max leaned forward, warming to the conversation. "For safety reasons, I always remove the mirrors, bells, and swings, and placed their wooden perches close to the bottom of their cages. And I keep bottled water handy for refilling their cups."

"Good to know." Dorothy shot him a tongue-in-cheek smile. "Not that I ever plan on purchasing a pet. My brother, Nicholas, owns Molly Belle, an overgrown pup who gets into everything. That dog cured me of owning any animals."

Max chuckled. "In some respects, birds are easier than dogs."

"Nicholas is trying to find a home for a puppy that showed up at the sheriff's station a couple days ago. Are you interested?"

"What type of dog?"

"He's guessing a mixed breed—a toy poodle and Yorkshire Terrier."

"A Yorkipoo."

"Maybe. He's a real cutie, brown with silvery-white markings." She paused. "Wait. I'll be right back."

Dorothy emerged two minutes later clasping a puppy to her chest. She set him down and the puppy bound forward in little jumps, then stuck his nose under the counter. Furiously, he tugged on a pencil that had fallen.

"No, no. He loves to chew." At the sound of Dorothy's voice, the little ball of fur rushed headlong down an aisle, apparently unheeding of her calls. He turned a corner and almost lost his balance. Dorothy scooped him up and brought him over to Max. He licked Max's outstretched fingers as he petted him.

"He's a cute pup, isn't he?" Dorothy asked.

"He's also a bundle of charming, unrestrained energy."

"Any chance—"

"Sorry." Max shook his head. "I'm only in town for a month." Plus, he'd vowed never to own a dog again. He'd missed Tinsel too much after he'd been placed with another foster family.

Dorothy returned the puppy to the back room, then placed Max's harmonica and a complimentary candy cane in a bag. "I'm sorry it's such a short stay, but this town is welcoming, especially during the Christmas season."

Max expected he'd enjoy spending December in Cherish. The lease on his apartment in New York had ended, and he'd preferred to travel in early December rather than January.

"Are you a musician?" she asked, offering an irrepressible grin. "Naturally you are—considering you're in a music store purchasing a harmonica. Ryan and I are—"

"Concert artists."

She handed the bag to him. "I'm a pianist."

"And Ryan is an opera singer."

She tipped her head. "How did you know?"

"My friend Gerry Adams lives in Perrytown. He often shops in your store."

Unlike many of the undergraduate students Max taught his online Joy of Birdwatching class to, Gerry had been interested and engaged. Most of Max's students selected his course as an easy elective.

Not Gerry. In his fifties, he'd developed an increasing appreciation for Max's expertise that had led to a friendly rapport between the two men. Gerry had become a sort of guru, offering guidance and awareness on another subject that interested Max: music.

"I know him." A smile dawned on Dorothy's face. "Gerry sings in the choir at Memorial Street Church."

No comment on the church part, though Max had recognized the wooden sign mounted above the store's entrance.

Proverbs 19:21.

He once knew the proverb, but could no longer recall the words.

Dorothy cast her gaze heavenward. "'Many are the plans in a person's heart, but it is the Lord's purpose that prevails,'" she recited.

Max kept silent.

Memories of sitting in a stiff pew during Sunday services came back in a blink. He'd tried, but he'd never pleased God as a child. He never pleased God as an adult, either. Where was the path to peace God promised? It remained elusive.

The successes Max had achieved hadn't been enough. Thus, at the age of twenty-five, he'd given up on religion.

As far as his career, he sometimes wondered if he was on the right path. Was his research nothing more than a "fluffy" elective for uninterested college freshmen? Society seemed to think along those lines, and reports through the academic grapevine whispered that ornithology programs were soon to be scrapped.

Sure, Max was appreciated—which was the reason why he was in hamster-wheel performance mode—to continue proving himself to his colleagues.

"Gerry and I are in a band," he replied, when he realized Dorothy waited for him to say something. "We rehearse online."

"Online?" Her brow furrowed.

"You're a professional, so you expect frequent in-person rehearsals. But our band rehearses virtually every week. Technology is marvelous, isn't it?"

"Not as rewarding as live rehearsals, though."

Max had to agree. "There's a likelihood Gerry and I will perform this month, if we can find a venue."

"Inquire at The Garden Terrace restaurant. The owners book entertainment on Friday evenings. In addition, I'd be delighted to host you here at the store. Do you have any CDs for sale?"

"You're kidding, right?"

"What's the name of your band?"

"The Bearded Elves."

"Hmm. Neither of you sports a beard."

"We change our name with the season."

She grinned. "When February hits, you'll become …"

"The Bearded Valentines. But I won't be here in February. My work takes me all over the US, and I'm headed to Florida in January."

"Well, I look forward to hearing you perform this month."

"Thanks. Gerry encouraged me to rent a place in Cherish. He believes all this down-home goodness is beneficial for me."

"You're on a vacation the entire month?"

"I'm rarely on vacation."

"No wife or children?" Pointedly, she peered at his left hand.

"Neither. You're looking at a forty-year-old bachelor."

She granted a conspiratorial smile. "The right woman will come along and change your mind."

"I doubt it. Women can be … exasperating."

She chuckled. "Will you travel to New York for Christmas?"

"I'll spend Christmas day with Gerry, his wife, Melissa, and their newborn colicky son. They're first-time parents."

Dorothy rolled her eyes. "So I've heard."

Besides Gerry, there was no one else, Max thought. Unless Max's foster brother, John, who resided in a faraway Portuguese village, counted.

It didn't matter. The season had lost its meaning eons ago. December twenty-fifth was just another day that passed in the flicker of an eye.

Dorothy's fixed smile didn't vacillate. She seemed the sort who put immense emphasis on the holidays.

He shifted. "I'm grateful for the opportunity to hunker down with my research this month."

At Dorothy's quizzical glance, he added, "On birds."

"Along with performing a live gig or two."

"Gerry and I aren't expert musicians like you and your husband, or that Slater worship singer guy. Our specialty is performing at roadside diners for a free meal."

"I well remember those days." She shook her head. "Since you'll be working here for the month, do you need any assistance with your research?"

"Can you recommend someone who could go birding with me tomorrow morning? I'd appreciate a guide."

Dorothy studied him. "I picture you in a forest, some-where more suited to your rugged looks, rather than writing papers. You must spend a great deal of time outdoors."

"I try." He pushed a hand through his thick hair. When had he last gotten it cut? "The Carolinas have various bird species I'd like to listen to."

"Your parakeets will truly mimic other birds?"

"Optimistically, although I haven't had much luck with them imitating anything."

Except "*God bless us, every one.*"

"I know the ideal woman," Dorothy said.

"She likes nature?"

"Absolutely, and she's passionate about hiking." A gleam of mischief shone in Dorothy's eyes. "She works at Thumbs Up, a local florist, but might be off tomorrow. I'll text her."

"What's her name?"

"Sarah Hartman." Dorothy snatched a cell phone from beneath the counter. "She dropped out of college to care for her elderly aunt, then went on to pursue a degree in floral design."

"How old is she?"

"Sarah turned thirty last month. She's the type who juggles a half dozen projects, numerous details, and never gets frustrated. And …" Dorothy paused to accentuate the words. "Her flower arrangements are exquisite."

He'd never purchased store-bought flowers in his life. The most magnificent blossoms—miniature red roses, deep violets, and pale blue ivy—spilled alongside brooks or grew wild in a field.

A response flew across Dorothy's phone screen. "Sarah confirmed she's not working until tomorrow afternoon," Dorothy read. "She had plans but is happy to change them. What's your address, Max?"

"I rented a house a couple blocks from here. It's 8 Poplar Lane. Tell her I'll bring the hiking essentials."

Dorothy typed into her phone, then delivered the response. "She'll pick you up in the morning."

"A hiker and a florist is an attractive combination."

"Oh, and she's plenty more. Animals love her. The cat at the greenhouse that handles mice won't let anyone near her except Sarah. Likewise, dogs practically grovel at her feet." Dorothy glanced up. "Remember Molly Belle?"

"Your brother's unruly dog?"

Dorothy choked a giggle. "She adores everyone and is beyond energetic, although remarkably calm and obedient around Sarah."

"Does Sarah own any pets?"

"Are you giving away birds?"

"I'd never part with my parakeets. Angel is the oldest, and she's been with me for several years." He lifted a quizzical brow. "What about Sarah?"

"She owns a few animals."

"Is she married?" He didn't want an irate husband or boyfriend on his tail for going birdwatching with Sarah.

"She's coming off a sorry relationship, but you'll discover she's a stunner."

Another word for mantrap. He understood the type well after dating a flirtatious woman who'd been beautiful enough to be on the cover of *Vogue* but who abruptly ended their month of dating with a cursory text.

From that point forward, he'd avoided any romantic overtures from beautiful women. They were interested in a guy's money and power. As soon as they realized Max had neither, they hightailed it out of his life.

"You'll learn all about her tomorrow." Dorothy peered at the phone screen, grinned, then snapped it shut. "She drives a yellow pickup truck and said she'll see you at eight."

CHAPTER 2

The following day, Max rose before dawn to wash and dry the parakeets' food bowls and water bottles, then placed a slice of kiwi in their cages. Angel, a female, occupied her own cage, while the two males shared a cage.

"God bless us, every one," Angel chirped.

Max covered three sides of the wrought-iron cage and faced her on the open side. Over and over, he enunciated, "Angel. Angel. Angel."

"God bless us, every one," Angel repeated.

"You can say that entire sentence, but you can't pronounce your own name?" He threw his hands up and surveyed the other two parakeets. The blue-winged roommates perched on their respective swings, then burst into a flurry of activity for no apparent reason, effectively distracting Angel.

And thus, the lesson was over.

Max choked on a laugh. Some things never changed.

Regardless, he was in jovial spirits. Although his new bed was lumpy and the bedspread a musty chenille, he had slept well and left his window open a crack. The whisper of a floral-scented breeze had provided him with a comfortable, peaceful slumber.

He flicked a fatigued glance at his handwritten notes, twenty pages and counting, spread out on the computer desk. His suitcases still sat on the floor, waiting to be unpacked. He'd rummaged through them for a clean pair of jeans, a blue button-down shirt, boots, and his favorite bow tie.

A half hour after he'd showered and passed on shaving because he couldn't find his razor, he heard an engine and peered out the window.

A yellow pickup idled in the driveway. The truck boasted reindeer antlers attached to the windows and a red nose on the front grill.

The woman in the driver's seat caught his stare and waved, her smile bright and pleasant.

Sarah Hartman, he assumed. Punctual at eight o'clock in the morning.

Admirable. They were off to a promising start.

He had filled a thermos with fresh coffee and stuffed thermal cups, peanut-butter banana sandwiches, and his favorite brand of frosted sugar cookies in a bag. Hoisting a backpack over his shoulders, he headed out the door.

He opened the passenger door, smiling in at her. "Sarah, right?" he said. He put the food bag and his backpack in the back seat, then slid onto the passenger seat.

"Correct." She nodded to him. "And you're Max?"

"Indeed. Max Archer." He set his thermos in the truck's oversized cup holder. "And you're driving Rudolph."

She laughed, gentle and musical. "I love Christmas."

"Let me guess, you're a sentimental movie junkie too." He gestured to her glittery pine tree earrings and the white snowflake steering wheel cover.

"Sentimental movies are the best." She tilted her head, studying him with sea-green eyes. "You look exactly the way Dorothy described."

"Not a reindeer covered in snowflakes, I hope?"

She swallowed a chuckle. "No."

"How did Dorothy describe me?"

Sarah stared at his lips. "She said you had dark hair, silvery-gray eyes, wore a bow tie and would probably have a backpack."

"A battered and weathered one." He twisted and motioned to his backpack, its ripped seam fixed with duct tape. "Today, it's filled with necessities—bottles of water, a first-aid kit, binoculars, and my fully charged phone."

She nodded. "Sounds like you've got everything you need."

"Yes. I've brought my microphone and recorder too. To record birdsongs, I'll demonstrate the setup when we arrive at the mountain."

"Okay."

"Are you carrying a cellphone?" he asked.

"I always carry one for emergencies, but I also use my phone camera to take photos."

"Photos of wildlife?"

"Mostly deer, although I can never get closer than fifteen feet before they bolt."

"Deer aren't always the sweet, docile animals you may imagine. Be careful around them."

"I am."

Those green eyes fringed with thick russet lashes, and her creamy complexion, enhanced by light freckles across her nose, stopped him from responding with anything other than "Good."

She continued to watch him, and he returned her stare.

This beautiful, intelligent woman hadn't been scooped up by a guy?

Wearing a hooded red jacket, gloves, and brown hiking boots, she was small and slim. He estimated no taller than five feet. He found himself staring at her delicate lips before his gaze wandered down to the silver cross necklace around her slender neck.

Preoccupied with an attraction he hadn't expected, he picked up his thermos. "Another requirement for a morning outing is caffeine. Do you like black coffee?"

She nodded.

"Then we share commonalities—coffee and hiking. I also brought a package of cookies. They're store-bought because I'm not a baker. The cookies, not the coffee." He returned his thermos to the holder. "Juniper Mountain is our first stop."

"There's another?"

"Crandall's Mountain, depending on our time frame."

"Okay. My morning is free," she replied.

"Mine too."

With a quick bob of her head, she backed out of the driveway.

He stretched out his legs. "It will be good to go for a long hike. I arrived in town yesterday, driving down from New York. I'm here for the month, then heading for a job in Florida."

Another nod. She probably already knew that because of chatty Dorothy.

Because he liked to have music playing, he asked her if he could switch on the radio. She hesitated and then said yes, and he scanned the stations, on a quest for something other than a holiday tune. He settled on Jon Bon Jovi singing "Please Come Home For Christmas." Not typically merry, but more of an expressive classic.

Satisfied, Max drew out his cellphone. "Do you need directions to the mountain?"

She twisted. "Say that again?"

"Directions?" He spoke louder.

"No. I've hiked Juniper for years. It's part of the Carolina state park systems."

"I mapped the distance to Crandall's, because the mountains are within a few miles of each other."

Another glance. He repeated that Juniper and Crandall were near each other.

Each time he talked, she swiveled to look at him. At one point, he almost advised her to watch the road, not him.

He lowered the volume on the radio. Possibly, music distracted her when she drove.

"I brought a knapsack," she said after a few silent minutes. "It's on the back seat."

Don't turn around to show me, Max silently implored.

He didn't initiate any further dialogue, spending the time glancing sideways at her appealing profile.

After they arrived at Juniper Mountain and she parked, they got out of the truck and he poured two cups of coffee, handing her one. He grabbed a swallow, pleased the coffee was still hot, and scanned their surroundings.

Today might provide a breakthrough in his research, an ultimate realization of success. That is, if his parakeets cooperated and actually repeated the birdsongs.

He gazed at the gorgeous woman beside him, leaning against her truck, and smiled. Surely, Sarah would bring good fortune.

When they finished their coffees, they detoured to the visitor center and procured a map. Sarah lingered at a Christmas ornament display, sputtering in disbelief when the park ranger stated that the store was sold out of a particular ornament featuring a bear, hiker boots and the inscription, "Take a hike."

She pointed to an exhibit on the wall. "The ornament is hanging right there and will go perfect on my holiday tree."

"Those are display items only and can't be sold," the ranger responded. "More should arrive by the end of the month. Check back."

She stuffed her gloves in her pockets and tapped her fingers on the counter. "By then, Christmas will be over."

Eager to lighten the mood, Max steered her out the exit to a wooden bench. "Let's study the map. There are eleven trails." He beckoned her to sit and settled beside her, indicating a twisty pathway. "The Maple Tree route is strenuous with rocky terrain and unsuitable for beginners."

"Fortunately, I'm not a beginner," she replied matter-of-factly.

"Neither am I."

"Maple Tree isn't difficult, but I recommend …" She ran her finger along a trail marked Oak. "This one passes through Walnut Forest, down to the Nanchee River's edge, up through a meadow, and finishes on a grassy path leading back to the visitor center."

She peered at him for a deciding opinion.

Based on the fact she'd resided in Cherish for many years, Max readily approved.

With her so close, her scent reminded him of an elusive flowery fragrance, similar to the breeze floating through his window last night. Rosewood, perhaps. Peaceful and serene.

He liked that. He liked *her*.

Their gazes merged, and he couldn't stop staring. She was stunning—high cheekbones and a flawless complexion—the type of beauty that prompted people to gape.

"You're the expert in these parts, Sarah." Max thought he spoke, but he wasn't certain, because the world had become unfocused, and she was at the center. He moved his index finger alongside hers, along the map, a light brush of fingertips.

And the attraction. His heart did a backflip.

He forced himself to concentrate on the map and swallowed. Surely, she felt it too.

An easy smile worked its way across her features.

Was she interested in him?

With any luck, she was.

At the same instant his brain shouted no, no, no. He was here for research purposes, and Sarah Hartman was a romantic complication he could ill afford. He had enough conflicts in his life—a stressful job, and no relationship at all with religion. Her necklace signified she was a Christian, and before he knew it, she might be declaring, "'This is the day that the Lord has made.'"

He'd believed that psalm once upon a time. Not anymore.

He pulled his extra pair of binoculars from his backpack and handed them to her, then hung his own around his neck. Next, he retrieved his recording device, a pocket-sized digital recorder and the microphone.

She rose. He automatically stood too.

"Your gear is more sophisticated than I envisioned."

"After years of trial and error, I finally realized my equipment had to be top of the line." He plugged the module into a mini jack cable. "The shotgun microphone has a powering module containing a battery."

She gazed at him with wide eyes and a wider smile. "I'm impressed with you and your work, Max."

"I'm impressed by you too," he replied.

"I haven't done anything remarkable."

He pressed his fingers on her forearm, lightly, to make his point. "There aren't many women who'd change their plans to assist a newcomer in town."

"I'm always happy to help."

He told himself to finish readying the equipment rather than gaze at her lovely, upturned face. He covered the microphone with a wind sock. "This reduces the noise created by the wind."

She acknowledged his description with a nod.

He scanned the sky, checking the angle of the sun. The haze was beginning to clear, gray clouds giving way to shades of pink and lavender. "Sunny days are ideal, but overcast is also fine," he said.

In the wash of the morning light, her complexion glowed. "Birding is a first for me."

"I was under the impression you're an animal lover."

"I am. Usually, I bring my dogs here."

"How many?"

"I have two dogs."

He noted her smile. "Is something amusing, Sarah?"

"I was thinking you're remarkably efficient and obviously an expert in your profession. I admire a man who makes things look easy and effortless."

Her compliment caught him off balance. He uttered a heartfelt, "Birds are my life and my career."

A December breeze rustled the trees and blew her shiny hair across her face. He smoothed an auburn lock from her cheek, and she stepped back out of his range.

"In any case ..." He cleared his throat and passed her a protein bar.

"Is this lunch?"

"I packed sandwiches. This is a snack."

Before he could say anything else, she whispered a prayer, asking God to bless their food, Max's career, and the picturesque day.

Max scratched his neck. Nothing made him feel more like

a fraud than thanking an imagined God. For what? A protein bar? A clear day?

God had never granted any of Max's requests.

Nevertheless, he bent his head and studied the protein bar's wrapper while Sarah prayed.

After finishing with an amen, she said, "I love animals too," as if their conversation hadn't been stalled by prayer.

His response was a dull nod.

She nodded to the knapsack on her shoulders. "Are you interested in what's inside?"

He took a bite of the protein bar. "Sure."

"I have sunscreen and used tea bags."

At his questioning look, she clarified, "Tea bags are a natural alternative to commercial products and will ease the sting of bug bites. Or, for instance, if you walk into a poison ivy plant."

"A person doesn't walk into a poison ivy plant."

"Sure they do. At least, I have."

He grinned. "We're both protected and covered." He surveyed her hooded jacket and jeans. For a petite woman, her legs were long and shapely.

"A slight brush of poison ivy leaves on your skin is all it takes for a rash," she said.

"I'll protect you."

She wrinkled her nose. "From poison ivy?"

"From anything." Protectiveness for her stirred inside him, an unforeseen response. He'd blurted the words aloud before forming the thought in his mind.

Her dubious gaze leveled on him.

"You don't believe me?" he asked.

"We hardly know each other, and I certainly don't need protecting. In addition, I packed bear repellent."

"I doubt we'll come across any bears."

"Let's hope not, but just in case." She withdrew a soup can

from her knapsack and shook it. "It's full of pebbles and makes a handy noisemaker."

"A bear weighs a lot more than we do, and we can't outrun one. Bear that in mind." He chuckled. "Pun intended."

The joke seemed to slide past her. "I've read about bear encounters," she answered. "There are certain rules to remember, such as to speak calmly, not make direct eye contact, and never run."

"If your handy deterrent doesn't scare away a bear, the loud noise will no doubt encourage any birds in the area to take flight."

"That's not a good thing if you're trying to record bird-songs," she replied with a grin.

They burst out laughing, then started down a gravel trail.

He stood on the forest's edge and watched for motion. "Look. Listen. There's a golden-winged warbler in the trees." He raised his binoculars and encouraged Sarah to do the same.

She regarded him blankly.

He held up his microphone and began recording. "The warbler has suffered the steepest decline of any songbird."

"Why?"

"Loss of habitat for breeding."

A sharp *chip* and a melodic *warble* diverted him. He signaled toward a metal-gray and yellow bird hopping between bushes in a cluster of thick ferns.

"You're hearing an adult male Canada warbler," he said.

"Oh."

Oh? *Oh?*

"Some people pish to encourage birdsong." He imitated the sound. "I don't. I've found birds will come out no matter what and I wait for their natural behavior."

As they continued along the path, he was absorbed in recording and figuring out what birds he heard, and Sarah offered no help in identifying any of them. Every few minutes, the hushed air was fragmented by a high-pitched cry, and Max stopped to record.

Well into their walk, an outbreak of wings sounded louder than the crunch of leaves beneath their feet. Before he raised his binoculars, a bird flew out of range and into the brush. Max skimmed the shorter branches to find the bird, disregarding a group of energetic high school students breezing by with their teacher guide.

A second stir of motion in his peripheral vision had Max rushing to record.

Each clue necessitated an intermission, an awaiting, a heeding.

The appeal of ornithology. Search and find.

Max had become engrossed in the study of birds when Mr. Lenny, a foster parent, had brought him birding. He was a kind man with wavy gray hair and tortoise-rimmed eyeglasses. He was the only adult who'd shown a true interest in Max, and they started a tradition of birding every Saturday morning. For a child with precious few traditions, the man was a father figure. Lenny had made a lasting impression, inspiring a young boy who had no real home.

A woodpecker ripping through the brush, accompanied by three cardinals singing *cheer, cheer, cheer,* snapped Max out of his reminiscing. He spun and monitored their calls, tip-toeing through the undergrowth, peering above and below.

Sarah, on the other hand, seemed anxious to move on. She pointed her binoculars skyward and rarely spoke.

That is until they reached the Nanchee River's edge.

"An ideal spot for a picnic." Max nodded to the waterfall beyond and fished in his bag for sandwiches.

The weather had changed, and clouds covered the sky.

"I'll keep my cellphone handy," Sarah remarked, "in case I see a deer."

A crash came from somewhere he couldn't pinpoint. Max whirled around, searching for the source, and glimpsed a large animal emerging from the river.

"I can finally take a close-up photo of a deer," Sarah declared. She stepped toward the river, but slipped on a patch of wet grass and clung to his hand.

It wasn't a deer, Max thought. A deer would shy away.

It was a bear. A wandering yearling male by Max's estimate.

The bear started for them on all fours.

Sarah's breath burst—an inhale, an exhale.

Seconds froze.

"Where's your deterrent?" Max abandoned his equipment and drew her close. She grabbed her knapsack and pulled out the soup can.

The bear came up on hind legs, almost eye to eye with them, and with one hand, Max flung his peanut butter sandwiches, the cookies, and the protein bars as far as he could. Sarah shook the can, yelled, and tossed it near the bear.

The bear backed away, then turned and ran.

Sarah licked her trembling lips, her eyes damp. "Thank you, God."

Max kept his arm around her tight shoulders and provided a reassuring squeeze. His heartbeat raced, his mouth dry. "We're safe."

"These things happen in books and movies. Not to real people." She attempted a feeble stab at humor.

Despite her ashen complexion, he was impressed she'd lost none of her composure and had reacted quickly. Still, her rounded green eyes shone luminous beneath her russet, delicate eyebrows.

Max didn't have a boatload of experience with women, but he'd lived with enough foster sisters to know when a female was on the brink of tears. Sarah bravely tried to hold them at bay, blinking ferociously.

He wavered between his male instinct to sidestep any prospect of a sobbing woman—or the reasonable desire to offer support.

Her lips parted, her smile sluggish. "Countless questions are running through my mind," she said quietly.

"Let's begin with the most important. Are you okay?"

"Yes." He heard the quiver in her tone. "We've established we're both fine."

He lifted her chin. "Let's celebrate how grateful we are."

"By prayer?"

"A consideration for a Christian, I assume, but I thought of something more like this." He brought her closer. Unhurried, he kissed her.

Her expressive eyes gazed into his. When she veered, his hands tightened, and his mouth moved more firmly.

"Max."

"Hmm?" he murmured.

The air was hushed, the only sound the babbling river.

She slid her fingers up the collar of his jacket. "Nothing." Hesitant, she returned his kiss.

Max got so caught up in kissing Sarah, a moment went by before boisterous talking penetrated his brain. He lifted his head and glimpsed the same high schoolers from earlier.

With a self-conscious shift, Sarah pulled from his grasp. "I see we have company," she said.

"Right." *And at a most inopportune moment.*

He darted a glance at his watch, retrieved his equipment, and pushed out a sigh. "I suppose we should head back."

As they retraced their steps, Sarah glanced up at him. "Max, I can't believe …"

"I wanted to kiss you as soon as I saw you this morning," he said.

She bit her lip. "Did we do everything right?"

"The kiss was perfect."

A rosy blush tinted her cheeks. "I'm referring to the bear."

He chuckled. "All I remember is throwing food at him."

"Thank you for protecting me."

He hadn't, really. If anything, *she* had protected *him*, protected them *both*, with her bear deterrent.

"Thank *you*." He reached for her hand, soft and delicate, and a rush of emotion made him smile.

In silence, they returned to her truck.

Still dazed by the whirl of emotions between their fear and the resulting kiss, they spoke little on the drive back to Cherish. Max didn't bring up hiking Crandall's Mountain, and he kept the radio off.

When she pulled into the driveway of his home, he didn't encourage her to join him birding again. Nor did he invite her inside—something he had considered along the entire route.

"The sandwiches are gone," he said. "Sorry. No lunch."

"We could have been lunch for the bear."

"Thankfully, we weren't. Besides, he was young and not very aggressive."

"Even when he charged straight for us?"

"He's undoubtedly partying right now, devouring cookies and sandwiches and protein bars with his friends." Max tried a laugh, then sobered. "Sorry you didn't get a picture of a deer."

"I took a rapid sequence of photos with my cellphone."

"Did they come out?"

"I haven't had the opportunity to check yet."

"You had time. I knew we were safe all along," Max declared.

"Uh, huh." She became absorbed in tracing the pattern of

snowflakes on her steering wheel. "As long as the bear didn't swat the ground with his front paw."

"Or snort," Max countered.

"Or lunge."

He answered with a smile. She was lovely, amiable, and attractive, and his instinctive reaction was to lean over and kiss her again.

However, other instincts warned to keep his distance. A short-term romance didn't benefit anyone, and Sarah deserved more. With his relentless studies, travel, and limited financial resources, he had little to offer her.

He told himself he was wed to his profession, as a girlfriend from long ago had once accused him.

The mood in the truck became quieter.

Let's face it, he reasoned. Sarah wasn't excited about his profession, anyway. She'd responded to his interest with little more than a few nods. Birding was his passion, and he wanted someone to share his enthusiasm.

Satisfied with his decision, he grabbed his backpack and opened the passenger door. "Thanks for the ride and for being my guide. Have a marvelous afternoon."

Their experience would be remembered as a memorable exploration. A couple hikers who scored a birding, or rather, a bear adventure.

And their kiss? Yes, there was that. Delightful, tender, and exquisite.

Like Sarah.

*a*fter dropping Max off, Sarah stopped by her home to tend to her animals before continuing on to Thumbs Up, the nursery/garden center where she worked.

To her intense relief, the garden center's parking lot was nearly empty. Many customers, particularly older gardeners, preferred to shop for plants in the morning. She blew out a thankful breath. She needed the quiet to revisit her moments with Max.

She'd admired his home when she drove up to the neat and tidy rental, encouraged that he didn't have a bird perched on his shoulder as she'd half imagined.

Dorothy had texted Sarah the previous evening, detailing Max's plans. He didn't intend to stay in Cherish forever—only a month to explore the area for information supporting his research.

December is an unusual month for research, Sarah had texted, *considering the holidays.*

Apparently, any close family is nonexistent, Dorothy replied. *Plus, I asked if he was married and he isn't.*

Sarah could scarcely believe that the brilliant, handsome

man, his muscular physique filling out his twill jacket, was so approachable.

On closer range, his eyes, brimming with kindness, shone light silver beneath dark, straight eyebrows. His hair was thick and longish, and she was tempted to brush back the waves that constantly fell across his forehead.

Of course, she didn't. They hardly knew each other.

Besides his intellect (she'd looked up his profile on an ornithology university website), he was amicable, humorous and thoughtful. She made the blunder of staring at him often to hear his words more clearly, and her gaze had been drawn to his firm mouth.

Then the kiss had happened.

Oh my, such a kiss! At first, she'd been tentative and self-conscious at their closeness. His mouth had sought hers with cool expertise, then persistence, then increasing claim. Her heart had responded in rapid, thudding beats.

If the teenagers hadn't entered the scene, would she still be kissing him?

Her cheeks warmed. They must have seen her and Max together.

Almost unwillingly, Max had lifted his head to end the kiss.

A kiss she never should have allowed. What an imprudent, impulsive thing for her to do—in the middle of a public state park.

Yet, his lips had been persuasive and tender.

A part of her insisted she should have ended the kiss first. The other part maintained that she and Max had shared a distressing incident. Subsequently, their mutual fright had drawn them closer.

When the bear came upon them, Max had held her. He'd kept his promise, prepared to protect her.

Once they had begun the hike, Max had been fixated on

his work. For her, the birdcalls that excited him had been faint and distant.

Why?

Why couldn't she hear the birds Max was obviously eager to record? He was so in tune with them.

Lately, she'd found that if she didn't watch people's lips while they spoke, she sometimes missed what they said.

Regardless, she appreciated Max's spontaneity, fairly bouncing on his toes as he dashed through the brush. She was accustomed to sitting on the sidelines. Her loud, raucous, older brothers had consistently stolen the spotlight, and her parents often overlooked her.

She fingered the silver cross on her neck.

Max gave the impression of being uncomfortable when she offered a prayer before eating, whereas she was a Christian and faith was important to her. By his quick exit when she'd taken him home, he obviously wasn't interested in her, anyway.

As she always did in moments of confusion, she turned to God to set her course.

The psalmist in Proverbs 4:23 had written, "Above all else, guard your heart, for everything you do flows from it."

She'd had her heart broken by a budding architect. Their relationship had ended quickly, although she'd wept for days. Since then, her emotions were precarious at best.

Nonetheless, she'd vowed to reset her path after that painful experience. Her heart wouldn't be broken a second time. Not even by Max.

Her eyes squeezed shut, and she uttered a prayer. "God, set me free from my reservations and uncertainty. Please show me the way." She always felt better after praying. Her God was a big God, bigger than her hurts and disappointments.

Taking an easy breath, she exited her truck and pushed

opened the nursery's heavy steel doors.

"Good afternoon, Sarah." Bonnie Ellerman, a coworker, tapped Sarah on the shoulder. "You're fifteen minutes early. I'm on register today, and you're working the floor. The amaryllis flowers are thriving, and timing the bulbs to bloom for Christmas worked like a charm. No wonder the garden center relies on your expertise. You have a magical green thumb."

"Hardly magical." Sarah tied a blue employee apron around her waist. "If the rest period for the amaryllis begins in late summer, the bulbs will respond. Customers appreciate the extensive blooms, thus it's worth all the planning."

Sarah picked up a warehouse broom to sweep soil off the concrete floor. She tackled the chores she disliked first, before arranging the pink, white, and red poinsettia plants for Memorial Street Church.

An unexpected thickness formed in her throat as she gazed at the tastefully decorated Christmas trees lining an entire side wall. The prospect of returning home to spend another night by herself during the Christmas season … during any season … Well, she yearned for more.

To cheer herself up, she organized a Christmas gift list in her mind. Uncle Gerry, her great-uncle in Perrytown, played guitar. Accordingly, a gift from Musically Yours would be ideal.

An insistent voice in Sarah's ear interrupted her thoughts as Dorothy Edwards came into view.

"Hello," Dorothy said. "I stopped by to purchase a pink poinsettia plant for Musically Yours." Dorothy grinned mischievously, and Sarah knew at once that Dorothy had come into the nursery for more than a poinsettia.

"Who's minding your music store?" Sarah asked with a chuckle.

"Emmanuelle." Dorothy changed the poinsettia from one

arm to the other. "So, how was your hike together?"

Sarah quirked an eyebrow. "With …"

"Maxwell Archer."

"Enjoyable."

"That's it?"

"That's it." A wry smile touched Sarah's lips as she navigated the subject back to Dorothy. "Is Ryan in Atlanta?"

"He's preparing for a classical concert there. He's the lead in a chamber choir and singing a sacred text in Latin. The concert will be live-streamed next weekend." Dorothy paused. "You know I love gushing about my husband's accomplishments, but now I want to find out about your date details."

"Hiking a mountain is hardly a date." Sarah attempted to compose her features and disguise her attraction to Max. He was so different from the architect she'd dated, who'd had arrogant qualities and a slight build. Max, on the other hand, exuded strong masculinity. He was also smart, passionate about his work and gentlemanly.

And the kiss.

The sigh-worthy kiss.

Animated chatter from customers swirled nearer, blending with the clink of a clay pot as Bonnie handed Sarah a paperwhite narcissus and requested a price check.

Dorothy trailed Sarah to the stand of blossoming paperwhites. "What are your thoughts regarding Max?"

Sarah focused on Dorothy's mouth in order to lip-read.

She'd been ignoring the polite remarks from friends about having her hearing checked. A woman of thirty was *not* hard of hearing. For the time being, she'd employ all the tools at her disposal, and one was lipreading.

"He seems nice," she replied.

"Nice. Nice?' Dorothy flung a hand to her hip. "What sort of description is *nice* for a handsome, well-versed man?"

"He's well-versed on birds." Sarah gave Dorothy a good-natured shove. "Period."

Well, no, that should probably be a comma. He was also well-versed on kindness. Similarly, he's sweet and understanding, with a romantic nature she hadn't anticipated.

"I can tell by your reddened cheeks there's more to the story." Dorothy smothered a laugh. "You're attracted to him."

"He's polite and humorous." Sarah's gaze veered to Bonnie, who was frantically signaling another employee over to the narcissus plants.

Sarah's attention swung back to Dorothy.

"Am I right?" Dorothy asked, grinning.

"Maybe."

"I knew it!" Dorothy's expression went from happy to happier.

"My reactions are mixed. He's brilliant, yes—"

"Plus, he's an animal lover, just like you."

"Let's not forget he's taking a position at a Florida university in January."

"Yes, yes." Dorothy moved to the side to allow the employee to pass. "You actually start working here at one, right?"

Sarah nodded.

"So, we have a couple more minutes. Have you considered adopting the adorable dog that Nicholas and the Cherish sheriff department are caring for? An officer is complaining they are on call 24/7. The dog has a tremendous appetite and eats a lot of puppy chow."

"Have they named him yet?"

"They're waiting for the right person to adopt him. We all agree you are the perfect new owner."

"Who are we?"

"Me, Nicholas, and Emmanuelle."

"I adopted two abandoned dogs, two cats, a goldfish and a

hamster," Sarah said. "Plus, my house is a one-story bungalow."

"You'll adore him when you see him."

"I'm touched, and would love to help ... but I can't."

Dorothy sighed. "Notify Nicholas if you change your mind. Deal?"

"Deal."

"One more thing." Dorothy glanced at her watch at the same time Sarah did.

"Go on."

Dorothy pulled in a breath. "One of the reasons Max decided to stay in Cherish this month is because he's friends with Gerry."

Sarah stumbled back a step. "My great-uncle Gerry?"

"The men play in a band together. Max told me when he was in my store yesterday to buy a harmonica."

"Uncle Gerry never discussed Max before. How long have they been friends?"

Dorothy winked. "Ask Max."

With that, Dorothy waltzed to the cash register with her blooming pink poinsettia.

Sarah was left staring at the paperwhite in her hand, trying to remember Bonnie's request. Was the flower supposed to be restocked or bedecked with a ribbon?

No, no. A price check. But another worker had taken care of it.

Sarah stifled a quiet moan. Her focus was fractured. And all because of a man named Maxwell Archer. A sensitive, fascinating and accomplished man.

And then another thought formed.

Perhaps, just perhaps, she could enlist her great-uncle's help to meet Max again.

With a radiant smile and a lively step, Sarah clocked into work at exactly one o'clock.

CHAPTER 4

A week later, Max strode into his living room and ducked as Angel flew by. He allowed the parakeets to fly at least an hour a day and kept the doors and windows closed for their safety. The routine kept them healthy and happy because they needed to explore. He'd limited their time the first week, in order for them to get used to the unfamiliar environment of the rental.

For now, the roommates were back in their cages, which left only Angel perching on a curtain rod. He'd trained the budgies to return to their cages, but Angel sometimes preferred not to.

Earlier, Max had compiled his notes and organized the pages in a computer file. He'd worked eighteen-hour days all week, although emailing his file to the ornithology department in Florida hadn't produced the desired accolades. The university had demanded additional bird recordings—particularly of his budgies repeating the birdsongs.

Except his birds hadn't responded or repeated any of the songs.

After Max received the university's reply, he didn't trust

himself to respond. His ideal job. How could the department question him?

Perhaps he was in the wrong profession after all. Published studies demanded reliable facts, and budgies, as well as birds in general, were unpredictable.

Budgies mimicked humans and the sounds of their mates. However, their response to his recordings had brought distress and frustration. They peered around, attempting to establish where the birdsongs came from. When they failed to locate their perceived new friends whom they suspected were close by, they became anxious.

Max contemplated his options.

He wouldn't return to New York City, and the Florida university position didn't seem as appealing anymore, considering the head of the ornithology group wanted Max to work round the clock for little pay.

At any rate, another hike to Juniper Mountain was in Max's forecast. He considered contacting Sarah and asking her to accompany him.

During the past seven days, he'd given the morning they'd spent together deeper consideration. He remembered her face going pale when the bear charged. He also recalled how sweet she was, and how fearless. He admired her beauty, but was more intrigued by her modest and steady presence. She'd bravely held back frightened tears after scaring off the bear.

Society sometimes displayed a cynical indifference to the wonders of nature, but Sarah appreciated the unspoiled forest. He had recognized the romantic interest whenever she gazed at him, and it melted him with surprising tenderness as he recalled their affectionate kiss.

And how did he repay her kindness after she'd given up her morning to hike with him?

Why, he'd departed with a quick, "Thanks for the ride and for being my guide. Have a marvelous afternoon."

Who said such words after sharing a morning with a beautiful woman?

Apparently, he did.

He rubbed a hand over his face. After their tender kiss, what must she think of him? Their hours shouldn't have ended with such finality. He blamed his cool farewell on the fact that he was weary after the lengthy drive, his move, and endless unpacking.

Nevertheless, he needed to rectify any misunderstanding because she fascinated him.

But how?

He lifted a cup of wassail to his lips and swallowed, and a familiar comfort surged through him. Years earlier, Mr. Lenny's wife, Amanda, had mixed homemade wassail using ingredients on hand—apple, orange, and cranberry juice.

Ultimately, Max had come to realize those long-ago times of assembling in Lenny's cheery kitchen drinking wassail with him, his wife, and their son, John, had resulted in Max's fantasy of heart-warming holidays surrounded by loved ones.

That fantasy never materialized. Still, he felt a sense of allegiance and gratitude to Lenny that exceeded every other emotion. Which was why, he supposed, he drank wassail.

A few short months after Max's placement with Lenny and his family, Max had been returned to his birth mother's care until she was hospitalized with liver disease. By then, the water and electricity in their apartment had been shut off. He never learned what happened to his father, who had never been a part of Max's life.

A loud knock on the front door sounded, and Gerry's voice bellowed, "Anyone home?"

"Just me and a bird flying around the living room."

A snicker. "You've been around birds so long you learned to fly?"

"Hang on while I catch Angel."

"Will it take a while?"

"Anywhere from five minutes to an hour, depending on if she cooperates."

A loud guffaw. "The weather is comfortable and I'll wait on the porch. I brought you a housewarming gift. A bottle of blackberry brandy."

"Really? I don't normally drink brandy … but thanks."

From experience, Max knew coaxing Angel to her cage was no easy task. Parakeets were flock animals, and keenly aware of a person's body language. They were, after all, low man on the food chain and had learned to be cautious.

Max chatted quietly and walked nonchalantly, coaxing her down from the curtain rod. After he picked her up, he held his hand lightly over her wings and carried her to her cage.

A half hour later, he and Gerry sat in Max's tiny kitchen drinking cups of wassail. Gerry poured a shot of blackberry brandy into his cup, claiming he needed something to calm his nerves, being a spanking new father and all.

Max declined the brandy. He wanted to keep his wits about him while he engaged with the birds. Tonight, he planned on playing the harmonica—perhaps a scale followed by a soulful ballade. Maybe they would mimic the musical sounds.

He leaned back in his stool as Gerry brought him up to date on living with a newborn and how he embraced father-hood in his fifties. Then Gerry poured himself another shot.

Max's initial thought upon seeing his friend in person for the first time in years was that Gerry's hair had turned a bushy stark-white—whiter than it appeared on screen—framing a robust, pink-cheeked face. His glacial-blue eyes were piercing, yet friendly. His once crusty exterior had softened.

By day, Gerry worked in a pet store in Perrytown. By night, his passion was music. Over the course of their Internet jam sessions, Max discovered that Gerry had a powerful bass voice, and his guitar skills were disciplined and focused.

Gerry raised his cup for a toast. "To the Bearded Elves. Forever may we sing."

"Forever may we sing … anywhere?" Max clinked cups.

"An opportunity will present itself."

"Dorothy Edwards suggested The Garden Terrace."

"We'll check it out." Gerry ran his tongue over his lips. "Hey, this is tasty wassail for a bachelor."

"Wassail is my holiday indulgence. I learned how to make it from my foster mother and father."

Max tapped a relaxed fist against his heart. "They were the epitome of kindness."

"I've known you many years, my bird singing comrade. You don't celebrate Christmas. Wassail is Christmas."

Amused, Max drank a final gulp. He too appreciated the irony of savoring wassail, rather than, say, a cold beer. Avoiding answering Gerry, he looked into the living room. The parakeets were busy quibbling with their toys and preening.

Gerry took the hint. "Any luck with the birds repeating your recorded songs?" he asked.

"None, even though I play different tracks for them every day."

"Maybe your birds would respond well if there was another animal around. I hear there is an adorable puppy in need of a home."

"A puppy galloping through my legs every morning, and keeping me up half the night?" Max shook his head. "This house is a rental, and a puppy is known to chew everything in sight. I already bumped up the place when I lugged my suitcases inside."

"My wife and I have discussed pet ownership, but newbie parenting is enough for now." Gerry commiserated with a nod, then gestured to the parakeets. "What do they mimic?"

Max shrugged. "Nothing."

As if on cue, Angel blurted loud and clear, "God bless us, every one."

Gerry swiveled on his stool. "Is that your bird?"

"You're hearing Angel's favorite, and only, sentence."

"Ho, ho, ho. You own a budgie who celebrates the holidays." Gerry chuckled. "Have you seen the Cherish town square transformation?"

"Too busy."

"Those little wooden houses lined up around the ten-foot Christmas tree resemble a Norman Rockwell village when lit at night. There's also a craft fair selling local wares. My wife prefers cranberry-scented candles and pine-smelling soaps."

"It's going to be challenging to shop with a newborn."

Gerry linked his hands behind his head. "Barring the matter that neither of us has slept more than three hours since little Freddie's birth, my answer is yes, it will be. Are you up for any babysitting?"

"Perhaps when he's a little older. He cries a lot?"

"He's colicky." Gerry stared into his cup, then at Max. "I thought you always wanted children."

"Someday. In the meantime, call me when he turns five."

As Gerry rambled about the egalitarian share of chores in his marriage, Max's thoughts gravitated to his research. Should he expand his study to include cardinals? A recent article by a colleague had supported a claim to include natural-history habitats, and cardinals were the state bird in neighboring North Carolina. Perhaps the Jacksonville university would be more attentive if Max's study included additional birds.

He massaged his nape. Shouldn't the ache be gone? He'd moved in a while ago.

Stress, a little voice nudged.

No. An adamant no. Stress is a motivator.

In the meantime, didn't the department head realize Max couldn't *force* his budges to talk?

"Seen the live reindeer at the children's petting zoo?" Gerry asked.

Max's musings gravitated to Sarah. She loved taking photos of deer.

Aware his friend regarded him, Max shook his head. "No time." With a weary sigh, Max picked up their cups and rinsed them in the sink. Then he led Gerry into the living room. "I'll let the birds fly around if that's okay."

"Suits me. I let my cat roam throughout my house."

"Just don't bring your cat to my house when the birds are out."

"You'll meet my new baby before you ever see my cat. I can bring little Freddie over anytime."

"Looking forward to it," Max murmured.

At the far end of the room, beyond a scarred wooden coffee table, stood a cushioned sofa and a side chair. Two large cages were hung at chest level on the opposite wall, situated near the window so the birds could see outside.

Gerry pushed his hands into his jean pockets. "I identified the recordings you sent—a golden-winged warbler and a Canada warbler."

"You're correct. You were always a top-notch student."

Gerry knew his birds. He could have found the information using birding apps, but a conscientious and deliberate Gerry most likely had done his research.

"All the birds were recorded at Juniper Mountain?" he asked.

"Yes. And the setting is superb." With an airy wave of his hand, Max gestured toward the threadbare sofa for his buddy to get comfortable, then opened the doors to the bird cages. "I enlisted the help of a local guide."

"Who?" Gerry took a seat, shooing away a bird that quickly decided to roost there. "A park ranger?"

"A woman named Sarah Hartman. She lives in Cherish and—"

"Sarah Hartman? Sarah is my great-niece."

Max stared in surprise. "You never mentioned that."

"Why would I? Our conversations center on birds and music. So, what's the consensus?" He sounded so matter-of-fact that Max grinned.

"About Sarah?"

"Who else?"

"She's lovely. Absolutely lovely." *Okay, yes, that was an understatement.* His vision of her lustrous hair cascading over her shoulders, the red highlights glistening in the sun, served as a reminder of her beauty. "And plucky. We had a close encounter with a bear and she was magnificent."

"A real live bear?"

"Big and breathing, but Sarah's quick thinking came to our rescue. She's marvelous under pressure."

"Sounds like her. She's a wunderkind with animals."

"I've heard."

Gerry leaned in. "Can I tell you something about her I've noticed lately?"

"Should you betray her confidence?"

"It's more of a speculation shared by me and a number of her friends. We believe she has a hearing deficiency she's denying."

Thoughtfully, Max nodded. That would explain her

occasional hesitancy to speak and the way she kept looking at him when she was driving, as if she had trouble hearing him.

He felt a clutching in his heart. He, more than anyone, should understand. Not exactly the same, but Mr. Lenny had worn a hearing aid, saying it helped him listen and communicate—mainly in noisy situations.

Max waited while Gerry went into the kitchen and refilled a fresh cup—all brandy and no wassail.

When he returned, he stopped short and regarded Max for a suspiciously long time. "Well?" he prodded.

"Well, what?"

Gerry took a quick swallow of brandy. "Did you and my divine niece get along?"

Max cleared his throat. "Of course." He turned, a clear sign he wasn't willing to make any small talk when it came to his feelings toward Sarah. Some subjects were personal, and she was special.

"Alrighty then." Gerry's laughter rippled through the room. "Next topic. Church."

"Let's close that topic before you begin." Max flipped open his computer, scanning the files, calculating how successfully he could change the church subject without Gerry asking a thousand questions.

"Let me reword. Not church, necessarily, but the Cherish church *choir*." Gerry hesitated for emphasis, his tone growing insistent as he touched on the real issue. "A strong baritone voice is needed for our cantata. The choir is performing at the six o'clock service on Christmas Eve."

"If you're hinting for me to join, I haven't set foot in a church in years."

He'd attended as a child, since Mr. Lenny had served at the local church as an associate pastor, but Max had gotten away from anything religious once he heard of Mr. Lenny's death. None of his other foster families, nor his birth mother, had favored religion.

"Come once to rehearsal, Max, and see if you're a decent fit. I think you are, though it's your call. The choir members are good people and—"

"No one's refuting their goodness."

"Then help us out." Gerry extended a sheepish smile.

"Isn't Ryan Edwards your main singer?"

"Normally, although he's conducting the choir on Christmas Eve. And right now, he's in Atlanta rehearsing. Another member is stepping in for the next couple of weeks."

Max hesitated, ready to cut off any additional arguments from Gerry with a shake of his head.

"You're here for Christmas, correct?" Gerry asked. "And staying through New Year's."

"I am. However—"

"You'll recognize the traditional hymns: 'Away in a Manger,' etc. You'll catch on quick. You're a fine note-reader."

Max's eyebrows furrowed. His friend knew he wasn't a churchgoer, yet he was asking him to sing in a church choir. He considered Gerry's earnest expression as his mind scrambled for an excuse. At a loss for how to decline, he returned to the computer files.

"Did I mention Sarah is usually at the church when we rehearse?" Gerry added. "She designs and arranges the altar flowers. Sure looks pretty all decked out in red with green velvet ribbons."

"The church or your great-niece?"

Gerry winked. "Both."

Max sprang to his feet. "When are the rehearsals?"

"Thursday evenings at seven o'clock."

"Sarah is usually there?"

"Usually."

"I'll give the choir a try."

"I thought so." Gerry sent Max a knowing grin. "Oh, and bring your harmonica."

"Why?"

"The finale is a rousing rendition of 'We Wish You A Merry Christmas.' I'm playing guitar and a harmonica would be a nice touch."

"What about Joseph Slater? He's a professional guitarist."

"He and his wife, Scarlett, are flying to Australia next week for a worship conference. They asked me to step in."

"No one else plays harmonica in this town?"

"None that I know of. Consider it an honor to be asked. I wanted to add a sixteen-measure solo at the end."

Max digested this and considered reverting to his earlier decision. Singing in the choir was one thing. Playing the harmonica in front of Ryan Edwards, a world-renowned opera singer, was quite another. He opened his mouth, but Gerry interrupted.

"The other day, Sarah mentioned hanging wreaths on all the church windows on Thursday night."

Max chuckled. "I'll bring my harmonica."

Gerry drained his cup. "I knew you wouldn't let the baritone section down."

CHAPTER 5

*H*armonica tucked in his pocket, and his favorite bow tie in place, Max arrived at the white-painted Memorial Street Church on Thursday evening. Night had darkened the winter sky, forming a blanket of black velvet, and the steeple soared proud and magnificent against it.

An outdoor nativity scene took center stage. The life-size creche included the Holy Family, two white lambs, kings and shepherds, and a wooden stable.

Gas street lamps were wrapped in fragrant pine boughs, and a trembling wind rustled the tree branches.

Inside, an assemblage of youthful and older men and women were taking their places on the risers, and a small group of women hung wreaths on the arched church windows.

Looking around, he spotted Sarah balanced on the third rung of a stepladder.

He strode over to her and tapped her on the back. "Good evening, Sarah."

She whirled and almost fell into his arms. A burst of

delight lit her face, and everything around him—the stained glass depicting Bible scenes, the whiffs of incense and candles, the other people's voices—faded away. The intensity of her gaze did funny things to his insides. Regardless of the way their last time together had ended, she looked pleased to see him.

"Max!" She clung to the sides of the ladder for support. "I chatted with my uncle Gerry this week and he claimed you're singing in the church choir."

"Temporarily," Max corrected.

"You're also in a band with him?"

"The Bearded Elves." Max steadied the ladder as she climbed down.

"The Bearded Elves? That's … different."

"Don't get hung up on the name. It will change soon."

She tilted her head to the side.

"When you're *not* a number one hit band, you're granted some flexibility." He grinned. "Wait until February. You'll see."

But then, he wouldn't be here in February, which left him with a sense of sadness.

She didn't reply, accepting his explanation without question, not even with the prompt of "What happens in February?"

Then again, maybe she hadn't heard him.

"Uncle Gerry raved about your superb baritone voice and perfect pitch," she said instead.

"He's biased since he was an undergrad student in my bird-watching class." Max removed his jacket and placed it on a pew. "Besides, doesn't every choir member sing in tune?"

"I'm not certain. Based on my great-uncle's comments, some don't." Sarah stepped to a side table and gathered red spray roses and luxuriant ivy, creating an elegant bouquet in a green glass vase. "The choir is all volunteer. These folks aren't professional except for Ryan Edwards and a few of the others."

Max turned her to face him. "Are you brave, Sarah?"

She looked startled by his unexpected question. "I try."

"You're the most courageous woman I've ever known."

Her cheeks pinkened. "Thanks."

"I intend to explore Crandall's Mountain next weekend. Will you join me? I hesitated inviting you, considering our adventure last week."

"You mean, because of the bear?"

"Because of me. I apologize for my rudeness. We didn't part on the finest note."

"You're here now. The present is all that matters."

"Is that a yes?"

Her nod of affirmation was accompanied by a smile of delight. "Let me check my work schedule, but it sounds like fun."

She was full of life. Eager. Forgiving. And stunning. The hiking gear she'd worn the previous weekend hadn't done her justice. She'd looked anything but glamorous in a hooded jacket, snowflake gloves and boots. The woman gazing at him now was entrancing. By the light of numerous church candles, the jeweled sparkle of her emerald eyes mesmerized him.

"For the record, I like hiking more than ever," she said.

Her statement thrilled him, sending a rush of gladness straight to his heart.

Before he could reply, Gerry called him to the choir to begin the warm-up.

Max nodded at Gerry over his shoulder, then curved back to Sarah. "The rehearsal runs an hour. Will you be here when it's finished?"

"Most likely. There are thirty windows in the church."

"I'll see you after rehearsal then?"

She chewed her lip. Glanced away.

He stared at her in eager silence. "Well?"

"Sure. If I'm done beforehand, I'll wait."

The recognizable first notes of 'Joy To The World' led by the sopranos, announced the beginning of choir practice.

Max hurried to the risers and took his appointed place between Gerry and a gray-bearded man. He retrieved a hymnal and thumbed through the selections until he located the correct piece.

The uplifting lyrics and melody, published by Handel in the 1700s, plucked him backward to a tiny church, sitting on a hard wooden pew as he listened to Mr. Lenny's heartfelt sermon.

Max focused on the associate conductor for the most part during the rehearsal.

However, he often stole glances at Sarah. She wore black slacks and a shimmery candy-red sweater, and her slim figure kept drawing his attention.

Whenever she caught his gaze, she quickly looked away. However, she smiled first, and he reciprocated with a responsive grin.

The final selection called for a guitar and harmonica. The "honor" of playing a harmonica solo in front of the other musicians was one that Max would've happily forgone, but when he was done, he was satisfied with his performance.

"What's your decision?" Gerry asked once the rehearsal ended.

Max slid the harmonica into his pocket. "I'll join."

"What was the deciding factor? The beloved hymns, my brilliant persuasion, or my great-niece's presence?"

"The latter," Max assured him.

In a refined southern drawl, an elderly woman introduced herself as Mrs. Marge Addyson. Her gray hair was neatly coiffed, and her rouged cheeks plumped with her smile as she held out a freckled hand. "Your baritone voice is as fine as a sunny winter's day. Welcome to Cherish. I'm the associate pastor."

"Thank you, ma'am. I'm Maxwell Archer." He shook her hand, frail yet sturdy. He was surprised at the callouses.

In a deafening stage whisper that garnered the notice of the remaining choir members, Marge announced, "You're the professor birdman who went hiking with our Sarah."

Our Sarah?

Intent on sidestepping a discussion involving Sarah that might be overheard, Max replied, "I'm affiliated with an ornithology department at a university."

"Birds."

"Ornithology is a branch of zoology," he clarified, "and is a discipline involving the study of birds."

"Impressive, and a distinctive description."

"Animals are important in my life and profession."

He expected Marge to rhapsodize about the significance of pets. She did just that, but offered a particular recommendation.

"Nicholas, the town sheriff, is looking for someone to adopt a cuddly homeless puppy," Marge said. "Considering your animal expertise, you're ideal."

Although both startled and pleased by her consideration of him as a candidate, he replied, "I've already been asked by the woman who owns the music store."

"Dorothy Edwards?"

"Yes, and I declined."

"Aren't you a fan of stray mongrels?"

"I should be, because I'm one myself." He regarded her with an ironic grin. "I used to live in Cherish."

"When?"

"Three decades ago, and for a brief spell. My foster family's last name was Monroe."

"I don't recall a Monroe family, although oftentimes my memory fails me." She pursed her lips. "I'll remember something that happened a decade earlier and forget something that happened a minute ago."

By the looks of Marge Addyson's well-heeled style and demeanor, Max assumed she resided in the wealthy outskirts of town. The Monroe family had occupied the impoverished fringes.

"I'm in no position to take on the responsibility of a dog," he said. "I move around a lot and my three parakeets are a literal handful. In January, I begin my dream job in Florida. I've struggled for ages to be on the faculty of a prestigious university."

"I express the feelings of the entire town when I say I'm overjoyed you're in Cherish." Marge reached for her handbag and tugged on a pair of flowered red gloves. "Regardless of your job, I hope you're here a long, long time."

"I appreciate your hospitality."

It warmed him—this undeniable sense of community, a welcome transition from big city living.

"Our church holds services on Saturday afternoons and Sunday mornings. On Christmas Eve day and evening, we offer several services." She studied him with an astute gaze. "Christmas is an opportune season to honor our Lord."

For a split second, their exchange grew awkward. Max wasn't about to divulge his lack of faith to the elderly associate pastor in the middle of a church.

He opted not to reply, although he recognized the wisdom flowing from her heart.

"You need honest and caring people in your life," she said.

He managed a grim smile.

"Do you serve God?"

Surprised at her bluntness, he answered truthfully. "I tried the religion route when I was younger. It didn't go well. The people in my circle …" He shrugged.

"Perhaps the season has come for a different circle." She squeezed his hand, her intelligent eyes exuding care and friendship. "Press on, Max. We're all here for you in your journey."

Journey to where?

"'Thanks be to God for his indescribable gift,'" she proclaimed.

"Second Corinthians 9:15." At her lifted eyebrows and inquisitive gaze, he avoided eye contact. "My special foster father was a pastor," he said.

"Special?"

"Yes."

"Was?" She grasped her blue tweed coat draped over a music stand.

"Mr. Lenny died many years ago."

She fiddled with the silver bell brooch on her coat's lapel as she studied him. "You miss him."

"Very much." Max glanced toward Gerry, who was collecting choral music.

Gerry picked up his guitar, slicked back his white hair, and approached them. "Hi, Mrs. Addyson."

"Hello, Gerry." Marge smiled up at him. "I just asked our newest choir member if he was interested in adopting the stray pup that wandered into Nicholas's office."

"What was his answer?"

"I'm right here, Gerry." Because they were close friends, Max caught the drollness in Gerry's tone. "As much as I'd love a puppy, I can't commit."

"I refused as well because my plate is full. Sorry." Gerry flashed a guilt-ridden smile. "However, let's all go out for a celebratory drink at The Garden Terrace."

"What are we celebrating?" Max inquired.

"You joined the church choir."

"Don't you have to rush home to your new baby?" Caught between amusement and confusion, Max and Marge inquired in unison.

Gerry shot them a look filled with emotions—including self-reproach and longing. "My mother-in-law is visiting and insisted on rocking the baby to sleep. She holds the magic touch."

Max grinned. "Therefore, your and your wife's roles aren't egalitarian tonight?"

"Little Freddie giggles from head to toe whenever I make faces at him," Gerry replied. "Or raspberry kisses. I'll do both in the morning."

Mrs. Addyson left shortly afterwards, pleading tiredness, and shaking her head in refusal at the invitation. She reminded them that she was past retirement age and went to bed early.

A bang of the ornately carved doors signaled the last of the choir members filing out.

Max peered around. Sarah was hanging a final wreath on a window.

"Go ahead to the restaurant," he instructed Gerry. "We'll be along shortly."

"We?"

"I'm hoping Sarah will join us."

Gerry clapped a hand on Max's back. "I'm rooting for you, my friend. I'll inquire about a gig at the restaurant while I'm waiting."

"Do you think the management will agree?"

"Simple logic. We order a meal and they'll hire our band."

"Just because we eat there doesn't mean they'll want us to *play* there," Max countered. "Hundreds of customers dine at the restaurant every day."

"It's a start."

"Will we get paid?"

"I was thinking more along the lines of free drinks."

Max bit back a grin at the logic he didn't see at all, pulled on his jacket and hurried to Sarah.

"Perfect timing," he declared.

"For what?"

"You're finished, and I am too."

"I'm *nearly* done." She swerved around him to a table and secured buckthorn berry branches into florist foam, then arranged the branches with a trail of ivy in a copper vase.

He followed her as she set the vase near the altar. "Will you join us?" he asked.

"Where?"

"The Garden Terrace."

"It's after eight o'clock."

"Hardly late."

"There's cleanup here. In addition, I'm scheduled for a double shift tomorrow."

"I'll finish." To Max's relief, a short, heavyset woman spoke up. "Sarah, you go on and enjoy yourself with this handsome newcomer."

Max turned to her. "How do you know I'm a newcomer?"

"Cherish is a small community." The woman reached for the last two poinsettias. "Word travels fast."

"Thank you, Rosemary." Sarah's shoulders lifted as she turned to Max. "I'd like to, but—"

"Do you have any noteworthy plans on a Thursday night?"

"After I tend to my pets, I planned to catch up on some reading."

He persevered. "Did you drive here?"

"I walked. I don't live far."

"There's a chill in the air, Cinderella. Ride with me, and I

58

guarantee you'll arrive home before midnight. Besides, I don't know where the restaurant is."

She laughed. "I'm certain you can find it without my help." In the flick of a few seconds, her mood had switched from indecision to humor, and it struck him that no matter her disposition, he appreciated her companionship.

"I have it on excellent authority you're the ideal guide," he said.

She gathered a half dozen stemmed red roses and placed them in a bucket filled with water. "From whom?"

"Me."

With a sideways smile, Sarah retrieved her jacket, then tucked her hand through his arm.

He couldn't help grinning as he escorted her out the wooden doors and down the church steps.

CHAPTER 6

The Garden Terrace wasn't the restaurant Max imagined. Certainly, the Monroes hadn't been able to afford such luxuries as dining out.

He'd pictured a genteel garden, a sparkling fountain, and an abundance of plants. After all, the restaurant's name alluded to a *garden*.

Instead, he and Sarah were welcomed by lively waitresses, a boisterous clatter of dishes, and heavenly whiffs of mesquite smoked chicken. An oversized sign at the entrance stated in bold letters, "The holidays are for barbecue." Multicolored lights were strung from the ceiling and pine cones and faux red berries wound around rustic poles, accentuated by tan burlap. A keyboardist provided a background performance of "Carol of the Bells."

"This restaurant doesn't subscribe to minimalism," he joked.

"They're renowned for sugar-free lemon cake and sweet tea," Sarah told Max as he led her through the crowd and ushered her to a booth Gerry had claimed.

Somehow, Max remembered that about this restaurant.

He'd eaten a slice of the cake in his youth and had savored every bite. Another aspect of this appealing town were that things stayed the same. A time machine rewound to an era without the push and shove of big-city living.

"Sugar and sugar-free." Max helped her off with her jacket, tugged off his, and hung both on a coat hanger. "Isn't that a juxtaposition?"

"An oxymoron." Sarah teased him with a nudge. He noticed that she had watched his lips as he spoke. The restaurant was noisy and even he strained to hear their conversation. "Or rather, one cancels out the other. The calories in sugary tea—"

"Is a paradox," Gerry interrupted, indicating the guitar on his seat. He motioned them to sit across from him.

"Wrong," they contradicted him, which produced lots of laughter.

In the minutes between ordering and waiting for their meals—hot chocolate topped with marshmallows for Sarah, a slice of the sugar-free lemon cake and tea for Max, and a draft beer and two platters of French fries for Gerry—Max arrived at several important deductions.

First, Gerry wasn't, as Max earlier had presumed, merely a first-rate student, a talented musician, and a newbie father. Gerry was also candid and clever. While he inquired about Max's and Sarah's hiking adventure, he closely observed the way Max draped an arm around her shoulders.

And Sarah, with her delicate features and lilting voice, had a remarkable gift. She was charismatic, and she gave an enthusiastic account of the bear adventure, flavoring it with enough elements to engage Gerry. By doing so, she successfully avoided any reference to the kiss she and Max had shared.

Smiling at her wide-eyed gaze as she described the

babbling river, he felt inside him the stirring of a sentiment so remote, so foreign, he gasped in denial.

He was falling for her.

Not in the cards, he told himself. He was leaving in January.

Even so, the sentiment prompted him to curve a lock of shiny hair behind her ear. Her glittery gold star earrings winked back at him.

"You forgot our interruption by the teenagers," he said.

Her eyes glistened with laughter. "If they hadn't approached, we would still be ..."

"Kissing," he whispered in her ear and squeezed her shoulders, a gentle reminder in case she'd forgotten.

Oblivious to the direction of the conversation, Gerry pulled out his cellphone, concentrated on a text and frowned. "My wife," he muttered.

"Is little Freddie sleeping?" Max inquired.

"Almost." Gerry tried for a smile that said all was well, although he didn't entirely convince Max.

After their drinks and food were served, Gerry took a deep pull from his beer and set it down. "Incidentally, my friend, management agreed."

"To what?" Max handed him a bottle of ketchup and watched him smother the fries, then slid the platter to the middle of the table for all to share.

"To us performing here a couple Fridays from now." Gerry broke off a fry and chewed. "The Bearded Elves are back in business."

Max helped himself to an ample portion of fries after scarfing down his cake. He'd forgotten how much he liked lemon. "We weren't ever *in* business. Nonetheless, your news is exciting. Are they paying us?"

"Our gig is doubling as a debut audition and management is requesting familiar holiday tunes." A smile quirked Gerry's mouth. "I'll organize a playlist. We can rehearse separately, then together before our unveiling."

Sarah joined in with a chuckle. "Am I invited?"

"Absolutely. We'll perform in that far corner. There's even a dance floor." With his half-eaten fry, Gerry gestured to where the keyboardist played on a small stage.

Once their table was cleared, Gerry insisted on paying the bill, then peered at his phone and announced, "I'm heading home before my wife and her mother murder me."

"Did the baby wake up?" Max asked.

"The baby never went to sleep."

"No magic touch from your mother-in-law?"

"Our next option is to phone Merlin the Magician. Evidently, little Freddie is offended by the idea of sleeping."

Sarah surged up as quickly as Gerry did. "I should leave too." She peered at the restaurant's rustic wall clock, which showed after nine o'clock.

"Don't rush on my account." Gerry waved toward the dance floor. The keyboardist had begun a jazzy rendition of Ray Charles's "That Spirit of Christmas," and a handful of couples swirled to the rhythm.

Max slid his arm around Sarah and led her to the intimate dance floor. She was so petite, scarcely five feet tall, her head hardly reached his shoulder.

She gazed up at him with a jesting smile. "Are you the type who steps on your dance partner's feet?"

"Exactly." He chuckled, tempted to kiss the edges of her smile. "You?"

"The same, so watch out." Her laughter was mellow and melodic. He loved her ability to laugh at herself, as well as with him.

"Has anyone ever described you as a wonderful, caring man?" she asked.

"I dislike labels."

"I do too, but my intuition tells me you're a good person."

"Never tell a man he's good. Strong, maybe, or marvelous—"

She rested her head against his chest, and he whirled them around and around. Her steps were agile, gliding to the rhythm. Above them, the multi-colored lights sparkled, creating a wondrous, otherworldly effect. Her hair spun with each pivot and twist, and he kissed her forehead, her cheeks, her lips.

"What a wonderful feeling," he sang, adlibbing the lyrics, "to waltz with a precious, vivacious woman who is as sweet as a sugarplum."

As they danced, he reviewed the plan he'd conceived within the past half hour. While he lived in Cherish, he'd see her as often as possible.

Her descriptions of him—good and caring—were poignantly familiar. Mr. Lenny's wife had often called him a "caring little boy." Once, his outlook on life had shone optimistic.

His timeworn thoughts now were shadowed with the awareness that a future with a loving wife hadn't come to pass.

He blew out a labored breath.

He'd gotten over the injustice of being born to birth parents who couldn't focus on anyone except themselves.

Some children were born lucky. Other weren't.

But now he'd met Sarah.

How wonderful they could spend a few weeks together.

How awful they could only spend a few weeks together.

Seeming to sense the dipping of his mood, Sarah muttered she was sorry for stepping on his foot—she hadn't —but her comical expression portrayed her attempt to cheer him and her refreshing humor. But then she added, "I should get home."

With a nod, he maneuvered her off the dance floor and retrieved their jackets. Outside, the streets were dark and quiet. Gas lamps flickered, forming pools of warm light.

"How far do you live from the restaurant?" he asked.

"Three blocks." She turned right. "My house is in the center of town."

"I'll escort you. It'll give me a chance to walk off my fried-food coma."

Plus, it would take longer than a quick drive in his car, and he wanted to enjoy every precious minute with her. He pointed toward the town square as he heard voices rise in harmony. He recognized the "Silent Night" refrain.

"What's going on?" he asked.

Sarah hesitated. "Going on?"

"The singing."

"Oh, singing. It's carol singing," she replied. "The town's Christmas committee sponsors caroling three nights a week in December. Anyone can join. Afterwards, they serve hot apple cider and roasted chestnuts."

Now that she had mentioned it, he recognized the scorching charcoal aroma, rich and nutty, permeating the air, along with the hint of woodsy fireplaces.

Beams of silver fell around them. A full moon graced the sky, and a smattering of stars twinkled in shimmering beauty.

A chilly burst of wind tugged at their jackets.

Sarah bowed her head and closed her eyes to avoid the sting.

His gaze fell to her long, thick eyelashes, an unmistakable reddish-blond. Her copper-colored hair, as smooth as the finest silk, fell loose around her face.

"I recalled Carolina weather being warm all year round," he said, "but my remembrances are from a youngster's perspective."

"How long were you here?"

"Briefly." He shifted the subject, in no mood to upset the fine balance of a pleasant evening by being reminded of his tumultuous upbringing. "I assumed the climate was comparable to Florida."

"Do you like hot weather?"

"In all honesty, no." His reflective pause initiated a jab from his conscience. *Dream job, remember? You're moving.* "How about you?"

"I've lived here my entire life. I know everyone and am comfortable here. Still, I sometimes wish to see other places."

"Like Florida?"

"Are there more palm trees than the Carolinas?"

"Probably."

"You'll receive a pay raise with your new job?"

"Not necessarily, although I'm optimistic my research will resonate with people avid about ornithology. That is, unless my appointment is cancelled. Universities are tightening their proverbial belts, and bird study isn't at the top of their budgets." He shrugged, sighed. "If it happens, it happens."

"You work a lot of hours. It's a considerable workload." She seemed to choose her words carefully.

"Which will become heavier once I take on more responsibility."

"I'm sorry you're not a hot-weather fan."

"I don't particularly like cold weather, either. Nor do I care for synthetic snow, the kind the outdoor fairs manufacture for gala events."

"The Carolinas enjoy four distinct seasons," she replied. "I eagerly wait for snow on Christmas Day. No assurances, though. The weather here is unpredictable."

"I lived up north for years. If it doesn't snow, we're surprised."

She grinned. "In Cherish, if it *does* snow, we're amazed."

Several of the shops' single-paned windows had frosted over, and they peered through the glass, admiring one-of-a-kind gifts—a man's handmade striped red tie, a vintage green and gold pinecone necklace, and jars touting themselves as a "One-Stop Spa." An innovative store advertised a pet-friendly dog bakery, and Sarah commented on the unique toys, ranging from whimsical Merry Christmas bandanas to tail-wagging elf sweaters.

While they strolled, she was more outgoing than the day of their hike, regaling him with hilarious stories of her pets, beginning with what happened when she returned from work each day to a houseful of welcoming animals.

"My two dogs and two cats wait by the door until I arrive," she described. "Even if I leave for ten minutes to get the mail at the post office, they're under the impression I've been gone for hours, and the greeting parade begins anew."

She grew more gorgeous by the second. Her cheeks had grown rosy from the cold, her wide-set eyes sparkling a deep emerald. When she chuckled, tiny puffs of her breathing filled the air. He couldn't look away.

"My budgies are happy," he said. "They spend their days singing or talking."

"Uncle Gerry told me they haven't mimicked the birdsongs you recorded."

"Nothing yet."

Max went over the endless hours he'd spent with his birds. Why wouldn't they mimic other birdsongs or harmonica music? He reined in his frustration and focused on Sarah. "My budgies have individual temperaments. One male is timid, the other bolder, and the third, a female, speaks her mind."

"Hurray for the female. What does she say?"

Max pushed out an exasperated breath. "'God bless us, every one.'"

"From *A Christmas Carol*? Tiny Tim?"

"Exactly. She's a rescue bird. An elderly woman owned her."

"What's her name?"

"Angel." He resisted the urge to laugh. "Don't be fooled. She's the most unangelic bird of the three."

"Is unangelic a word?"

"It is now."

"We all have distinctive personalities, because God created variety and uniqueness."

"You're saying He knew what to do."

"Exactly."

"But how, Sarah? I'm not at peace with all this religious jargon."

"Don't search for peace." Her tone softened, and he felt his expression grow less rigid. "You already are at peace. God is inside you."

She expressed herself with her body, gestures, and expressions rather than a deluge of words.

He had appreciated her artistic flower arrangements at church and he knew she was hard working and industrious. Her faith in God was clear, and he sensed she possessed what Mr. Lenny had called "a new creature in Christ." Combined, these attributes contributed to her magnetic personality.

In the sparkle of twinkling lights dancing from nearby homes, the sadness in his heart diminished. Sarah carried the same unique gift—to enhance the world around her merely by her presence. She was an extraordinary, special woman.

Soon, they reached the gaily decorated Musically Yours. Although the music store was closed, they paused to admire the window display of the polar bears, treble clef signs, and model train.

How many hours, Sarah mused aloud, had it taken Dorothy and Ryan to dress up the window with such flair?

"Maybe they had help," Max said.

"From who? A polar bear?"

"Maybe Beethoven himself." Max curled his fingers around hers. Happiness lifted his spirits, and, judging by Sarah's contented sigh, the holiday atmosphere of the winsome town affected them both.

"Cherish Hills Inn also has particularly noticeable decorations. The inn is located farther up the street." Sarah gestured with her chin. "The innkeeper, Tom Canning, is a long-time resident, and strict about who he rents to."

"I tried to get a room there, but Tom wasn't keen on renting to me and my birds for the entire month of December."

"Not surprising. The inn is posh and unconducive for pets."

"Ah. That explains Tom's half-hearted response."

"What did he say?"

Max grabbed a mouthful of air and shouted, "No."

"That's why Tom doesn't have anyone currently staying at his inn. He's choosey and a stickler for elegance."

"Thank you." Max picked her up and twirled her around.

"What for?" She giggled. Wriggled.

"For sticking up for me."

"I did?"

"Yes. You stuck up for me instead of Tom."

"I'm getting dizzy. Put me down."

He continued to spin, but slower this time, holding her close. "Not until you guarantee me something."

"You expect an assurance after that?"

"Promise me you'll never change." He gazed at her amazing face, trying to ignore the flip in his pulse.

She met his stare. "Our lives, our paths, take many forms, Max."

He spoke clearly and deliberately, as he had done all evening. "Not with us."

He set her down and reached for her hand, whistling the entire last block to her house. It was set back from the road and surrounded by bare-branched trees. The front door was painted gray and bedecked with shiny pink ornaments and a garland heavy with silver tinsel.

"You're a true holiday-lover," he remarked. "I hope the porch doesn't collapse under the sheer mass of the decorations."

At her doorstep, with barking dogs and loud meows in the background, he slipped his arms around her. So close their foreheads touched, he tipped up her chin and kissed her.

She stood on her tiptoes and yielded to his hungry mouth. Her lips were plump and inviting, fitting together with his, two pieces of an intricate puzzle matching perfectly. Her hands reached up and her slim fingers tangled behind his neck.

Her enticing sweetness obliterated his concerns—an uncertain job market, his research, his turbulent past—and he savored every second of their kiss. The promise of December, creamy hot chocolate and tart lemon cake—he'd hit the jackpot when he met Sarah.

He was filled with anticipation and gladness.

And a spark that completely surprised him.

A spark of love.

CHAPTER 7

*T*he following day, Sarah clocked in at the greenhouse at ten o'clock in the morning. Fragrant whiffs of lush evergreens never failed to bring thoughts of sparkly white lights and an array of gaily wrapped gifts.

That morning, she'd secured her flyaway hair with a green headband because it always frizzed after shampooing, even when she used her favorite rosewood shampoo. Then, she'd tugged on a cream-colored cable-knit sweater, jeans, and snowman dangle earrings.

After a wave at Bonnie, who had positioned herself at the cash register, Sarah sorted Christmas cactus. She lavished care on each showy red and white flower. Many had been overwatered, which led to root and stem rot.

While she tended to the first plant, she tried to ignore the butterflies in her chest as memories of her previous evening with Max kept surfacing.

His animated features when he chatted about his birds, his quick-witted banter, his musicality, were all part of his personality. He was bold yet vulnerable; humorous yet sensitive.

And she loved every minute she spent with him.

He'd dismissed his upcoming Florida job with a casual "if it happens, it happens" as he rubbed the dark stubble of his beard. Nonetheless, his dismissal had only confirmed that he cared about the prestigious position more than he let on.

The plants, she reminded herself. The plants.

She tended to the next one and again, her mind meandered.

The mouth-watering food and drink at The Garden Terrace, her intimate dance with Max, their leisurely stroll ending in an earth-shattering kiss—all those memories came back in a rush. Rational thought had a way of abandoning her whenever she was within two feet of him.

She pressed a finger to her lips. Was last night a first date? After all, he'd invited her to a restaurant. Or was it a second if she counted their hike on Juniper Mountain?

"Do you have any noteworthy plans on a Thursday night?" he'd asked her.

Um, no, unless scrubbing the kitchen floor and vacuuming were considered noteworthy. In any event, she was glad she'd accepted his invitation.

At the end of the evening, he'd requested her phone number and had promised to text, phone, and see her often.

He was a man, he assured her, who never reneged on his promises. True to his word, he'd texted a few minutes later, telling her how much he'd enjoyed their hours together. That text had resulted in an hour's worth of conversation.

Was his kiss the beginning of something extraordinary, something lasting?

As quickly as it came, she released the thought.

He was in Cherish for one month. He'd made that fact abundantly clear.

Nevertheless, his affectionate words and tender actions were sincere.

Weren't they? What if he didn't call or text again?

A favorite passage from the Bible, Matthew 6:34, reassured her: "Do not be anxious for tomorrow, for tomorrow will be anxious for itself."

She wondered about Max's past, because Marge Addyson had left a voice mail for Sarah that morning when Sarah was in the shower.

"I scoured the Big Brothers Big Sisters files," Marge said. "I believe I've found a photo of your Max, probably taken close to thirty years ago when he lived in Cherish with his foster family. You'll want to see it, I'm sure. I'll stop by your home … I'm assuming after six o'clock? Call me if that's not okay."

Her Max.

Sarah's heartbeat had drummed at Marge's reference, and she scarcely paid attention to the rest of Marge's words.

Wait.

Big Brothers Big Sisters.

Despite Max's brilliant mind and academic demeanor, his background apparently wasn't silver-spoon. She considered him handsome, but there was a blunt masculinity to his square jaw and muscled physique. Had he been the type of boy who'd been in many brawls?

She knew he wasn't afraid of anything.

Not even a charging bear.

By the river, his strong, chiseled arms had held her tight.

Images of a Christmas spent with him brought comfort to her lonely world, a breathlessness whenever she recalled the glimmer of interest in his gray eyes. His dark hair, a tad too long, curled at the nape, and she'd wanted to smooth the adorable cleft on his chin.

By far, he was the handsomest man to set foot in Cherish.

He's leaving, her sensible side was quick to remind. *Do you honestly want to get hurt again?*

A jarring announcement over the store's loudspeaker called for a price check. Quickly yanked back to the present, Sarah surveyed the rows of cacti, trying to recall which plants she'd tended. White blooms or red?

The nursery door opened, and a blast of wintry air hit her.

Nicholas, the town sheriff, accompanied by Molly Belle, his rambunctious golden retriever, strode toward her. Molly Belle's leash didn't prevent her from romping away from him. She knocked over a bunch of plants in her hurry to chase … nothing.

"Stop." Nicholas tugged on the leash and peered at the spilled soil on the concrete floor. "Sorry, Sarah."

"It's a fast clean-up." Sarah grinned at Molly Belle. "Are those doggy obedience classes helping?"

Nicholas shoved a hand through his blond hair. "The instructor recommended she get lots of exercise. What an understatement." His moan was part sigh, part frustration. "We take her out often, although she's easily distracted."

The dog beamed up at them with expectant black eyes, then went back to lapping the water spilled from the plants.

"Here, Molly Belle." Sarah grabbed a water bottle, foraged for an empty container, and poured water into it. "You'll find this is tastier."

Nicholas crossed his arms and turned to face her. "You're one of only a handful of people Molly Belle will listen to."

Sarah appreciated that aspect of living in a small community. Folks were now using strong, clear voices when talking to her. Needless to say, it wasn't because she had a hearing impairment, despite what her friends hinted. They merely needed to speak louder, especially when she was in a crowded place with many voices.

Perhaps another reason why Dorothy had recommended Sarah as Max's hiking companion was because she knew that Sarah preferred the quiet solitude of nature.

"Molly Belle isn't obeying your commands?" she teasingly asked Nicholas.

"Once in a while. Once in a *great* while."

Sarah laughed, wiped her hands on her employee apron, and grabbed a broom. "Are you purchasing anything in particular today?"

"I'm here for two reasons. First, my wife wants a live wreath for the front door, rather than the fake one I purchased at the grocery store."

"The wreaths are all hung outside. You passed them when you entered." Sarah swept the soil into the dustpan and discarded it. "What's the second reason?"

"I hoped to discuss the puppy who wandered into the sheriff's office—"

"We discussed the subject. My answer is no."

"Sarah, you're the ideal choice."

"I can't, Nicholas. My house is overrun with pets."

He kneaded the back of his neck. "You have two cats and a hamster."

"Plus two dogs."

"Your dogs are friendly."

"You didn't remember I owned dogs until a second ago. My Shih Tzu is ten years old and set in her ways, and the other dog is a cocker spaniel who thinks she owns me rather than the other way around. I'm confident someone will welcome the puppy as the perfect addition to their family."

"Who?" Nicholas muttered, half to himself. He tugged his phone from his pocket, scrolled through it, then drew her attention to a tiny puppy with fuzzy silver-colored fur. "Do you agree he needs a loving home for Christmas?"

"Absolutely." She scrutinized the photo. "He?"

"Yup." Nicholas eyed Molly Belle, who had secured a place on the concrete floor in a spot of sunshine. "He lacks a safe, loving environment. Here's some videos. Doesn't he look like he's ready to take on the world?"

A bouncy puppy filled the screen, a roll of fat evident under his chin. In the second video, he chased Nicholas and nipped at his pant legs. This was followed by a short bark as the puppy rolled onto his back and stared into the camera with sweet doggy eyes.

"We've had him vet checked and he's healthy. Plus, he's handled daily and exhibits a devoted personality." Nicholas pointed to the screen. "Look at that shiny coat."

"That puppy is in constant motion. Wagging his tail and wriggling all over the place."

"He's a gem, right? The vet estimated he's eight weeks old, and vaccinated him for the first series of shots."

Sarah smiled and leaned in. "Nicholas, you're persuasive, but—"

A tap on the shoulder caused her to whirl.

"Hi, Sarah." Max stepped within a foot of her. He smiled at her and scowled at Nicholas. "Am I interrupting something?"

"Max." She touched her fingers to her throat. "I didn't expect to see you today."

He shoved his hands in his pockets. His lips pressed together. "I wanted to say hello and—"

He looked sinfully handsome, and the thought crossed her mind that Nicholas might book Max, because it had to be illegal to be that good-looking. He wore black jeans that accented his toned legs and a chambray shirt. His familiar bow tie peeked beneath the olive-green twill jacket.

The time showed mid-morning—the hours when Max normally pored over research.

Yet, he was here, and her heart did a slow flip.

Max's scowl stayed on Nicholas.

"You're not interrupting a thing." Nicholas clicked his phone shut and shoved it back in his pocket.

Sarah flinched, sensing an unmistakable hostility between the two men.

"I'm glad you stopped by the store, Max." She gave an uneasy laugh and swallowed. "Let me introduce you to the Cherish town sheriff. Nicholas Thompson, meet Maxwell Archer."

At the same height, six feet tall, both men's features were similar—sharp and athletic and wary.

They shook hands, although Max treated Nicholas with chilly courtesy. He bent to pet Molly Belle. She responded with a gleeful tail wag.

"I'm Dorothy Edwards's brother," Nicholas clarified as Max straightened. "My wife, Emmanuelle, teaches harp lessons at Dorothy's store."

Max's expression eased. "You're off duty today, sheriff?" He sized up Nicholas' casual attire of khakis and a sweater, then positioned himself between Sarah and Nicholas, bracing a hand on a pole above her head. Although the men's verbal volley might have ended, Max was sending Nicholas a clear message.

He was interested in Sarah.

Because he was jealous. Jealous of *her*. The knowledge brought a wry smile.

"Nice bow tie," Nicholas said flatly.

"Thanks."

Okay, so it was unusual to wear a bow tie into a garden center, but Max was unique. The tie made him unforgettable, offering an air of distinguished academia. Although, considering his disheveled hair, he reminded her of an absent-minded professor.

"Today is my day off." Nicholas offered a scarcely

disguised smirk. "You don't, by any wild chance, break the law, Max, do you?"

"Never, sheriff. I'm new in town, and my rental is begging for a little holiday cheer." His gaze rested on Sarah. "I'm here to purchase flowers. Can you help me, Sarah?"

"Definitely."

"Dorothy mentioned our little town had acquired another fine musician," Nicholas said. "The other day, a man stopped by her store to buy a harmonica. I assume that was you?"

"I'm an average musician and a temporary resident," Max corrected.

Nicholas narrowed his gaze. "So, you're here *temporarily*."

"Yes."

Nicholas glanced at the pole where Max still braced his arm. "You won't want to get too familiar with folks, then, if you're leaving them soon." With a crisp nod, he turned toward the entrance. "Well, I'm off to grab a wreath. C'mon, Molly Belle."

The dog didn't move and stared up at Nicholas with a kindly expression.

"Come." Gently, Nicholas pulled the leash.

Again, no response.

"Up, Molly Belle." Sarah ducked beneath Max's arm and stepped over to the sunny spot where the dog sat. "Up Molly Belle. Obey your master."

Molly Belle immediately stood. Her tail wagged with so much enthusiasm her entire body shook.

"You do have a way with animals, Sarah." Nicholas extended a rueful laugh, then regarded Max. "Don't forget that she's an exceptional woman, and well-loved by everyone in this town."

Max gave Sarah a teasing wink. "I've already discovered she's extraordinary, and she's hands down the bravest woman I've ever known."

Sarah felt her cheeks flush pink. She blamed it on the heat and sun in the garden center.

As Nicholas and Molly Belle headed out the door, she set down the broom she hadn't realized she still held. "What types of plants are you looking for, Max?"

"My birds are happiest around dazzling flowers."

"The poinsettias this year are brilliant." She signaled for him to follow her. "Any particular shade?"

After he selected two vibrant red poinsettias and a purple cyclamen with upswept flowers and silver foliage, he said, "A bike was left in my rental and I rode it here. Any chance you can bring the plants by my house when you get off work?"

"I'm done at six o'clock."

He nodded. "Excellent. I'll prepare dinner for us."

"I can't." She bent to pick up Molly Belle's water dish. "I haven't decorated the inside of my house for Christmas and I planned to start hauling decorations down from the attic tonight. Although I don't know why I do both inside and outside decorating. The cats think the artificial tree is a scratching post, and the dogs chew the ornaments. And don't get me started on holiday baking. Why, the dogs will eat everything in sight and …"

She was babbling, and Max was grinning.

"Can decorating wait one more day?" he asked.

Something in his tone prompted her to study him.

A couple of customers wandered over, asking how to care for a Christmas cactus.

"My specialty," Sarah exclaimed. She cut her conversation with Max short and bustled over to show them the array of cacti. When they had chosen one and carried it to the register, Max was standing exactly where she'd left him.

She intended to refuse his invitation, but an entirely different answer emerged from her lips. "I need to stop home first."

"No problem. Say, seven o'clock?" His expression had softened. He looked pleased.

"You cook?"

"No. Fortunately, The Garden Terrace offers a delicious barbecue takeout."

"If you drive to the restaurant, you can easily swing to the nursery for your plants."

"Hmm." He shuffled his feet.

"Hmm?"

His gaze leveled on hers, the teasing evident. "I'll grant that your idea makes sense, although it ruins my excuse."

"Which is?"

"To see you tonight."

A giggle escaped her. "It would be a true calamity if your excuse was ruined."

"Is your answer a yes?"

"I'd love to have dinner with you."

Her spirits soared madly beneath the brilliance of his ready smile.

CHAPTER 8

*A*nother December night had fallen in the Carolinas, and stars emerged in the sky one by one.

When Max ushered Sarah inside his slightly messy bungalow, she immediately noticed the three colorful blue, white and green budgies near the window—two sharing one cage, the other alone in a separate cage. Mounds of scientific and bird magazines were stacked on a desk, the floor, and various shelves.

He kissed her tenderly on the cheek, thanked her for delivering the flowers, and rushed to take her coat. "Come. Sit on the sofa. It's comfortable. I made chip and dip."

Although he set the poinsettias and cyclamen on a tall pedestal table, she felt his probing silver gaze drift over her.

"I bought sandwiches, slaw, and a gingerbread cake for dessert." He gestured to the kitchen beyond. "Homemade wassail is simmering in the crock pot."

The cinnamon and apple aroma of the wassail made her mouth water. She grabbed a chip.

"I assumed you didn't cook," she said.

"I don't, but this is an easy family recipe."

Ah, so he had a family. When the subject had come up while they'd texted the night before, he'd veered to other topics—the weather, his research, his birds.

"Well, it smells delicious." She skimmed her fingers across her brown leather tote bag, which contained a precious manila envelope. When she'd stopped home after work to feed her animals and change into dark-wash jeans and a red striped sweater, Marge Addyson had met her at the door.

"Here is the photo from Big Brothers Big Sisters. Max looks young." Marge pressed the sealed manila envelope into Sarah's hands with excessive care. "He's very sweet and that worries me."

"Then or now?"

"Both. That sweet boy has become a charming, caring man."

"Why are you worried?"

"At choir rehearsal I stood across from him, and he could hardly keep his eyes off you. I wasn't sure the interest was mutual, but then I saw your return smiles. He cares for you a great deal."

"We've been friends only a short time," Sarah reminded Marge.

"But long enough. I know you, Sarah, and there's not a mean bone in your body. Do you believe in love at first sight?"

"Is there such a thing?"

"Certainly." Marge paused. "Max tries to hide it, but he's wearing his heart on his sleeve. I was at The Garden Terrace this afternoon for a bit of tea and cake, and he was there, ordering dinner for the two of you. He drove everyone crazy, asking about your favorite foods, obsessing about creating a splendid meal. It was almost as if the queen of England was coming to dine. He insisted on an exceptional holiday dessert."

"Lemon cake?"

"Gingerbread."

"He is very sweet." Sarah offered an affable grin, the kind that pacified fussy customers. Nonetheless, Marge wasn't easily placated.

"And?" Marge asked.

"I care for him a great deal too," Sarah replied. "However, he's leaving in January."

"Is he?"

"A promising career opportunity awaits him in Jacksonville. He's looking forward to it."

"Uh huh." Marge nodded perceptively. "Remember the Bible verse from Corinthians? 13:13?"

Sarah recited along with Marge. "And now these three remain: faith, hope, and love. But the greatest of these is love."

Now, standing in Max's living room, Sarah adjusted her leather tote bag.

"I finished another page of my research paper a few minutes ago," he was saying "This timing worked out well. Dinner at seven is an ideal fit for me."

"Me too."

"Do you often eat alone?" he asked.

"More often than not. You?"

"It depends." He exhaled. "Who am I kidding? I always eat alone." He ran his thumb and forefinger along the edge of a laptop computer, then firmly closed it. "Would you like to meet my uncooperative birds?"

She chuckled. "Sure."

"I want to tell you, Sarah, I'm thrilled you're here."

The question in his persuasive gray eyes was well-defined. *Do you feel the same?*

Slightly, she bobbed her head, a silent response he immediately understood.

He took her in his arms and kissed her. Long and sweet. Her eyes closed, and her breath came in a sigh. He kissed her again and again. Deeply, exquisitely, and soundly.

After the kisses, with her head against his chest, Sarah smiled. Things were so good.

But only for now.

She lived in Cherish, worked at a job she enjoyed, and embraced her church, family and friends. He was off to a promising career opportunity in Jacksonville.

She was a Christian.

He was not.

She loved Christmas.

He tolerated Christmas.

Therefore, she must steel herself for their imminent separation.

She pulled out of his arms, brushed a hand over her hair, which she'd secured in a French braid, and approached the bird cages.

The parakeets squawked as she peered inside.

"Hello, pretty birds," she said.

All three began chirping at once. Vibrant birdsongs flooded the room.

Max came beside her, looping an arm around her. "Fascinating," he said, staring at the birds.

"What's fascinating?"

"The birds. Their reaction to you. I've never seen such behavior from them before."

LATER, they dined in his tiny kitchen on scrumptious barbecue served on his finest white ceramic plates, drinking bottled water. When dinner was finished, he ushered her into the living room and switched on the overhead pendant light.

"Would you like a mug of my homemade wassail with our dessert?" he asked. "The gingerbread is from the restaurant."

"You didn't make the gingerbread too?" she joked.

"My contribution to a festive meal is wassail." He retreated to the kitchen, then returned with two steaming mugs of wassail and slices of gingerbread on a tray. The consummate host. He set the tray on the coffee table, handed her a mug, and took the other for himself. He tapped a seat beside him on the sofa, waited for her to sit, then settled so close their legs touched.

She sniffed appreciatively. Fruity, spicy aromas rising from the mug conjured images of Christmas. The perfect warm drink for a brisk winter night.

She happily sipped and nibbled. The gingerbread tasted fresh out of the oven—sugary, buttery, and delectable. She expressed her compliments aloud, then added, "You touched on the fact that wassail is a family recipe."

Max smiled, but it was distant and distracted. His forehead tensed, and he gave the impression of wrestling with her statement.

Into the beat of an uncomfortable silence, she said, "I have a surprise for you from Big Brothers Big Sisters. Marge Addyson came by my house." Sarah drew the envelope from her tote bag. "She brought this."

Max frowned and pushed his plate of half-eaten gingerbread to the side. "Which is?"

She noted the hesitation in his voice and dipped her head toward the envelope. "A photo of you when you lived in Cherish. You were … maybe twelve years old?"

He faltered. "Close enough."

"You attended Big Brothers, correct?"

"Every afternoon after school when the Monroes worked

late." He managed a sardonic laugh. "Or rather, when they forgot about me, which was often."

Knowing she might be placing him in an awkward situation, she handed him the envelope with the same care as Marge had handed it to her.

"You don't have to open it if you don't want to," Sarah said.

"I'd like to." Yet he flinched, as if gearing for a disappointment.

He shoved out a breath, then withdrew a black-and-white glossy photograph.

Sarah peered over his shoulder. "Is that you?"

He nodded. The dark-haired boy staring back at them held a stoic expression. His fingers grasped the collar of an enormous dog who stood by his side.

Her heart turned over at the boy's brave demeanor, despite the uncertainty in his eyes. She wanted to hug the photo to her chest, hug the young boy and never let him go.

"Your features haven't changed." Emotions welled inside her, although she managed to keep her tone even. "I'd recognize you anywhere with that determined expression. It's been what, over thirty years?"

Max sipped his wassail, a deceptively casual gesture. "I remember when this was taken, right around Christmas."

"Is that your dog?"

"Not mine. The Monroes." His gaze swung to the parakeets, who perched silently on their swings. "I missed that dog more than anything when I was moved to another foster family. More than I missed the Monroes. Much more."

Sarah swallowed the lump in her throat. "What type of breed was the dog?"

"A Labrador husky." Max rubbed his eyes with his forefinger.

She waited for him to continue, but he showed every sign

of being lost in troubled reflections. He stared at the photo, then looked away.

"What was the dog's name?"

"Tinsel."

She studied the photo. A young Max stood outside Big Brothers Big Sisters. His jeans were five inches too short for his long legs. He looked thin, almost undernourished. But his eyes were warm. Max's eyes.

"Want me to refresh your wassail?" he asked.

"I'm good, thanks." She held a hand over her mug. "Did you want to discuss the photo?"

"Nope. I'm a foster kid, Sarah. I moved around a lot. I had some good foster parents, and some not so good." He choked on the words. "The Monroes were not so good."

"And the family where you learned to make wassail?"

"Mr. Lenny's family."

"Where are they now?"

"He and his wife died. My foster brother, John, lives in Portugal. A few years ago, I gave up trying to stay in touch with him."

"Why?"

"What's the point? He lives so far away." Max didn't move a muscle. He cleared his throat. "Do you suppose it's in a man's best interest to suppress unhappy events, to keep them hidden from the woman he's falling in love with?"

Sarah's cheeks warmed. *Max was talking about her.* "The question is, how can that woman help a man repair those inner hurts?"

"I don't know. Sometimes I want relief from all the past pain." His face was expressionless. "My heritage, or rather, lack of heritage."

Now she understood where his resolve to make something of himself had been formed. It had started with the photo.

Or perhaps years earlier. Perhaps in other photos, in different towns with different families. Perhaps with different pets. And every single heartbreaking situation had strengthened Max with the fortitude to break free and make something of himself.

"Try prayer," she said softly.

"Been there." He linked his hands behind his head and peered at the ceiling pendant. "Done that."

"Try again."

His memories, unwelcome and agonizing, would continue to haunt him until he released them.

He dragged in a breath. "Years ago, I prayed to God to grant my foster brother a successful surgery."

"Go on."

"John only got one shot at a basketball scholarship. I knew how much it meant to Mr. Lenny."

She measured her words. "What happened?"

"God didn't listen. A week before Christmas, John's last surgery left him with a distinct limp and one leg shorter than the other."

"A physical disability." Sarah slid her fingers through Max's. The appeal, the warmth of his hand ... this attraction only grew stronger each time they were together. "A handicap."

"Handicap? Ask John how much of a handicap. He didn't attend college. Now he lives in a faraway village, and I haven't seen him in years."

"How did Mr. Lenny react after the failed surgery? You obviously hold him in high esteem."

"He didn't share my anger and frustration at God. He was a pastor—a virtuous and noble man. After listening to my ranting, he reminded me that John was alive and healthy, which was all that mattered."

"Lenny was right."

"At what cost?" Max tore his hand from hers. "Why were the other athletes on John's team strong and whole? He had a promising pro basketball future."

"Lenny was a man of faith."

Max stared straight ahead. He didn't seem aware any longer that she sat beside him. "Lenny declared that John had God on his side and God was all he needed."

"You don't agree?"

"I can't shake my resentment toward a God who plays favorites."

"Try again. Try prayer," she repeated.

"Prayer will make the hurt go away?"

"God will. Reflect on the healing truths of His words every day."

Max lifted his arms and surveyed the room. "I don't see God anywhere."

"Just because you don't see Him, doesn't mean He isn't here."

His expression gradually relaxed, and her chest still ached for him. He had erected a barrier around his heart. A barrier that was impossible to breach until he put aside his resentment and anger.

Pushing up from the sofa, he carried himself stiffly as he walked to the computer.

A moment later, birdsongs floated through the room, the same songs he'd recorded during their hike.

She came to stand close and motioned to the parakeets. "They aren't repeating anything?"

"Nothing. Not even when I play my harmonica."

The single green and white budgie in a wrought iron cage flapped her elegant feathers. In a clear, bell-like voice, she said, "God bless us, everyone."

CHAPTER 9

a few hours later, Sarah headed home.

Max sat on his living room's threadbare carpet and leaned against the sofa.

She was exceptional, fascinating, and extraordinary. More than extraordinary.

The Big Brothers photo had transported him back to the land of unfulfilled dreams. Life with the Monroes had been intolerable, specifically during Max's difficult adolescence.

He wasn't certain why Marge Addyson had gone to the trouble to find that photo and then give it to Sarah. A woman of well-meaning honesty, she may have wanted him to confront past issues in order to move forward.

But he'd done that already, hadn't he? He was accomplished. He'd succeeded in establishing a noteworthy career. Besides, life-altering injustices could never be forgiven.

He shook his head, a rueful smile. His thoughts harbored the very bitterness he thought he'd overcome.

Days ago, Sarah had encouraged him to reflect on the truths of God's word.

"Start with Psalms," she had advised. "The verses will promote healing, comfort and well-being."

"All that?" he questioned.

"All that," she echoed an assurance.

He'd heeded her advice about reading the Bible, although he hadn't told her. It wasn't a subject that came up in daily conversation. Although he could have told her tonight …

Sarah. Sarah. Sarah. They were friends, and there were times when she kept him at arms-length. But there were other times when an electrical current, a snap of lightning, flowed between them. Even when they were a few feet apart, it seemed as if they touched.

He unfolded himself and straightened. He embraced the tranquility he felt when he was with her, and their evening had passed in a blur of laughs and kisses and a hint of rose-wood perfume from her fragrant hair.

Peace was indeed a part of her, a serenity and contentment he attributed to more than her excitement for the upcoming Christmas season. It was her Christian faith. This woman, this town, was a shift for him, when his daily life was filled with more duties than he could accomplish.

He mentioned as much to Gerry when they met a few days later for an impromptu jam session at Musically Yours. Dorothy had afforded them an after-hours studio, and the men had gratefully accepted.

A grin on his weather-beaten features, his fuzzy eyebrows raised in a tickled question, Gerry responded by saying, "So, you're in love?"

Max pulled back, disconcerted. "Who said that?"

"You did."

"When?"

"By your eyes, words and actions."

Max navigated to safer ground. "You sure you don't mind

meeting here to rehearse? The drive from Perrytown is a haul for you."

"You and I share a passion for music, and rehearsing in person is a blessing."

Max tugged out his harmonica. "I assume your wife is understanding about the hours away from little Freddie?"

"Totally. As long as I'm home by ten o'clock." Gerry set an amp on the floor, then searched for an outlet. He plugged one end of a cable into the amp, the other into the guitar. Snaps and shrill bangs followed, and Gerry switched the volume down.

Because Max lived a few blocks from the store, he had walked, admiring the decorations on the way over, likening them to a Christmas postcard.

The temperature had dropped in the past few days, and blades of grass peeked through a frost of white. Holly bushes were in vibrant red-berry bloom, and blinking red, green, and white lights were everywhere.

He passed a busy coffee shop with folks bustling in and emerging with large cups of hot chocolate topped with creamy whipped cream. Aromas of fresh brewed coffee and toasty chocolate brought scents of the season to mind. A vendor on the corner peddled roasted chestnuts in paper cones. Giggling youngsters ran by him, their laughter high-spirited over the chatter of adults. On side streets, flickering candles gleamed from residences, and vibrant lights from their evergreen trees shone from the windows.

Max never remembered decorating a pine tree, except for the year with Lenny and his family. The snapshot of that one perfect tree, the one perfect Christmas, lived forever in his mind.

When he reached Musically Yours, he was immediately immersed in the harmonies of guitar music sounding from the speakers, the cozy overhead lights, and the warmth of an excellent heating system. After greeting Gerry, who was already there, he asked what they were listening to.

"Joseph Slater's newest worship song, a contemporary Christian arrangement," Gerry noted. "He slowed the tempo, kept the instrumentals simple, and let his voice do the heavy lifting. He's an awesome vocalist."

"Awesome, indeed." Max tilted his head, and allowed the poignant lyrics to wash over him.

"'Mary Did You Know?' is one of my favorite pieces," Gerry said. "Are you aware that the composer took seven years to complete it?"

"Good things are worth the wait, time, and effort," Max replied. "And when you find something good?"

"Never let her go."

Max regarded Gerry. "I'm assuming you mean Sarah?" he asked, and then went on to talk about her in such a way that Gerry told him he was in love.

Gerry brought on a grin and didn't reply.

Focus on the music, Max told himself as Gerry finished tuning his guitar.

They decided on a playlist for their upcoming perfor-mance—a medley of carols that included, "O Christmas Tree," "Santa Claus Is Coming To Town," and the finale, "The Twelve Days of Christmas."

"A fun holiday singalong," Gerry said. "For the encore, we'll perform "All Is Well," which is uplifting and inspi-rational."

"You're certain we'll get enough applause for an encore?"

"Stranger things have happened," Gerry mused while he plucked his guitar. "On another note, my wife and baby are attending. My mother-in-law too."

"How's little Freddie lately?"

"I anticipate my wife's hasty exit after our first song."

"Hopefully, we won't sound that bad."

"We're fairly decent. Besides, my wife deserves a night out."

"With little Freddie," Max reminded with a grin. He pointed to an autographed album hanging on a wall, the cover depicting Joseph Slater and an acoustic guitar. "Musically Yours sure promotes this guy."

"He's a big-name artist who lives in Cherish."

"Joseph settled here," Max mused, arching a single eyebrow.

"Same goes for Ryan Edwards. Love is like a fairy-tale, at least that's what my wife parrots. Joseph met Scarlett when he was here for a music promotion. He decided to put down roots after all those years of touring and married her last year."

"Because of Scarlett, he gave up his career?"

"Hardly. Life is a compromise, my friend, and you're clearly smitten too. Are you still coming to my house on Christmas Day for dinner?"

"Unless you're having second thoughts."

"On the contrary, I'm thinking about inviting my great-niece to join us."

Max beamed. "A tremendous idea."

"I suspected you'd be receptive." Gerry smirked, then leaned back in a wooden chair he'd snagged from the student waiting area. "Now let's rock-and-roll to some favorite Christmas carols."

ON THE FRIDAY evening of The Bearded Elves' debut, Sarah grabbed a seat at a round table near the band, along with Dorothy, Ryan, Gerry's wife and son and mother-in-law, Nicholas, and Emmanuelle.

She'd dressed with care for the evening—a fit and flare lace dress, strappy-leopard print heels she already wanted to kick off, and sparkly gumdrop-red earrings. She'd topped her outfit with the fine royal blue wool coat she wore on special occasions.

During the past two weeks, lighthearted conversations and dinners with Max at The Garden Terrace, their stolen kisses, their bantering texts, had become routine. Max invited her on another hike, and she'd happily accepted.

Each time they parted, he promised to see or text her the following day.

And he always did.

She should have been joyful. She was. But a heaviness weighed on her spirit because the days flew too quickly. Soon, January would arrive.

Refreshed by endless glasses of sugar-free lemonade, she sang along to the familiar carols with the others, especially during Ryan's sidesplitting rendition of "The Twelve Days Of Christmas."

As he reached the final, "And a partridge in a pear tree," his operatic voice swelled through the restaurant.

Max confirmed his ability as an excellent harmonica player. He'd been too modest, she thought. Whenever he hit an imagined wrong note, he glanced at her with a chagrined smile. The keen, honed bite of blues he produced on such an inexpensive instrument proved him a man of many talents, and pride flowed through her.

Can you believe the tunes a person can produce from such a modest instrument? he had texted a few days earlier. *Wood, two pieces of metal and minute brass reeds.*

The only thing I can play is the radio, she'd texted back in jest, despite his assurances that he would teach her how to read music.

When? she'd wanted to ask. However, she remained silent.

Wait till you hear our encore, he'd responded.

What's the name of the song?

It's an inspirational piece. It'll bring tears to your eyes.

She was seeing a side of him she hadn't envisioned beneath his polka-dotted tie, chambray shirt, and jeans—a look she'd catalogued as distinctly Max.

During each fifteen-minute break between sets, he'd made it a point to sit next to her. He drew her close, his arm draped around her shoulders in a gesture that seemed possessive, but delighted Sarah immeasurably.

After the band's first set, Melissa, the baby, and her mother left. Little Freddie had been fairly well-behaved, and Melissa and her mother had taken turns walking around the restaurant to soothe the baby.

Sarah surprised herself by offering to help. She'd never been an active participant in group situations, and had felt increasingly uncomfortable in even small crowds now—reticent to speak in case she'd misheard someone, and hesitant to ask people to repeat themselves.

In any case, she wasn't used to these feelings—the attention from Max, the joy of being among a welcoming, friendly group. This was camaraderie, sharing jubilant hours with friends and family who cared.

After the rousing rendition of "The Twelve Days of Christmas," Gerry and Max grinned and bowed to enthusiastic applause. As calls for an encore rose, Max stepped down from the small stage. Dorothy stopped him, saying something to him. Sarah couldn't see Dorothy's face, but she could see Max's, and she couldn't resist eavesdropping by reading his lips.

"January first," he seemed to be saying, "I'm eager to leave for Florida and head up an ornithology department."

January. Leave. Eager.

Sarah's stomach tightened.

She half rose in her seat. But no, she shouldn't be

surprised. He'd repeatedly cited his new Jacksonville job. His time in Cherish was temporary.

Unexpectedly weak, she braced her hands on the arms of her chair. She'd been a fool for falling for him. Hoping against hope, while knowing the romance would come to an end in January.

Questions surfaced with no answers. He was a man of his word and had accepted the university position months ago.

Nevertheless, confronting the pain of his departure brought unexpected heartache. They'd never actually discussed him leaving. It was a point in the future neither had chosen to broach.

No matter. She'd slip into the background again, a pattern she'd honed over the years. Loneliness encroached so swiftly she couldn't react, save for tugging on her shoes and scouting out the quickest path to the exit.

She'd been unmoored by the attentions of a stranger. She'd only known him a few weeks. *A few enchanted weeks.*

She swallowed hard and stood to leave as soon as Max and Gerry returned to the stage to more applause. The diners had awarded the men a standing ovation, and the enthusiastic applause soon quieted.

Max angled a glance at her with a broad smile. *Success*, he seemed to say. *Thank you for supporting me and my music.*

She grabbed her coat and turned away, then rounded to glimpse him one last time. His chin drew in, perplexed, as he lifted the harmonica to his lips.

Dorothy caught her hand. "You're leaving? What about the last song?"

"It's later than I thought." Sarah made a show of peering at her watch, aware of how quiet everyone at her table had become. However, she couldn't face another conversation with Max.

From the onset, he'd spoken the truth. Nonetheless, truth

was difficult to confront, especially when it waylaid you at the happiest moment of your life.

Nicholas stood and excused himself from the others. "Sarah, I'll walk you to the door."

"Thanks. I can manage." She veered left, away from him, struggling to keep her emotions in check.

"It's no bother. I have an ulterior motive."

They passed straggling diners, plates of food being cleared from empty tables by tired-looking waitresses, while Max's bluesy harmonica accompanied Gerry's vocals.

"'All is well all is well, ... Sing Alleluia.'"

"It'll bring tears to your eyes," Max had said.

And it did.

The lyrics were hopeful and encouraging, and Max harmonized with Gerry, his baritone voice complementing the uplifting words.

A Christian song. Max was singing a Christian song.

"What's your motive?" she asked Nicholas when they reached the entry. "The abandoned puppy?"

"Yep. And if I don't find a home for him, he'll end up in an animal shelter. It's a no-kill shelter, but still ..." His words trailed off.

She opened her mouth. Closed it. She was about to refuse when she paused. A darling puppy would be the ideal distraction for her hurt heart.

"I'll take him," she burst out.

"Sarah, thank you! Why did you change your mind?"

"I can't let a lovable puppy spend the holidays in a shelter."

"I'll bring him over to your house in a couple days." Clearly, Nicholas was uncertain whether he'd understood her. "I realize Christmas Eve is almost here ..."

"No worries. The puppy has spent too many nights alone already."

CHAPTER 10

On Christmas Eve, Sarah sat alone.

Only for tonight. Tomorrow, she would drive to Perrytown to dine with her great-uncle, his wife, and little Freddie. He'd phoned her, and she'd gratefully accepted the invitation. In years past, she'd spent Christmas Day with her parents and brothers, traveling to their homes in the Carolina mountains. They'd moved away from Cherish, and she was the only one who had remained.

This year, she'd elected to stay home with her growing number of animals.

She had already attended the three o'clock church service. She'd done so purposely, in order not to run into Max, who would be singing in the choir at the six o'clock service. Right about now, he would be entering the church to get ready.

She'd returned from the service invigorated and encouraged. The sermon had touched on how God didn't free people from traumatic situations, but rather, He was there walking with them every step of the way.

Yes, she'd experienced troubles and challenges. However,

any expectations fixed on the Messiah to grant a person's peace came from within. God didn't promise an easy life, and Sarah couldn't experience peace when she had been anticipating a textbook Christmas with the man she loved.

Her mind traveled back to the loving way Max had regarded her—by the river, at the restaurant, in his home. His tenderness when he kissed her.

No. She couldn't allow him into her thoughts anymore. He belonged to the huge, widespread world of birds and his research, not the microscopic town of Cherish.

Yet she'd felt loved and protected when his lips pressed against hers—his strong arms shielding her when they'd encountered that bear.

She hadn't wanted to lose that, the sense of being cherished and safeguarded.

But Max's love was never hers to begin with.

She peered at the roly-poly puppy nestled in his crate. Already, he'd created a wealth of joy in a short period of time.

He was beginning to eat solids, and she'd continued the transition of soaking the food in warm water, then blending it to the texture of gruel. A fresh supply of water was ever present.

The past couple days, she'd brought his toys into her home first for the other animals to sniff. When the puppy arrived, the dogs ignored him except for an occasional sniff. She'd rewarded their unaggressive behavior with upbeat praise, and had placed the resident dogs' toys and food bowls in a separate location.

Likewise, the cats wandered over for a sniff, then dismissed the puppy.

Sarah's goal was to allow the animals to learn to trust each other. So far, so good.

She switched on a holiday radio station, and The Mormon Tabernacle choir sang "Adeste Fideles" in Latin.

Max would've appreciated the arrangement. He was so musical.

Sighing, she looked at the framed photo on her side table. When she had finally scrolled through the photos she'd taken with her cell phone the day of their hike, she found a wonderful one of Max. It was a profile picture. His face had been near the camera, and every handsome quality was evident—the dark stubble of his beard, his silver-gray eyes, his determined demeanor.

She'd also gotten a surprisingly good photo of the bear. She'd auto-merged them into a silly collage, the bear and Max staring at each other, eye to eye.

She'd planned to gift him the photo and had bought a wooden frame depicting the great outdoors with the words Into the Woods on it. She'd captioned the photo, "I knew we were safe all along."

Max's words.

She would never hear his voice again. She squeezed her eyes shut and took a deep breath. "I love you, Max," she murmured, vowing to rely on time and faith to heal her broken heart.

She slid the photo into a bag and placed it in a drawer in the side table.

As Max looked around the church on Christmas Eve from his vantage point on the top riser, his heart dropped. He scanned the pews—the exquisitely appointed windows and altars bedecked with the brilliant display of flowers that Sarah had arranged. But Sarah was not there.

"Surely, she'll attend church," he muttered to Gerry, as the men took their places in the baritone section.

Marge Addyson, standing near the altar, turned. "She attended the earlier service," she said.

She did? Why?

Two days ago, Sarah had left The Garden Terrace before The Bearded Elves' performance was over and without a farewell. Thereafter, Max's phone calls and voice mails had gone unanswered.

The previous morning, he'd stopped by the nursery. Her coworker, Bonnie, declared that Sarah was in the greenhouse dealing with seedlings and couldn't be disturbed.

The service ended with the cantata and Max's harmonica solo. When the service was over, he exited the church with his heart touched and his spirits lifted. The sermon had delivered a message of optimistic goodwill.

"God's son appeared in the least likely situation and to humble people," the pastor had addressed the congregation. "Forgive and let your resentments go. What will prevent your happiness is to strive for perfection in yourself and others."

Hadn't Max always sought excellence? Blame it on his upbringing, but he'd endeavored to become top-notch in his profession. But what good was that perfection without someone to love?

Unwilling to accept the end of their relationship, he strode from the church to Sarah's house. In a short time, he'd become accustomed to small-town living, where most places were within a few blocks' walking distance. He'd purchased a special present for her and held the package securely under his arm.

When he reached her house, he stood silently on her front porch. Although he didn't move, wild barking sounded from inside before he could even knock.

Then the barking ceased.

He knocked, hesitant to ring her doorbell. Okay, maybe

he shouldn't have dropped by unannounced, but what else could he do when she kept slipping away from him?

Suppose she was sleeping?

At eight o'clock on a clear and cold Christmas Eve? Sarah? Unless she wasn't home … But where …

Tiny yelps sounded. A yipping.

The door opened a crack, and a wobbly puppy shoved his nose through the opening, wagging a fluffy white tail.

Sarah scooped up the puppy, then gasped as she stood in the doorway. "Max?"

"Merry Christmas."

"How long were you standing on the porch?"

He shrugged. "A while."

"What were you doing?"

"Praying."

"Praying? What are you praying for? An extraordinary gift on Christmas Eve?"

"I'm praying for the most extraordinary of gifts. You."

Her striking green eyes glistened with tears, her features a flood of emotions. "Merry Christmas."

"May I come in?" She couldn't just stand at the door holding a puppy.

"Yes. Please."

He stepped inside and brushed a kiss across her temple. She cuddled the tiny Yorkipoo to her chest. He grinned at the pom-pom tail, the paws reminding him of a hedgehog, and the molten-brown eyes peeking beneath half-closed lids. Perhaps he wasn't a Yorkipoo …

"Apparently, Sheriff Nicholas convinced you?" Max asked as he stroked the puppy's velvety fur.

"Careful," she warned. "His teeth are like little needles." She set the puppy inside a blanketed crate. The two older dogs settled. The cats walked away.

And Sarah walked into Max's embrace.

He drew her closer, pressing his lips to hers, fearful to break the hold for fear she might disappear.

When the kiss ended, she rubbed her cheek against his jacket. "I'm glad you're here."

Her home wasn't decorated for the holidays, which surprised him, considering her festive porch.

"My fake tree and ornaments are in the attic." She seemed to read his mind. "I haven't had time."

Or rather, had she felt like him, and didn't have the heart to decorate?

She was gorgeous in a crimson cashmere sweater and form-fitting black pants. Her figure was trim with curves, a wreath of dark russet curls framed her perfect face.

"I do have appropriate holiday cookies and eggnog, if you're interested," she said. "And both were bought from the grocery store."

They shared another commonality besides coffee and hiking and a love for animals. They appreciated store-bought items when homemade wasn't an option. Or, he supposed, even if it was.

He smiled, removed his jacket, and adjusted his bow tie. For the Christmas Eve service, he'd elected to wear black dress pants and a crisp white shirt.

"Can I be direct?" he asked, after she'd taken a jug out of the refrigerator, poured him a glass of eggnog, and set out a platter of frosted vanilla sugar cookies in the shape of snowmen.

"I wouldn't expect anything else."

He placed his gift on the coffee table. He'd wrapped it in plain brown paper tied with twine, topped with a green and white parakeet ornament.

"Why did you leave the restaurant without saying good-bye?" His hand slid up her arm in a caress. "Furthermore, why were you avoiding me? Is my singing that bad?"

She smiled. "No."

"I'd like to continue seeing you."

She fixed her gaze on a point beyond him. "I can't deal with a long-distance relationship and you're leaving for Jacksonville in a week."

He heard the hurt in her tone. His gaze stayed on her.

He invited her to sit on the sofa in the living room and he settled beside her. "Who said I was moving to Jacksonville?"

"You've mentioned little else since you arrived in Cherish. The other night at The Garden Terrace when you spoke with Dorothy, you declared your eagerness to leave for Florida in January and head an ornithology department."

And then it hit him. Sarah cared about him. Deeply. So deeply, she couldn't face him leaving.

And he was delighted.

He pulled her nearer. "I said I was eager to greet the new head of the ornithology department in Florida in January."

She blinked. "I don't understand."

"I declined the position. The latest candidate is a colleague from my New York university days who's done amazing research on zebra finches. She's a workaholic and will be an excellent fit."

"So much for my lip-reading abilities. And eavesdropping." Sarah sat straighter. "You didn't accept the position?"

"No."

"I made an appointment with an audiologist to test my hearing. I've read that I won't be as fatigued at the end of the day if I haven't had to struggle with the effort of listening."

"If you indeed have a hearing loss, it should be addressed." Max smoothed his lips over her hair. "I should've been clearer about my feelings. I would've been if you hadn't vanished."

"I haven't gone anywhere."

"This project has involved numerous researchers working

around the world. My bit with budgies is only a small part of the larger study on birdsongs."

"And?"

"The paper will take a couple years to complete, especially as current research sends scientists in different directions. Which means I'm not going anywhere. I can continue my research here and will receive a full-time salary."

"You're staying in Cherish?"

"I renewed my lease on 8 Poplar Lane."

"Does this mean more hiking adventures?"

"Weekly." He grinned. "This place, and you, have allowed me to slow down and reflect. However, I will have to travel to Jacksonville twice a semester to meet with other members of the department. I'm hoping you'll accompany me."

"I'd love to."

"I'd also like to visit the university I attended in New York."

"I've never seen a big city."

"New York is filled with diversity, culture, and excitement. I'll take you to see the famous landmarks."

"I'd like that," she said softly.

"And I have a brother in Portugal."

"Yes."

"I need to reach out to him again. If he invites us to travel to Portugal to visit him, will you accompany me?"

She nodded. "Happily."

"Good." He peered upward. "Where's your attic?"

"You're looking in the right direction."

"I've only decorated a Christmas tree once in my life—with Lenny and his family."

"Is that a hint?"

"A broad hint. But first." He nodded to his gift.

Glancing at him, she unraveled the twine. In the box was

an ornament—a bear, hiker boots and the inscription, "Take a hike."

She smiled, smoothed her fingers over the words, then curled near him. "You remembered?"

"Of course. After numerous phone requests to the ranger, a shipment finally arrived."

"Thank you." She slid open a drawer in the table beside her and handed him a bag. "I'm sorry it isn't wrapped. By the time the order arrived, I assumed I'd never see you again."

"Yet here I am." He pulled the frame out of the bag and read aloud her caption. "I knew we were safe all along."

"Because we'll do life together."

For a long while, he held her. "I missed you at church tonight. Mrs. Addyson remarked on the preacher's outstanding sermon."

"Yes. I thought so too."

"I played the harmonica. The choir was beautiful."

"I'm sure they were. I'm sure you were awesome."

"You'll hear me play and sing again because I joined the choir." He tipped back his head, as if he were gazing toward heaven. "I was distracted—by my bitterness, and by life. I'm starting to realize that God is for me, not against me. My perspective was messed up, but finally, at forty, I'm seeing more clearly."

"God has always been your champion. He is never against you."

She whispered a word of praise, and Max joined in.

"Gerry declared that dinner tomorrow is at two o'clock, give or take a few hours," she said.

He returned her smile. "He told me the same. I guess it depends on little Freddie's schedule."

She hesitated. "I didn't realize you were dining there too."

"He didn't mention it?" Max chuckled. "He must've forgotten when he phoned you."

"You knew he called?"

"I stood next to him when he made the phone call."

"So, you figured between tonight and tomorrow, we'd see each other?"

"That's one of the things I love about Christmas. All this togetherness." He reached for his jacket and pulled out a handful of wildflowers from his pocket—intense violets and pale blue ivy. "These grow at the edge of town. I'm impressed that plants bloom here in the winter. I'd forgotten. In any event, I picked them for you. Sorry they're wilted."

"They're not. They're beautiful."

He muffled her protest with a deep kiss and drew her into his arms. "I can't give you much, but I'll give you my love."

"I love you too."

The puppy whimpered, and Sarah freed him from his crate and nestled him in her arms. When Max extended his hands, she placed the tiny bundle in his lap.

"What's his name?" he asked.

"Tiny Tim."

Max swallowed the thickness in his throat, the emotions overcoming him.

He drew Sarah near. She was all he needed, all he'd been searching for. The woman he loved by his side, a reverence for a God who was no longer elusive, and a significant, heartwarming Christmas.

"Merry Christmas, Max," Sarah whispered. "And God bless us, every one."

The End

AMANDA'S EASY WASSAIL

Ingredients:

2 cups apple juice
  2 cups orange juice
  2 cups cranberry juice
  2 cinnamon sticks

Add everything to a crockpot, mix, and warm until the desired temperature is reached.

For a larger batch: (almost a gallon)

5 cups apple juice
    5 cups orange juice
    5 cups cranberry juice
    3 or 4 cinnamon sticks, as desired
    Enjoy!

A NOTE FROM JOSIE

Thank you for reading my holiday romance, A Christmas Puppy To Cherish. I hope you enjoyed this heartwarming, inspirational story. This is the fourth book in my contemporary "Cherish" series.

You don't need ears to hear God's plan. All you need is an open heart...

This story is set in the charming fictional small town of Cherish, South Carolina. The book follows A Love Song To Cherish, A Christmas To Cherish, and A Valentine To Cherish.

In A Christmas Puppy To Cherish, I introduce two new characters to our beloved mix of familiar heroes and heroines. Many of you may know that music is an important part of my life, and many of the characters are musicians.

I also researched the hero, Maxwell's, fascinating profession of ornithology. (The study of birds.)

And the heroine, Sarah, with her kind heart, is the perfect match for him.

If you loved this story as much as I loved writing it, please help *other people find it by posting your review.*

A Christmas Puppy To Cherish is available in ebook, Paperback, Hardcover, Large Print Paperback, and Audiobook.

My Spotify List for A Christmas Puppy To Cherish is here.

PAWFECT CHRISTMAS
HEARTS

JOSIE RIVIERA

Christmas in the Air

PUPPIES
FOR
CHRISTMAS

PRAISE AND AWARDS

USA TODAY bestselling author

Top 10 Amazon Romance Collections and Anthologies
#17 Amazon Romance Collections (Books)
#47 Amazon Holiday Romance (Kindle Store)

PROLOGUE

$\mathcal{P}$enelope Reid sat glued to her seat.

Breathe in. There's nothing to be nervous about. Flying in an airplane is routine for many businesspeople.

And she, unfortunately, was a businessperson.

She attempted to smile at the flight attendant who walked past, before resuming her pep talk to herself.

Virginia to Hilton Head Island is a short flight.

She considered texting her brother, Lincoln, with a 'mission accomplished' message, though he wouldn't get the message until she had cell service again. He'd encouraged her to take the flight to secure a toy shop location. She'd complied, albeit reluctantly, though she'd been successful with the negotiations and closed on the deal. Nonetheless, when she finally arrived home, she intended to wring his neck. He knew how much she dreaded flying.

She cut a glance at her handsome seatmate's profile. She'd admired the angle of his face—his sharp jawline and straight nose—throughout most of the flight. Framed by the afternoon sunlight streaming in the window, he seemed relaxed.

Of course, he seemed relaxed because he was sleeping. In fact, he'd slept almost non-stop.

She coughed and nudged him with her elbow. She needed someone to talk to and take her mind off the flight. She'd already breezed through every magazine in the seat pocket.

"Hmm?" He took off his aviator sunglasses and turned toward her. His eyes were a deep shade of brown, warm and mesmerizing, rimmed with black eyelashes. His skin exuded a healthy golden glow. "Have we arrived?"

"Hardly."

He peered out the window. "Cloudy day."

"The weather forecaster called for rain."

"He was probably right."

"*She* was probably right," Penelope corrected.

He grinned. "Touché."

Penelope sat up straighter. "Before you fell asleep, we were discussing our jobs."

"Were we?"

"We were about to." Her seatbelt tightened as she leaned toward him. "I've managed a toy shop business ever since I was a teenager."

"Sounds fun."

"I hate it."

His dark eyebrows curved upward. "Why?"

"Do you want the truth?"

"By all means."

"I shouldn't be telling you this, but I've never been good at deception."

"Bravo." He gave her a thumbs-up. "So, do tell."

"I'd like to do something else."

"Nothing wrong with that. I'll keep your secret." He flashed her a positively magnetic smile.

Her heart stilled. Here sat a good-looking man who had listened to her rattle on about her life whenever he opened his eyes. At least, she assumed he listened. She'd held him captive because he couldn't escape. They were seated next to each other in first class. Still, she'd begun to assume they were friends, and he was an attentive guy.

At his assessing gaze, a flush warmed her cheeks. "I'm bored with my job. I want to create, not manage."

"Create what?"

"I'm not cut out for left-brained, logical analysis anymore. Let's call it a midlife crisis."

"Let's." Another smile. "Do you have another job lined up?"

"No."

"Is your job difficult?" His tone lowered. Thick, wavy hair fell across his forehead, and he pushed back the strands with his hand. His features were a bit weathered, his jawline and cheekbones prominent. A rugged man who apparently spent time outdoors if appearances were any indication.

The thump of attraction in her chest surprised her. She hadn't felt an interest in any guy since her divorce.

"No, my job isn't difficult," she said. "Just repetitive."

"Playing with toys can't be all bad."

She stiffened at his off-hand remark. If he was teasing, he wasn't funny.

"I don't play with toys and they're not mine," she clarified. "I *manage* the business and we sell toys."

He cocked an eyebrow. "We?"

"My brother and I."

"No husband?" He sounded as if he accused her of something—she wasn't sure what—because of her marital status.

"No husband."

"So, you're in the family firm. Come on, mate. Toys are heaps of fun."

Mate? Inwardly, she shook her head.

"Bloody tough, then?"

Bloody? Who used these terms?

"I've done the same job forever." She gave herself a second to regroup. "Since I was a teen."

"When you decide what you want in life, focus on it and let go of the old ways," he replied. "Embrace your creativity."

"At my age?"

"At any age."

He scratched a finger along the shadowy bristles on his jaw. Wasn't it time he shaved? Come to think of it, he looked as if he hadn't slept soundly in a week. His jeans were clean, though his green cotton shirt was rumpled.

He paused to consider her—regarding her cream-colored crepe blouse, which she'd managed to spill coffee on that morning—and her stretchy brown slacks. She hadn't had an extra minute to put on an ounce of makeup before rushing through the Richmond, Virginia, airport to catch the plane to Hilton Head Island. In her hotel room, she'd only showered and added a light spritz of her favorite lavender-scented perfume.

She hardly traveled anywhere anymore, and a commute to Virginia was a last-minute meeting she couldn't avoid. She didn't even like going to Virginia, because it reminded her of her old life and her ex.

To make matters worse, she'd overslept. The evening before, she'd overindulged in fried food and two glasses of celebratory wine.

Conversation was easy when her seatmate didn't stare at her. But now that he was wide awake, she was unprepared for his assessing gaze.

She brushed nonexistent lint from her slacks. "What should I do for a living? Any suggestions?"

Mr. Too Handsome for his own good, she added to herself.

"There are heaps of books on the subject. Whatever suits

your skill level and interests." He gave a short nod, turned back toward the window, and slipped on his sunglasses.

"I'm excellent at parenting, although my son disagrees," she said. "I'm a single mother of a soon-to-be teenager and life isn't easy."

"No matter the age of the child, parenting calls for patience."

"Do you speak from experience?" she asked.

"Nope."

"Do you have kids?"

"Nope. Never will."

Why? she wondered. She grabbed a candy bar from her purse and took a nibble, debating on whether to ask him to explain. However, he kept his face turned toward the window. In under two minutes, she detected soft breathing. Most likely, he was asleep again.

"I'm divorced and my ex has remarried," she said. "His twenty-something wife was a coworker, and she is decades younger than me." Penelope added another fact that continually gnawed at her. "They're blissfully happy and expecting a baby."

"Are congratulations in order?" her seatmate mumbled.

"Not on my end." She tried to push down her snide comment and found she couldn't. "I find it all a bit odd, considering my ex's age." Resentment boiled inside her when she least expected. "He'll be in his seventies by the time their child graduates from college."

"What's your ex's name?"

"Roy."

"Mmm."

She stopped speaking for a second to gain control of her voice. "He moved to another state, making our shared custody agreement for our son trickier than ever."

Her seatmate nodded slightly.

"You know what else?"

He still faced the window. "Hmm?"

She bit off a piece of candy, chewed, and swallowed. "All the guys I've seen since my divorce are cads. I subscribed to an online dating website, but my first date proved an embarrassing bust." She didn't elaborate, and he didn't ask. She'd also dated an art teacher at her son's school until the man gave up. He was a pleasant guy, but her feelings for him had been absent. Plus, he'd acted as if her son didn't exist.

She'd resolved herself to the fact that she wouldn't commit to anyone ever again. Her heart couldn't recover from another broken relationship. Living inside the cocoon of a quiet, safe environment was preferable and assured no one got hurt.

"In summary," she finished, "I've decided to stop dating altogether."

"An archaic term," he replied.

"Dating?"

"Cad."

She waved a dismissive hand. "I refuse to be forced into any more awkward conversations at the local pizza joint."

"You don't like pizza?"

"I like all food."

"Then never say never."

"What's that supposed to—"

The plane jerked. Several shrieks from passengers rang throughout the plane.

Penelope joined in the shrieking, louder than the rest. Her half-eaten candy bar dropped to the floor.

Her seatmate swiveled to her and pocketed his sunglasses. "Are you all right?" His gaze darted about the plane's cabin before landing on her.

"Didn't you feel the plane?" she asked.

"It's just a bump."

"I'm afraid of heights."

"You're on a plane," he reminded.

"I had no choice. I was forced to close on a business deal." She hadn't had a spare moment for anxiety to grab hold when her brother had booked the last-minute flight, and hindsight did little good. She'd assured herself there was nothing to fear.

Envision floating above pearly fluffy clouds while drinking a glass of sparkling water, she told herself.

What was it about reality that proved so different from your imaginings?

She indicated the window—they were flying above *gray* clouds, not pearly, and they weren't at all fluffy.

"To keep my mind off of the fact we're thirty-five thousand feet in the air, I've babbled constantly," she said.

"You talked. You haven't babbled. Talk all you want." He reached into his pocket and handed her a clean white handkerchief. Despite the plane's cold temperature, she was sweating. He'd noticed the sweat beads on her forehead before she had.

"You haven't told me anything about yourself," she prompted.

"What would you like to know?"

She glanced at his left hand. No ring. He wasn't married, although the lack of a wedding ring didn't mean anything.

Regardless, she asked, "Are you married?"

"Absolutely not. Once was enough."

"You're divorced?"

"Thankfully divorced. Marriage isn't for me."

"Why not?"

He shrugged. "My career is important and all-consuming. Romance, women, and marriage got in the way."

She took several seconds to digest his information.

Got in the way of what? she wanted to ask.

"Planes are remarkable if you stop to analyze the mechanics," he said.

"Now is not the time to analyze how planes stay in the air." She dabbed at her forehead with his handkerchief. Her hands were clammy. "Never again," she muttered.

"You won't ever fly again?"

She twisted her wristwatch. "I'll drive or take a bus or a train."

"Have you always been afraid of flying?"

"No. Only the past few years."

"Suppose you're traveling overseas?" he asked.

"Are you kidding? I'll never fly overseas."

When the plane bounced from side to side, she grabbed hold of his arm. Her throat went dry. A fresh start of panic stunned her as the fasten seat belts sign flashed.

Flight attendants buzzed through the cabin, reminding the passengers to buckle up, before scurrying to their own seats. The captain came on the intercom and assured that the plane was flying outside of a thunderstorm, and the occurrence was brief and passing.

Penelope tugged at her seatbelt, ensuring she was secure. Her seatmate patted her shoulder, making no attempt to move away or disentangle his arm from her death grip.

He was tuned in to her fear.

Maybe he was attracted to her—despite the deepening lines around her mouth and the dark circles under her eyes. She didn't need to peer at herself in a mirror to realize she looked a sight. She never seemed to get a sound night's sleep anymore and blamed her restless, worried thoughts on her son for keeping her awake at two a.m.

She dropped her hand and passed him his handkerchief. "Is Hilton Head Island your final destination?"

"No. You?"

"I'm staying overnight on my brother's houseboat, then

driving on to Roses in North Carolina," she said. "You may have heard of the town."

Roses combined small-town charm with big-city conveniences. The tidy homes blended with the landscape of the scenic mountains. In the summer, the town was renowned for bubbling hot springs and comfortable mountain temperatures.

A look she couldn't read flickered across his tanned face. "You're staying on a houseboat?"

"Southern summers are intense, and the ocean breeze is a welcome respite, especially at night."

"Houseboat living is ... different; I'll grant you that. As for me, I'll stay on land, thank you very much."

"Or in the air," she reminded.

He laughed out loud. "You live in Roses?'

She nodded. "Roses is my childhood home. I moved away after college and got married, then returned after my divorce. Since then, I haven't made many friends."

At first, familiarity had enfolded her like a generous hug. Now, things had changed.

"Why not?" he asked.

"Friendships are difficult. The women at my son's school have a close circle reaching back to when their kids were in kindergarten. I missed all that." She cast a glance at him. His expression was unreadable. "Don't get me wrong. Roses is lovely. The main street is lined with local shops, and the park boasts a bandstand for outdoor concerts."

"I prefer big cities. I like all the restaurant options and public transportation."

"Roses is unique and has loads of restaurants."

"I'm sure the town is a beaut." His gaze lingered on her face. "Care for a cold one?"

"I don't drink," she said. "Correction. I don't drink often."

"I used to say that."

"And *now* you drink?"

"Depends on the circumstances."

"The flight attendants are buckled in." She indicated them with her chin.

"They'll be up and about soon."

"You fly a lot?"

"Sometimes," he said. "I've experienced turbulence, though flying is safer than any other form of transportation."

"A quote from …?"

"Me." He smiled. "In all fairness, I read the statistic in *Popular Science* magazine."

"Are you trying to reassure me with a magazine quote?"

"I'm a pro. My job is all about counseling and prevention."

He opted for a caffeinated soda when the flight attendants came to their feet and began serving passengers one last time. He picked up Penelope's candy bar, murmuring, "Your sweet fell on the floor," and handed the candy to the attendant to discard.

"No cold one?" she asked him.

He raised his glass. "I'm a fan of America's free refills."

She'd noted his accent. Probably Australian.

Penelope ordered a low-calorie lemon-lime sparkling water.

"I prefer coffee," she informed him. "In fact, I'm obsessed, and drink six cups a day."

"You didn't order coffee."

"I take my coffee with loads of cream and sugar. Low-calorie soda has no calories, while sugar and cream add hundreds. It's clear sailing for healthy eating now since the fourth of July is safely behind me."

He regarded her with a quizzical frown. "The fourth of July is a problem?"

"If you love hot dogs, hamburgers, and potato salad." She

extended her hand. "Introductions are a little late, but I'm Penelope Reid."

"Jacob." He shook her hand. His fingers were strong. She wondered what he did for a living—his all-consuming profession. Perhaps he was a professor of some sort—teaching psychology courses or counseling. He projected an air of professionalism, despite his casual appearance.

"Here's to the next holiday, Penelope."

"And will-power." She slipped her hand from his. "Fortunately, there are no holidays until my birthday in November."

Her fiftieth birthday. She left that noteworthy detail out, although she guessed this guy's age close to hers. A few threads of silver in his dark-brown hair caught a sliver of sunlight, and subtle lines were etched on his forehead. Men's ages were often difficult to determine. Many men grew handsomer with age. Jacob was apparently one of them.

"What kind of cake do you like?" he asked.

She paused. No one had ever posed that question to her before. "Carrot cake is my favorite."

"Me too. With cream cheese frosting?"

She gave a thumbs-up. "The best."

After her birthday, and much worse, came Christmas. These past few years, her saddest memories were at Christmas. She struggled hard not to think about her ex's unexplained absences when he'd begun having his affair. They were lonely. And now, with Evan readying to visit his father in Florida by flying there by himself, the days preceding Christmas would be lonelier still.

In truth, she couldn't wait for the holiday to be over. Silently, she shook her head, guilty about her lack of Christmas spirit.

By the time they landed, she realized she had told him the month of her birthday, her hometown, her parenting situation, and her single status.

When the plane stopped at the terminal, Jacob hoisted her carry-on luggage down from the overhead compartment. All Aussie charm, if Australia was indeed his homeland, and chivalrous to a fault.

He followed behind her as they exited the plane, and a blast of sultry air greeted them. A reminder that summer still held a firm hold on the Carolinas.

"A pleasure meeting you, Penelope Reid," he said.

She met his gaze as they stepped into the bustling terminal. "The feeling is mutual, Jacob."

"Safe travels to Roses."

"Thanks. You, too." For wherever he was going. She slung her handbag over her shoulder and grabbed her carry-on bag.

He walked backwards a few steps. "Penelope?"

"Yes?"

He drew out his cell phone. "May I take your picture?"

"Why?"

"Truth?"

"By all means."

"You're a lovely woman."

She hesitated. "Okay."

"More than okay. Perfect." He snapped a photo and pocketed his phone. "Well, cheerio."

"Goodbye, Jacob."

She watched as he departed. Broad shouldered, he held himself tall, self-assured as he disappeared into the swarm of passengers.

Somewhere in her gut, she regretted the fact she wouldn't see him again.

After two hours of non-stop conversation, admittedly one-sided and except for when he was sleeping, she'd only learned his first name.

CHAPTER 1

*W*hat a way for her son to start the second month of seventh grade.

Penelope studied herself in the tall gold mirror propped in her bedroom. She'd dressed professionally—a bohemian style midi dress and strappy sandals, because she planned to head to work after seeing to Evan.

She suspected he had strep throat. Again. What twelve-year-old boy got strep throat every other week?

She'd been surprised the previous evening when he hadn't finished the chocolate ice cream she'd brought to soothe his throat. She'd finished it instead because she couldn't let the ice cream go to waste. She'd used a clean spoon, assuring herself that whatever virus he had wasn't contagious.

"I'm not sick, Mom. Everyone gets sore throats." Evan stood in the living room of their eighteenth-century Victorian home wearing his customary saggy jeans. He shrugged on his black leather jacket and crossed his chubby arms. His cheeks shone a bright red, a sprinkling of freckles across his nose. His stout build reminded Penelope of herself, though his legs were too long for his body—a promise—if her ex's height was any indication, of the tall man Evan would someday become.

Her thoughts swerved to Jacob and his muscular, sturdy physique. She scolded herself to stop thinking about him—yet he remained in her thoughts. He was a curve in the road, a curve in her life she could ill afford. She didn't know why she'd told him so much about herself.

"Did you hear me, Mom?" Her son interrupted her musings.

The humidity of a Southern October afternoon should have deterred him from wearing a jacket. And what was it about dark colors these days? A kind of rebellion, she supposed. She kept her opinions to herself. No use fighting over small battles like a black jacket.

She placed her hand on his warm forehead. "You have a fever."

He pulled back as if she'd branded him with her touch. Where had her apple-cheeked, angelic son gone? Once Evan hit twelve years old, he'd turned into a mini monster.

"Are you driving me to the doctor's office?" he asked.

Did he try to avoid being seen with her, or was this all her imagination? He sure didn't act like a kid who wanted to go places with his mother. "We can't walk from the outskirts of town. Besides, my throat is sore, too."

"You made two appointments?" He groaned. "We'll be there forever."

"Just one. I'm hoping the doctor will recommend an over-the-counter medicine for me."

"I'll ask him for you." Evan jutted out his chin in defiance. "Then I can go by myself."

"Dr. Williams' office is past the Roses' recreation center." She vacillated, remembering the numerous swim meets Evan had once participated in.

"So?"

"You used to love to swim." Happy memories flooded her thoughts. "The coach said you were a natural at the butterfly stroke."

"I guess the butterflies flew away," Evan muttered.

"Swimming is a lifelong sport. Exercise builds endurance and will keep you healthy and slim." That last bit slipped out, and her son frowned. She hadn't meant any inference to his weight gain over the past year.

"I like ocean swimming," he said quietly. "The rec center's indoor pool is too closed in."

She wondered how their conversation had gone from strep throat to swimming, but a dialogue, any dialogue, with Evan, was welcome.

"We never lived near the ocean, but we'll visit during the summer." A thought came to mind; overseeing the Hilton Head toy headquarters instead of the shop in Roses, commuting if she was needed in the office. "I'll homeschool you next semester and we can live on Uncle Lincoln's houseboat."

"How will I be able to spend spring break with Dad and Victoria?"

"Your stepmother will be absorbed with the newborn baby, and I'm sure your father and I can work out a congenial solution."

"Oh, right. Like that would ever happen."

A solution might be possible, if her ex was even remotely agreeable, and they didn't get into an argument whenever they discussed custody. Only Roy would move clear to another state to please his young wife, forsaking the needs of his son.

"A houseboat in a harbor is a fishbowl, like living here," Evan said.

"Well, we can rent a cottage farther out. How about

Daufuskie? The island is only a short ferry ride from Hilton Head's mainland and surrounded by the Atlantic Ocean."

"Oh, great. Then everyone at school will call me a freak."

She sighed. There was no pleasing Evan, though she tried and tried. "You're a freak for living on a houseboat?"

"For being home schooled."

She faltered. "Have your classmates called you a freak before?"

"Try every day, Mom. I just want to swim where no one is staring at me. Especially my teammates from the swim team."

"Why on earth would they stare at you?"

"Because I'm fat and ugly and a slow swimmer."

"That's ridiculous."

"Don't say it's not true, because we both know it is. The popular kids don't want anything to do with me." His shoulders hunched, yet his gaze was astute. "You competed in championship competitions. Uncle Lincoln showed me the newspaper clipping when you won first place in freestyle."

"Perseverance pays off."

"You always say swimming is a lifetime sport, but you never swim anymore."

That was her life eons ago, before her college years, her failed marriage. In high school, she'd immersed herself in competitions.

Everything had changed after her marriage.

But not at first. Blissful happiness came first.

And then she'd begun to suspect her husband was unfaithful, though Roy had denied her suspicions. If she ignored the signs, perhaps his affair would go away, she told herself.

It hadn't.

Since the betrayal, heartbreak, and subsequent divorce, she'd fortified herself with an impenetrable barricade. She was serene and no-nonsense. In her youth, she'd been known for her sense of humor, but hardly anything made her laugh anymore.

She breathed in. Nothing was going to topple her hard-earned and sensible equilibrium.

She recalled the comradery with her teammates and the late-night swim meets. She loved belonging to a tight-knit group of friends she relied on. Was Evan missing out on those same memories because he'd abruptly quit the team?

Why hadn't she realized his withdrawal from all extracurricular activities since her divorce and their move to Roses? The signs were clearly there if she'd only taken the time to notice.

You're a bad mom, her conscience reprimanded.

I try my best.

Still, she should've encouraged him more. Instead, she'd become more involved in the business and neglected her son in the bargain.

She took in Evan's appearance—sandy-brown hair and vivid blue eyes, and her heart squeezed. His heavy-set build would thin out as he grew, and his resemblance to her good-looking brother, Lincoln, was striking. Someday, Evan would become a young man with more girlfriends than he could count.

He wasn't aware of that yet and didn't care. He was interested in the present. She prided herself on identifying issues at the toy shop and fixing them. Now she needed to focus on her vulnerable son and fix whatever was causing his problems. She hoped she wasn't too late.

"Make sure your hamster's cage is secure," she said. "Yesterday, he got out and ran all over the house."

"Giblet is a girl, Mom," Evan replied. "Besides, I want a puppy."

"Let's see how well you care for your hamster first. Last week I rescued her from behind a shelf where she got stuck."

Evan obeyed while muttering under his breath for having to do chores when he was sick, and they walked out the front door.

"Won't you be late for work?" he asked.

"Are you still trying to get rid of me?"

He stooped to pick up a loose stone and sent it hurtling across the lawn. "Maybe."

"It hurts when you speak to me like that."

"Sorry, Mom," he muttered.

"I phoned Uncle Lincoln and told him to expect me by midmorning." Penelope kept her voice calm. "He and the staff can easily handle my absence. Besides, I make my own hours."

Penelope and Lincoln shared ownership of New Beginnings Toys, a well-known toy company noted for producing heirloom wooden rocking horses and organic toys. In addition to the Roses shop and headquarters on Hilton Head, the business distributed toys across the United States. Her flight to Virginia had been to finalize the acquisition of another property for expansion.

Since the plane trip, she'd pushed aside her confession to Jacob that she hated her job. Just keep on living and working in a no longer challenging career, was her motto. She led an isolated life, the fate of soon turning fifty, and had come to accept the sad truth.

As a pastime, she'd begun making wooden dolls that children seemed to love, but the craft, though easy and enjoyable, was time-consuming.

"I'll be late for school," Evan said.

"All this concern about lateness. You don't even like school," she said.

Throughout his elementary days, Evan had aced classes and scored straight A report cards. The past couple of years, his grades had slipped. He had no friends, at least none who came over to their house anymore. He stayed in his room, munching on bags of potato chips, and played video games for hours.

Her once athletic son.

"I'll get behind in school if I don't go," he protested. A last-ditch effort, she supposed.

"You'll catch up. This is the only appointment available with the new doctor in town. Emphasis on the word new. Everyone is raving about how gentle and patient he is. The mothers at your school say he's excellent with kids and won't rush us. He'll answer all our questions."

"You mean *my* questions, Mom, not *our*. The appointment is mine. I'm not a kid anymore."

True. He was turning into an adolescent, and she doubted she could live through the next few years.

"Why aren't we seeing Dr. Damian?" Evan asked as he slipped into the front seat of their truck and buckled his seat belt. "I'm used to him."

"For one thing, Uncle Lincoln and I remember Dr. Damian treating us, which goes back decades. For another, Dr. Damian has thankfully retired. I was beginning to question whether he was thorough enough."

"I liked him."

"I was comfortable with him, too. However, I assume Dr. Williams is up on the latest medical techniques."

"Aunt Shanice said he is good-looking."

Shanice was Lincoln's wife. They'd been wed a few years and still displayed a delightful newlywed affection for each other.

Penelope grinned. She'd heard an earful about the handsome Dr. Williams, but romance was the last thing on her mind. He was probably fresh out of medical school, married, with a couple of kids.

When she found a spot in the crowded parking lot, she

parked a distance from the entrance, declaring the walk was beneficial for both her and Evan.

Once they stepped inside the office, the receptionist, clearly flustered, greeted them with a distracted hello and ushered them to a packed waiting room.

"We're behind at least forty-five minutes," she explained. "Dr. Williams was called in for an emergency at the free clinic he established in town. He has returned and is seeing patients, and we apologize for the delay."

Considering the time, Penelope surmised that Dr. Williams kept early hours. Unlike her. She was the opposite of a morning person.

She'd read about the clinic. He'd secured a donated warehouse facility near the hospital and solicited donations from businesses and additional funding through a state grant. He provided free health care to patients who couldn't afford otherwise. Open on weekdays and weekends, the word was spreading, and evening hours were being extended.

After filing their paperwork, the nurse called Evan's name.

Penelope stood, and Evan stuffed his hands into his pockets. Much to Evan's frowning dismay, she followed him into the examining room.

She pointed to her throat, her excuse to accompany him. "You'll get the swab done and tested, and we'll leave with a prescription for your antibiotics in hand. Couldn't be easier."

CHAPTER 2

*E*van plunked onto the examination table and yanked his phone from his pocket.

"Why are you constantly absorbed with your cell phone?" Penelope seated herself on an empty chair across from him.

"Everything is on the internet, Mom. Everyone famous, and whatever is going on in the world."

Penelope pulled out her own cell phone and gestured toward the window. "Isn't the world happening outside and all around us? Your screen doesn't tell the truth."

"You're on *your* phone."

"I intend to get some work done."

He stared straight ahead, his features impassive. "Then why are you always watching me?"

"I don't mean to. I'm worried about you."

"I've had strep throat four times."

"Exactly." In fact, her nerves were frayed. Evan had never been a sickly child, but this year, things were different, beginning with his unhealthy diet. She vowed to make changes in her grocery shopping and eliminate the candy and chips they'd both grown so fond of.

The door opened abruptly, and Penelope reminded Evan to put his phone away.

"G' day, mate. Evan, is it?" A tall man stepped inside, his deep male greeting filling the tiny room.

His voice. That accent. She'd recognize him anywhere.

Penelope snapped her phone shut and slowly rose to her feet. An email she'd been typing to an employee was halted in midsentence.

Evan swung his legs back and forth, clearly impatient, still wearing his black leather jacket. He glanced up from the latest video on his phone, a tower defense game he'd tried to explain to her once. At her stern frown and second sharp reminder, he shoved the phone into his pocket.

"I'm Dr. Williams." This attractive doctor, wearing a white coat and khaki pants, exuded competence as he closed the door behind him. A stethoscope hung from around his neck. He looked up from the chart on his clipboard, gave Evan a sincere smile, then turned to Penelope.

Her heart did a double flip.

"You. Here?" she asked.

A beat of silence passed.

"Penelope Reid." He smiled. "I recognized the last name."

"What are you doing in Roses?" She found herself staring. Why couldn't she shake off this attraction to him? Since they'd met on the plane, she continued to envision his slow, discerning smile. His voice had been gentle when he'd leaned close and assured her that he didn't mind her babbling.

He set down the chart. "I bought the practice from Dr. Damian."

"I thought you preferred big cities."

"I changed my mind."

Whoa. Not because of her. No, of course not.

"You never mentioned anything on the plane," she said.

"What plane?" Evan asked.

"Dr. Williams and I met a while ago when I … we … flew back from Virginia."

"I visited several physicians' practices before making my final decision." Jacob studied her. "I interviewed in Virginia, then planned to fly on to Florida. I made a detour in Hilton Head."

"A detour," she echoed. "To Roses. You never mentioned any interviews."

Why would an older doctor buy another doctor's practice? Had Jacob lost his own practice due to incompetence?

He offered a half smile. "I believe you did most of the talking on the plane."

He was hardly the young, recently out-of-medical school doctor she'd anticipated.

He turned to Evan, who assessed their conversation with a peculiar, thoughtful scowl.

"Anything you'd like to talk to me about, Evan?" Jacob asked. "How's it hangin'?"

"My throat hurts."

"You're how old?" Jacob scanned Evan's chart.

"I'm twelve."

"Almost an adult, mate. Shall we ask your mum to leave?"

"No." Evan shot a glance toward Penelope. "She can stay. She has a sore throat, too."

"I'm fine." She waved off his remark. She didn't want to discuss any illness of hers with Jacob Williams. She intended to keep her replies brief and avoid any personal connection. "My sore throat went away."

"Did it?" Jacob pressed the back of his hand to her forehead. His touch was warm and firm. Her cheeks heated.

"She wants you to recommend an over-the-counter medicine for her," Evan chimed in.

Jacob quirked an eyebrow. "Does she now?"

"If a recommendation isn't too much trouble," she said.

Jacob dropped his hand. "No trouble at all. Let's have a look at your son first." He lifted his stethoscope and listened to Evan's heart and lungs. "Nothing of concern there." He flipped a page on his chart and made a note. Then he produced a swab and instructed Evan to say "ah." Much to Penelope's surprise, Evan didn't gag. His usual sullen expression vanished. In fact, he urged Jacob to explain the test.

"Evan is tossing around becoming a physician or a veterinarian when he gets older," Penelope explained.

Evan crossed his arms. "I want a puppy."

"Do you like dogs?" Jacob asked.

"I love dogs."

"Is that why you're interested in becoming a vet?"

Evan shrugged. "Maybe."

"I'm encouraging him." Penelope turned to Jacob. "What mother doesn't hope her son will someday become a doctor?"

"I can name one." Jacob looked away before meeting her gaze. "You're a sweet and caring mum, Penelope Reid."

"I don't know about the sweet part." Evan was scowling at her again. Flustered, she groped for a subject change. "Evan loves all animals."

People ... well, not so much.

"The medical profession needs bright young minds," Jacob said.

They returned to the waiting room while awaiting the results, then were summoned back to the examining room. As Penelope suspected, the test confirmed strep throat.

Evan's eyes widened. "I've got strep for the fifth time?"

"You're obviously susceptible to strep," she replied. "Does your throat still hurt?"

"Are you kidding? Yes."

She turned to Jacob. "Our previous doctor recommended a tonsillectomy for Evan."

"Weigh the pros and cons of a tonsillectomy at Evan's age," Jacob said. "There's always a risk of complications from the surgery. A recent study suggests patients are more prone to long-term respiratory disease afterwards."

"I don't want an operation," Evan said.

"I agree, at least for now." Jacob extended a hand to Evan and shook. "Have a good one. I'll send a prescription for antibiotics to the local pharmacy, and you should start feeling better in two or three days. And this is my recommendation for your mom." He scribbled on a sheet of paper and handed it to her.

She scanned the instructions. "Tea with honey and lemon and loads of rest?"

"Works like a charm."

"When should Evan return to school?"

"I'd advise he stay home for at least forty-eight hours after he starts the antibiotics."

"Good," Evan said. "If I don't ever have to go to school again, my life will be a lot better."

"Quitting isn't an option, Evan," she broke in. "You'll never be a doctor if you can't finish junior high."

Evan opened his mouth.

The last thing she needed was her son spilling more of their personal affairs. Jacob Williams knew enough about her already.

She cut Evan off with an abrupt nod.

"Thank you, Doctor," she said.

"Please call me Jacob."

She felt torn. She really wanted to keep up the formality in a doctor's office, but she really, really liked calling Jacob by his first name.

She nodded. "Okay."

"Thanks, Dr. Jacob," Evan chimed in.

"Not you," she replied. "To you, he's Dr. Williams."

"Why? That's not fair."

"Life isn't always fair. We're adults. You're a kid, and you must be respectful."

"Why would your life be better if you didn't attend school?" Jacob's gaze swayed to Evan.

"Because all the kids hate me, and I hate them."

"I could use some help in my clinic. Do you ever volunteer?"

Evan lifted his shoulders. "Not much, unless I go with my mom."

"Oh, where do you go?"

"She and Uncle Lincoln donate toys to the homeless center in town."

"Several of the families I see are refugees from other countries," Jacob said. "They come into my clinic for free health care."

"We hang out with the kids at the shelter and help them with homework and stuff," Evan continued. "Mom was bringing in the wooden dolls she made, but not anymore."

"I'm tied up at work," she murmured.

"Admirable, and very creative. I encourage you to get back to it." Jacob shot Penelope an approving glance, then turned to Evan. "Would you like to lend a hand in the clinic, mate?"

Evan fixed his gaze on the tile floor. "Doing what?"

"Whatever the moment requires because the patients' needs change minute by minute. How are your phone skills?"

"Okay."

"We need more beds and chairs. I'll give you a list of the other clinics in the area," Jacob said. "Do you speak Spanish?"

"He doesn't, but Evan took a signing class last year," Penelope put in.

"I'm in seventh grade." Evan rolled his eyes. "I can communicate all by myself, Mom."

Jacob concentrated on Evan. "Signing will be helpful for my deaf patients."

"Okay," Evan mumbled.

Penelope's eyebrows raised. *I can't believe my son agreed so easily.*

"Excellent." Jacob patted Evan on the back, and she caught Jacob's smirk as he winked at her. "I'll ask the nurse to provide the details. She volunteers at the clinic every Saturday morning. Will Saturday work for you, Evan?"

"I guess."

"Can you arrive by seven?"

Evan blinked. "A.M.?"

"Yep."

"Evan doesn't usually get up until—" Penelope tried to keep her voice neutral.

Jacob made eye contact with her and gave a subtle shake of his head.

His silent message, to allow Evan to answer for himself, stopped her. She knew what Jacob surmised. She was an overprotective, hovering parent.

Evan broke the ensuing silence. "All right. I'll get up early."

"Let's plan on a week from this upcoming Saturday, so you have several days to recuperate."

As they exited, Penelope's chest filled with encouragement over the conversation. Jacob Williams had accomplished a great deal during their short office visit. Whether he realized or not, and she had a sneaking suspicion he did, he'd given her son a purpose.

At the pharmacy, Evan waited in the car. Penelope hastened inside and collided with Candee Winchester, a local realtor. Candee was a striking woman with wavy auburn hair and an amiable personality. She'd married Teddy, one of her clients and a real estate investor. They'd adopted his nephew, Joseph, who loved horses.

"What brings you to the pharmacy on a weekday morning?" Candee slung her handbag over her shoulder and juggled a bag filled with cleaning supplies. She explained that she and Teddy were redoing her office.

"I'm picking up a prescription for Evan," Penelope said. "He has strep throat again."

"Did you see the handsome new doctor?"

"The guy everyone is fixated on?"

"Who else?" Candee had made a name for herself as the town matchmaker, and Penelope recognized her cupid grin from a mile away. "I'm working to find him a house here. In the meantime, he's renting an apartment at the old Roses Hotel."

"Lincoln never mentioned anything."

Lincoln and Penelope had purchased the rundown hotel and renovated it. Besides an investment, the hotel provided housing for their toy shop employees. A couple of years ago, though, they'd sold the hotel, preferring to concentrate on their business rather than real estate.

"I've shown Dr. Williams numerous properties, though he's very particular." Candee fingered the gold cross earrings she always wore. "He wants what he wants, all wrapped up in a certain low-price range."

"I assumed a doctor's salary was more than ample."

"For whatever reason, not in his case."

Penelope picked up the prescription. Before she headed out the door, she bought three chocolate candy bars. She earned them, she decided, foreseeing a challenging week ahead while caring for her cranky son.

CHAPTER 3

$\mathcal{T}$he following day, Jacob grinned at the remembrance of his brief conversation with Penelope and her son in his office. He'd never met a teen who liked to get up early, and Evan proved no exception. He admired the boy's commitment when agreeing to volunteer at the clinic. Of course, the real test was yet to come. Would Evan show up at the assigned hour?

Jacob scanned his mile-long to-do list for the evening. More house-hunting with Candee Winchester can wait, he concluded, as he closed his office.

He looked up Penelope's address, discovered she lived on the edge of town, and decided to drive to her home. He'd purchased a ten-year-old yellow four-door Volkswagen when he'd moved to Roses. Driving wasn't his thing, and he'd never gotten used to seeing cars on the wrong side of the road in America. He'd relied on big-city transportation in Atlanta, and Roses didn't boast subways. Fortunately, traffic here was minimal.

He didn't make house calls, and strep throat wasn't usually a cause for concern. However, Evan was a new patient, and, for lack of any other reason, rational or otherwise, why not? He was attracted to Penelope and wanted to get to know her better.

Reservations stirred. He'd vowed to keep his life simple ever since his niece's death. He'd vowed to prioritize what was important. He'd vowed to devote his career to serving people.

Eighteen-hour workdays had worked well throughout his successful career. He had shouldered all responsibility with unrestrained energy, though he had never achieved his goal.

Success and kudos aren't necessary anymore, he reminded himself.

He'd quit his job; walked away to reassess and refocus, searching for more simplistic goals.

His thoughts gravitated to Penelope.

From what he'd learned from their plane conversation, she was anything but simple. However, she was unassuming and vivacious. In fact, she was a stunner.

Penelope revealed that Evan's father didn't see his son much anymore. Although he didn't intend to become a surrogate father, Jacob made a mental note to engage with Evan, and volunteering at the clinic proved a positive beginning.

He located Penelope's home and parked at the curb, viewing the expansive driveway, and surrounding half acre of land. Inhaling, he breathed in freshly mowed grass and the honeyed scent of late-blooming flowers.

Her home was a beaut. A splendid, old-fashioned Victorian, classic, with a rectangular shaped, sloping roof, and boasting a veranda.

He got out of his car and scanned the property. This was the house he envisioned for himself. This was exactly the type of house he was looking for.

The few Candee had shown him were out of his price

range. He'd poured a lot of money into helping his sister, Kylie, rebuild her life after his niece's death, and even more money setting up his clinic.

He paused to study Penelope's home. He wasn't certain what to expect when he stepped inside, but based on the exterior, he assumed the interior was gorgeous.

All the homes he'd viewed in Roses had lacked one specific requirement. He wanted to have a medical practice in his home, and most weren't big enough. This home, painted in colors of vivid blue with gold trim, resembled a doll house. Standing two stories, with a stained-glass window facing the street and a rounded turret, the architecture was a reminder of the historic Victorian era, where nothing came cheap.

He surveyed the area. The house was located at the end of a main road leading to town.

Penelope hadn't exaggerated when she'd described Roses. Storybook wasn't an adequate description. The town was idyllic, a scene straight out of a Norman Rockwell painting. In addition, from his early morning jogs, he'd discovered something even better than a wholesome culture. He'd observed the heart.

The people.

Young and old alike were kind, interested in others, and respectful. Honest and polite and middle America at its best, where church was at the center.

He scanned the block. Other homes and businesses were located nearby Penelope's house. Surely the area was zoned for both business and residential properties.

Not only would a home office reduce his overhead, but he could treat more patients on evenings and weekends. He liked the idea of a short commute from his kitchen to his office instead of driving to town.

Trouble was, this house was hers, not his.

You'll never be able to afford anything on this scale. Occasionally, his mother's voice echoed in his ears, and his chest tightened. He allowed the mental numbness to take hold and shook away his contemplation.

He *could* afford a lovely home.

Eventually.

He stepped onto the porch. After seeing patients at his office all day, he'd stopped at his rental apartment at the Roses Hotel to shower and change into dark jeans and a clean T-shirt.

He rang the doorbell. From inside, a squeal sounded.

"Giblet, get into your cage this instant." The sound of rushing footsteps. "There, I've got you. Come with me, it's probably the postman with a late toy delivery." She opened the front door with a tiny hamster nestled in her hands.

She gaped. "Jacob?"

"Hello, Penelope." He caught his breath. He'd forgotten what she'd been wearing on the plane, or in his office, but it wasn't a stunning striped dress that flared at the waist.

That generous figure. Her bare toes peeked out from a pair of beige sandals. He'd be thinking about her for the rest of the evening. Oddly, her sharp blue eyes, focused on him, were even more captivating.

Her gaze narrowed. "Why are you here?"

"I'm not delivering any toys."

"I can see that. Is Evan supposed to report to your clinic tonight?"

"I hope not, unless he intended to expose my patients to strep throat."

"Then why?" A slight breeze lifted her dark hair, shaped in a short bob style. Classy and elegant silver highlights framed her round face. He wanted to tuck one of the stray strands behind her ears. He wanted—

He cleared his throat. "You drink coffee, right?"

"Every day."

He held out a bag of ground coffee he'd picked up at the local shop in town. "Did you reach your quota for today?"

"That will never happen."

"Care to brew us a cup?"

Fearing she might protest, he held up a hand to hold her off.

"You like coffee, too?" she asked.

"Very much." He had her compete attention.

"You didn't mention anything about coffee on the plane."

"No?"

Her delicate eyebrows came together. "All you said was that you liked to drink."

"I do, especially ginger beer."

She tilted her head. "What is ginger beer?"

"A beverage made from ginger, sugar, and water."

"Is the beer alcoholic?"

"Sometimes. Where I come from, ginger beer is a local favorite."

"Australia?"

"Yea. Down under."

"I suspected you were from Australia but couldn't place your accent for certain." She peered out the door. "You drove here?"

"I didn't ride my kangaroo. In fact, riding a kangaroo is forbidden in Australia."

"Probably in America, too."

"Why did you suspect I was Australian?"

She offered a half-smile. "Your accent is a dead giveaway."

"I've never been able to shake it."

"You've lived in America a long time?"

He stroked his fingers over the hamster's caramel-colored fur. "Uh-huh."

"A man's foreign accent is usually appealing to a woman." She stared at him while holding the wriggling hamster.

"Usually?"

She didn't reply and pushed the door open wider with her hip. "Would you like to come in?"

"I was hoping you'd ask."

"I don't have any ginger beer."

He shook the bag. "I'll provide the coffee."

She ushered him inside and cradled the hamster. "Are you afraid of hamsters?"

"Is he going to race about?"

"Not if I can help it, and I've been informed that Giblet is a she. Evan refilled her water bowl a while ago and didn't secure the cage." Penelope placed the hamster in a cage situated on a table in the hallway and secured the latch. "Are you comfortable with animals?"

"Animals are my passion." Jacob closed the door behind him. The gorgeous Penelope was becoming his passion, too. "My family owned a dog, a golden retriever."

"In Australia?"

"We moved to the States when I entered primary school and gave the dog to a friend. My mum and dad announced that our dog was too old for a big trip and a bigger change."

"Didn't your parents like Australia?"

"Australia is awesome, from what I remembered, and they both grew up near Melbourne, where I was raised. Unfortunately, my father went bankrupt."

"I'm sorry," she said quietly.

He shifted. Alrighty, then. If he was trying to make a good impression, blurting out his family's descent into poverty wasn't the best way to go about it.

"We struggled, but we landed on our feet," he replied.

"What happened?"

"The bankruptcy? Long story. My father packed up my

mum, my sister, Kylie, and me and then found a job in Maryland. We've lived in the States ever since."

"Do you see your parents often?"

"My mum, on occasion. My sister lives near her but is considering moving back to Australia."

"Do you visit your mother?"

"Not as often as I should."

"Is your sister older or younger?"

"Kylie is younger than me. She and her husband split soon after …" He swallowed the lump in his throat. The expected tears came to his eyes.

Penelope studied him, giving him no place to look but straight at her. She didn't press him for any more details, and he didn't offer an explanation.

"I'm sorry," she said simply.

"Thanks." He couldn't say more. After a difficult and uncomfortable minute with no words, he relaxed. That was extraordinary. He never relaxed when he spoke about his adorable niece, Linda, and her tragic death. Normally, he tensed and felt worse.

"If you ever need to talk with someone." Penelope offered a tentative smile. "I'm a good listener. I don't usually babble on and on. Honest." She attempted to lighten the mood with a disparaging wave at herself. She'd noted his sadness and responded with empathy.

He moved from one foot to the other. "I won't be discussing the subject again but thank you."

"I talked nonstop on the plane."

He couldn't help his smile. Quiet filled the air, spun with kindness and understanding. He recognized the whiff of lavender, her scent.

"I liked your stories." He kept his expression neutral. "Do you want to hear a truth?"

"This truth business again?" Her lips twitched. "Sure."

"You're a remarkable woman." His observation surprised himself. He truly was interested in her. In fact, he planned to learn everything about her.

He surveyed the expansive living room, the cushioned window seat overlooking the side yard. A cherry-wood coffee table and armchairs were cluttered with books. People called him a neatnik. Maybe so. He pressed down the inclination to straighten the stacks, so all the book edges aligned.

"Gorgeous home." He peered up at the high ceilings, the gold-carved wooden mirror hanging over the marble fireplace. The room was painted a rich hue of chocolate brown. He assumed to his left was the music room, judging by the ebony-black grand piano. No white or beige walls anywhere.

"You play piano?" he asked.

"I tried. I struggled. I couldn't get the hang of reading the notes in the bass clef, so I quit."

"On the plane, you mentioned you wanted to create something."

The corners of her eyes crinkled. "If you ask my piano teacher, she'll assure you it wasn't a Mozart sonata."

He gestured toward the wooden beads, paint, sharpies, newspaper, and glue on a separate table. Several beads were painted in various neutral shades and stood upright. "Are these the dolls you're making?"

She shrugged. "I've put the craft aside."

He stepped into the room and picked up a miniature doll. Her black hair and blue eyes were intricately drawn, her hands clasped together. Two yellow silk hair bows were glued on either side of her head above her ears.

"She is precious." He fingered the hair bows.

"I name all my dolls after spices. Hers is Cinnamon."

"Nice name."

"Our business has a large amount of scrap wood I can use."

"Right." He'd looked up her toy shop on the internet.

"I brought the dolls to the homeless shelter Evan mentioned. My brother Lincoln donated several rocking horses, but I decided each child needed something simple."

Simple. There was that word again.

"Congrats on a worthwhile project," he said. "I'm learning simple is best."

"Me too. Life is all about balance. So many material things are relatively useless."

"Like big expensive cars."

She grinned. "And designer purses."

"You're an inspiration, Penelope."

She picked up a tiny blue silk scarf and handed it to him. "I love this craft. Of course, you're familiar with my story."

"Some parts. Remember, I'm an excellent listener, so keep talking."

"When you're not sleeping," she reminded. "I prefer to keep my story to the parts you've probably memorized, so don't press me, okay?"

"Apologies." He draped the tiny scarf over the doll's shoulders. "Sometimes I lose my finesse around beautiful women. Women who have survived hardships and heart-break are even more …"

She snatched the doll from him, readjusting the scarf before setting the doll back on the table. "You should've stopped when you were ahead with the word 'beautiful.'"

"You're also fun and creative."

"I'll brew your coffee, and you can tell me the reason you're here." She breezed down the hallway, and he followed. The wooden floor creaked as they stepped into the kitchen.

"I dropped by to see Evan," Jacob said. "How is he feeling?"

"So, this is a house call?"

Truth? Well, he wasn't ready for the blatant truth, because he hadn't come to terms with it yet himself.

"You can call it a house call," he replied.

"Evan is resting." Penelope surveyed the hallway, as if Evan might materialize at any moment. "Correction. He's playing video games. Do you want to go upstairs and check on him?"

"You're his mum." Jacob moved beside her. "What do you suggest?"

"Stay down here." She nudged him, a lighthearted nudge. "He'd probably prefer to run a 5K race than see you. He's a bit prickly when he's interrogated." Though she joked, her face beamed whenever she mentioned her son. Her delight exposed a wide-open fracture in his own defenses and his attraction to her. Again, he questioned himself. What was he really doing here?

"I blame his change in disposition on the rough road to adolescence," she finished.

When she opened the bag, Jacob inhaled the scent of fresh ground coffee.

"Is the antibiotic working?" he asked.

"Antibiotics are a miracle drug." She scrutinized him, peeling away more and more layers of his resistance. "You realize, Jacob, that not many doctors make personal house calls anymore."

"I'm new in town." Same old excuse, and he debated whether he should elaborate. "This is a way for me to get to know my patients better."

"Do you make calls often?"

"Not very often." In fact, he never had.

She spooned four scoops of coffee, then measured filtered water into the coffeepot. "Your interest means a lot. Most physicians won't take the time."

"My patients are the reason I'm a doctor."

"You look like a doctor." She switched on the coffee machine, then appraised him from head to toe. "I should've realized that on the plane. I imagined you—"

He stepped closer to the counter. Why was he so fascinated with her?

A difficult remembrance of his marriage and subsequent divorce resurfaced.

"I'm having a baby," his wife, Janet, had declared. Tears had poured down her cheeks. He'd assumed they were tears of joy, and he joined in with ecstatic tears of his own. Before he could bring out the champagne glasses, she'd added, "The baby isn't yours." And thus, the marriage had ended.

Her unfaithfulness had killed his pride and left him stunned.

"Where did you go, Doctor?" Penelope's steady voice drew him back from the devastating remembrance.

"Down memory lane," he said.

"Joyful times?"

He tapped his chin. "No. I was thinking about my ex-wife."

"You mentioned you were married."

"A decade ago, and for a couple of years. She's an anchorwoman on a national network. You'd probably recognize her. In fact, she was awarded an honor for investigative journalism."

"I'm impressed."

"Don't be." He blinked. "Let's discuss something else. You were in the middle of imagining me."

"I'd like to hear more about you."

He'd severed all recollections of Janet from his mind, though when he caught a glimpse of her on a cable television show, a slight pinch of awareness went through him. Thankfully, nothing more. He'd made peace with the hurt she'd caused and resolved never to get his heart all twisted up again. He dated women casually, and the women knew not to demand any emotional entanglement from him.

So, for the umpteenth bloody time, what on earth was he doing in Penelope's kitchen?

As a concerned physician, I'm here for Evan.

"I'm a doctor," he said aloud.

"At first, I imagined you as a professor who worked in academia."

"Why?"

"You cited statistics about airplanes."

He stepped back as she reached around him to grab two mugs from a high glass cabinet. She handed them to him, one by one.

He set the mugs on the wooden kitchen table. "A single offhand remark, and you pegged me as Professor Jacob."

"Now that I think of it, you don't fit the stereotype."

"Which is?"

"Shirt, tie, and tweed jacket."

"Another cliché." He folded cloth napkins she handed him and placed the napkins next to the mugs. "Are you interested in how I pictured you, Penelope?"

"After we went our separate ways?"

"While you were working at your job."

"Probably sitting on the floor and playing with tiny toy trucks."

"Gorgeous blue eyes, brown hair, and drop-dead gorgeous." He followed her back to the counter and grabbed two spoons. "I checked your website and saw your photo. You own New Beginnings Toys."

"The photo is old." She pushed back her hair, the hint of silver strands. Her cheeks turned crimson. "How did you realize I was one of the owners of the toy shop?"

"I asked Candee to verify for certain. The custom, hand-made rocking horses are ..."

"Our specialty."

"Right. And now you can sell your charming wooden dolls there."

"Hardly a specialty, and I don't sell them. If I had my way, I'd gift them to every child in the world." Her gaze shifted to the stairway. "Evan is returning to school in a couple of days. He's not thrilled about going back."

"Why doesn't he like school?"

"Peer pressure. Twelve years old is a challenging age." She placed sugar and a creamer on the table and poured steaming coffee into two mugs. Once she sat, he claimed the chair across from her.

"I met one of Evan's friends at the office today," he said. "He came in for a checkup."

"Oh?"

"A polite kid named Zack. He mentioned he was in seventh grade, and I asked him if he knew Evan."

"Zack was once Evan's best friend."

"Not anymore?"

She cupped her hands around her mug. "Not anymore."

"Zack inquired about volunteering at the clinic, and I encouraged him. He seems an ambitious chap. He is trying out for the high school swim team." Jacob spooned sugar into his coffee and stirred. "The coach accepts students in junior high."

"If the swimmer is good enough. A big *if.*"

"Is Evan trying out?"

"He'd rather wash dinner dishes for a week." Penelope circled the rim of her mug with her forefinger. "A couple of years ago, he was the star of the team. Now he doesn't seem to belong anywhere, and I have no idea how to help him."

Let Evan find his own way. The consideration came to Jacob's mind, and he quickly dismissed it. He had no right to tell Penelope how to raise her child.

An hour passed quicker than anticipated—an easy hour, filled with friendly conversation. She discussed the toy business and explained that everything had to be worth the cost of the retail value. Business was business. However, toys were unique and personal to each child. Discerning parents chose specialty toys for their children, believing in the value when cheap plastic toys were readily available at every big box store.

The perfect toy was designed as an heirloom for the child and family, Penelope went on, though she and her brother were businesspeople, and profit was a consideration. Excited parents gushed to their friends that they were being mindful of what they bought for their children, so everyone was satisfied.

Success meant Penelope's employees continued to work, and the toy shops remained open. It also meant that Penelope and her brother could continue to enjoy a comfortable lifestyle.

When Jacob stood, she walked him to the front door. "As usual, I did all the talking."

He smiled. "I always liked making house calls."

Evan never materialized, and Jacob didn't press the issue. After all, Penelope assured him that Evan was getting better.

"Thanks for the coffee," she said.

"You're welcome. I like your home. It's exactly the type of place I'm looking for."

"I met Candee in the pharmacy. If anyone can find your dream house, she's your realtor."

"Considering my hectic schedule," he said, "I've had only a few hours to scope out Roses and the surrounding area, and my house-hunting is hindered."

"I've lived here most of my life."

He knew that from their conversation on the plane.

"Where is the best place to find a home?" he asked. "Any suggestions?"

"Well, I—"

At the doorway, he turned to her. "May I call you?"

"Why? I don't need another prescription. In your professional opinion, I needed tea with honey and lemon and lots of rest."

He grinned with satisfaction and squeezed her hands. "Did my prescription help?"

"The tea is a blessing, though I couldn't manage the 'lots of rest' part."

"Can you show me around the area this weekend? Candee is good, but you're better."

She withdrew her hands and stepped backward. "I'm not a realtor."

"Doesn't matter."

"Evan is sick."

"If he continues to take the antibiotic, he'll make a full recovery by Saturday," Jacob replied. "Perhaps he can stay with your brother and sister-in-law for a bit. They live in Roses, right?"

She looked flustered. "I'm not sure. I suppose I can ask them."

"After I leave the clinic tomorrow, I'll phone you to firm up our plans."

"Phone?"

"Or I'll text you." He asked for her cell phone, texted himself, then handed the phone back to her. "Afterwards, we can go for dinner."

"You mean to eat?"

"You aren't on a diet, are you?"

"I'm trying to choose healthy. Look, this probably isn't a suitable idea."

"Order a salad."

She shook her head. "You're Evan's doctor."

"Are you dating anyone?"

"I told you." Her gaze sharpened. "I gave up dating."

"No pizzerias. I promise."

Her cell phone pinged, and she read the text with a concerned frown. "Sorry, Jacob, I need to contact the supervisor at our Roses location." She tapped a number into her phone. "A shipment is delayed because of stormy weather in New York, and the delay is causing repercussions to our stores along the East Coast. With the holidays approaching soon—"

"No worries. I'll let myself out." As she put the phone to her ear and began instructing the supervisor, Jacob mouthed, "I'll call you."

He closed the front door behind him before she could protest.

Penelope Reid was a remarkable woman. Despite her rather slapdash appearance on the plane, and the untidy state of her house, she was quick, conscientious, and decisive at her job. Too bad it was a job she hated.

CHAPTER 4

*P*enelope didn't know why she'd agreed to Jacob's request, and she dissected their conversation as she pulled into the driveway of Lincoln and Shanice's farmhouse on Saturday.

Shanice had inherited the farmhouse from her grandmother, Jasmine, and the house even had a name—Jasmine's Joy.

Evan had missed the entire week at school, declaring he wasn't feeling well enough to attend, and his accommodating teachers had sent online assignments to him. Penelope hovered over his shoulder, offering to help.

"What a great idea, Mom," Evan said. "As if the teachers won't realize it's your work and not mine."

"I didn't say I would do the work." She reached for the homework papers her son had printed.

"I've got this covered, okay? Science is my favorite subject."

Science had always been her worst subject, so she agreed.

She could only trust that he'd completed the assignments.

"I'm showing Jacob Williams the town of Roses and

prospective houses for sale," Penelope began, after Lincoln opened the front door and welcomed her and Evan inside the farmhouse.

Evan disappeared into the living room and dropped his backpack onto the floor. He clicked on the television set, and Penelope heard a delighted squeal when Shanice's cat and Lincoln's dog jumped on the couch beside him.

The couple had no children and frequently discussed adoption. Currently, they devoted their free time to expanding New Beginnings Toys and renovating the rambling farmhouse.

"I think showing him the town is a wonderful idea," Shanice remarked when Penelope stepped into the kitchen.

"He trapped me into this," Penelope replied.

"Trapped is when you're stuck inside for days after a snowstorm. Hanging out with Dr. Handsome is exciting."

"I'm not his realtor," Penelope said. "Besides, I can't choose the right house for him."

Shanice tucked a stand of thick ebony hair behind her ear, then grabbed plates from the glass-fronted cabinet. "For some reason, he prefers you. I wonder why?"

"Short explanation. I'm a native of Roses."

"Honestly, Penny." Shanice referred to Penelope by her nickname. "Jacob is a dream come true. Rumor has it that he's single and in his early fifties. If he wants to spend time with you, don't fight it."

Because you're married to Lincoln, who clearly loves you. You have no fears of denials and infidelity and heartbreak, Penelope thought.

Shanice plated oversized portions of sweet potato pie and carried the plates to the table.

"Jacob Williams moved into town only a short time ago and has already established a free clinic," Shanice said. "He's committed to helping the community and is an exceptional doctor."

"He's interested in his patients," Penelope said. "How many doctors make house calls anymore?"

Shanice smiled conspiratorially at Lincoln, then beamed at Penelope. "None, and certainly not for a case of strep throat. Any ideas on what drew him to visit you?"

"He is new in town."

"We've established that," Shanice replied.

"Okay, he is admired." At her sister-in-law's obvious delight at her statement, Penelope amended, "I like him as a friend."

"He's an eligible bachelor."

"I see where you're headed, and the answer is, I'm not interested. After my nasty divorce, dating is no longer in the cards for me." Penelope forked a piece of pie and smirked at Lincoln. "Are you aware your wife has already married me off to this guy?"

"She's a cheerleader for your happiness. We're both thrilled you opened your life to a man. Give him a chance. You're finally excited about dating someone. With the holidays approaching—"

"Lincoln, we're not dating. You're envisioning Jacob and I under a mistletoe, kissing, and married by New Year's Day." She peered around the expansive kitchen. "You've started to decorate for Christmas. I love the reindeer salt and pepper shakers. And the poinsettias from the garden center are gorgeous, especially the red and pink ones. I noticed them by the fireplace when I walked in."

"And we celebrate Kwanzaa, too." He looked fondly at his wife, then back at Penelope. "Don't you want to spend the holidays with a special someone? You've been alone too long."

"Maybe, sometimes."

"That special someone may be right under your nose." He studied her intently. "You blush whenever his name is mentioned."

Her warm face gave her away. "Jacob is originally from Australia."

"Ooh, I love an Australian man's accent," Shanice said.

Lincoln's eyebrows furrowed. "More than mine?"

"You don't have an accent."

He drummed his fingers on the table. "I have a Southern accent."

"So do I, and that doesn't count because a Southern accent isn't exotic. I've heard it my whole life. However, I love you anyway." Shanice leaned over and kissed him on the cheek. He placed his fork on his plate, pulled her closer, and kissed her back.

Penelope grinned when Shanice broke the kiss. "You two are an inspiration."

Their infectious laughter wafted throughout the kitchen.

Lincoln was Penelope's younger brother—square-jawed, considerate, and generous, and he and Shanice had been granted a second chance when he'd returned to Roses. He'd pursued her, married her, and they planned to raise a family.

When Penelope regarded them, a twinge of longing went through her chest. They'd found each other and enjoyed a loving marriage.

Meanwhile, her ex had cheated on her with another woman—someone decades younger and much prettier.

Jealousy knocked, though not followed by grief. Penelope refused to jump into the courting game again, and she'd declared her decision to everyone who would listen. In her defense, she'd tried dating, both online and in person, and both were unsuccessful.

Shanice shifted her gaze to Penelope. "I can't wait to meet Dr. Williams."

"He's a pediatrician, so I doubt you'll have the opportunity for a while."

"Oh, you'll introduce us well before that." Shanice wiggled her eyebrows. "Seems as if you two are spending oodles of time getting better acquainted."

Penelope leaned back in her chair. "We only spent a few hours together because his visit to my house was a—"

"House call," the husband and wife chorused in unison. "And don't forget the plane. Remember, you told us all about it."

Penelope noted the glints in their eyes and laughed.

"Did the good doctor examine Evan while he was at your house?" Shanice asked. "Water, anyone?" At their nods, she stepped to the refrigerator and grabbed several bottles.

"No, although Jacob inquired about him," Penelope replied, accepting a bottle from Shanice. "We didn't want to bother Evan because he was in his room playing video games."

"Makes perfect sense. Not." Lincoln chuckled. "Either way, we're delighted. Your divorce was difficult, and I … we … Shay and I, are pleased you're interested in a good man."

Any mention of Penelope's ex set off a chain of reactions, and she sternly fought to keep her sadness under control. She sliced her pie portion in half and slid the pie onto Lincoln's plate. "My birthday is coming soon," she explained at his quizzical expression. "I've been eyeing a lovely dress, though it's quite short and clingy. My figure could use a remodel."

"Don't shortchange yourself." Shanice placed her hand on Penelope's forearm. "You are beautiful."

"I appreciate you handling the snafu with the shipping problem the other day." Lincoln took a swig of water. "You put in a good deal of effort to solve it. I don't say it often enough, but you are vital to our company's success."

I hate my job. Penelope's words to Jacob echoed in her mind.

However, if she examined her statement, she didn't hate her job. She'd simply grown tired of doing the same tasks day after day, year after year.

Initially, she'd assumed the responsibilities of the family business to please her father. She'd worked at the toy shop throughout high school, and then slipped right back into the business after college.

When had she become indispensable? How could she ever leave when her brother depended on her? Equally important, what would she do instead? She was proficient at organizing, yet not overly adept at shaping her own life.

Her inferiority stemmed from her ex's cheating. A major hit to her self-confidence.

Old news. Old excuses. Look ahead. Refuse to dwell on the past.

"Evan assured me that he finished his science essay, though you may want to double-check," she said. "He brought his backpack, but he won't allow me anywhere near his assignments."

"He only missed a few days of school." Lincoln steepled his fingers together. "He is responsible."

She gazed out the window. A rustic barn was framed in the distance, along with a firepit, and the rolling hills of Roses beyond. "Why won't he let me help him?"

"Because he needs to learn some things by himself. Think how proud he'll feel when he turns in the assignments."

"He hates school. I wish he loved seventh grade as much as I did."

"You loved seventh grade?" Shanice smirked. "I never met anyone who loved seventh grade."

Penelope craned her neck toward the living room and observed her son. He seemed so vulnerable sitting on the couch between the dog and cat. So solitary. Her foolish fear of him failing stemmed from her own difficulties in school, she rationalized. She'd struggled and never been able to achieve the high grades her younger brother attained with ease.

Logically, she knew Lincoln was right, and she was grasping for excuses to hold on to her only child. If only time stood still, or at least slowed down.

She speculated. Had the past year flown by for Evan, as it had for her? Likely, the twelve months had been interminable.

"I want Evan to be confident in himself," she murmured.

"You're doing a fine job raising him," Lincoln said.

Then why didn't Evan have any friends?

Her thoughts tangled. When things weren't right in Evan's world, they weren't right in hers, either.

She wanted him to enjoy the childhood she never had. Her father was a taskmaster who set impossible standards. A workaholic, aiming for success at all costs.

Evan shouldn't be held back because of her—a woman who might never recover from humiliation and hurt caused by sorrow and misgivings.

"He's acting like a preteen," Lincoln said. "He's perfectly normal."

"He's down on himself," she murmured.

"He has gained weight this year," Shanice broke in, then put a hand to her mouth. "I'm sorry. I shouldn't have mentioned anything."

"It's okay." Penelope blew out a breath. "Sometimes I feel helpless. I'm trying to eliminate junk food in the house, although I'm equally guilty. Lately, I've been encouraging him to be more active. He's touchy and snappish if I mention swimming."

"He is welcome to keep us company any time. We have chickens in the barn, a dog, a cat, and more plants than we can count." He grinned at his wife. Shanice was a professional landscaper.

"Evan wants a puppy for Christmas," Penelope said.

"Get him one. He's at the perfect age, and dogs are wonderful companions."

"I work a lot. It isn't fair to the dog. Dogs love people."

"I'll give you the time off." Lincoln teased. "And Evan gets off many school holidays. It seems like the kids are hardly ever in school. Now in my day …"

"Things were exactly the same. However, it's food for thought and you're both too kind." Penelope was grateful for their welcoming invitation, though it meant she would be alone if Evan spent nights at his uncle's house. And what about the days before Christmas when he was scheduled to visit his father? The visitation stipulated every other year, and this was Evan's year to visit.

The prospect tied her stomach in a knot. Christmas was such a special season, and she would be missing those precious days with her son.

How would she cope when he left for college in a few years? Kids went to college all the time, though the possibility of Evan leaving ripped at her heart.

Then she would truly be by herself.

From across the table, Lincoln grabbed her hands. "Start living your life again."

"I'm trying. It's difficult."

Her brother's advice was sound. Why did she refute him? Perhaps the best path for Evan was to allow him room to grow.

She carried her plate to the sink. "Thanks for the pie, Shanice. I'd better run. Jacob is picking me up at two o'clock."

Shanice grinned. "You're on a first-name basis with Dr. Handsome."

Penelope stood quietly for a moment before she nodded,

recognizing the meaningful smiles exchanged between her brother and Shanice. She crossed to the living room and instructed Evan to help his aunt and uncle on the farm because the tasks were endless.

He bristled before agreeing, reminding her that Uncle Lincoln had an adorable dog *and* a cat, *and* chickens, though Evan didn't have any pets.

"You own a hamster," she reminded.

He stroked the dog beside him. The cat had settled in his lap. "Christmas is coming, right? And a puppy?"

"Let's get through this semester first." Penelope planted a kiss on top of his hair.

"Say hi to Dr. Williams," Evan called out. "Tell him I'll volunteer next Saturday morning."

"I will." She stepped to the door. She planned to meet Jacob at her house because he'd insisted on driving.

She'd told Evan she was taking Jacob house-hunting, and he hadn't remarked one way or the other. She'd wondered at the time if he'd even heard her. Apparently, he had, and didn't have a problem with it.

Dr. Williams. Jacob. She was spending the afternoon with Jacob. Her stomach tightened, full of odd flutters she couldn't define.

CHAPTER 5

*A*t exactly two o'clock, Penelope peeked out the living room window just as Jacob drove up to her house in his bright-yellow Volkswagen.

She'd changed when she'd returned home, deciding on lightweight linen slacks and her favorite flowered blouse. She left the blouse untucked to cover her generous waistline.

For the next hour, she slid in and out of Jacob's car to view different areas of Roses, and soon discovered that her slacks and blouse were completely wrinkled. Fortunately, her sneakers were comfortable.

She'd worn this same outfit behind a desk in an air-conditioned office several times in the past. Today, she'd imagined driving by a few neighborhoods with Jacob, then sitting across from him at her favorite coffee shop while sipping a vanilla latte.

He, on the other hand, was dressed more appropriately in khaki shorts and a green cotton golf shirt.

"You look gorgeous," he'd said when he arrived at her front door. She'd flushed with the compliment, though now she felt plain. Her blouse had soiled when they'd peered into the grimy window of an abandoned, dilapidated house on Brook Street. Dusty sunshine filled the interior.

"I like the house," he remarked, when they were once again settled in his car and headed back to town. "I like Victorian homes."

"You're joking," she said. "I wouldn't know where to begin except to hire a bulldozer."

"I'll grant the house is in dire need of repairs. But it has good bones."

"Bones? Let's start with the roof."

"What's wrong with the roof?"

"It's caving in," she reminded. "Are you handy with tools?"

He smirked. "I don't even own a tool kit, though I guess I should put it on my Christmas list if I buy the house. However, this location is excellent."

She surveyed the street. "There are several mom-and-pop stores in the area."

"The home is big."

"Unlike your car," she observed.

He chuckled and patted the dashboard. "Can't beat compact and reliable."

He switched on the radio to a contemporary station. She recognized the holiday tune, remarking that it wasn't even Halloween yet and they were playing Christmas music. Jacob tapped the rhythm of "It's the Most Wonderful Time of the Year" on the steering wheel and sang in a deep baritone voice.

"The house has what I want most," he continued when he'd finished singing.

"Which is?" she asked.

"Besides you?"

"Get outta here."

He grinned. "I'll tell you when we arrive in town."

Despite the outfit mistake, she enjoyed the hours with

him. He was interesting, with a grand sense of humor and a clear disdain for the other homes they drove by. He seemed to gravitate to the old, rundown house.

Finally, they took a break for cups of sweet lemonade from a sidewalk stand.

"Soon, the downtown will decorate for the holidays." Penelope gestured up and down the street. "We even hold a bake-off contest."

"We?"

"Yes. I'm a resident of the town." She admonished him with amused severity.

He grinned. "Me, too."

"Keiran and Desiree, a husband-and-wife team, own O'Malley's Irish pub. Keiran bakes whiskey cakes. He usually wins the contest because his cakes are delicious, although Desiree's pistachio cake is equally delicious."

"I've never baked so much as a cupcake, but I'll patronize a good bakery any day." Jacob chuckled. "I lived in Atlanta for many years and there are several well-known bakeries specializing in smiling gingerbread men and chocolate Santas around the holidays."

"I love sweets," she admitted with a sigh. "However, I'm set on healthy eating in order to lose a few pounds."

"I agree with the healthy eating part." Jacob swept an arm around her shoulders and gave a caring squeeze. "In Atlanta, a spectacular Stone Mountain Christmas serves all sorts of food. Some might be healthy."

"You'll love the holiday events here, too," she said. "Food trucks line the streets on weekends in December. If you're up for a thirty-minute drive, an entire town lights up every house for Christmas and is utterly charming."

"I look forward to seeing it. So far, Roses reminds me of a Rockwell painting." Jacob placed a hand on the small of

Penelope's back while directing her toward a bench. "I hope you'll accompany me to Atlanta."

Her heart thumped a joyful beat. Jacob wanted to include her in his Christmas plans.

"On one condition." Penelope balanced the cup of lemonade in her hands and situated herself on the bench. "You allow me to treat."

"Nope."

She took in a breath, about to object, and he shook his head. "I'm aware you don't date, so we won't call it a date. Like today. Today isn't a date."

"Today is a house-hunting day."

"Exactly."

Good. He'd gotten the message, though she suddenly felt empty despite her firm assertions. Apparently, her emotions hadn't gotten the same message.

No, no, no. She couldn't be falling for him. Wasn't her unsuccessful marriage, her pathetic attempts at dating, evidence enough?

"Romance is off the table for me," she declared, to firm up her assertion. "My last attempt was dating a teacher at my son's school. I wanted to like him because he was a great guy. He was fun, but we always ran out of things to talk about. I wondered after I broke it off with him if it was him or me. Either way, I wasn't willing to commit to anything beyond a shared pizza."

"No dates. No pizza." Jacob saluted her. "Romance memo received, loud and clear."

She drew a long breath and groped for a subject change. "Candee mentioned you were a discriminating house buyer. Today I witnessed firsthand what she meant."

"I'm certain she used a stronger word than discriminating."

"Her description was 'picky.'"

"Completely true." His mouth twisted in amusement. "I intend to establish a practice in my home, and my choice is important both professionally and personally."

"You're looking for a house big enough to live in *and* practice medicine?"

"Yes. A neighborhood made up of both businesses and residential." He gestured up and down the block. "Similar to your area."

"Why?" she asked.

"Homey. Convenience. I'll be more available for my patients. In Atlanta, my practice was becoming more of a business. Something happened … several things, and I realized I needed to make a change."

She offered a murmur of acknowledgement when he didn't supply any additional information. "Why did you become a doctor?"

"As I mentioned, my family moved to the States, and because of the bankruptcy, all we could afford was a mobile home in an impoverished area. We had nothing at first, not even furniture. We'd sit on the living room floor and pray." At her quizzical expression, he explained, "Me, my mum, father, sister."

"And then?"

"And then God delivered. We worked odd jobs and eventually scraped up enough money to purchase several acres of farmland." He drained his lemonade, then gazed at her. "My mum wanted me to stay on the farm and help. In fact, she suggested I quit school early. She doesn't believe education is important."

"And?"

"I refused. When I graduated, I got out of town as soon as I could and never looked back."

"Your parents still live on the farm?"

"My mum does."

"Your father?"

"He disappeared several years ago. He's not the sort of guy who sticks around when the going gets rough."

"Who helps your mother with—" Penelope began.

"My sister lives in Maryland." He closed his eyes for a beat. "I understand my mum's concerns. After all, she's alone and running a farm. But I couldn't. I just couldn't stay, only to please her."

Penelope gazed back at him, giving him her full attention. "You're not a farmer?"

"Hardly. I can't even grow an herb."

"One can never have too many herbs."

He grinned, obviously appreciative of her attempt to ease the conversation, but soon sobered. "There were few doctors or dentists where I grew up. My sister married young, and her daughter, Linda, … an accident occurred when she was seven."

He breathed in a deep lungful of air. His silence, a heartfelt emotion, was so palpable she could almost taste it.

"Go on. I didn't intend to ask so many questions." But yes. Yes, she did.

She waited for his reply and scanned the park across the way, the children running and playing tag. Autumn was a magnificent season. Gold and red leaves twirled to the ground, and the landscape was splashed with color.

She acknowledged several parents as they pushed their toddlers on the swings. This was the advantage of small-town living. Some called it a downside, though she understood both sides.

"Linda didn't receive the adequate care required for her condition, at least, not in my opinion," Jacob continued. "Our community lacked quality medical doctors. Soon afterwards, I decided to become a doctor and make a difference. Somewhere along the line, I got sidetracked while climbing the ladder of success. I strove to be the best in my field."

"That's a good thing."

"Maybe I wanted to prove something."

"To whom?"

He didn't reply for a moment. "Maybe my mum. Maybe myself."

"Were you the best?"

"I accepted a position at one of the country's leading children's hospitals." He opened his cell phone and scrolled to the photos, tapping a picture of a hospital sign to make it larger.

Penelope recognized the Atlanta hospital immediately. "Impressive. Congratulations."

"Thanks. I was passed over several times when I applied for the position of public health and administrative leadership. This last time was the final straw. I was experienced, and the most qualified for the job."

"So, you quit?"

"An administrative role was my biggest dream. I worked my entire career for the opportunity. I wanted more, more, more." He met her gaze. "I sound bitter, don't I?"

"A little. You're human." She tilted her head back to view him better. His recklessly handsome features regarded her. His face was captivating, almost boyish, especially when the strong jawline and keenly carved mouth were changed by one of his devastating smiles.

Beyond them, bluebirds flew through the air, spinning and diving from tree to tree. She had the urge to slip off her shoes and relish the cool grass tickling her toes.

"I'm learning how to be content and follow my focus to help people, though I may disappoint others," he said. "Life is an interesting balance."

"Balance between what?"

"Contentment and complacency. I never want to be complacent."

"Like me?"

"You're not complacent."

"I haven't changed jobs yet," she reminded him.

"Your job is important." He tucked his cell phone back in his pocket. "Just remember not to limit yourself."

"The family business is what I know."

"All my life, I questioned my career choices and long hours," he said. "I couldn't put my finger on what needed to change. When I quit my job in Atlanta, I visited several areas in search of a medical practice to purchase. Then I learned Dr. Damian's office was available, and here I am. It's odd how things work out. I never considered a small town setting before ..."

"Because a small town is beneath your big city aspirations?"

"Thanks, Penelope."

"The salary and benefits are obviously greater in Atlanta."

"No question. My job was becoming soulless, though."

"Do you ... intend on settling here permanently?"

"Yes." He regarded her. His expression changed, turning thoughtful. He rubbed his thumb along her palm and raised her hand to his lips.

Her heart lurched. "Why Roses?"

"Hard-working, down-to-earth folks are the best." Lightly, he kissed her fingers, and her hand tingled. "I'm a medical man and serving in a large hospital was rewarding for two decades, but circumstances led to my change of heart, and the end result is a blessing."

Her eyes widened as she digested his remark. "What circumstances?"

"What do you mean?"

"Circumstances suggest more than one thing happened."

She slid her hand away and tucked it securely behind her back. "You mentioned being passed over for the higher hospital positions. What was the other circumstance?"

"Sad, sad story." He suddenly became absorbed with studying the brick pavement. "A family tragedy."

"Your niece?"

He didn't reply.

"Your mother?"

"She's okay. We only talk when I reach out to her."

Penelope set her cup down and touched his forearm. Whatever the tragedy, he preferred to keep the heartache to himself.

"I'm glad you chose to land in Roses," she finally said.

"Me too." His intense brown eyes locked with hers, and a quiver of attraction shot through her.

"Lucky you."

"Why?"

"You heard all my problems on the plane." A thought occurred. "I'm surprised I didn't scare you off."

"If anything, I was more intrigued." He pointed to a simple, wood-sided building. "Look. Roses has an animal shelter."

"I'm well aware. Evan reminds me every day on the way to school when we pass by."

"Have you ever stopped in?"

She nodded. "We've visited several times. The precious animals break my heart and I want to bring all of them home. Almost two months ago, the shelter took in a pregnant stray. They think she is a terrier mix, mostly Scottish."

"How soon is she due?"

"She had her puppies."

"An entire litter for Christmas?" He tried to suppress a smile. "Evan will be thrilled. How many?"

"On average, dogs have five to ten puppies. She had six." Penelope swallowed a bubble of laughter. "Good try, Jacob."

"All that pleasure in one litter and you're still deciding? Psst. Cats are easier." Playfully, he nudged her. "Let's go see for ourselves."

Penelope picked up their cups and discarded them in the trash. A few minutes later, they climbed the stairs and walked through the shelter's doors.

"Be forewarned," a volunteer teasingly wagged her finger. "You'll probably fall in love."

"I'm inquiring about the terrier mix," Penelope said. "She recently had puppies."

The volunteer bobbed her head. "The dog is out back. The vet is examining her. Are you ready to bring a sweet furry friend home today? She is on our VIP status."

"Meaning?" Jacob asked.

"She's been here a while, and we don't want her to be overlooked." The volunteer met Jacob's gaze.

"I'm interested in possibly adopting one of her puppies," Penelope said.

She and Jacob peered into the cages as they walked down the aisles. Dogs with expressive, adoring eyes stared back at them. Penelope wanted to pass her fingers through the soft fur of each dog—colors of apricot, gray, silver, brown and black. Whether the dog's characteristics resembled a pug or a husky, they all had the cutest faces.

The volunteer announced that the mother dog, named Nutcracker, had been brought back to her cage, and they all stepped over. The dog's compact build and short legs, distinctive white coat and overall sturdiness, brought a heartfelt smile to Penelope's lips.

"This dog is more precious every time I see her," she said.

"I agree. She is gorgeous." He glanced at the volunteer. "May I pet her?"

The volunteer opened the cage and the dog stepped out. "Sure. Nutcracker will sniff you until she approves."

"Right." Jacob bent down and held his hand in a fist. He averted his gaze so that he wasn't looking directly at the dog. Once he passed the sniff test, he gently petted the dog's shoulders.

Penelope crouched down with him and smiled. "You're comfortable with dogs," she said.

Nutcracker, apparently satisfied, turned and found a cozy spot in her cage.

Six squirming, wriggling puppies with pink markings on their tiny paws, playfully romped and wagged their tails. Though wobbly on their feet, their liveliness knew no bounds. All the puppies had white fur, their coats velvety and fluffy. They yipped and yelped, boisterous, and paying no attention to Penelope and Jacob.

"Two boys and four girls," the volunteer declared. She warned the puppies weren't old enough to be picked up and handled yet, as they were only approaching four weeks. Furthermore, the puppies weren't adoptable before seven to nine weeks of age.

"Which puppy are you choosing for Evan?" Jacob asked, after he thanked the volunteer. He clasped Penelope's hand and they walked back to their bench across the street.

"When the time comes, the decision will be up to him. A puppy is a huge commitment, and I'm still not certain whether Evan is up to the task," Penelope sighed. "Or if I am because I'll probably assume the brunt of the work. I'm still weighing the pros and cons."

"Tough to do."

"Depends on which side of the fence you're on. Practical, like me, or more laid-back and irresponsible, like Evan."

"I try to agree with the parent, except in this instance."

Jacob studied her for a long moment. "A puppy will teach Evan responsibility."

"You're a big help. Then I'll have a puppy and a hamster running around the house. Or six puppies, if you have your way. Please don't encourage Evan when he's at your clinic."

"I wouldn't dream of it." Jacob chuckled. "Though there's something about puppies that triggers empathy." He rested his arm along the back of the bench and turned to her, his gaze focusing on her lips.

"I can't discuss my puppy dilemma when you stare at me." She dabbed at her chin with her forefinger. "Am I dripping lemonade peel?"

He leaned toward her and rubbed his fingers along her chin. "Penelope Reid. You are lovely and I can't stop looking at you. You've successfully diverted my attention away from the puppies."

"I'm not doing anything except sitting next to you."

"Reason enough to break my concentration."

"Quit joking." She jabbed at him with her elbow.

She tried, though she couldn't tamp down the bewildering yet indisputable flurries in her chest. She felt like a teen again, all nervous and agitated and captivated by a guy.

Oh, no, she firmly reminded herself. She didn't intend to date any man, and besides, Jacob wasn't interested in her. He intended to keep things simple, if that was the correct word he used, plus he was committed to his career.

However, her impractical brain shoved the thoughts to the side.

His gaze ran along her face. "Gorgeous," he murmured, giving her an admiring smile.

She heard herself inhale but didn't move.

He bent his head. Softly, he kissed her, his lips touching hers. "You taste so sweet," he whispered.

"Lemons are sour," she teased.

"But lemonade is sweet."

"We can't begin anything, Jacob. I'm not looking for a relationship."

"Neither am I."

At least he was honest, although for some reason, his admission disappointed her. She covered her disappointment with a topic switch. "Roses needed an excellent pediatrician and all-round doctor. The residents are thrilled you're here."

"All the residents?"

"Every single one."

"Good." His lips were still close, his gaze hooded. Evidently, he wasn't self-conscious about kissing her in the middle of town. His scent was clean—the outdoors coupled with a trace of male. She pushed down the urge to wrap her arms around him, to feel the hard muscles of his forearms, his cotton shirt pressed against her cheek.

"I plan to serve the community, then I will ease up to pursue things I enjoy," he murmured. "I hope you'll do the same."

If he referred to her wooden dolls, she'd moved the craft to a back burner. "Things like what?"

"Things like—" His eyebrows drew together as his cell phone pinged. He read the message and stood. "I'm sorry, Penelope, but we'll have to forego our dinner plans for another evening. An emergency has come up at the clinic."

She stood alongside him. "Nothing serious, I hope?"

"A preteen girl swallowed a bee." He typed a response into his phone. "I recommended to the head nurse that the girl drink water, but I'll see her just in case."

"Will she be okay?"

"I look for localized swelling, though she may suffer mild pain."

Penelope matched his long strides to the car. Several times, his hands brushed against hers. When he parked at the curb of her home a few minutes later, he cracked the windows open, letting in a breeze, and apologized again.

"Such is the life of a pediatrician. I'll double my efforts to wow you by treating you to the fanciest place in town. There is an exquisite farm to table restaurant getting rave reviews." He flashed a grin before dashing around to the passenger side to open the door for her. He'd opened the door when he'd picked her up earlier, too. He was a polite, considerate man. She liked that about him.

"Please, Jacob, don't apologize, and a fancy dinner isn't required."

"It's not a date, Penelope," he said. "We'll call our time together something else."

"Like what?"

He kissed her temple, then whispered in her ear, "I'll think of something."

CHAPTER 6

*S*unday mornings meant church, and this Sunday was no exception. As always, Penelope and Evan attended the eleven o'clock service. The church hadn't begun to decorate for the holidays yet, though a live nativity was planned for December.

Penelope chose a long-sleeved jersey-knit dress in sage green and topped the dress with a shawl-collared coat in a light khaki. She wore her hair loose, and when she peered at herself in the mirror, her smile was bright. She looked forward to her upcoming "undate" with Jacob.

After church, she and Evan opted for lunch at Kathleen's Tea Shop, a popular eatery.

Kathleen, the owner, had decked out her restaurant in Thanksgiving finery. Autumn-scented candles, miniature pumpkins and oranges, and golden-colored napkins created an inviting ambiance. Kathleen and her husband, Rob, were hands-on restauranteurs, and the nod was always there as a tribute to Kathleen's Irish heritage. The shamrock-green walls lent a festive flair.

As Penelope and Evan entered, the scent of yeast rolls and

fresh-brewed coffee filled the air. An Irish tenor's voice crooned a holiday tune, accompanied by a harp and fiddle.

"November is too early for Christmas music," Evan said.

"It's never too early." Penelope hummed the melody of "Holly, Jolly Christmas" along with the Irish tenor. "November is the magic time between Thanksgiving and Christmas. You can sense the spirit of anticipation. It's almost palpable."

After they were ushered to their table and seated, Evan pulled out his cell phone.

"No cell phones at the table," Penelope reminded.

With an exaggerated sigh, he tucked away the phone, perused the menu and selected pancakes, scrambled eggs, and orange juice.

"Hey, there's Dr. Williams sitting all by himself." He indicated a corner table. "Let's invite him over."

Penelope's heart skipped a beat. "I'm going out to dinner with him tonight," she replied.

"He told me when I volunteered at the clinic yesterday." Evan smiled. "He seemed excited. You do, too."

"I do?"

"Yeah. You're fun when you smile and hum Christmas songs."

She drew a quick breath. Evan was obviously more astute than she gave him credit for.

"His clinic is short-staffed," Evan said. "He wondered if you'd volunteer there in your spare time."

"He did? What spare time?"

Several days had passed since Penelope had last seen Jacob and life had marched on. He texted often, quick texts when she least expected, apologizing for his busyness. Sometimes he texted in the early morning, and she was surprised she was on his mind in the hours before dawn.

He usually began his texts with a question.

Are you awake?

Unfortunately, yes, she replied. *I hardly ever sleep.*

Same here. Once I secure more staff, I'll ease up on the hours.

Work overload. Remember why you moved here?

To help people, he typed.

From the talk in town, you've reached your goal and I'm impressed, she said. *You're an overachiever.*

How would you feel if I told you I moved here because of you?

If she were honest with herself, his question brought dreams. Dreams of a relationship. She dismissed the consideration as quickly as it surfaced. She wouldn't risk having her heart broken again.

Knock it off, she replied.

I'm looking forward to seeing you soon for our ... undate.

Is that your new favorite word?

Definitely. BTW, how is your creativity level these days?

Nonexistent.

Evan brought some of your wooden dolls to the clinic. The kids love them.

I haven't had any time for more woodcarving.

Make the time, he said.

Whenever her mind focused on him, which was often, she was touched and impressed by his story. He'd left a successful career behind to relocate to a postage-stamp community and lend a helping hand with his physician skills. In all honesty, she'd been a bit envious that he'd decided to go after what he wanted. Why couldn't she be more like him?

You're gifted, he added.

Gifted? Hardly, though she knew her cheeks flushed at his compliment.

Not easy while balancing a full-time job and raising a preteen. She stared at the phone screen. *Are you doing any more house-hunting?*

I'm fixated on the dilapidated house on Brook Street.

Why?

It's big and cheap and in an excellent location.

She sent a thinking face emoji. *Better buy that tool kit. You'll need it.*

LOL. I haven't had a chance to drive by recently. Should I make an offer? I'm pondering pros and cons and all that. Thanks again for the tour of the town.

I'm happy to assist, she said.

Truth?

Always.

The other day, I was more fixated on you than on the houses.

"How do I answer him?" she muttered to the empty room. How could she tell him *she'd* been fixated on him? Think quickly, Penelope. Start a new topic.

You seem the type of person who is quick and decisive, she typed.

Truth?

Again?

I'm decisive at work. In my personal life, not so much.

A few hours later, Jacob texted:

Good news. I've secured extra help at the clinic. I'm free on Sunday night.

For more house-hunting?

For dinner at the farm to table restaurant. Will you join me?

Somehow, he'd avoided the word date.

Sure.

See you soon, beautiful.

Please, Jacob, don't flatter me.

Why not?

I'm unaccustomed to compliments.

Get accustomed ... you are beautiful.

A smile overtook her face when she bid him a good night. He always closed his texts by calling her beautiful. He made it clear he found her attractive, and he boosted her self-esteem. She recalled the numerous instances when her father, or her ex, had muttered slighting comments about her weight. They were hurtful and hadn't helped in her effort to lead a healthier lifestyle.

She smiled. Seeing Jacob at the restaurant and thinking of his texts brought a flip of excitement she could hardly hide.

"Mom?" Evan craned his neck and waved at Jacob. "Can Dr. Williams join us?"

"Sure."

Evan jumped to his feet and hurried toward Jacob's table.

She closed the menu, deciding on coffee and toast, then looked around at the beaming couples and chatting relatives. She did love this little town. Life was slower, summer and fall had waned, and November brought a decided crispness to the air. Nearby, a toddler chortled with laughter as her father tickled her and the young mother smiled in approval.

Such a precious family, Penelope mused. Christmas will be extra special for them.

She'd always wanted more than one baby and envisioned celebrating noisy, over-the-top Christmases, but her dreaded birthday loomed, and her child-bearing years were over. The only child she had to hang onto was Evan.

She set aside her contemplations and gave her attention to Evan as he advanced with Jacob in tow. Jacob paused at a couple near them, apparently recognizing their child. He conversed with the parents and squatted beside the boy. With a broad smile, he playfully interacted, and the boy's dimples flashed. Jacob seemed genuinely interested and concerned, lingering, and chatting. He was excellent with children.

He wore navy-blue pants and a checkered button-up shirt. Again, she was struck by his athletic physique and confident manner. When he approached, he greeted her with a twinkle in his deep-brown eyes.

Sometimes, though, she detected sadness in those same eyes.

With an undisputable flutter of magnetism, she greeted him. "Hi, Jacob. Please have a seat."

"Thanks." He claimed a chair between her and Evan. "I heard a lot about this place and wanted to check it out after church this morning."

"We were at church, too. I didn't see you."

"I sat in the back."

"We sit in the front."

"Fortunately, we ended up in the same restaurant."

She lifted a brow. "What a coincidence."

He grinned. "Definitely."

He distributed the coffees and orange juice that the waitress placed on their table. "Are we still on for tonight?"

"Uh-huh."

"Two undates in one day."

Evan gulped down his orange juice. "What's an undate?"

"Private joke, mate," Jacob replied.

He poured cream into his coffee. Penelope did the same and added sugar.

"We can take a raincheck," she said.

"I wouldn't dream of it." Jacob's eyebrows furrowed, silently telling her no excuses were allowed. "I moved schedules for this evening. Sickness doesn't stop on Sundays and the clinic is well staffed. They'll do fine without me."

They placed their orders, and the waitress returned shortly and set plates of eggs, pancakes, and melted toasties on the table. A toastie was an Irish specialty sandwich, featuring cheddar cheese, ham, and onion. Complimentary Irish soda bread was also provided.

Penelope bowed her head to say grace, and Jacob and Evan followed suit.

As soon as she finished her prayer, Evan poured a gallon

of syrup on his pancakes and dove into them. When he was done, he gave her a rueful glance. "Did Dr. Williams tell you that when you finally give me permission to get a puppy, he'll go with us to the shelter to help us choose?"

"No, he never told me that."

Jacob shrugged. "I meant to."

"Dr. Williams also reminded me that Candee and Teddy Winchester raise beagle puppies." Evan finished the rest of his orange juice in one gulp. "Did you know that, Mom?"

She sighed. "I did, indeed." In a moment of weakness, she'd phoned Candee to inquire if any of her pups were available. Candee had replied that she and her husband were concentrating on their son's horses and hadn't had any time to devote to breeding or raising any more puppies.

AFTER THEIR PLATES WERE CLEARED, Evan asked to be excused and walk home.

"The tea shop is quite far from home," Penelope protested.

"Don't freak out, Mom. You encouraged me to get more exercise."

She eyed her son. Despite church that morning, he'd insisted on wearing his usual baggy jeans and an oversized T-shirt of a band she'd never heard of. Once, he'd prided himself on clean, stylish clothes, which she'd deemed remarkable for a young boy. Sometime this past year, she'd couldn't pinpoint exactly when, he'd stopped being concerned about his appearance.

Now, as he slumped back in his chair, he didn't seem surly or rebellious. He just seemed reconciled to the fact that there was no use in arguing with her.

Jacob pushed his coffee cup to the side. "How about if he walks to my clinic instead? Only a few blocks from here and two nurses are working this afternoon." He waved his cell phone in the air. "I'm on call, as usual."

Evan met Jacob's explanation with a bland expression. "Will I have to work?"

"I expect you'll make yourself useful," Jacob said. "Zack is volunteering today. You can carry out a list of phone calls together."

Evan's eyes narrowed. "You just gave me a good reason not to go."

"Why would you say such a thing?" Penelope folded her hands in her lap. "Zack is your friend."

Evan stared at the floor. "You wouldn't understand."

"Try me."

"I'm a joke to the other kids, Mom, remember? They tease me all the time."

"Treat your mum with respect, mate," Jacob said. "She asked you a question."

"Sorry, Mom."

"The other kids tease you?" Penelope leaned forward. "Even Zack?"

"Not him so much. But some of the boys at my school push me around."

A flicker of alarm added to the despair creeping up her chest. Evan was too young to defend himself. Why hadn't he confided in her? No child should be harassed, and she had a good mind to phone Zack's mother.

She brushed his arm. "Are you telling me—"

Evan flinched at her touch. His ears burned a bright red. "I don't want to talk about it anymore, okay?"

"You were bullied at school?" Penelope demanded. "When?"

"In the boy's locker room after gym practice. One of the guys pushed past me so hard I fell on the floor."

"Why didn't you tell me any of this before?"

His gaze lowered. "I'm telling you now, Mom."

Jacob regarded Evan with a quiet expression. They fastened eyes before Evan fixated his gaze on the window.

"Did Zack see any of this?" she asked.

"He was in the locker room." Evan refused to meet her gaze. "When I fell, the other kids laughed, but Zack just walked away."

"He should've defended you. You two are friends."

"Yeah, like when we were ten."

Penelope placed a hand on Evan's arm again. "I'll call the school and complain."

"Are you kidding? Everyone hates me. Let me quit and we can live on Uncle Lincoln's houseboat forever." He swiped at his eyes and shoved back his chair. "May I leave now?"

"Where are you going?" Penelope pulled her cell phone from her purse.

"I'll go to the clinic and ignore Zack."

"How will you get home? Do you want me to pick you up?"

"I'll drive him," Jacob put in.

"Thanks." Evan turned to Jacob. "I'll finish phoning more hospitals for supplies, right, Dr. Williams?"

"You're a born salesman." Jacob trapped Penelope's wrist. "Who are you calling?" he quietly asked as they watched her son leave the restaurant.

She shook off his hand and scrolled through her phone. "I might have Zack's number in my contacts. I'll talk to his mother."

"Don't." He caught her gaze and held it. "The more you try to mediate the situation, the worse his friendships and school will be. Let him and Zack work it out for themselves."

"Are you an authority on children now?"

"Kids can be cruel." He broke eye contact, his conviction flat and firm.

"Evan is an innocent child. He doesn't deserve to be picked on."

"No one does." Jacob lowered his voice. His expression was strained. "I grew up dirt-poor. I didn't wear the right clothes. I talked funny because of my Aussie accent, and not a day went by that I wasn't teased or bullied."

"You couldn't help your family's situation."

"True."

"I still feel sad for Evan."

"He'll be okay." His cell phone buzzed with an incoming text. He read the text. His dark eyebrows furrowed as he pushed back his chair. "I need to head to the hospital."

"An accident?"

"A woman was washing a glass in the sink and the glass broke. She needs stitches in her hand."

"Dr. Williams?" A striking, well-groomed woman in a figure-hugging red pantsuit, a woman Penelope recognized from Evan's school, stopped at their table. "I'm Meredith Sinclair. Do you remember me?"

Jacob inclined his head. "Of course."

"I assume I'm not interrupting anything." She flipped back her shiny blond hair and granted Penelope a quick scan. "Do you two know each other?"

"We're best friends and tell each other our deepest, darkest secrets." Jacob smiled at Penelope. His joking tone conveyed a note of fun, though his gaze was serious.

Penelope was ready to refute him, but he grabbed her hand across the table and squeezed. "Right, mate?"

His amused expression irked her. "You wish, mate," she refuted sarcastically.

Meredith cut her eyes to Penelope, then back to Jacob. "I wanted to personally thank you, Dr. Williams. My daughter, Annabelle, recovered quickly from the bee incident."

"I'm glad. How is she feeling?"

"Your quick thinking made all the difference." She gave him a flirtatious smile. "I'm speaking for the entire community when I say we're thrilled you set up a practice here in Roses."

He paused, seeming to reflect on her words. "My pleasure. Annabelle is a lovely girl."

"Thank you." Meredith turned to Penelope, finally taking more than a passing interest. "All the mothers in Annabelle's class are having a Christmas cookie exchange next month at my house. Would you like to join us? I know Evan is in her homeroom."

"If I'm free, I'll try to be there," Penelope said. "Please send me the details."

"Annabelle will give Evan the information."

Meredith Sinclair had never been one of Penelope's favorite parents. The man she'd recently divorced was a flagrant attorney, and the family had a high-class air not lost on Penelope. From what she recalled, Annabelle was pretty and popular in school.

Once she swished away, Penelope remarked, "The girl who swallowed the bee was Annabelle?"

"Yup. Do you know the family?"

"A little, though Meredith snubbed me, as usual," Penelope said. "Our kids have been in the same classes ever since I moved back here."

"She didn't snub you. She invited you to a cookie exchange."

Penelope fumbled, dumbfounded that Jacob stuck up for Meredith. She checked her watch. "Evan should be arriving at your clinic by now."

"He'll see Zack," Jacob reminded. He picked up the check. Despite her objection, he firmly shook his head and placed several bills, plus a generous tip, on the table. "I'll stop at the clinic after I finish at the hospital."

"Let me know if he and Zack talk at all."

"Please, Penelope, allow him some freedom." Jacob bent down and kissed the top of her head before she could turn away.

She stiffened.

"Is anything wrong?" he asked.

"Of course not." She'd heard a sermon once about being a stuffer and keeping her emotions inside, instead of letting them out. She'd honed that skill to a tee.

"Remember," his puzzled smile confronted her, "I know everything about you."

"Almost everything," she corrected.

"You can't hide your emotions from me."

"Try me."

"I'll pick you up at seven o'clock tonight for our undate."

"Where are we going? The farm to table restaurant?"

"Nope Dress casual." He gave a lopsided grin. "The location is a surprise."

CHAPTER 7

*I*t was a surprise all right, because the "undate" never occurred.

Jacob phoned an hour after Penelope arrived home. She'd changed into a red sweatshirt, as a nod to the upcoming holidays, and black sweatpants for comfort. Now she stood in the kitchen and clicked her cell phone on speaker as she pulled a tray of cream cheese Christmas cookies from the oven. The recipe had been handed down from her great-grandmother, Teresa, and she baked a double batch every year, mindful to send a plate to the first responders in town. Later in the season, she'd hand-deliver a batch to the local police station, too.

"I can't apologize enough," Jacob began. "Unfortunately, I need to cancel tonight."

She lowered her head and pressed her lips tight. "Another emergency?"

"A head injury. A ten-year-old child fell off his bike and is experiencing confusion. The parents are beyond worried and a little crazy."

Sternly, she reminded herself that her disappointment stemmed from selfishness.

He'd committed himself to serving people, and his kind and concerned attitude showed. He had so many good traits, which made her care for him even more.

She tossed a dishtowel over her shoulder. "Are the parents overreacting?"

"They're sensitive, though I tried to explain the situation. The child is being transferred to the hospital to be monitored overnight. Once I finish at the clinic, I'll stop by the hospital to check on him."

She placed the tray on top of the stove. "Your patients come first."

"I appreciate your understanding. I didn't anticipate a nurse calling in sick or a child's worrisome head injury."

Juggling the difficult emergencies a pediatrician dealt with daily was difficult to imagine. He never complained. He strove for a work-life balance, though parents were emotional and easily upset when it came to the well-being of their children.

"I'll make it up to you," he said.

"Don't be ridiculous."

"Do you like flowers?"

"Everyone likes flowers."

"What's your favorite?"

"No one has asked me the question before because ..."

"Don't stop now."

"Because no one ever brought me flowers." She struggled between maintaining her self-respect and answering truthfully. An irrefutable pang of sadness twisted her gut.

"You haven't answered my question."

"Roses. I love red roses."

He chuckled. "Befitting, considering the town we live in."

She grabbed a cookie off the tray and bit into it. Mmm. Delicious. She swung her arms as she made her way to the sink. Food always cheered her up.

"I'm baking Christmas cookies," she said.

"For Meredith Sinclair's cookie exchange?"

"Possibly." She bristled at the woman's name, a wave of unfounded jealousy causing her to pause. "In any event, I'll freeze the cookies for now."

"I'd be tempted to cheat and pull them out of the freezer. There wouldn't be any left by Christmas."

Slightly pacified, she laughed. "Last year, I ate a half gallon ice cream along with the cookies I had baked," she admitted.

She flicked a glance out the kitchen bay window framing her sizable backyard. The pergola-covered patio was brick paved and the table and chairs carved from teak wood. She and Evan hardly used the outdoor space. Though she paid a landscaper to mow the lawn, the curved flower bed in the corner was sorely neglected.

In fact, her entire house was untidy.

She vacillated. Should she sit beneath the pergola devouring a tray of cookies while feeling sorry for herself because of the change of plans with Jacob, or work on her housekeeping skills?

Dappled sunshine shone through the trees, and the sun began to set.

A sudden worried thought made her stomach clench. "Is Evan at the clinic?"

"He phoned several hospitals for equipment we might be able to use, then went off with Zack and his mother to the rec center."

She wasn't certain if Jacob was teasing or serious.

Evan left the clinic without phoning her?

"Oh?" Her voice swelled.

"Oh?"

The stillness between their connection troubled her. She expected a quick, clear response and shook her head in disapproval.

"Evan didn't call or text me?" She cupped the phone to her ear and paced the kitchen. Her tone was accusatory, but she couldn't help herself.

"Does he need to ask your permission first?"

"He was supposed to ride home with you."

"I told you I'm working late. There was a change of plans."

"Without informing me? His mother?" Conflicted thoughts swept through her. She'd anticipated seeing Jacob. More importantly, her son was in a car with someone else and hadn't consulted her.

"Zack's mother is a responsible adult," Jacob continued.

Restless, she shifted and didn't immediately respond. Jacob was a pediatrician, not a parent. Therefore, he wouldn't understand.

"Is Evan headed home after the rec center?" she asked.

"I assume so," Jacob said.

"That's it? No concern?"

"Look, Penelope, let me share something with you. I over-heard the two boys talking about the locker room incident. It sounded like Evan shoved the boy first. Then the boy pushed him back and Evan landed on the floor."

She slumped in a chair. "I believe my son's side of the story."

"There are usually two sides to every story."

"What should I do?"

"Be aware of the situation. Junior high is challenging for most preteens, and Evan faces a bigger hurdle because he lacks a father figure."

She bristled. Jacob made it sound like Evan's home environment was lacking, though she didn't have a choice. Roy had cheated on her. As a single parent, she strove to raise her son properly and conscientiously. However, some part of her acknowledged that Jacob's words were true. An involved, interested father figure in Evan's life might make a difference, and Roy lived too far away for more than an occasional visit. Maneuvering the tricky landscape of adolescence required Evan to sort difficult decisions, and a male brought different parenting qualities than a female. Could a man bring extra value to Evan's development?

Her job as a mother was to protect her son. After all, Evan was her only family. They were a team.

"Evan and Zack spoke at length," Jacob said. "They installed a new diving board at the pool and Zack wanted to show it to Evan. Zack's mother said it wouldn't be for long."

"Okay."

"Penelope?"

"Yes?"

"Evan won't live in a bubble forever and you can't fight every battle for him. Young people solve problems without our interference all the time and turn out just fine."

She massaged her temple with both hands. "So, you're saying I should force him to man up and tough it out?"

"No one's forcing Evan to do anything."

Isn't that exactly what you're inferring? she inwardly refuted. Jacob's statements were absurd, though she told herself not to be rude and argue with him.

Offering a stiff goodbye, she clicked off the phone, arranged the cookies on a plate, and set them on the kitchen table.

She plopped on a chair and perched her chin on her hands.

She didn't like the idea of Jacob interfering in her

parenting decisions, especially when he disagreed with her, or his judgmental inference. Surely, he meant well, but she was decidedly sensitive regarding anything to do with Evan.

In what had begun as an encouraging Sunday, discouragement washed over her. She'd looked forward to the evening with Jacob more than she'd recognized. She liked the idea of a surprise dinner. She liked the romantic idea of an "undate." And she might not like to admit it, but she was sorely disheartened she wouldn't be seeing him.

Oh, no. I'll not be getting involved in a relationship that only leads to heartache.

Jacob, whether he realized it or not, had upset her with his parenting inference.

After a deep breath, she peered at the unwashed dishes and cookie sheets cluttering the sink. The floor needed sweeping. But how could she accomplish any tasks when she lacked the drive and motivation to overcome her frustration?

She sunk deeper into her thoughts, and only one emerged.

Jacob.

Feeling emotions she could hardly rationalize, she was caring for him more and more despite their differences.

He was an earnest person. His appealing smile, his charming accent, his gentlemanly mannerisms—were all qualities she longed for in a man. He was indisputably interested in Evan and wanted to build a rapport with him. Securing a bond between them seemed important to him.

She'd tried to act like it wasn't any big deal Jacob had moved to town, but even her son had noted she smiled more often, and her brother inquired if she had spent a recent afternoon soaking up the sun because of the rosy color in her cheeks. Shanice joked that Penelope must be drinking an abundance of wine for dinner.

Though now, the reality of her life threatened to consume her.

Jacob couldn't be counted on. Her son would be leaving soon to see his father. All that added up to loneliness at the holidays. Again.

She eyed the cookies on the table and pushed the plate away. She wasn't hungry anymore.

Sure, she could stuff herself with cookies … or … she could be more like Jacob. He'd pressed aside his former ambitions and was pursuing a lifestyle change. He'd determined what he wanted and was going after it.

Why couldn't she be as brave?

Filled with renewed energy, she refused to brood. Instead, she'd harness her disappointment and grow.

She placed the cookies in a freezer bag and stashed them in the back of the freezer.

A scan down the hallway was a stark reminder of her untidiness. She was never the neatest person, but she wasn't a slob, either.

She peered down at her outfit. Sweatshirt and sweatpants. Before her divorce, she'd dressed stylish and sophisticated.

She fixed her hands on her hips and studied herself in the mirror over the stove. "It's time," she declared, "to begin an overhaul Penelope project."

She began with her upstairs closet and spent time organizing and tossing handfuls of drab, plain clothes into bags to donate to Goodwill. The next hour she straightened the house.

While she waited for Evan to return, she wandered to the living room and grabbed a book she'd purchased about changing careers. She sat on the plush couch and penciled in her preferences, first and foremost creating toy dolls out of wood, though she found herself writing Jacob's name on the corner pages.

Her next book choice was a romance novel she'd read several times. A woman could read these books over and over, she decided. She skimmed her favorite emotional scenes and closed the book with a happy sigh.

She glanced at her watch. Hmm. Evan still wasn't home. Should she text him?

No. She'd heed Jacob's advice and wait.

She selected another book on the coffee table she'd recently purchased: *Change Your Holiday Menu, Change Your Life.* She curled up on the couch perusing healthy, nutritious meals.

Career choices, cleaning, and cooking were all steps to confront her concerns and get a handle on poor eating habits. Inspired, she marched into the kitchen and chose fresh spinach and a bag of potatoes from the pantry.

Thirty minutes later, Evan still hadn't arrived. Surely, the center was closed by now. Her concerned thoughts were interrupted by her ringing cell phone.

Her heart jumped.

"Penelope?"

She bit down on her bottom lip. "Yes?"

"This is Zack's mother. We stopped at the rec center after the clinic."

Penelope could hardly focus. "I'm aware."

"Well, we were in an accident."

"Is everyone okay?" The terror in Penelope's throat altered her breathing. She could hardly catch her breath. "Is Evan hurt?"

"We're all fine. Evan will explain. I'm dropping him off at your house shortly."

. . .

WHEN A PINK-CHEEKED Evan arrived home a few minutes later, he greeted Penelope with a smile.

"Zack's mother phoned. Thank goodness you're all right." Penelope lunged to hug him. He seemed to tolerate her for several seconds, then moved away.

"Tell me you're okay," she said.

"I'm okay, Mom."

She flopped on a chair. "What happened?"

"Zack's mother drove into a mailbox when she was making a U-turn near the rec center."

"She should've called me sooner."

"No reason to. In a few years, I'll be driving."

"We'll see about that."

"In our state, I can drive as soon as I'm sixteen."

She held her tongue and refused to comment.

Evan had processed her divorce from his father with stoic naivety and seemed to grasp that his world would never be the same. Friends had commended his strength, and Penelope was grateful to her brother and the toy shop. They'd given her a solid purpose to return to Roses and piece her life together.

With a pang of guilt, she recognized her own strict childhood, coupled with the realization that life was tenuous, might be the reasons she was holding her son back.

With a quiet exhale, she knew there were few powers more potent than a strongminded, soon-to-be adolescent.

"Dr. Williams called to let me know where you were." She stood, telling herself not to dwell on the accident. She tossed the spinach into a salad with boiled eggs and a light vinaigrette dressing. "So, how was your afternoon with Zack?"

"It wasn't as bad as I thought." Evan placed his jacket on a chair. "You'd be surprised at the rec center's transformation. The entire place has been remodeled."

"I'd like to see it some time." She set the salad and potatoes on the table. "I haven't been there in over a year. Not since you quit swimming."

He didn't react, though he stepped farther into the kitchen and surveyed the food. "Looks good, Mom."

"Thanks. Did you guys go anywhere after the rec center?"

His face blanched. "We stayed for a while, stopped for hamburgers and milk shakes, and then Zack's mother ran into the mailbox."

You're lying, she thought. But about what? She decided not to pry and gestured to the table. "I roasted potatoes, too."

"Yeah. I'd prefer chips, though."

She grabbed the cookbook. "I'm trying out new recipes for Christmas Day."

"I'll be home by then. Don't we usually eat lasagna?"

"Different foods make life interesting, Evan." She cocked her head to the side to take in the sight of her sweet son. "I'll miss you while you're visiting your father."

"You'll only be alone a few days."

"Your father said that baby Christina weighed eight pounds and eleven ounces when she was born." Penelope's voice quavered. "Childhood is so precious. Remember when I used to read the Christmas story to you on Christmas day?"

Evan went to the sink to wash his hands, then turned to search her face. She forced a smile, although he obviously noted the sadness in her expression.

"You can read the story to me again, Mom. I like it. In the meantime, visit with Uncle Lincoln and Aunt Shanice if you miss me."

"They're flying to New York City on an extended holiday." She flipped through the pages of the cookbook and came across a recipe featuring quinoa and bell peppers. She held it up for him to see. "I'm still concerned about you flying all by yourself."

"I'm finally twelve," Evan said. "It's legal for me to fly without an adult."

"I'm still not comfortable with the idea." She flopped down on a chair. It seemed as if she was more protective of him than ever.

"What about Dr. Williams?" Evan sank into the chair across from her, whispered a prayer of grace, and scarfed down a baked potato. "You can hang out with him at the clinic. When I come back on Christmas Eve day, we'll invite him over. I bet he doesn't want to be alone, either."

"We'll see." She regarded the spinach salad. "Try some."

"Later." He eyed the salad and stood. "Aren't you and Dr. Williams going out to dinner tonight? That's why you're not eating, right?"

"He canceled. An emergency after you left."

Evan placed his dish in the sink. "What are you going to do instead?"

She had a mountain of office work to tackle. However, the living room screamed for a dusting.

An idea occurred. There was something else. Something to distract her. Something that never failed to trigger happy, nostalgic memories.

"Evan?"

"Hmm?" One foot in the hallway, he swiveled toward her.

"Let's lug our Christmas tree down from the attic."

"Mom, it's November. We always wait until after your birthday before we trim the house. Last year, we hardly decorated."

"Decorating is a lot of work," she reminded. She'd decided there wasn't much to celebrate once her family had split up.

She reined in her previous emotions. Was her resentment toward her ex-husband hurting her son? She shouldn't be going through the motions of Christmas. She should be truly appreciating the holiday.

"Lots of families decorate early." She hauled in a decisive breath. "This year, let's be one of those families."

AN HOUR LATER, Penelope eyed the living room with satisfaction. Sparkling white lights twinkled from the dark-green artificial spruce. Garland, in earthy tones and decorated with pinecones, dangled from the tree branches. On her front door, she hung a cedar faux wreath adorned with red berries and gold metallic bulbs, then tied a velvet ribbon to the top.

She clasped her hands to her chest and stood back to admire the results. As she'd anticipated, the holidays brought optimism and her mood lifted.

She clicked on the stereo system she seldom used and searched for a radio station playing Christmas music. "Rockin' Around the Christmas Tree" sung by Brenda Lee, wafted through the house.

"I've never heard this version of the song," Evan noted.

She laughed. "It's one of the best, and Brenda Lee was only thirteen years old when she recorded it."

Evan foraged through a stack of boxes on the floor marked *Christmas*. "Mom, where's the ceramic nativity you painted a couple of years ago?" His voice was bubbly, his appearance relaxed.

The set, painted in a light blue, depicted Joseph, Mary, and baby Jesus.

She picked through another box. "I think I gave the set to Uncle Lincoln and Aunt Shanice."

And she remembered why. She'd intended to carve wooden dolls into a miniature nativity but never got around to it. Why couldn't time stand still? Why was she always pulled in a million directions and left the activities she enjoyed for a later time? And why did that time never come?

She surveyed the wooden dolls. They sat where Jacob had last placed them when he'd made his "house call" to check on Evan's strep throat.

A smile flickered. Jacob hadn't even seen Evan that day. He was an excellent doctor, but surely, he had come for her, and the realization brought a quiver to her heart.

Evan propped open the window seat and peered inside. "The nativity isn't in here, either." He snatched his bookbag by the stairs. "If we're done, I should go upstairs to finish my homework."

"Your hamster needs feeding," she reminded. "Tidy your room. I cleaned and straightened the house but didn't touch your room."

Audibly, he groaned. "I'm busy, Mom."

"If you want the responsibility of a puppy who requires feeding, exercise, and grooming, you must prove you're ready."

"Dr. Williams said the best time to get a dog is when a kid is eleven years old. I'm twelve, so I'm a year late already. He also said that owning a dog helps you live longer."

"You or me?"

"Both of us, I think."

"He is a fountain of information. I'm surprised either one of you gets any work done if you're chatting all the time."

"He's awesome, Mom."

Observing her son's animated expression, she knew she was running out of excuses to be upset at Jacob. Her own senseless fear of being hurt affected Evan, and he deserved the right to have a positive male role model.

Nonetheless, Jacob was a diversion, an imaginary character in her life. She'd resolved to avoid any commitments. She'd warned him that a relationship between them was out of reach. So why did thoughts of him constantly fill her mind?

In truth, he seemed hesitant, too. Sometimes, he showed more interest in Evan or the dilapidated house than in her.

She curved toward the table in the living room. Evan had homework to finish, and she had wooden dolls to carve. Another positive step in the Penelope Project. If she felt better about herself, then everything else would fall into place.

*T*wo weeks later, Jacob drove to Penelope's house and parked at the curb. It was a special day. It was her birthday.

He hesitated, taking in a deep breath. A beat of apprehension coursed through him. He'd taken a bold move by coming to her house, but she hadn't left him any other choice.

She'd avoided him lately, and he wasn't certain why. He'd kept his texts general, inquiring about the dilapidated house and if she had heard anything. She invariably responded by advising him to contact Candee, the realtor.

He'd boasted about Evan's ability to juggle several tasks at once when he volunteered at the clinic, and how proud she must be of him. He suggested the boy pursue other activities, too, such as choosing a favorite holiday-themed book and reading to the younger children in his school or making and sending Christmas cards to troops overseas. She'd thanked him, then told him that she and Evan participated in Toys for Tots.

I appreciate your focus on my son, but I'm his mother and have things well in hand, she'd added in her text. *Oh, and I would've appreciated it if you had advised him to call me before he got into the car with Zack.*

This again? Jacob thought.

I assumed Evan would be fine, he replied. *Zack is Evan's friend, and his mother is responsible.*

Don't assume you know everything, just because you're a doctor, Penelope had countered.

Then, she had shut down the conversation.

Alrighty then. He'd nearly given up trying to get through to her. She appeared to understand the clinic's emergencies. Though how could he develop a relationship with her that had nothing to do with her son if he couldn't talk to her without her getting all offended?

Also, he'd hidden a secret, and a pain settled in the back of his throat whenever he went over his decision.

He'd opted not to tell her that he and Evan had visited the animal shelter when the clinic closed on Saturday. The shelter needed volunteers to clean cages and dog dishes, and to interact and care for the animals. Jacob and Evan also bathed and walked the dogs.

Jacob rationalized this was an important and practical first rung in Evan's learning ladder. In addition, Evan was learning more about dogs and puppies.

Well, she couldn't avoid him any longer. Fortunately, her birthday had landed on a weekday, and he figured she wouldn't celebrate until Evan arrived home from school.

He strode to the front door and rang the bell.

"Happy Birthday, beautiful," he said, when she opened the door.

Her gaze narrowed as she eyeballed the cake topper numbers on the cake he held.

"You knew I was turning fifty?" She plunked a hand on

her hip. "All I told you on the plane was that I had a birthday in November. Besides, you were sleeping."

"My eyes were half open under the sunglasses," he teased.

"So how—"

"Evan mentioned it several times. By the way, where is he?" Jacob peered toward the stairway.

"In his room, where else?" She shrugged. "He should be downstairs shortly."

"May I come in?"

"Of course." She opened the door wider and ushered him inside.

"No birthday is complete without a carrot cake topped with cream cheese frosting."

"You remembered?"

"Naturally."

"I wonder if Evan did." She preceded Jacob into the kitchen. "He's been acting awfully quiet and vague."

"He knew I was bringing the cake," Jacob confessed. "We planned your celebration ahead of time."

"When?"

"Last week." He went back to the porch, returning with a bouquet of red roses he offered her, and a six-pack of ginger beer he set on the kitchen counter. "The flowers are for you. The cake too, of course. The beer is for me. Care for a cold one?"

"No thanks." She lifted a delicate eyebrow. "How?"

"I discovered the local grocery store carries ginger beer. I opted for nonalcoholic."

"Not the beer." She shook her head. "How did you—"

He winked. "You mentioned the flowers in a text. However, lately you've become almost impossible to reach." He hoped he didn't sound overly accusing.

"I've been busy."

The age-old excuse.

He sensed her winding up more excuses and changed the topic.

"Your house looks great." The ebony-black piano gleamed, and books were stacked neatly on the coffee table. He strode into the living room, perused the stack, and held up a paperback. The front cover was a bright-blue, and a couple were in a heated embrace.

"*A Tale of a Forever Heart?*" He read the title.

She followed him. "I love sweet romance novels."

"Who is the tale about?"

"A man and a woman." She snatched the book from him and set it on top of the stack.

"Have you finished it?"

"Not this one yet. I know the ending, though."

He quirked an eyebrow. "How?"

"The sweet romances I read guarantee a happily ever after. Hearts are broken, but always mended at the end."

"You like romance."

"I love romance. The novels make me happy."

Her smile, her natural vitality and exhilaration, drew him to her. His mind drifted to the upcoming holidays and spending every waking free moment together.

On a nearby table, a line of miniature wooden dolls stood straight and colorful.

"White pants, blue coats, and red detailing," he said. "The toy soldiers are ready to march in formation. What are their names? General Admiral Oregano, Private Basil …"

She poked him in the side. "You're a regular comedian these days."

His deep chuckle resounded through the room. "You name your wooden dolls after spices."

"You have a memory like an elephant."

"And your carved dolls are extraordinary, a work of art."

"Thank you."

She wore a short, clingy green dress that accented her figure. Her shiny hair fell to her shoulders in gentle, dark waves. She gazed at him with soulful blue eyes, a perfect complement to her light creamy complexion.

"Crikey." He almost forgot his words. "You are gorgeous, especially on your birthday."

She opened her mouth, and he held his palm up. "Don't disagree. A thank you is sufficient."

"It's not that. I've waited for you say the word *crikey*. The term is utterly Australian."

"A cultural assumption," he said. "The word is hardly used anymore by younger Australians. I'm part of the old guard."

"You and me both."

"At our age, we can leave our cares and worries behind. Now our job is to welcome our world and savor every moment."

Her full lips curved into a smile. Her dimples were adorable. "Wise words, Dr. Williams."

She was even more gorgeous when she smiled.

"I always imagined life would be better when I reached fifty," she admitted.

"It is."

"Is it?"

He bent closer to her. "Yes, because I'm here, your son is here, and we are all together."

"True."

There was no challenge in her tone, though her chin quivered, and she averted her gaze.

His heart lurched. Awareness of her sense of humor, her zest for life, shot through him. He didn't want her despondent, especially on her birthday. He felt a surge of something he'd yearned for and recognized the emotion for what it was.

Attraction. To her.

He'd left his ex-wife far behind when he'd learned of her infidelity. Since then, he'd harbored ambivalence about close relationships. He struggled, but with each passing day, realized that Penelope was the woman he could contentedly live the rest of his life with. Nevertheless, how could he overcome his uncertainties if she wouldn't allow him to get any closer?

"So, let's light the candles," he announced.

"HAPPY BIRTHDAY TO YOU, Happy Birthday to you."

Jacob grinned at a smiling Penelope when he and Evan had finished singing.

"Time to blow out the candles," he teased. He'd debated placing fifty candles on the cake, but decided on the numbers five and zero, respectively.

She held back her hair, half-closed her eyes, and the two candles were extinguished in one blow.

"Hurray!" Jacob and Evan laughed and clapped.

"Mom, whose birthday comes next?" Evan asked.

"Well, yours is in February." She regarded Jacob as she began brewing coffee, then returned to the table to cut the cake. "When is your birthday?"

"January," Jacob replied.

"Really, Dr. Williams? Only a couple months away?" Evan blurted.

Jacob nodded.

"Truth?" Penelope asked Jacob skeptically. "Or did you just want the first slice of cake?"

"Truth." He offered a slight smile. "Although I'm happy to be served the first slice, regardless."

"And you'll be how old?"

"Fifty-one. Welcome to the fifties."

"I didn't realize you were older than me." Penelope

blinked, seeming to take several seconds to mentally regroup.

"Because I look so young," he joked.

"You and my mother are the same age for a few weeks!" Evan said. "Your birthday is next, Dr. Williams, so you can pull out the knife."

Jacob placed his palm over Penelope's delicate fingers. Surely, she felt the invisible magic shimmering between them. Otherwise, how could a woman's small hand push his heart into such a rapid beat?

"Make a wish." Penelope slid her hand away. "Keep it a secret or it won't come true."

Jacob closed his eyes for several seconds. "Secrets are difficult for me."

Especially when his secret wish stood directly in front of him. His feelings for her were shattering any final reservations. The awareness seemed sudden because he'd only met her a few short months ago.

He sat on a chair, cracked open a ginger beer, and downed half.

"No coffee?" she asked.

"I'll stick with beer."

He needed something to quell his nerves. Lately, he couldn't sleep, pondering his feelings. Could he get married again at his age? Penelope was a divorcee with a preteen boy. In the past, he'd stepped away from any conflicts. He'd attended college rather than deal with his family. Their problems and goals were too different from his. Same was true of his hospital job in Atlanta. However, he believed his decision to relocate to Roses was the right choice, and the reason was standing in the same room.

Penelope poured herself a cup of coffee and sat across from him. "Earth to Jacob Williams," she said.

"Sorry. I was thinking."

"About?"

"Your festive home." He gestured toward the living room. "The decorated tree inspires me. I wish the holidays were already here."

"I love Christmas." Despite her words, her eyes were sad.

"Me too."

"Me three," Evan chimed in. "Mom, did Dr. Williams tell you he plans to dress up as Santa Claus at the clinic next month?"

"No, he didn't." She plated a heaping slice of cake for each of them while Evan rummaged in the freezer for a carton of chocolate ice cream.

"I thought it would be fun for the kids," Jacob said, "though I haven't found a Santa costume yet."

"You will," she replied. "The children will call you Doc Christmas."

"I love Christmas," he repeated.

"Bah, humbug," she half joked. "You're Doc Christmas but sometimes I feel like I'm Mrs. Scrooge."

"Dr. Williams, did my mom mention we are spending Thanksgiving on Uncle Lincoln's houseboat on Hilton Head Island?" Evan brought the carton of ice cream to the table. "Our neighbor watches my hamster when we go away. When I get my puppy, we'll take my puppy with us."

"Oh, we will, will we?" Penelope crossed her arms.

"If my mother says it's okay, you can join us. Unless you have other plans." Evan beamed at Jacob, then glanced at Penelope.

"I don't have anything special planned." Jacob set down his fork. *Whoa. Wait. Wasn't a houseboat a boat on the ocean? Since his niece's accident, he'd avoided pools and lakes. This scenario was even scarier. This was an ocean.*

A smile flickered across Penelope's face. "Of course, you're invited, Jacob."

"Are you staying all week? I'm working until Wednesday." Inwardly, he grappled with his words. He wanted to celebrate Thanksgiving with them, but a houseboat wasn't part of the equation. Somewhere on land, a cabin, for instance, sounded infinitely better, and much safer. "I always phone my mum and my sister on holidays."

She scooped ice cream onto each plate and handed him and Evan a spoon.

"Call them from the houseboat," she replied.

"You have cell phone service?"

"The boat isn't sailing anywhere because it's not motorized. It stays in one place—docked at the marina. Water and sewer and electricity are provided by the shore power. Houseboat living is like staying at a vacation home. Do you swim?"

"Why?" He tilted his head and tried to contain his shudder. "Will I need to?"

"Not unless you want to."

"I'm not a strong swimmer."

"You won't need to wear a life jacket while you eat Thanksgiving dinner." She grinned. "The boat hardly sways."

"Hardly." He blew out a speculative breath and met her gaze. "I'll make a deal."

"What kind?"

"While I'm talking to my mum and sister, I'll introduce you and turn the phone over to you."

"Fine. I'm thrilled to chat with them both."

He gave an ironic laugh. "You're in for an adventure."

Boy, was she ever.

She wandered to the sink to wipe her hands on a dishtowel, then stepped to him. "You're completely off work for a few days?"

"I'm close enough to Roses to drive back if there is an emergency, though Dr. Hannaway, the town GP, is taking on extra shifts as we've expanded. Even though we have different specialties, the limited number of doctors here makes it possible for us to cover for each other if needed. She's excellent and no-nonsense. Plus, we use each other as a sounding board." He hesitated. "The drive from Hilton Head to Roses is what ... around three hours?"

"Depending on traffic. I imagine the Thanksgiving holiday is busy at a clinic."

"Most common is a condition doctors call holiday heart." He finger quoted. At her curious expression, he explained. "It's caused by excessive drinking. The patient usually comes in pale and sweaty and smelling of alcohol."

"Is the condition serious?"

"It can be, if heart palpitations are rapid."

"Let's pray no one sees any of that," she said.

Evan piped in after he'd finished the cake and ice cream on his plate. "Can we take a ferryboat to Daufuskie Island for the day? The trip is short from Hilton Head."

"We'd have to ride on another boat to get there?" Jacob inquired.

"The ferry is small, Dr. Williams."

Jacob scraped a hand through his hair. Irrational thoughts flooded his brain. Suppose there was a strong wind and the small boat overturned?

"Not everyone is comfortable on boats," Penelope replied to Evan. "Each of us wrestle with our own fears." She nodded conspiratorially at Jacob. An understanding nod, and he tipped his head back to take in her sweet face. "My fear is planes."

He smiled. "I remember."

"Lincoln and Shanice won't be around, as they're taking an extended holiday," Penelope went on. "They hardly use the houseboat anymore. Did you know my brother is also an author?"

"What does he write?"

"Children's books. *Tuggy the Tugboat* books are his best-loved series, which is the main reason why he wants to hold on to the boat."

Jacob downed the rest of his ginger beer. "Which is?"

"Inspiration, I imagine." She sat again and sipped her coffee. "The weeks between Thanksgiving and Christmas are hectic for toy shops. I'm spending hours ordering inventory and managing invoices. Fortunately, our employees are more than capable, though with Lincoln gone, I'll be on call if anything goes wrong."

A wide grin spread across Evan's face. "We'll decorate the houseboat for Christmas. Wait till you see how we tape red stockings to the kitchen cabinets, Dr. Williams. Uncle Lincoln has an artificial pine tree in a storage unit, and we hang tinsel everywhere." Evan placed his dish in the sink and bounded toward the hall. "We also cut out paper snowflakes for the boat's windows. Don't we, Mom?"

Before Penelope answered, Evan skipped up the stairs.

"Lots of sparkle and flair." Jacob offered a bemused smile.

"This entire conversation has caught me by surprise." Penelope returned to the sink and began loading the dishwasher.

"Which part?" Jacob placed his bottle in the kitchen's recycling bin. "The paper snowflakes?"

"Not funny."

"Have I been uninvited for Thanksgiving?"

"You're still invited. A deal is a deal."

"You'll cook a turkey?"

"Roger's Diner, my favorite restaurant on the island, offers a spectacular takeout spread. The entire turkey with all the trimmings. I don't cook large meals on the boat, because the oven heats up the boat too quickly. However, there is a full kitchen, complete with a stove, refrigerator, and microwave."

Jacob strode close to her, the delicate floral whiff of lavender flooding his nostrils. The scent was calming, lightening his mood, and quelling his reservations about a sinking houseboat.

Her back was to him, and he wrapped his arms around her waist. "I missed you," he whispered in her ear.

"Yet here I am."

"I tried texting."

Her lips pursed. "Busy," she murmured.

"Are you still upset about the accident with Zack and his mother?"

"I was concerned and worried."

"I hope you don't blame me. I got caught up with patients and—"

"Don't be silly."

"However, you've avoided me."

"Busy," she repeated.

"My birthday girl has a lot of the same excuses I don't buy."

She tilted her head toward him. Her lips were slightly parted. "What don't you buy?"

The expression on her features mirrored his own, confirming his feelings. Her eyes were teasing and appraising, and his pulse thrummed a steady beat. In that moment, he realized she cared for him as much as he cared for her.

"Your excuses for avoiding me," he said. "I forgive you. Please forgive me."

"Of course." She inhaled and turned to him. "Jacob, whatever you're thinking … this isn't a good idea."

"The best idea I've had in a long time." He cradled her face in his hands and kissed her gently and thoroughly. "In fact, I have an even better idea."

She gazed up at him. "I can only imagine."

"No more of this "undate" stuff. From now on, we're officially dating. We're a couple."

She trembled in his arms, slightly, as if he had stirred an emotion she was trying to suppress. "Promise me you'll never turn into a Roy."

He wanted to bury his lips in the curve of her neck. She brought gladness and love into his life. She was fresh and vibrant, witty, and delightful.

"I promise." He sealed his assurance with an affirming kiss.

CHAPTER 9

A houseboat wasn't Jacob's idea of the ideal place to observe an American Thanksgiving. First and foremost, he was petrified of being on a boat.

Okay, not petrified. Just not totally comfortable swinging back and forth on a floating "vacation home."

The America part? He loved the country and was thrilled to celebrate the traditional holiday. After relocating, his family had become US citizens, and he appreciated having dual citizenship for both Australia and the United States.

At present, totally stuffed from Thanksgiving dinner, he placed his cloth napkin to the side and pushed back from the galley table. "Best meal I've ever had, and so much food it took two hands to carry the turkey platter to the table. My compliments to Chef Roger."

"I doubt the diner is still owned by a guy named Roger," Penelope replied.

"At least the cooks carried on Roger's legacy." Jacob patted his stomach appreciatively. "Especially the mashed potatoes with loads of butter."

Seemingly caught between laughter and agreement, she smiled and didn't protest.

"If we're done, I'll get the Christmas trimmings." Evan's face flushed with excitement. "Mom and I hauled the tree out of storage before you came on board, Dr. Williams, but there are plenty of decorations left."

Penelope gazed out the window. "The unit is on the other side of the marina."

"I know where it is, Mom. We've been here a thousand times."

"Soon, it will be dark," she said.

"Yeah, in like three hours."

"Go ahead, then." She clutched her hands together. "We'll finish cleaning, and when you return, let's start trimming the boat for Christmas."

After Evan shrugged on his leather jacket and skipped out the door, Jacob pulled her into his arms. A flow of heat passed between them, a crackle of attraction he couldn't deny. Her heady feminine fragrance called for a kiss.

"Thank you for a wonderful Thanksgiving," he said.

She licked her lips and regarded him with unabashed affection. "My pleasure."

Those lips. A rosy tint from his kisses enhanced her full mouth. He'd be thinking about those lips all evening.

He sighed and glanced at his watch. "This may be a good time to phone my mum."

Penelope brought their dishes to the sink. "Do you want some privacy?"

"No." He stepped to her, claimed her hand, and squeezed. "You're part of the deal."

"Are we video chatting with her?"

Curtly, he shook his head. "A phone call is sufficient."

Jacob peered around, admiring the boat's interior. Penelope had explained her brother had opted for white paint to make the space look bigger. The open floor plan on the upper deck featured a dining room, kitchen, and living room, and the reclaimed wooden floors were originally crafted and removed from an old school. The lower deck offered bedrooms, three bedroom, two full-sized bathrooms, and a half bath. In total, the houseboat was two thousand square feet.

The ocean views from the docked boat were jaw-dropping. Waves swished, and the cries of seagulls squawked as their wings beat through the air.

With his duffle bag slung over his shoulder, he'd admired the gorgeous wooden and rope walkway when he'd arrived. The handmade door boasted an antique porthole. "I didn't envision this type of luxury," he admitted.

"*Shay's Secret.*" He'd read the boat's name engraved over the entry and asked, "Who is Shay?"

"Shanice. Lincoln's wife," Penelope said. "Shay is his nickname for her."

"What's her secret?"

"They have a history together. They dated in college and then broke up. She left him because of our father, who didn't approve of their relationship. She never explained her reasons to Lincoln. Fortunately, they ended up finding each other again in Roses and thus, true love."

"The best kind." Jacob offered a nod of approval. "Just like your romance novels."

On Thanksgiving morning, he'd woken to a golden sunrise streaming into his bedroom window. He'd stepped outside and relaxed on the deck while savoring a cup of fresh-brewed coffee. The mouthwatering scents of roasted turkey, sweet potatoes, cranberry sauce, and warm-from-the-oven bread filled his nostrils.

"Smells like turkey day!" Evan exclaimed, and Jacob heartily concurred.

Now as he rinsed dishes, a cloud of impending doom descended over him as he anticipated the upcoming call.

"I'd prefer you're here with me when I phone my mum." He wiped his hands on a dishtowel and started toward the living room sofa with Penelope. He beckoned her to sit next to him and she complied, snuggling against his shoulder. He smiled down at her, and his breath quickened at the delightful sensation of her closeness. He drew her tighter and pressed a kiss on her lips. Her gaze lifted to meet his, and the gentle yielding in her magnificent eyes almost made him forget about the dreaded upcoming phone call altogether. He wanted to keep Penelope in his arms forever.

She'd taken extra pains with her appearance and wore a cable knit blue sweater dress. Cozy, yet casual, the dress enhanced her smooth complexion, and her dark hair shone in the afternoon sunlight.

Jacob had opted for jeans and a chambray shirt.

"Don't you want to talk to your family alone first?" Penelope asked.

"Nope." Jacob loosened his hold around her shoulders, fighting the impulse to keep her as near as possible. "My mum is ... well ... my mum. Our relationship is rocky, at best."

"What about your sister?"

"Kylie has had a hard go of it these past few years. She's been angry with me, though we've begun to mend our fences."

"Part of your long, tragic story?" Penelope inquired.

"The very same." He responded with a small nod. "Kylie is considering moving back to Australia."

"With your mother?"

"Possibly." He studied his cell phone, as if searching for answers. "My mum can't handle all the farm chores on her own, though my sister has frequently helped. However, now that Kylie and her husband have split, only the two women are holding onto an old, rundown farm."

"You seem to gravitate toward rundown things yourself."

"Or rush away from them. I apparently have a love-hate relationship going." He narrowed his eyes. "Are you trying to analyze me?"

"I have enough on my plate trying to analyze myself."

He hesitated. Should he phone his mother now, or wait a bit? Speaking about his mother revealed his ambivalence more than he realized.

There was no time like the present, he encouraged himself. Rubbing a hand over his jaw, he clicked on her number.

"Hello?" an elderly woman's voice answered.

"Happy Thanksgiving, Mum," Jacob began.

"Who is this?"

"Your son, Jacob."

"Nice of you to remember your mum and ring me once in a while."

"I call you every week and text whenever I can." He gave himself a small shake. "Happy Thanksgiving."

"We're not American, Jacob."

"We've lived in the States longer than Australia and we're American citizens." A familiar emptiness overwhelmed him. No matter what he achieved, he could never please her.

He peered at the stereo system in the corner. Perhaps if he was armed with relaxing music in the background, the music would subdue his anxiousness instead of being surrounded by silence. As if reading his mind, Penelope grabbed a remote. She tuned into a station of holiday classics, and "Oh Come, All Ye Faithful" sounded, sung by a male choir.

He gazed at her, curled up on the sofa beside him. She

looked the opposite of how he felt. Her features were determined and resilient.

His protector.

He smiled at that. Penelope, rising to his defense in any storm.

"Are you working today at your fancy clinic?" his mother inquired.

"Another doctor is on call, Mum. And you're confusing the clinic with the hospital in Atlanta."

"Are you all moved into your new place?"

"I'm renting an apartment. I'd love if you visited me for the holidays."

"You're a big shot doctor. You don't have time for your mother."

"I have plenty of time for you, mum." He pressed his lips tightly together.

"You didn't have time for the farm. It could've collapsed all around you and you wouldn't have cared."

"I'm not a farmer. I wanted to be a doctor and I couldn't turn down the full scholarship for being valedictorian of my class. Besides, I want to help people."

"Doesn't charity begin at home?"

His stomach churned, and he reached for the glass of water Penelope had placed next to him. "Did you receive my check this month?"

"The money was a little less than usual."

"I'm sorry. The clinic was more expensive to start up than I anticipated, and coupled with the expense of moving from Atlanta and buying another doctor's practice ..."

He rubbed his forehead, then slung an arm around Penelope's shoulders. "Look, the weather is warmer in the Carolinas than in Maryland. Roses sponsors a Christmas parade and features a holiday sing-along concert in the park."

"I like snow at Christmas."

"I haven't lived here long enough to forecast for sure." He glanced at Penelope. "I'm certain they get snow sometimes."

"Sometimes," she mouthed.

"I prefer a white Christmas," his mother said.

He sank deeper into the sofa. He'd had this type of discussion often and instructed himself to remain upbeat. Nonetheless, if he liked red, his mum would say the opposite and like blue. The past was a mere breath away, and he clearly sensed this conversation was resembling all the others.

"I'm considering purchasing a home in Roses and setting up my practice in the house." He struggled to find the right words to describe his dream. "It needs work, but the house has character."

"Our farm has character."

"Is Kylie there?" He briefly closed his eyes. "She is welcome to visit for Christmas, too."

"She's busy in the kitchen and can't talk."

"Some other time, then. Please wish her a lovely Thanksgiving." He sat still for a moment. "Mum, I'd like to introduce you to a very special someone. I'm officially dating a wonderful woman, and her name is Penelope. She wants to say hello."

"Now?" Penelope whispered.

He nodded vigorously.

She rubbed the back of her neck, then accepted his cell phone. She exchanged light pleasantries with his mother, then handed the phone to him for a final goodbye.

When he clicked off, he leaned back against the sofa. Still holding Penelope close, his body sagged.

Some conversations rendered people speechless. This conversation with his mum was one of them.

"'Deck the halls with boughs of holly.'" The following morning, Evan belted out the carol in a faultless tenor voice while he taped paper Christmas stockings to the kitchen cabinets. His wide beam of delight lit his entire face.

Penelope grinned. She loved seeing him happy. These were precious memories she'd tuck away and revisit forever. These were the festive times chipping away at her insecurities and resentments toward her ex. These moments brought optimism for a brilliant future.

She'd picked out a pair of linen joggers and a dazzling red sweater. She'd decided to grow out her hair, and loose brown waves framed her face. She'd parted her hair in a deep side part.

She followed Evan into the living room, where Jacob, squatting on the floor, was setting up a three-foot artificial tree. The scents of a Christmas candle, balsam pine and cedar, wafted through the air.

"Can I ask you a question, Penelope?" Jacob stood, his tall, commanding frame dwarfing the tree. He brushed silver tinsel off his jeans, though tinsel still stuck to his hair and green polo shirt.

"Sure." She smothered a giggle and reached up to pluck the tinsel from his hair. "Are you planning to turn into a Christmas tree?"

"I'm Doctor Santa, remember?" He brushed the tinsel from his shirt. "When is the soup done?"

"A few more hours. It's simmering on the stove."

Earlier in the morning, she and Jacob had picked over the turkey carcass, then sliced extra vegetables—onions, carrots, and celery—to a turkey broth. A rice cooker supplied the rice they would add later.

"Smells homey and delicious." He stepped toward the kitchen and sniffed the heavenly aroma. "All we need is a bag of sticky caramel corn to munch on while we binge watch holiday movies. I vote for *National Lampoon's Christmas Vacation*."

Evan fixed a sparkling white angel to the top of the tree. "That movie is one of my favorites. Let's stream it tonight."

Penelope stood back to admire the decorations. An eclectic mix of humorous, stylish, and handmade ornaments brought a fun, understated elegance to the boat. It was a shame, she thought, that she wouldn't be back here to enjoy the festive ambiance. However, Lincoln and Shanice declared that they would stay on the houseboat in January and celebrate the holidays then.

By late morning, red and green bulbs sparkled around the fake fireplace, and a blinking *Ho, Ho, Ho* sign hung over the corner bar. Penelope hadn't observed a true, merry Christmas since her divorce. However, she imagined the upcoming weeks with Jacob as picture-perfect opportunities to awaken her sense of joyousness in the season.

As if reading her thoughts, he reached for her hand and gave a light squeeze. His warm smile filled with love.

Love. For her. The thought brought unexpected flutters to her chest.

"Can I play video games in my bedroom?" Evan asked when he finished hanging the last strand of tinsel on the tree.

"Sure." Penelope turned to Jacob and reciprocated his smile. "Thanks for all your decorating help."

"You're very welcome," he replied. "My pleasure."

"Later I want to go swimming," Evan said. "I brought my swimsuit."

"Swimming?" She expressed her disbelief aloud. Evan hadn't asked to swim in months. "The water is cold." She hesitated to say more, though she didn't wish to discourage him, especially with Jacob staring at her.

A wistful look crossed Evan's face. "I'll just take a quick dip."

"Not in the marina," she replied. "Long gone are the days when you can jump in from the boat. This water is dangerous with electricity and fumes and operators unable to see you." Her hands gripped the chair, a myriad of accidents that might await Evan flashing through her mind. "There are *No Swimming* signs posted everywhere, and any further discussion on this subject is nonnegotiable."

"Message received, Mom. You've given me a thousand lectures about the dangers, but Pelican Beach is a short walk from here. I'm a strong swimmer. So are you. Come with me."

"I'll pass."

"What about you, Dr. Williams?" Evan asked.

Jacob's entire body stiffened. "Your mother and I will sit and chat." With that, he led her to the outdoor deck overlooking the harbor.

The view of the ocean beyond was spectacular, and she'd noted he'd taken in every detail of the houseboat, both inside and out.

"In December, the holiday lights take to the water," she said. "Hilton Head holds a twinkling boat parade."

Jacob raised a dark eyebrow. "Sounds marvelous if I can watch from the shore. However, if you invite me, then I'll be there."

They stood by the handrails, an ocean breeze cooling her cheeks.

He wrapped an arm around her. "Simply breathtaking," he breathed, as he gazed down at her face. The same breeze ruffled his dark, thick hair as he studied the sunlight glinting off the water, then contemplated the sapphire blue sky.

He looked incredibly handsome, and nothing took away from the peacefulness and pleasure of standing with this conscientious, dashing man. Earlier, he'd jogged around the marina shirtless, and she'd admired his hard chest and flat stomach as sweat pooled along his muscular arms. After returning to the houseboat and showering, he'd responded to numerous phone calls from his staff. He'd assured Penelope that Thanksgiving at the clinic had been thankfully without any alarming incidents, save for grease burns from frying a turkey, upset stomachs from overeating, and a bout of food poisoning.

"Dr. Hannaway is keeping an eye on a holiday heart patient," he said. "She's monitoring his abnormal heart rhythm."

"Is she on call the entire weekend?" Penelope asked.

"Yes. This weekend is officially my vacation. However, I'm scheduled to work at the clinic on Christmas Eve day and on Christmas Day."

"Perfect for your Santa outfit," she teased.

He chuckled. "Meanwhile, how is the toy business?"

"We fussed with our window display, and it features a lighted carousel and several handmade elf puppets. I insisted on background Christmas music to be played in the store."

"Is "Jingle Bells" the standard fare?"

"Jesus is the reason for the season, and I prefer to keep Christ in Christmas. So, "Oh, Little Town of Bethlehem" is perfect."

"I agree." He rubbed his thumb over her wrist and kissed her hand. "In addition, I like giving and receiving gifts, too."

Her hand tingled from his warm lips. "We also devoted one floor of the shop to wooden rocking horses in all shapes and sizes. There's a rocking horse convention this weekend and a couple of busloads of people are expected to tour our store."

"There's such a thing as a rocking horse convention?"

"Apparently." Penelope had checked with several of her toy shops and the holiday season was off to a promising start. Lincoln had texted from New York City and declared that he and Shay were having a splendid time seeing the famous sights.

"This is the first year Lincoln and Shanice won't be hosting a Christmas party," Penelope mused.

"I'll host a Christmas party," Jacob said.

"You will?"

"Absolutely." He searched her face. "Will you attend?"

"I'd love to."

"Good. I'm throwing a Polar Express party at the clinic and will serve hot chocolate. I requested new sleepwear donations for the children, and the outreach from the community has been overwhelming."

"Another advantage of living in Roses." Grinning, she settled on a deep-cushioned teak love seat and Jacob nestled beside her. He looped an arm around her shoulders, and her heart leapt in her chest when he nuzzled her neck. A glow of exhilaration and affection surged through her.

"This is a wonderful life," he whispered as his lips gravitated to hers. "The island is genuinely peaceful. A real corker."

"Corker?" She gave him her undivided attention. "What's that mean?"

"Australian slang for really good, mate." His eyes gleamed wickedly, and she couldn't prevent a broad smile from spreading across her face.

"This entire harbor will decorate for Christmas," she said. "Red bows on all the lanterns, and many owners will string colored lights on their boats." Her gaze roamed over the glistening water. Smooth waves followed various boats as they motored out of the harbor.

She inhaled. A whiff of salty air never failed to invigorate her.

"Why are people drawn to the water?" she mused.

"Some people," Jacob corrected with a grim smile.

She looked up at him. "What do you mean?"

"Some people are, some people aren't."

"You mentioned you aren't a strong swimmer."

He shrugged indifferently. "I can hold my own. I'm not a champion like you or your son."

"We've grown up around the water."

"Crikey, I'm an Aussie guy." He broke out in his thickest Australian accent. "My family's farm in Maryland isn't near the sea."

Penelope stood to check the soup.

"There's something I want to tell you." His gaze pinned to hers. "My story involves swimming."

Her chest tensed at his serious tone, and her voice rose in pitch. "What is it?"

"Sit for a while longer." He patted the seat and pulled her back down beside him. "I'm ready for you to hear my long, tragic tale."

By his decree, she'd assumed the subject was closed and shot him a questioning glance. "Truth?" she inquired.

"Always. You're a good listener."

"I try." He leaned back against the cushions and stretched out his long, muscular legs.

"At least when I'm not talking constantly." She managed to keep her tone joking to lighten his suddenly pensive mood.

He inhaled a lengthy breath and then released it. "My sister, Kylie, had a daughter."

Had. Penelope noted the past tense and her heart constricted.

"Linda," she said. "You mentioned she never fully recovered. What happened?"

"A swimming accident when she was young. She nearly drowned."

"How old was she?"

"She was in elementary school. The accident occurred in a friend's pool. My sister sat by the pool and looked away for a few seconds when Linda suddenly went under the water. Kylie dove in and rescued her, and her quick thinking saved her daughter. However, Linda's brain suffered from a lack of oxygen. The doctor in our little town diagnosed the injury as not severe."

Penelope reached out and patted his hand.

"The doctor was wrong." Despite Jacob's somber expression, his voice remained calm. "Linda began having seizures. A couple years ago, she took a turn for the worse and suffered from amnesia and muscle spasms before she died."

His voice cracked, bringing tears to Penelope's eyes. "Jacob, I'm so sorry."

"I miss my sweet niece. We all do." He shuddered, as if a memory from the past was ever present. "Kylie was an excellent caregiver."

Penelope's stomach twisted in a sharp knot. "The … the remembrances must be difficult for you to process and—"

"I was working in Atlanta and left as soon as my sister phoned." His gaze focused on the horizon, where the water met the sky. His voice trailed off. "I didn't arrive in Maryland on time."

"I'm certain you got there quickly."

He bit down on his bottom lip, seeming to ponder his next words. "Not quickly enough. Kylie never forgave me. She never forgave me for not being at the pool that day, either. I had visited for the weekend but had stayed back to lend a hand on the farm."

"Don't blame yourself. There was nothing you could do in either case." Penelope swallowed as the risk of tears passed and the thickness in her throat began to dissolve.

"Explain that to my sister. I'm a doctor. I should've been able to do something."

"She'll come around eventually." Penelope still reeled, and her tears flowed again. Her heart ached for Jacob and Kylie, and his family. She pictured his niece, perhaps with the same dark hair and deep-brown eyes as he had.

"Continue to reach out to your sister," she said, dabbing at her wet cheeks.

"I will. Since then, I've been uncomfortable around the water. Coupled with the difficult memories, the dangers seem more pronounced than ever." He touched one of Penelope's tears with his fingertip. "Thank you for listening. Thank you for caring."

She gazed up at him, surprised at his heartfelt thanks. She wasn't accustomed to a man who wore his feelings on his sleeve. She wasn't accustomed to the emotions he woke inside her.

They sat for several minutes, watching the hypnotic rise

and fall of the ocean, and she burrowed her face against his chest.

So that explained why his expression had paled when she'd mentioned the houseboat. He'd been leery, cautious, and a bit skittish. Now she understood why.

A while later, her cell phone buzzed, and she recognized the number immediately. *Roses Toy Shop*. The manager was capable and would only phone if an emergency arose.

She stood. "Jacob, I apologize. I have to take this call."

"We lost power on the street because a transformer went out," her manager began without preamble when she clicked on. "Two busloads of folks from the Rocking Horse event are scheduled to pull up within the next few hours."

"Are you closing the store?"

"We plan to stay open, although it's dark here with no lights. I sent the staff out for flashlights, though I anticipate cash register sales will be a challenge."

"Thankfully, it's daylight," she replied. "Do you want me to come help?"

"We're shorthanded and the rain is coming down in sheets," the manager said. "Our parking lot is tight, and someone needs to direct traffic."

Mentally, Penelope estimated the time it took to drive to Roses. Three hours. The store was open until eight o'clock, though they might close early once darkness fell. Still, she'd be able to assist for a good portion of the day.

"I should leave now," she murmured, half to herself.

"Leave?" Jacob was on his feet. "Where? Why?"

"The toy shop in Roses." She rubbed her palms across her linen joggers and irritably shook her head. Her job was interfering with a wonderful weekend, although she had no choice. Her business came first, particularly during the holidays, and especially with Lincoln out of town.

"The shop lost power because a transformer is out in the area," she said. "The staff is buying every flashlight in sight."

"What can I do?" Jacob asked.

She stared blankly out at the ocean. "Will you stay with Evan? And stir the soup?"

His lips formed a smile as he placed his hands on her shoulders. "Whatever helps."

"Thanks." She rushed inside the houseboat to grab her keys and shrug on a cotton jacket. "I'll direct cars in the toy shop's parking lot. Believe me, in the pouring rain it's the job no one else wants. I'm the owner, and I must lead by example."

"You're a professional and selfless woman and absolutely amazing."

"I hate leaving Evan."

She also hated leaving Jacob.

"Evan is fine." Jacob clasped her cold hands. "We'll play board games, walk the marina, and eat soup. Tonight, we'll watch the movie, unless you want us to wait for you."

"Don't. Sounds like a plan." She turned toward the stairs and called out. "Evan, I'm driving to Roses but should return around ten. Dr. Williams is here."

"Awesome," came the quick response.

"Drive carefully," Jacob said. Their gazes met and held. He hugged her, and she relished the solidness of his muscles, the warmth of his hands on her back heating her insides. He brought "tidings of comfort and joy," like the lyrics of her favorite Christmas carol, "God Rest Ye, Merry Gentlemen." Her breath paused for a beat at the wonder of Jacob's embrace, the wonder of *him* to make everything right.

"I'll keep your son safe," he promised, pressing a tender kiss on her lips.

He made her feel sheltered and adored, and nothing could

dampen her excitement at the upcoming weeks with him by her side.

Because nothing was as important as security and ... love.

Willfully, she lifted her chin. Love was the last feeling she wanted, and contemplations along those lines only betrayed her. Still, what was more exhilarating than love, especially during the most magical season of the year?

She refused to feign indifference to him any longer. If anything, she cared for him more than she ever dreamed possible.

"No reservations about leaving Evan," she reassured herself as she withdrew from Jacob's hold. As she walked along the narrow dock to the parking lot, she scuffed at a shiny pebble in her path. "My son is in Jacob's capable hands," she said aloud. "What could possibly go wrong?"

CHAPTER 11

acob strode into the kitchen as soon as Penelope left. He stirred the turkey soup simmering on the stove and sipped a spoonful. Savory and delicious, and he sprinkled a dash of salt and pepper into the broth.

Penelope had placed the rice cooker, a box of rice, and a measuring cup on the counter.

He grinned. She was certainly a planner, and wow, did she look gorgeous. She was everything he could ever ask for. Efficient, brilliant, and stunning. Was that why he couldn't form a coherent thought whenever she entered a room?

"Dr. Williams, I'm going swimming," Evan announced. He emerged from his bedroom and bound into the kitchen wearing swimming trunks, sandals, and a faded T-shirt, with a towel thrown over his shoulder.

Jacob checked his watch. The time showed past noon, and Penelope had most likely driven over the bridge connecting Hilton Head Island to the mainland and was well on her way to Roses. A glance out the window promised blue skies and a clear afternoon.

"Where are you swimming?" Jacob placed the spoon on a spoon rest on top of the stove.

"Pelican Beach. It isn't far." Evan bobbed toward the window and pointed to a sandy beach beyond. "My mother said it was okay."

"I'll walk with you." Jacob covered the soup pan with a lid and turned off the stove.

"Did you bring a swimsuit, Dr. Williams?"

"No." Nor did he ever intend to swim again if he could help it, Jacob thought. He stepped to the closet and retrieved a beach towel, then two water bottles from the refrigerator. "I'll sit on the sand and watch you."

They hiked through a stretch of pine trees and a planked wooden path and soon arrived at Pelican Beach. High grass grew between silky, golden sand dunes. Waves crashed against the rocks. A field boasted yellow and pink wildflowers.

Evan paused to pick up fragments of seashells and flat stones, then shook off his sandals. Jacob followed suit, and they fell into step across the wet sand as they neared the ocean.

Jacob scanned the beach, deserted except for a young couple cuddling, and a child digging in the sand. A scattering of fishing boats anchored in the distance.

"No lifeguard?" he inquired.

"In November, not many people are at the beach," Evan replied. "Plus, this beach is hidden from the main boardwalk. Only the locals realize it isn't private and open to everyone. My mother can probably walk to every inlet blindfolded because Grandma and Grandpa lived here."

The ocean was an exceptional turquoise-blue, and the sun lit the water all a glitter. Jacob tasted the briny tang of salt and vegetation on his tongue.

Yes, this glorious island was a beaut, and his insides gave

a peculiar little lurch. Hilton Head was a second home for Penelope, and he envisioned her as a young girl, sunburned and giggling while creating castles in the sand or swimming in the ocean.

"Mom loves the beach," Evan said.

"I can see why." A cool breeze whipped across Jacob's face as he smoothed out his towel and sat. "The sea is a magical place."

"She is a champion swimmer. She swam often when we lived in Virginia."

"Not anymore?" Jacob peered upward as several seagulls circled overhead, then flew past.

"Not since we moved to Roses. In Virginia, my mother was fearless. I remember going camping with my parents and she dove into deep lakes without thinking twice." Evan set his towel on the sand beside Jacob and pulled off his T-shirt. "Now she worries all the time. Take today, for instance."

"You asked if you could swim, and she didn't argue."

"Yeah, but she always frets about the tide pulling me under the water. I remind her I'm careful and not afraid and it doesn't do any good."

Jacob feigned polite applause. "Well, I, for one, approve of your bravery."

"Can I tell you something else, Dr. Williams?"

"Certainly."

"My mom seems happier now that you two are dating. I think this Thanksgiving is the best weekend of her life. Mine too!" Evan chugged from his water bottle, set the bottle on his towel, then headed for the ocean.

"Don't go far." Jacob pulled his knees to his chest. The weather proved cooler than he'd anticipated, and he shivered, regretting not bringing a jacket.

Evan stood by the shore before taking tentative steps, then splashing in the surf. "The water is cold!" he shouted.

"I can only imagine," Jacob said. His thoughts curved to Penelope. He'd risked exposing his vulnerability, showing emotion regarding his difficult relationships with his mum and sister. The loss of his sweet niece. Penelope was kind and gracious and seemed to absorb his sadness and blame.

Were introductions between his mum and Penelope over the phone the right approach? He wanted her to meet his family, assuming they would grow to love her as much as he did. A phone chat was a start.

Whoa. Backpedal. *Love.* He'd vowed never to fall in love again. He enjoyed dating, but one heartbreaking devastation in his life was enough. When had love come into play?

His thoughts shied away from studying his feelings too intently. After his divorce, he had little confidence in his ability to judge his emotions.

You fell in love with Penelope the first day you met her on the plane, his conscience prompted. She was brave and captivating, ambitious, and loving.

Not far away, Evan waded farther into the water and then dove in. With a deliberate scissoring of his legs, he swam forward, then drifted and floated on his back.

The wind whipped up, and Jacob stood, tucking the beach towel over his shoulders. If the air was cold, the ocean in November must be bone-chilling.

"Aren't you freezing?" he shouted to Evan.

Evan turned, but apparently didn't hear Jacob. The boy paddled to a rocky shore in an inlet, found a sunny spot, and sat beneath a ledge.

"Smart kid," Jacob muttered, seeking a sunny location on the sand for himself. His cell phone buzzed, and he yanked it from his pocket, assuming Penelope might be calling.

Instead, the phone number from the clinic floated across his screen.

"Dr. Williams?" a woman inquired when he answered.

"Hello, Dr. Hannaway." He recognized the woman's voice.

"Our holiday heart patient is complaining of chest pain," she said.

"What's the patient's age?"

"The man is in his sixties."

The wind picked up and the percussive sounds of the waves hitting the shore grew louder.

"His heart rhythm hasn't stabilized?" Jacob pressed the phone closer to his ear, turned away from Evan, and focused on the sand to concentrate. He noted that the young couple and the child had disappeared.

"His heartbeat is more rapid."

Jacob gnawed his bottom lip and weighed the options. "Let's use a beta blocker to slow the heart rate."

"I agree. Thank you," Dr. Hannaway replied.

Jacob clicked off and twisted back to view Evan.

The boy waved, then climbed higher on the rocks. The kid was adventurous, and Jacob debated whether he should discourage him.

When Evan neared the top of the ledge, Jacob watched in mounting fear. "That's far enough. The peak is too high!" Panic rose in his throat. Surely the rocks were slick.

"I'm okay. I'm gonna jump. I've done this before." Evan slipped and righted himself, then swiveled toward the water and stretched out his arms.

Weighed down by dread, a knot twisted in Jacob's gut.

"Don't!"

Afterwards, Jacob couldn't remember if his shout had been loud enough to carry.

A split-second later, Evan dove in.

All was quiet.

Jacob stood stock still, frozen in horror. Surely Evan would quickly break the surface and tread water. Uneasiness poured along his spine.

Drowning. His niece. Not again.

Twice, he hadn't been there to save Linda. But he would save Evan.

He could swim. Not great, but enough.

He cast his gaze across the shore. Still no sign of Evan.

Fear spiked. Time sped up, though his movements seemed to slow down.

No. He refused to be paralyzed. He flung his towel to the sand and raced toward the ocean.

RELIEVED that the power to the toy shop had been restored, Penelope hummed the melody of "Angels We Have Heard on High." A tabernacle choir belted the carol from her truck's radio as she headed back toward Hilton Head. The manager had phoned, and everything was under control.

As she stepped into the houseboat, she was still humming the carol. "Surprise! I'm back!" she called out.

Hmm. Her smile turned to a frown of dismay when no male voices greeted her. A quick search indicated that Evan had headed to the beach and Jacob had accompanied him.

As she swapped her shoes for a pair of beach flats, her mood elevated again. A rush of happiness spread through her at her son's decision to swim. He seemed to be gaining confidence and self-assurance, and she attributed both to Jacob's excellent influence.

Jacob was responsible and caring, intent on building a careful and considerate rapport with Evan. He clearly enjoyed the boy's company, communicating and focusing on him.

She closed the distance on the short path to Pelican Beach, following sandy footprints. She paused and shaded her eyes. Head down, Jacob stood talking on his cell phone.

Her gaze riveted on Evan poised at the top of a rocky ledge.

A wave of icy, stark fear flowed through her, and her blood froze.

Her son was a good swimmer. But—

Without warning, Evan lost his balance on the rocks.

"Evan, be careful!" She trembled. Her pulse skittered.

He righted himself and stretched out his arms.

Unease spun up her spine. She broke into a run at the sight of him diving into the water and heard herself scream. A lead weight took up residence in her stomach.

From her peripheral vision, she noticed Jacob. He'd clicked off his cell phone and stood motionless for a split-second. His failure to act didn't escape her.

"Jacob!" She caught up with him and grabbed his arm as he lunged toward the water with her. "What are you waiting for?"

A roll of waves washed up to the shore, as Evan broke the water's surface.

Penelope reached him first. "Have you lost all your common sense?" Her speech was mumbled, echoing in her ears. Her mouth was dry.

Evan's wet swimming trunks were plastered to his legs. He was drenched.

"Don't have a fit, Mom. I didn't fall in if that's what you're upset about."

Despite the coolness in the air, she was sweating. "Think about how high the ledge is. What you did was nothing short of reckless." She glared at Jacob as she wrenched a towel from him. Her hands shook as she wrapped the towel around her shivering son.

The threesome returned to the houseboat without speaking, their footfalls heavy in the sand. Evan pleaded tiredness, grabbed a protein bar from the kitchen, and headed to his bedroom.

Jacob walked with her to the living room.

"Wanna talk about this?" He crossed his arms, his hip perched on the side of the sofa.

Still fuming, she snapped, "No!"

"Okay. I understand." He gazed at her, waiting several seconds. "Are you certain?"

"More than certain."

"Right. Sure." Soundlessly, he strode from the room.

She stood alone. After a few minutes, her breathing returned to normal, and she no longer gasped.

"Penelope?" Jacob's voice was elevated enough to carry from his bedroom before he reappeared in the living room.

"What?" In the charged silence, she jumped at her name being called.

"I'm leaving." His duffle bag was slung over his shoulder. He unlatched the door leading to the outside walkway.

She regarded him. "You're leaving." They both knew she wasn't asking. She was telling.

"My decision is for the best." He paused, opened the door wider, then turned to watch her.

Her heart thumped louder in her chest. She imagined he might seek forgiveness for his negligence and beg her to let him stay. But he didn't assume any wrongness for allowing her son to attempt such a dangerous stunt. He didn't speak or beg. He said nothing.

"I assumed you were here until Sunday," she finally spoke.

"No reason to extend my holiday."

"Because of what happened at the beach?" She flinched at the renewed remembrance, and the terrible dreamlike pang in her chest when she'd viewed Evan's wild dive into the sea.

Jacob shrugged. "That's part of it. But I'll never be able to get through to you."

"Evan could have drowned."

"He didn't drown. He's safe. He's an excellent swimmer and he chose to dive in. He's old enough to determine his strengths and skills."

She pushed out a breath. Jacob was a doctor, a pediatrician, and worked with children. But he didn't have any children of his own.

"You should've stopped him when he started climbing the ledge," she said.

"I wanted to allow Evan some freedom. He's a fearless kid. That's a good thing."

Goosebumps traveled up her arms at the thought of what could have happened. "Is it?"

"Yes." Jacob turned on his heel and swung toward the door.

"Fearlessness doesn't keep him from danger." She lashed out at Jacob's retreating back. "You're not a parent. You could never understand."

He twisted. His dark-brown eyes flared with emotion. "This conversation isn't only about Evan. It concerns you. You're sheltering him too much and he can't be wrapped in cotton forever. What are you afraid of?"

She cringed. Jacob's remarks hit home, but she refused to admit he was right. "You don't know my whole story."

"I know enough. I know about your divorce and your move back to Roses. I know you hate your job and—"

How could she explain her childhood and her domineering father? And her loneliness after Roy's infidelity? Or her sadness and impending dread at spending the Christmas holiday alone—without a loving partner to share each special moment? She'd sound pathetic and needy, a side of her she refused to expose. He knew enough about her already.

She supported herself by leaning against the wall. She attempted to compose her features, though she was crying.

"Hey, beautiful." He stepped toward her, his expression softening. "You're carrying too much on your shoulders. You're a single mother and work too hard."

He offered consolation, though she refused to accept. She didn't need his pity. She was a competent woman who had learned to rely on herself.

"When Evan was young, he was afraid of heights." A tear trickled down her cheek. "Ironic, isn't it?"

Jacob caught her rebellious tear with his forefinger. Gentleness filled his eyes. "He overcame his fear."

"He was overly cautious. I was mindful and tried to encourage him."

"You obviously did a good job."

She inhaled and stepped back, eyeing the open doorway. The sun was beginning to set, and its fiery golden glow lit the harbor. Several boat lights flashed. A seagull perched on one leg on the handrail of the roped walkway. The bird seemed undecided whether to dive into the water or fly away.

"Evan is all I have," she said quietly.

"You have me."

She let out a sob as the bird flew up into the sky. "Do I?"

His gaze never left her face. "I'm here, aren't I?"

She took in his handsome features, those soulful eyes, and his firm, chiseled mouth. He was the epitome of maleness, and all she'd dreamed about since they'd met.

But then another thought forced its way in. She couldn't endure any more heartbreak.

Jacob moved forward. She moved backward. The gap between them stretched a few feet, though figuratively the distance could be measured in miles.

"Evan is a smart, intuitive kid," Jacob said. "He recognizes even more about you than I do."

"Like what?"

"He realizes you've never gotten over your divorce and your ex's betrayal. Evan worries about you because you worry about him. And too much worry isn't good for a kid."

"What you're saying isn't logical."

"Think about it, Penelope. I'm perfectly logical." The edge in Jacob's tone caused her defenses to rise. "And there's something else that drives me bloody insane."

"What?"

"I get that your marriage ended unhappily, and you felt betrayed." He stiffened; his entire body strained in an unbending line. "But why won't you give us a chance?"

"You're spouting opinions as if you were a psychologist." Words caught in her throat. "You're a pediatrician, Jacob."

Oh, but he was right. He'd scored a bullseye. She didn't allow any man to get too close.

"Why are you so frightened of a second opportunity for happiness?" he asked.

Why? Maybe because she was afraid her intense love for him might consume her. If something happened … if he broke her heart, he'd break Evan's heart, too. And Evan was too vulnerable.

"I appreciate your concern, but I'm well, and so is Evan." Her tone raised and her eyes smarted with tears she refused to shed. "Safe travels, and please don't try to contact me."

He paused, unmoving, forcing her to stare into his fathomless eyes. This wasn't the moment to remember his tender kisses, the upcoming festive celebrations she'd anticipated sharing with him. A happy Christmas, brimming with gladness and miracles.

He fished in his duffle bag and pulled out a gift, meticulously wrapped in red and green foil paper, and handed the package to her.

"I planned to give you this tomorrow. I envisioned us sitting under the tree with mugs of soup. Well, I'm some kind of fool, aren't I?" The sharp tone of his voice was tempered, though his words were weighty and significant. "In any event, Penelope, Merry Christmas."

CHAPTER 12

$\mathcal{B}$ack in Roses on the Monday after Thanksgiving, Penelope found that she could hardly concentrate. Although Jacob texted often, her replies were short.

Can we talk? he asked.

Nothing to say, she replied.

I'm sorry about what happened at the beach. I panicked. No excuses. I shouldn't have hesitated.

Apology accepted.

Wanna take a trip to Stone Mountain in Georgia? he inquired the following day. *I'll ask Dr. Hannaway to fill in for me. You and Evan will love it. There are millions of dazzling holiday lights and spectacular shows.*

Sounds like you're reading a pamphlet about the place.

LOL. I am.

No, thank you.

Are you busy?

Always.

What about the Christmas town you mentioned that's about thirty minutes away from Roses?

I can't, she responded.

He reverted to: *Can we talk?*

Nothing to say, she repeated.

Have dinner with me. You choose the restaurant.

Her fingers hovered over the phone's keyboard. She wanted to accept his invitation.

But no, she couldn't.

Not possible, she typed. *Please. Leave me alone.*

When one week turned to two, then three, and the calendar dutifully inched closer to Christmas, she came to terms with a cold, hard fact.

After several days of similar texts, Jacob had stopped contacting her. Since then, she hadn't heard a word from him. She drew her arms close to her body and stared down at her empty hands. Good. He was finally doing what she asked.

Then why did her chest ache, and why did she need to gulp air at every turn?

She cried herself to sleep at night and awoke to red eyes and a splotchy face.

When she casually inquired about Jacob after Evan's volunteering sessions at the clinic, Evan ran a hand through his shaggy hair, then tilted his head to study the ceiling, as if to deter her from asking any more questions.

Shanice phoned and confided that Evan had told her that his mother had fallen in love with Jacob, and then she'd sent Jacob packing after a big argument.

"Mom pretends she isn't interested in Dr. Williams," Evan stated. "Though it's obvious, she cares about him a lot." He also added that their disagreement was all his fault.

"Oh, no." Penelope gasped and denied, while a cold weight settled on her chest. "Evan made a reckless choice, but the argument wasn't because of him."

Or was it?

"Evan hasn't told you the entire story," she continued.

"Do tell," Shanice said.

258

"I left my son in Jacob's care, and Jacob was negligent." Penelope's voice thickened. "However, Jacob did apologize. Several times, in fact."

"Then all is well."

Yet there was more to the story. Penelope's every thought was of Jacob, and, because of her decision to end their relationship, she was forced to shoulder her hurt alone. Perhaps she should have asked him to stay on the houseboat and talk things out as he'd requested. Perhaps she should have answered his texts differently.

He should have persisted.

However, he was too much of a gentleman. He'd listened to her and eventually heeded her instructions. She wondered how long it would take for a handsome, eligible doctor to find someone new—just in time to celebrate the holidays.

Tears trickled down her cheeks, and she furiously brushed them away.

With inner regret, she recognized that Jacob was everything a man should be. He was intelligent, he made her laugh, he was ambitious, and supportive of her business and hobbies. He was dependable, and equally important, an excellent role model for Evan.

Though now he was no longer in her life because she'd pushed him out.

Seasons had changed for her once again, and slowly, her spinning world began to slow down. When she looked around, she realized she was blessed.

Through renewed determination, she threw herself into wood carving, and finished a dozen delightful dolls for Christmas. The dolls were unique, endearing, and no two were the same. The craft kept her mind and hands occupied, and she was grateful for the distraction.

She donated the dolls to the homeless shelter, and Evan brought several to the clinic.

Her toy shop was frenetic with activity, and whenever Penelope lent a hand during a shift, she couldn't help but compare the atmosphere in the shop to a jubilant party. Children were excited. Parents were thrilled. Everyone was kinder at Christmas.

She was busy beyond words.

And she was heartbroken.

Occasionally, Evan mentioned Jacob. She tried to act nonchalant, though her insides cracked. She avoided driving by Jacob's office or the clinic, fearful of encountering him. She never saw him anywhere.

Several days before Christmas, she paused in her kitchen and opened the window, allowing a light winter breeze to freshen the room. December brought unusually warm temperatures to the Carolinas, and, according to the forecast, the prospect of snow grew less promising by the day. Instead, the weather proved mild and wet.

She stood by her granite countertop, sorting two dozen frozen Christmas cookies. True to her word, Meredith Sinclair's daughter had given an invitation to Evan, and Penelope was invited to a cookie exchange on Sunday.

She pondered how to gracefully decline. The toy stores were demanding, but on Sunday every shop was closed, a decision she and Lincoln had made years ago. They gave their employees a break from the workweek to rest and worship God as they chose.

Her mind returned to the cookie exchange. The prospect of conversing with all the other mothers from Evan's class was awkward. They were an elite clique, and she didn't have much in common with them.

Except for one important point. They all had kids the same age and were struggling with the onset of their children's difficult adolescences.

. . .

"LET'S GO CHRISTMAS SHOPPING!" Candee phoned Penelope on a gloomy morning a couple of days later. "I'm looking for another gift to put under the tree for my son, preferably something with horses, and it finally stopped raining. Come with me. No excuses allowed."

Penelope cupped her cell phone to her ear. "I'm working at home today and drowning in paperwork."

"Take a lunch break. I insist. I'll pick you up at noon."

Quickly, Penelope changed her sweat suit for tailored black slacks and a green embroidered *Merry Christmas* sweater. She topped the outfit with a woolen coat in a light tan. She cast a quick appraisal of herself in the mirror and pulled her hair back at the crown, allowing a spring of curls to cascade around her face.

At precisely noon, Candee arrived. Candee welcomed the holidays and dressed appropriately in white slacks and a heavy knit red sweater.

"Nothing compares to the thrill of seeing Roses decorated for Christmas," she announced, when Penelope slid into the passenger seat of her car. "The tree in the square is gorgeous at night when it's lit up."

"I read online that the town is encouraging white lights for all the shops, to keep an old-fashioned holiday look," Penelope replied.

"Read? Haven't you seen any of the displays?"

"Not yet." Penelope batted a hand through the air. Her chest tightened around the ever-present heaviness. "The holidays aren't the same for me anymore."

"Make this a magical Christmas. You're the one in control." Candee's tone was confident, though her gaze was anxious as she scanned Penelope's features. "You look pale. Retail therapy will cheer you up."

"My shopping is done. Evan has everything a boy his age needs. Besides, he hardly ever asks for anything."

Except a puppy.

A few minutes later, Candee parked her car, and the two women jostled through the crowds and headed down the main street arm in arm.

Penelope sniffed a temptingly decadent aroma of dark chocolate, along with roasting chestnuts from a sidewalk vendor. The streets hummed with excitement, and Christmas was in the air. Each shop hung wreaths on their front windows, embellished with red and white ticking stripe ribbons. Several vintage wooden sleds stood propped by the doors. The women paused to admire bundles of fragrant garland adorning a clothing boutique's green window boxes.

A smart, fancy French poodle trotted alongside its owner. The poodle's curly-black coat was groomed in the traditional poodle style.

"Dogs are precious." Candee stopped to compliment the dog, then curved to Penelope. "Are you still adopting a puppy from the shelter for Evan?"

"Definitely. The terrier mix had her puppies, and one will be a surprise Christmas gift for Evan." Penelope brightened. "I've checked on the puppies often, and they're all so lovable. Their fur is mostly white, and they have the cutest expressive eyes and ears. Four puppies are still available from the litter and the shelter told me that Evan can choose his favorite."

"When is he flying to Florida?"

"As soon as school lets out. He'll return home on the morning of Christmas Eve."

"His visit is short," Candee said.

"I'll drive him to the airport. He's flying direct, and this is the first time he'll be alone."

"He'll be fine."

Penelope regarded her friend with a level look. "You sound exactly like Jacob."

The women ducked into a candy store, weaved through a

knot of people, and selected slabs of milk chocolate fudge. They claimed two wooden rocking chairs on the store's wide front porch, and remarked on the shoppers as they passed.

Candee bit into a piece of fudge, leaned back in her chair, and closed her eyes. "Heavenly," she moaned. "Now, speaking of Jacob …"

Penelope's stomach lurched. In the weeks since she'd last seen him, she'd considered texting him. Then she wondered why he'd stopped texting her.

She longed to share the incident on Hilton Head Island with her friend. Yet, she was hesitant to burden Candee with her problems.

"When is the last time you saw Jacob?" Candee asked.

"Thanksgiving weekend."

Exactly three weeks, four days, and twenty hours ago, Penelope thought. Not that she was keeping track, of course.

"Jacob bought the dilapidated house on Brook Street that you looked at together. He was able to snag the house for a steal."

"He did?" Infuriated because he hadn't texted to inform her, Penelope sat straighter and placed the fudge on her lap. "When is the closing?"

"The beginning of January. The house needs a tremendous amount of elbow grease, but he is thrilled and intends to set up his physician's practice there."

Penelope's next reaction was an inward burst of pride. Hurray for Jacob for pursuing his dreams. Nonetheless, he hadn't reached out to tell her the exciting news. And she'd been the person who had first showed him the house.

"He asked about you." Candee's quiet voice checked Penelope's thoughts.

"Oh?" Penelope felt her forehead knit into a frown. "What did he say?"

"He said he missed you. Very much."

Penelope shot up from the chair. Her fudge fell from her lap. "Not enough to phone me, though."

"If my opinion will make it easier to admit your feelings for him ..."

Feelings? The fact that she couldn't stop thinking about him? The fact she often played out their argument in her mind, and wished things had turned out differently?

Penelope picked up the fudge, threw it in the trash, and sat back down. How did a woman recover from a broken heart?

You're a professional and selfless woman and absolutely amazing, he had said.

You are beautiful.

No more thinking about him, she scolded herself, yet the memory of his attentiveness, his tender kisses, his kindness, lay suspended in the air.

"Knock, knock, my friend. Come back." Candee reached over and tapped Penelope's shoulder. "That man genuinely cares about you, and I believe you care equally for him. His feelings for you are so intense, it would astonish him if he stopped to examine them. Whatever your differences, please give him a chance."

"He was wrong. He needs to reach out to me again."

"Forgiveness is a powerful gift, especially at Christmas. Accept this gift, for it promises peace. Isn't the holiday all about reconciliation and good will toward men?"

Piped in music from the candy store spilled onto the porch, lyrics of "Tidings of comfort and joy, comfort and joy, oh, tidings of comfort and joy."

"God Rest Ye Merry, Gentlemen." Penelope's beloved Christmas carol. She rocked on the chair as optimism bloomed. Perhaps there a chance for her and Jacob, after all.

Candee finished her fudge, and the women continued

perusing the shops. Candee spotted an oil painting of a horse for her son's room, while Penelope skirted into a local hardware store.

"Are you handy with tools?" she'd questioned Jacob after they viewed the dilapidated house.

"I don't even own a tool kit," he'd replied.

She didn't understand why she considered buying him a Christmas gift and couldn't imagine when she might give it to him. Nonetheless, she purchased a kit featuring pliers, a hammer, and a screwdriver. It was a start at reconciliation, although later she would wonder what madness had possessed her to buy such a thing, especially when she requested the merchant to wrap the gift in winter wonderland foil paper.

"Did you need some tools?" Candee inquired with a laugh when the women met outside their respective shops. Her gentle prodding made Penelope feel churlish for questioning her purchase. Jacob's smile warmed her heart, and his thoughtfulness toward the community knew no bounds. He was level-headed and tuned into her emotions. Plus, he respected the boundaries she'd set. She couldn't fault him for that.

On the houseboat, he'd looked breathlessly handsome in casual jeans, and his polo shirt had fit his broad shoulders to perfection. She well remembered the thrill of gazing into his dark eyes when they'd captured and held hers.

"I promise," he'd replied when she'd asked him to never turn into her ex, and tenderness had swelled in her heart at his earnest response.

He'd sealed his words with a deep, toe-curling kiss that had left her breathless.

She wasn't certain he loved her, but he did care for her. And after all, it was Christmas. She'd write out a card and congratulate him on his home purchase, then send the gift to the clinic with Evan. She smiled, imagining Jacob unwrapping the gift and then texting her.

She clutched his gift close and strolled the sidewalk with Candee. She flashed her friend a smile when she kept inquiring about Penelope's "secret" from the hardware store, because Penelope refused to divulge the details. Some things, she decided, required a privacy of the heart.

A jarring note of laughter echoed from the steps of a nearby shop. Meredith Sinclair stood with a group of women, her stunning blond hair and slim figure reminding Penelope of a runway model.

"Dr. Williams is coming over for dinner soon," she told the women. "I didn't want the poor man to be alone during the holidays. I'm making my famous baked ham with pineapple and all the trimmings."

"Did he accept?" one of the women asked.

"He said it all depends on his work schedule, but he seemed more than a little interested." With a twitch of her checkered pencil skirt, she reminded that she'd see them all at her cookie exchange on Sunday.

Jacob's social life is none of my business, Penelope thought. She rubbed her forehead and closed her eyes. He was free to date whomever he chose. Besides, she shouldn't have been eavesdropping, though Meredith had spoken loud enough for the entire town to hear.

Penelope had listened to the conversation with annoyed sadness, wondering if Jacob would accept the woman's invitation. In that instant, Penelope resented the town, and all the women's gazes who now seemed focused solely on her.

Her thoughts scrambled. Perhaps she should return to Hilton Head with Evan and live peacefully on the houseboat.

With a look of feigned naiveness, Meredith sidled over. "Penelope, I didn't see you at first. Are you free to attend my cookie exchange on Sunday?"

While Candee looked on, Penelope met Meredith's gaze with measured composure. She took a brief mental pause and focused on the positive things in her life. She'd created an uncluttered, relaxing atmosphere at home. She and Evan were eating healthier, and she was looking forward to spending Christmas Eve with Evan and his new puppy. She was better than jealousy or ill will.

She straightened her shoulders. "Evan is leaving for Florida soon, and we'll be attending to last-minute details," she replied. "I'll donate my cookies to the first responders in town. Thank you for the invite, and I wish you and your family a Merry Christmas."

CHAPTER 13

a couple of days later, Penelope found her son in his bedroom, a half-empty, open suitcase on his bed. His phone was propped beside him, tuned to a pop station playing a rock version of "Jingle Bells."

"You haven't finished packing for your trip yet?" she asked.

"Florida is hot, and I won't need much."

"We leave in an hour," Penelope reminded, handing Evan a box wrapped in pink and white paper. "Please give this gift to your father and stepmother for the new baby. I carved a wooden doll for Christina."

"That was nice, Mom. She can't play with it yet."

"Someday." Penelope leaned over and smoothed Evan's dark hair. He sat on the bed with his legs stretched out. Lately, he'd been swimming at the rec center, perfecting his butterfly stroke, and training with the swim coach. He and Zack hung out after school, and Evan looked calmer and happier. He was coming into his own and finding his way.

He scanned her features. "I'll miss you, Mom."

"I'll miss you, too." She regarded her fine-looking son,

and her heart burst with pride. She reached out and gave him a quick hug, envisioning his thrill at the surprise puppy waiting for him when he returned.

"Dr. Williams is working overtime at the clinic." Evan adjusted the volume on his cell phone and the music muted. "You should see his Santa Claus costume. It's too big, and he holds up the pants with a wide black belt. He couldn't find a white beard, but he wears a red velvet hat. Everyone thinks he looks funny. Dr. Hannaway is always serious, but even she laughed when she saw him."

Penelope nodded. "I bet."

"He liked the Christmas cookies you sent, especially the ones with the chocolate filling. He snuck a few while I gave them out to the kids and he said you're an excellent baker. He's working eighteen hours every day between his private practice and the clinic."

They sat in silence for a minute, listening to the next selection on his phone.

"Silent Night." A quiet, peaceful song. Simple.

I'm learning that simple is best, Jacob had mentioned.

"What are we doing on Christmas Eve?" Evan asked. "Uncle Lincoln and Aunt Shanice aren't here."

"I'll pick you up at the airport and in the afternoon, we'll attend church service."

"What will you do when I'm in Florida with Dad?"

"There is plenty of work at the toy shop to keep me busy. Don't worry."

Evan worries about you because you worry about him, Jacob had said. *And too much worry isn't good for a kid.*

She squeezed Evan's hand. "I love you, and you've made me infinitely proud. When your father and I divorced, I was stuck, but you're here, we're together, and I'm happy it's Christmas."

"Okay, Mom, okay." His smile was affectionate. "Can I tell you something?"

"Of course."

He darted a glance at her and took a deep breath. "Remember when Zack's mother got into an accident?"

Her heart stilled. "How could I forget?"

"I told you she backed into a mailbox near the rec center."

"Right."

"I have a confession." He pulled at the collar of his T-shirt and shifted on the bed. "I lied to you, and I'm sorry. After we stopped for milk shakes that day, I asked Zack's mother to drive us to the animal shelter to see the dogs. I didn't want to get you upset and tell you. I knew we were already late, but I couldn't resist."

"You're forgiven for lying." Penelope fought against the impulse to reprimand him. Lecturing wasn't helpful, and she understood his underlying reason. "I love dogs, too."

"So does Dr. Williams."

Her emotions swung back and forth between desire and despondency at the mention of Jacob's name.

"If you're geared to homeschool next semester, we can live on Hilton Head Island," she offered.

"Are you kidding? I'm trying out for the swim team, and we practice every day after school." Evan drew his legs up and rested his chin on his knees. "Someday, when I go to college, I'd like to study abroad. Maybe I'll win a scholarship. My coach said there are loads of opportunities if I practice real hard."

The idea of Evan leaving and going to another country brought tears to her eyes and a discreet sniff she hoped he didn't hear.

"Not forever," Evan assured. "I'll come back often. I promise. Especially for Christmas."

"All kids should travel abroad." Her voice broke as she

pulled him into another hug. "Your experiences there will frame the rest of your life."

"You're a cool mother," Evan said. "Now I need to finish packing."

AFTER PENELOPE DROPPED Evan off at the airport with a tearful goodbye, she hurried home. Obsessing over the details, she'd set up a puppy checklist and purchased water bowls, a crate, puppy food, a dog bed, toys, and a leash. She'd hid all the items in the garage.

Satisfied the house was prepped and ready for the precious, cute addition, the next few days passed quickly. Evan texted when he'd landed in Florida. He assured he was having a good time and that baby Christina was adorable, although she cried a lot.

Occasionally, when Penelope passed the decorated Christmas tree in the living room, she glanced under it. Several bundled packages topped with gold ribbon were from Lincoln and Shanice, plus an assortment of gifts from her ex that he'd sent ahead for Evan.

Jacob's tool kit sat wrapped in the winter wonderland paper, and she pondered when she'd ever give it to him. Alongside was the gift he'd given her, packaged in red and green paper. She hadn't opened his gift. Obviously, he hadn't opened hers.

The realization made her want to pour out her sorrow, the pang of longing so strong, she felt weak. She wrapped her arms around her stomach and hunched over, overcome with sadness. Jacob was so impressive, so kind, so remarkably good-looking. If he'd only text her again, she'd agree to see him.

No, no. She couldn't waste her emotions on a man who didn't care. She deserved more from him. And he deserved more from her. Regardless, they couldn't give each other what they both needed because pride stood in the way.

Lincoln phoned and requested she fly to Virginia to tidy up loose ends from the recent acquisition. Though reluctant, she asked pointed questions and eventually agreed. Dismissing her negative thoughts, she pushed up the sleeves of her wool blazer and flew the short, round trip to Virginia the following day.

As PLANNED, Penelope picked Evan up at the airport on Christmas Eve day.

They stopped home to change and unpack. Mindful they were picking up his puppy after the afternoon church service, she dressed in gray slacks and a silvery sweater adorned with snowflakes. Lately, her clothes fit better, and she attributed her success to healthier eating. She had also initiated an exercise routine, which included a thirty-minute daily walk.

A Scottish plaid scarf, red quilted vest, and high leather boots completed her ensemble. Tasteful, yet casual enough to handle a wriggling puppy.

She paused to study her reflection in the hallway mirror before they left for church. When she tucked an errant tendril behind her ear, her faux diamond stud earrings flashed back at her. She'd styled her hair in a loose bun, adorned with a pearl clip.

Evan wore tan-colored chinos, a polo shirt, and his black leather jacket.

The rain had cleared out, and the forecast had changed. There was a possibility of snow for Christmas Day, the weatherman declared, which was a huge event for the Southern residents of Roses.

After pausing to speak with the pastor and admire the

live nativity after church, she drove to the animal shelter as early evening neared. A star-spangled sky promised clear weather, at least for now.

She'd checked ahead to be certain the shelter was open, and the volunteer assured two puppies were available for adoption.

"Mom, this isn't the way to our house," Evan reminded.

Hardly able to contain her excitement, she parked in front of the shelter. The interior lights blazed, cordial and welcoming.

She swallowed a laugh. "Are you ready to take your new puppy home?"

His eyes rounded. He clutched the door handle, then swiveled to her, his face beaming with elation. "You mean it?"

"Absolutely." She embraced him, envisioning his joy at seeing the puppies. "Merry Christmas!"

He burst into tears. "Don't mind me, Mom." He wiped his wet cheeks with a chagrined smile. "I'm just so happy."

A car pulled up and parked behind them. She stole a glance in the rearview mirror, and her hand went to her throat. A very yellow, very recognizable Volkswagen.

"Yay, it's Santa Claus." Evan threw a fist pump, then flung open the door and dashed from the truck.

Penelope got out and leaned against her truck. Her heart raced.

A tall, broad-shouldered man, carrying a bouquet of roses, strode toward her. A whisper of moonlight lit his path.

And he wasn't Santa.

"Hi, Evan." Jacob pulled off his red velvet hat and shoved it in the pocket of his rumpled Santa suit. "Hello, Penelope."

"Jacob." Incredulous, Penelope hung back in surprise. She searched for her voice and couldn't find it. "Are you here for a puppy?"

"I'm here for you, Penelope." He laid the bouquet on the hood of the truck. "Merry Christmas."

Breathe, Penelope, breathe. The fragrant scent of a dozen red roses wafted in the night air. "You're not working at the clinic?"

"I've seen patients all day. Dr. Hannaway stepped in for me."

"Mom is getting me a puppy, Dr. Williams!" Evan's eyes sparkled.

She gave Evan a radiant smile and nodded toward the animal shelter. "The volunteer is waiting for you. There are two puppies left to be adopted."

Evan broke into a run and took the stairs to the shelter three at a time. With a decided wave, he hurried inside.

"I'll meet you in a minute," she called out to him.

Jacob's posture was still. He released a sigh and stared at her. "Penelope, you are amazing."

"I planned this ahead."

"You're a planner."

He resembled a man who had just stepped out of her favorite romance novel, a handsome hero, though he had a full day's growth of a dark beard. He looked thinner, yet perhaps she imagined it.

"Why are you here?" Her voice shook.

"You ignored me. I waited like you asked, but when I didn't hear from you, I resorted to Plan B."

A thought niggled, then broke free. He'd done the gentlemanly thing, abiding by her wishes. And then he hadn't.

Curious, she tilted her head up. "What is Plan B?"

"It's my twofold puppy plan. Evan and I volunteered at the shelter, and I got friendly with everyone." His deep voice strengthened. "Sure enough, they mentioned you planned to surprise Evan on Christmas Eve."

He stepped forward. Curtains stirred in the windows of

nearby residents. Twinkling white lights shone from inside. The smell of wood-burning fireplaces permeated the air.

She gestured toward the homes. "There's the disadvantage of small-town living. Everyone knows everybody else's business."

"The advantages are a close-knit community and slower pace." Jacob's lips curved into a smile. "Oh, let's see, and a quaint, idyllic community, and a beautiful woman. A woman I'd really like to date again."

Tears swelled in her eyes. "You're working nonstop."

"I'm changing my schedule. Along with several other aspects of my life."

"You bought the house we looked at. Candee told me."

He chuckled. "A cheap house will allow me to work less, plus I'll be able to have an office there and see patients. The home is a start, but I need more."

"What do you need?"

"You." He caught a stray tear that trickled down her cheek. "Even though you broke my heart."

She inhaled, drawing a sharp breath. "I did? I didn't realize—"

"That I loved you? Well, I do. And I apologize for what happened at Pelican Beach. If you give me a second chance to prove myself …" He quirked an eyebrow and smiled. "After all, it is Christmas."

"Jacob, please don't apologize. You did nothing wrong. You care. That's not a fault."

The chemistry between them crackled. There was magic in the air. The magic that came with Christmas. The magic that came with love.

Her anger at him had been foolish and juvenile. She'd lashed out at him, though Roy had been the source of her hurt and insecurities.

"My mum and sister are moving back to Melbourne," Jacob said. "I told them I'd visit."

"Good."

"Will you join me? With Evan?" His words rushed together. "You can talk to me nonstop on the plane. I realize flying is involved unless—"

"Jacob, I … I need a second … I wanted to tell you I flew to Virginia recently." She dragged air into her lungs. "I was afraid at first, but then I realized there was something else I was even more afraid of than flying."

He gathered her in his arms and drew her close. Nearer, tighter. "What?"

She pressed a hand to his heart. "I was afraid I had lost you because I pushed you away. I love you, too."

"You'll never lose me. Roses is where I intend to stay." He traced her lips with his fingers. "Will you give me another chance?"

"I have a son."

"An amazing son. As amazing as his mother."

She ran her fingers along his strong cheekbones. She loved his good-looking features, his nearness, his solid hold. She turned her face into his chest and listened to the steady thud of his heart.

He lifted her chin and cupped her face in his hands. He kissed her, slowly at first, warm and emotional, then more intensely as his mouth captured hers. "I love you, Penelope. You're special, and when I lost you from my life, I knew I needed to find a way to bring us together."

She grinned. "Plan B?"

"The twofold puppy plan."

"Wait." Her grin widened. "What do you mean by twofold?"

A shout from the shelter's entrance startled her, and she pulled back from Jacob's embrace.

"Mom, are you coming inside?" Evan cuddled two fluffy, cream-colored puppies in his arms. "I chose my puppies!"

She shuffled back a step. "Puppies? As in, more than one?"

"They're brother and sister. They can't be separated because I named them." Evan's face was flushed and radiant. "Come and meet Kris and Kringle. Kris is the boy and Kringle is the girl. You'll fall in love. I promise."

"We're already in love," Jacob whispered. He twined his fingers around hers and led her toward the entrance.

"All this love at Christmas." She smiled and affectionately nudged him. She was at ease with her world.

"Doctor Williams, your dog is waiting for you," Evan declared as they approached.

Penelope touched her throat. Her breath stalled. "Jacob, you're adopting a dog, too?"

"Truth?" He grinned and kissed her temple.

"Uh-huh."

"I'm adopting Nutcracker." His dark eyes lit with an inner glow. "What better way to celebrate Christmas than with two puppies, a mother dog, a stepson, and a beautiful wife?"

"Stepson? And wife?"

"A fantastic stepson and a *beautiful* wife. Penelope Reid, will you marry me?"

She answered without hesitation. Her smile filled with love as she rested her trembling hand on his cheek. "My answer is yes. Yes, yes."

EPILOGUE

 *ne Year Later*

"WHO EATS quinoa and red peppers during the holidays?" Evan asked.

"We do." Penelope held up her *Change Your Holiday Menu, Change Your Life* cookbook. "Don't you want to continue to eat healthy?"

"This year I vote for cream cheese cookies." Evan looked to Jacob for backup.

Jacob chuckled and raised his hand. "I second the cookie vote."

His wife stood at the stainless-steel sink. The sink at his new house on Brook Street, Jacob thought with a satisfied smile.

Penelope drummed her fingers on the counter and grinned at them both. "Don't either of you like quinoa?"

"I tried it last year," Jacob replied.

"And?"

"I agree with my stepson. Cookies are better." Jacob strode to her and wrapped his arms around her waist. Strains of "It's Beginning to Look a Lot Like Christmas" wafted from the living room stereo.

She gazed at him over her shoulder. "I'm not baking any more cookies, because we're flying to Australia in a few days."

He pressed a kiss on her fragrant hair. Today, she held it back with a silver spangled clip.

"Fortunately, you froze two bags of your chocolate cream cheese cookies in November," he said. "They're my favorite."

She pulled from his embrace, stepped to the refrigerator, and rummaged in the freezer. "Then why is there only one bag of cookies left?"

Jacob and Evan pointed at each other, winked conspiratorially, then burst out laughing. "Recently, we had a late-night cookie festival," Jacob confessed.

She laughed, revealing her adorable dimples. She was gorgeous when she laughed. Her eyes were soft and shiny.

"I'm outnumbered by animals in this house." She gazed at the two sleeping dogs in the corner: Kris and Kringle. They weren't considered puppies anymore, though Kris still had puppy energy, and Kringle continued to chew on everything in sight. True to their breed, the dogs were willful, independent, and more than a little stubborn. However, they'd settled into the routine of life at the Williams' new home.

"What do Australians eat at Christmas, Dad?" Evan swiped three cookies from the freezer bag and placed them in the microwave to thaw.

Dad. Jacob took the word to heart. His stepson's acceptance and love meant the world.

"We usually begin with prawns at lunchtime. Lots and lots of prawns and they are massive. My sister is making lasagna, so at least we'll get our lasagna." Jacob gave a thumbs-up to Evan. "And my mum is serving a cold roasted chicken."

"Why cold?"

"It's too hot in Australia in December to cook a lot. Fortunately, my mum and sister bought a home with a pool, and you'll still be able to keep up with your swim practice."

Penelope caught Jacob's gaze and smiled. "Melbourne. Your hometown."

"Yea. I'm looking forward to showing you and Evan the sights." His chest expanded with each breath. "I remember restaurants by the Yarra River, and my mum is excited about the performing arts complex."

His mum had sold the farm at a profit, and she insisted that he no longer needed to send her money. Along with the savings on the inexpensive home purchase, he'd curtailed his hours at the clinic and hired another doctor. Seeing patients at his home office enabled him to spend more time with Penelope and Evan, the two loves of his life.

Spurred by Penelope's encouragement, Jacob had phoned and spoken with his mum and sister for hours. They'd shared stories about his niece, Linda, and grieved, while continuing to cope with the devastating loss. They sought comfort in their memories and had resolved to stick together.

"Australia is far away." Evan glanced at his two dogs. No longer puppies, Kris and Kringle resembled their mother, with white coats and almond-shaped eyes. Their paws turned out, and the distinctive pink markings they once had on their nose and paws had changed to black. "I'll miss them."

"Uncle Lincoln and Aunt Shanice will take excellent care of our animals," Penelope assured him.

"Nutcracker, Kris, Kringle, and Giblet." Evan grabbed the cookies from the microwave, shouldered his swim bag, and started for the door. "Gotta go. Practice begins in an hour and Zack's mother is picking me up."

"Have fun," Jacob and Penelope chimed.

Once Evan left, Jacob grabbed Penelope's hand and led her to the living room. Nutcracker, never far behind Jacob, took up her favorite spot by the fireplace.

They'd positioned Penelope's faux fir tree by the front window, and decorated it for Christmas in a tasteful, subdued flair. His tool kit sat under the tree. A thoughtful gift. Last year, they'd chuckled with the realization that it would take more than a tool kit to renovate a fixer upper on Jacob's limited budget. Together as a family, they'd painted floorboards, discarded the ancient front door for a new red one, and hung curtains. They'd left carpet, bathrooms, and kitchen appliance installation and remodeling to the professionals.

But renovate they had. Room by room, until the Victorian shone shiny and preserved. Jacob adored the home's character, the quirky light fixtures, and the unique woodwork and intricate moldings.

Penelope elected to place his Christmas gift to her from last year, the photo he'd taken of her when they'd first met at the airport, on the coffee table.

He smiled as he regarded the photo. His beautiful wife, wearing a cream-colored crepe blouse and brown slacks. Her dark hair, shaped in a short bob style, had grown longer this past year. Silver highlights still framed her lovely face.

The photo was placed in a glass frame alongside a stack of romance books. A row of carved wooden dolls, all named for various spices, were ready to be transported to the nearest hospital or shelter for children of all ages to enjoy.

After Penelope and Jacob had wed six months earlier, and his house was finally livable, she and Evan had moved in. Candee had secured a buyer for Penelope's house the first day she'd put it on the market. Success all around.

"I'm glad you decided to cut back your hours at the toy shop," he said, pulling her beside him on the sofa.

"Me too, yet the decision was difficult." She offered a tremulous smile that touched his heart. "I love my craft. Woodworking is infinitely rewarding."

"You're amazing and talented, beautiful." He brought her fingers to his lips for a kiss. "Do you know how much I love you?" His heart filled with more emotion than he thought it could hold—happiness, appreciation, and love.

"I hope looking after all our animals isn't asking too much from Lincoln and Shanice," she said. "They were out of town last Christmas—"

"And we'll be out of town this Christmas," Jacob finished.

She gazed up at him. "Are you certain the only flight you were able to book leaves on Christmas Day?"

"Yea. The trip takes about twenty hours, with two stopovers."

She shuddered and threw him an accusing stare. "Crikey."

He laughed. "Just sleep, eat, watch movies, and, most importantly, talk."

"Okay." She sighed and snuggled nearer him.

He gazed around his home. A beaut. His dream for a simple, rewarding life had come true. What a wonderful road he and Penelope had traveled. Eighteen months ago, he'd never have imagined a Christmas like this.

Though here he was, in this Americana town he called home, with a woman he loved more than anything in the world. When he'd surprised her at the animal shelter on Christmas Eve almost a year ago and declared his love, she'd cast aside her pride because she loved him, too. And that remembrance would remain in his heart forever.

He'd changed his lifestyle to accommodate his beliefs and found love in the bargain. Finally, he was at ease with his world.

"Jacob?" Penelope asked.

He gazed into her compelling eyes and outlined the curve of her jaw and cheeks. "Hmm?"

"How will we celebrate Christmas if we're not in Roses, or even in Australia yet?"

"Simple." He drew her close and kissed her. "We'll celebrate Christmas in the air."

THE END

RECIPE FOR TERESA'S CREAM CHEESE CHRISTMAS COOKIES

Ingredients:
   1 3 oz. package of cream cheese
   2 sticks of butter (softened)
   1 cup flour
   Shape into 24 one-inch balls and press into small muffin tins, and then add filling.

There are 3 different fillings:
   Filling One:
   1 egg
   1 tablespoon soft butter
   ¾ cup brown sugar

1 tsp. vanilla
Chopped mixed nuts

Filling Two:
6 oz. cream cheese
½ cup sugar
1 egg with a teaspoon of lemon juice

Filling Three: (chocolate)
6 oz. chocolate chips, melted
Add:
¼ cup sugar
1 tablespoon milk
1 beaten egg
1 teaspoon vanilla
1 tablespoon butter

Mix and half fill each cup with filling of your choice.
Bake at 350 degrees for fifteen minutes.
Enjoy!

A NOTE FROM JOSIE

Dear Reader,

Thank you for reading my sweet holiday romance, *Christmas in the Air.* I hope you enjoyed this heartwarming story, featuring Penelope Reid, the heroine, and Jacob Williams, the hero.

Christmas in the Air is the sixth book in my contemporary 1-800-series.

What if you told your innermost secrets to a guy you assumed you'd never see again?

This story is set in the charming fictional small town of Roses, North Carolina. Here, I introduce a new character and hero, Dr. Jacob Williams, to our beloved mix of familiar heroes and heroines. Penelope Reid was featured in 1-800-NEW YEAR, book 5 of the 1-800 series. She is a fun character who has relocated to Roses with her son, Evan, who is a soon-to-be adolescent.

Jacob is from Australia, and he and Penelope first meet on

an airplane bound for Hilton Head Island.

If you loved this story as much as I loved writing it, please help other people find it by posting your review.

Christmas in the Air is available in ebook, Paperback, Large Print Paperback, Audiobook, and Hardcover.

I'd love to meet you in person someday, but in the meantime, all I can offer is a sincere and grateful thank you. Without your support, my books would not be possible.

As I write my next sweet or inspirational romance, remember this: Have you ever tried something you were afraid to try because it mattered so much to you? I did, when I started writing. Take the chance, and just do something you love.

With sincere appreciation,

Josie Riviera

Love music?

My Spotify Playlist for Christmas in the Air is here.

Love the 1-800-series? Be sure to grab all the books in the series here.

I HOPE THESE SWEET
HOLIDAY ROMANCES
WARMED YOUR HEART.

Cocoa's Christmas Love

PUPPIES FOR CHRISTMAS

USA TODAY BESTSELLING AUTHOR

JOSIE RIVIERA

ACKNOWLEDGMENTS

An appreciative thank you to my patient husband, Dave, and our three wonderful children.

CHAPTER 1

*N*estled below the snow-capped peaks of the Blue Ridge Mountains, the tiny town of Evergreen Valley sparkled like a gem. With a population of only ten thousand residents, the tight-knit community and frost-kissed streets came alive during the Christmas season.

Inside the cozy confines of her florist shop, Ivy's Blooms, Ivy Bennett inspected the pale lavender flowers spread before her. Delicate and intricate, each resembled a hybrid between a rose and a lily. Some tiny buds peeked open, others sat fully flourished and fragrant. She intended to fashion several bouquets for the front window.

She twisted her long blond hair into a loose bun, wispy tendrils escaping to trail down her back. The simple style kept her hair out of her face.

Today, as usual, her wardrobe of choice was a taupe-colored blouse and khaki pants, perfect for the dirt and occasional spills she encountered during her workday. To protect her feet, she wore sturdy, low-heeled leather boots, ensuring she could comfortably stand, walk, and tend to her shop without any discomfort.

She breathed in the mingling scents of dreamy florals, cinnamon potpourri, and pine garland adorning her shop's walls. With practiced, callused hands that bore the evidence of a hard-working florist, she trimmed stems, arranged holly branches, and spun together evergreen wreaths dusted with Queen Anne's lace.

She noted the marks on her fingers by the occasional pricks and thorns from the blooms she carefully tended. With a soft smile, she felt a sense of pride in these small scars, symbols of the dedication she poured into her craft.

Here, she was completely at home, surrounded by her flowers and exquisite décor.

The bell over the door jingled as her friend Sophia hurried in, unwinding a cherry red scarf from around her neck. Her short dark hair was topped with a knit Santa hat, and her deep brown eyes brimmed with lively merriment.

"Ivy, I wanted to confirm the flower arrangements you're donating for the firehouse toy drive auction," she said. "Can you believe it's already the first of December?"

"Hardly." Ivy laughed. "I'm contributing four larger pieces —two Christmas themes and two winter mixes."

"Wonderful, thank you!" Sophia turned to exit, then paused. "What a shame that Eleanor's Toy Emporium closed its doors. We could've used Eleanor's antique toys in the auction. People always snapped them up."

"Eleanor moved to the coast," Ivy replied.

"And now there's a vacant storefront next to your shop."

Ivy nodded. Countless times, she'd thought about expanding her flower shop into that very space. However, the harsh reality held her back. She simply didn't have the funds to tackle such an endeavor.

"Well, I'm off." Sophia was forever in a rush, organizing various benefits. "Our goal at the auction is to raise five thousand dollars this year."

Ivy smiled, picturing parents picking out gifts with funds from the auction. Helping those in need—that's what the holidays were all about.

The shop filled with the jazzy notes of the classic winter song "Let It Snow! Let It Snow! Let It Snow!" playing from a vintage radio perched between two white lilies on a shelf.

Ivy swayed her hips and bobbed her head, getting into the zippy tempo. Even after the hundredth time, she couldn't resist smiling and sang along. "'Let it snow, let it snow.'"

From a far corner, her best friend and coworker, Amelia Green, snatched a broom. When the chorus began, Amelia swayed with her makeshift partner, swinging her trusty broom around the store while belting out the lyrics.

Ivy laughed until she was breathless. Amelia never failed to rouse her into giggles.

As soon as the song ended, Amelia set the broom to the side, and Ivy returned to placing finishing touches on the Wishing Blooms.

"Good afternoon, Mrs. Thompson!" Ivy pitched her voice to be heard as the elegant, older woman entered the shop. "How may I help you today?"

"I need a centerpiece for my daughter's engagement party, dear. She's coming in town for a few short days. And please call me by Harriet, my first name. No need for such formality." Deep crevices framed the woman's mouth, crow's feet fanned out from the corners of her soft gray eyes, and her red-rouged cheeks rounded up toward her silver hair.

Ivy smiled. "I'll try."

"Since my husband passed away five years ago, it's been difficult for me to truly enjoy life again." Mrs. Thompson stared down at the crumpled tissue in her hand, shredding the edges absently. "For the first time in a long time, I'm a little happier. My daughter is marrying a charming man."

"It must be hard living alone after sharing your life with

someone for so long. I can't even imagine how tough that must be," Ivy replied. "How can I make a bouquet to represent new beginnings and resilience?"

"I trust your judgment, dear."

Ivy's mind raced with ideas, her passion for creating delight and enchantment fueling her thoughts. "How about white roses mixed with baby's breath and eucalyptus?"

"Sounds lovely," Mrs. Thompson replied.

As Ivy busied herself with the floral arrangement, she reflected on the joy her flowers brought her—and, more importantly, the happiness they brought to others. She carefully selected each petal and stem, not only for their vibrancy and form but also to reflect the personality and preferences of her clients. Her talent came naturally, and she had nurtured and honed her ability over the years. As she worked, her mind turned to ways to help Mrs. Thompson beyond this small gesture and decided to schedule weekly fresh flower deliveries to her home to brighten her day.

Ivy glanced up. "Do you have any other shades in mind?"

"Maybe a few dashes of blush pink and gold." Mrs. Thompson adjusted the collar of her wool coat, a rich, canary yellow. "They're my favorite colors."

Ivy nodded. The artistry of her creations allowed her to connect with others in a way words sometimes couldn't. This was her gift—her ability to translate emotions and memories into arrangements that spoke volumes without uttering a single word.

Especially her Wishing Blooms. The petals' exceptional translucent quality enabled light to pass through and created an ethereal, otherworldly effect.

To many people in the town, the Wishing Blooms embodied the essence of the holiday season.

"Here we are." Ivy presented the completed project a few minutes later. The roses, baby's breath, and eucalyptus intertwined, were accented by subtle hints of blush pink snowflakes and gold ribbon. "I hope this makes your celebration extra special."

"Thank you." Mrs. Thompson eyed the flowers on the worktable. "Are you getting ready for your annual flower-wishing ceremony?"

"Absolutely. Tomorrow morning at ten o'clock."

"I wouldn't miss it. I plan to pick a flower and make a wish." As Mrs. Thompson exited the shop, Ivy turned back to her worktable. She finished the Wishing Blooms arrangements, then began a standing poinsettia order for another customer, Ethan Harrison.

She caught a glimpse of herself in the reflection of a polished glass vase. Her hazel eyes sparkled with a mix of passion and dedication, and her cheeks carried a healthy glow.

"Have you seen the latest issue of *The Evergreen Gazette* yet?" Amelia hollered from across the shop, letting Ivy know she was stepping into the storage room to grab more florist wire and picks. "Ivy's Blooms is on the cover!"

"The article is out so soon? I assumed we were slated for the January issue." Ivy reached behind the counter for a copy that a member of the *Gazette's* distribution team had delivered. She had gotten busy and set it to the side.

She paused, studying the front cover.

Indeed, there it was, a stunning photograph of her precious shop. Rays of sunshine streamed through the windows on either side of the cheery blue door, and her storefront was scenically framed by lightly falling snow. The shot captured the source of her happiness right there on the cover of the town's most popular monthly magazine.

Her gaze danced over the glossy pages, and she traced a finger over the elegant script describing her little shop.

She smiled broadly. This was even better than she imagined. Her creations, her passion, in print for all to see!

She flipped the pages, eager for more.

Mid-turn, her hands froze. Her smile vanished.

Any glowing satisfaction evaporated when her gaze landed on the bold, ominous headline splashed across the top of the page.

"Myth or Reality? Challenging the Enchantment of Ivy's Wishing Flowers."

She scanned the article's contents, and her breath grew short as she read the damaging words. How could this journalist make such cruel accusations? She had worked so hard to build trust with her customers, and this felt like a personal attack on her character.

The journalist, Britney Knox, had pivoted to a critical stance, an exposé that left readers questioning the authenticity of Ivy's renowned Wishing Blooms. The article claimed to demystify the enchanting claims surrounding the flower shop. Not to be outdone, the writer went on to highlight alleged incidents of subpar quality and late deliveries. The words didn't just paint a picture of the shop in a disparaging light, they tarnished Ivy's reputation with searing accusations of dissatisfaction, fraud, and deceit.

Five years of earning her patrons' trust and cultivating a spotless name had all been smeared in one cutting article by a journalist's hand.

Ivy's eyes glazed with tears.

Her Wishing Blooms had become a symbol of hope and good will. Each carried a whispered wish, a heartfelt aspiration, and a belief in the magic of the holidays.

Regarding the alleged incidents of subpar quality, Ivy reached back into her thoughts.

During seasonal peaks, she faced a higher number of orders than usual, leading to difficulties in managing all the requests promptly. Sometimes, limited availability of fresh flowers was due to seasonality or supply chain issues. And last year's severe winter weather had disrupted transportation and caused delays.

She'd apologized and acknowledged her customers' concerns, offering replacements and refunds. As a goodwill gesture, she'd compensated with small gifts and discounts on future purchases as a token of appreciation.

Her fingers shook as she set down the magazine. She leaned forward, head in her hands, and sighed heavily.

Britney Knox. The journalist had moved to town the previous year and been known to stir up drama to sell more magazines.

Shifting her focus back towards the poinsettias, Ivy tried to lose herself in shaping scarlet poinsettias and evergreen accents for Ethan's order.

But concentration eluded her. She found herself repeatedly fixating on the open magazine and offensive article. Visions of shelves overflowing with unsold products and silent phones during the frenzied Christmas rush flashed through her mind.

She clipped the stems, leaves scattering across the table. She began assembling the bouquet, more as a distraction than anything else. Her work seemed pointless while her reputation was under attack. She struggled even with a simple poinsettia arrangement, her focus divided between the flowers and the harsh article.

Had any customers seen the write-up yet? The *Gazette* reached every single household and business in the entire town, resulting in the distribution of over four thousand copies.

Her stomach lurched imagining loyal regulars reading the critique, frowning distrustfully at Ivy's friendly hellos, then turning and walking out, never patronizing her shop again.

She knew the importance of a solid standing in a tight-knit town like Evergreen Valley. The negative publicity could have a significant impact on her business, potentially driving away devoted shoppers and deterring new ones.

Returning from the storage room, Amelia approached, her reddish-brown eyebrows knitted together. "What's the matter, Ivy? Something seems very wrong."

Lost in thought, Ivy failed to respond.

Amelia rested a comforting hand on her arm. She waited patiently until Ivy redirected her attention to her friend.

"This is what's the matter." Ivy handed over the magazine, a frustrated rush of air escaping her lungs.

Amelia skimmed the contents and pressed her lips together. "Why would anyone write such a thing around the holidays? I thought this was the season of giving."

"I assumed I had rectified every one of those problems that Britney Knox listed." Ivy steadied herself. "I'll just make it a point to speak with her. She came into the shop a while ago but didn't stay long."

"Yes, I remember when you mentioned it," Amelia replied.

When Britney had stopped by the shop, Ivy recalled thinking she looked a bit out of place in their casual little town. She was tall and slim, dressed in an expensive-looking black pantsuit and wearing bright red lipstick—more high fashion than Evergreen Valley's laidback style. Her sleek ebony-black hair was pulled back in a severe bun.

When she smiled, it didn't reach her pale blue eyes, which stared at Ivy coolly. Ivy got the impression that Britney was meticulously studying her, looking for any misstep or moment of weakness. In their brief conversation, Britney spoke eloquently but with a subtle sharpness, like each word was carefully chosen to extract information. She seemed to be fishing for something specific, and oddly interested in Ivy's most popular flowers and products. Ivy sensed that this was a woman used to getting what she wanted.

"Ignore it. Ignore her," Amelia was saying. "Don't let that cynical newcomer upset you. Negative publicity is still publicity."

Ivy tried her best to understand her friend's optimism. However, despite her desire to brush it off, the accusations pierced her heart like daggers.

Tears blurred her eyes again. She quickly blinked, not wanting Amelia to see how much this affected her.

"You're right." Ivy forced a smile. "I shouldn't let this bother me." But on the inside, doubts continued to fester. Was this only harmless gossip? Or could these lies destroy all she and Amelia had worked for?

As Amelia prattled on about ignoring the article, Ivy's thoughts spiraled. She pictured walking into the shop tomorrow and facing accusatory glares from faithful customers. She imagined sales dwindling to nothing as the town turned against her. Her breath grew short, anxiety tightening its grip.

Amelia's pep talk only emphasized Ivy's powerlessness in this situation. She wanted to curl up and hide from the controversy because she was breaking inside.

Instead, Ivy turned back into Amelia's chirpy banter. "This will all blow over soon," she said, hoping she sounded more confident than she felt.

"Didn't the editor check these negative points before the *Gazette* went to print?" Amelia studied the last page. "Everett Shepherd is the name credited to the photos."

"I was so focused on the byline that identified the writer, I didn't think about anything else." Ivy examined the article again and noticed Everett's photo credit in the small text. "I remember looking up one day last month to see him standing there with his camera. He said *The Evergreen Gazette* had asked him to take some photos. I tidied up the shop and assembled several Wishing Blooms arrangements. He was professional, but very kind. He commented that I had a lovely little business here, and he hoped his photos did it justice."

Amelia grabbed the magazine, crinkled it up, and set it on the table. "He's a nice guy, but apparently he didn't have much say in the article."

"Apparently not."

"He owned a hardware store in town before he retired. Did you ever go there as a kid?"

Ivy frowned, trying to recall the store. "No. I don't have any memory of it."

"The store was on Riverstone Road for ages," Amelia said, sweeping her arm in one direction to indicate the street. "He ended up selling the lot a few years ago."

"We chatted for a bit, but mostly casual conversation."

"He freelances as a photographer. His grandson, Blake Shepherd, is famous. I think he works mostly out west, photographing those elaborate red-carpet affairs and high-end galas."

"Everett and I spoke about the town's upcoming Christmas activities," Ivy replied. "He never mentioned his grandson."

"I'm sure you dazzled him with that gorgeous smile of yours," Amelia teased, poking Ivy playfully with her elbow.

"He didn't take any photos of me, just the shop." Ivy's fingers lightly brushed the scarlet petals of the poinsettia. "What if our customers accept the article's claims as true?"

"They won't. I get why you're worried, but every single person in this town knows you." Amelia gave an encouraging shrug. "If you're still upset, communicate with the editor or Britney directly and put your side of the story out there. The regulars will stand by you."

"I appreciate what you're saying." Ivy searched beneath the magazine's masthead and jotted down Britney's phone number and email address.

With renewed conviction, she met Amelia's eyes. Then she scanned her shop, noting the overflowing baskets of peppery red carnations, emerald, green coils of ribbon and tissue paper, and shelves brimming with glass vases and ceramic pots painted with sprigs of holly.

Ivy's love for flowers budded in childhood when she tended her mother's rose garden. She became fascinated with floral arrangements while accompanying her mom to a local florist. In high school, she got a job at the flower shop, honing her natural talents over the years. She'd cultivated her interest by completing a two-year floristry degree.

Owning a floral business had always been her dream. Now in her mid-thirties, her lifelong passion had blossomed into her own thriving shop. Though the work was demanding, seeing the flowers she had nurtured and arranged with care reminded Ivy that this successful shop was the fulfillment of all her hopes. She was exactly where she was meant to be.

She paused, realizing Amelia's gaze was fixed on her.

She loved that Amelia was in her corner. Though right now, she needed time to process this betrayal and figure out her next steps. Plastering on a smile, Ivy started tidying up the shop, signaling the conversation was over.

As Amelia headed to the backroom, Ivy whispered under her breath, "I won't let this destroy everything I've built." She had to fight for herself and her business—no one else was going to do it for her.

As the afternoon progressed and more customers streamed in, Ivy pushed her negative thoughts aside. Evergreen Valley, already a picturesque location, transformed into a veritable wonderland of snow and ice each December.

When dusk fell, strings of lights illuminated every street corner. Gleaming tinsel and icy-blue ribbons embellished the lampposts, and no one could deny the air of celebration.

"Are you planning to attend the Christmas craft fair?" Ivy posed the question to a young couple as they selected a deep burgundy dahlia.

"Wouldn't miss it!" A flicker of excitement lightened the young woman's green eyes. "This is our first Christmas here, and everyone's been telling us about it."

"You're in for a treat." Ivy trimmed the dahlia stem and chose a gift sleeve in ecru to offset the burgundy shade. "The fair is held outdoors and in the high school gymnasium, and vendors sell homemade crafts and food. I'm a sucker for the maple fudge and cranberry orange bread."

The young man picked up a rosemary topiary shaped into a mini tree and inspected it. "We also heard a charity event is happening soon. Do you know anything about it?"

Ivy glanced at a calendar behind the check-out counter, mentally noting the date. "The fire department hosts a yearly toy drive to supply gifts for underprivileged children. The entire community comes together, and there's a real sense of camaraderie."

She proceeded to provide the couple with all the relevant information.

"We'd love to contribute." The woman reached for a flyer on the counter. "We want to do our part to support such a wonderful cause."

"Lovely. Thank you." Ivy positioned the trimmed dahlia stem in the center of the sleeve, allowing the large flower head to remain uncovered and prominent. Then she tied a raffia bow around the sleeve and handed it to the woman. "In fact, my store is donating a portion of our profits, so your purchase today is already making a difference."

As the couple departed, Ivy paused to stare out the shop

window that she'd decorated with multi-colored lights and strings of garland. Amelia had declared it a jewel-toned oasis of Christmas cheer, causing Ivy to exchange a smirk with a stationary Nutcracker, both silently agreeing that the display was probably a bit over the top.

Across the square, a Salvation Army bell ringer grinned at a passerby while children skipped around him, their breath fogging the air. People moved from store to store, bundled in scarves and mittens, their arms laden with packages.

Ivy envisioned the just-baked treats that tempted buyers at the adjacent bakery and cafe—sugary gingerbread men, foamy peppermint mochas, and pumpkin spice lattes. In this season, the square was redolent with the buttery scents of nutmeg and vanilla, as well as the keenness of freshly cut pine.

Her anxiety over the article receded as she took in the community's optimism. Facing her customers might be daunting, but this place and these folks were her heart. Come what may, she belonged here.

At six o'clock, she perused the shelves one last time before closing.

"Amelia, can you pass me those pinecone strings?" she asked. "I'll wrap them around the glass vases."

"Sure," Amelia replied. "Who said vases can't join the festive fashion trend?

Ivy tied the strings around miniature potted paperwhites, creating a dainty charm, while Amelia organized a parade of pink and bi-colored Christmas cacti.

"Remember when we made our own ornaments out of pinecones and acorns?" Amelia's hands moved with skill and precision, ensuring that the cacti looked stunning.

Ivy chuckled. "Our parents let us hang them on the tree, even though they were a tad …rustic compared to the store-bought ones."

"Speaking of trees, have you seen any that might be ideal for the store?"

Every December, the women decorated a modestly sized evergreen that graced a corner of the shop.

"Actually, I hoped we'd pick one out together next weekend." Ivy stole a glance at her friend, grateful for her nod of agreement. "It wouldn't feel right without your input."

"Deal! We'll spruce things up as a team. Get it? Spruce things up? Spruce?" With a humorous wink, Amelia placed a closed sign on the front door.

As the sign snapped into position, the women stood silent, looking around the shop that they had poured their hearts into—Ivy as a majority owner, and Amelia as a partner.

This was more than a business—it was a haven of creativity and friendship.

"Have you finalized your plans for the holiday break yet?" Ivy inquired.

"I'm flying home to Indiana to spend time with my family for Christmas and to bring in the New Year. And I truly miss Bailey, my mother's dog. She's such a sweet golden retriever —and never misses a chance to cuddle on the sofa while we watch movies. It'll be so nice to relax with her after being apart since last summer. I really wish I could get back there more often." Amelia pulled out her phone. "You gotta see the recent pictures that my mother sent me!"

She scrolled through her camera roll, cooing over shots of the retriever chewing on a toy bone or curled up napping.

Ivy smiled. "Look at those big paws!"

"I know, right?" Amelia pinched the photo to zoom in on the dog's fuzzy fur. "How can you not fall in love with those soulful eyes? Bailey is so loyal and kind."

"Okay, you're definitely selling me on the merits of dog ownership."

"That's not all!" Amelia tapped open her browser. "Check out this animal shelter site. So many cute dogs needing homes." She displayed photos of snuggly labs, peppy terriers, and a beagle with pleading eyes.

"Aww, they are all precious," Ivy admitted as Amelia clicked through.

"You'd give any pet the best home ever," Amelia said.

Ivy hesitated, but the adorable puppy pics had sparked a longing inside her. A dog would bring so much happiness and solace to her lonely lifestyle. However, owning a dog wasn't in her immediate future. Not with a florist shop to run.

"Bailey means the world to you," Ivy commented.

"Definitely." Amelia twirled a lock of her auburn hair. "And what are your plans over the holidays? You don't have any family here."

"I'm used to being alone. I should be able to carve out some time off, but year-end is usually busy. Thankfully, several college students can help on a part-time basis while you're away." Ivy let out an exasperated huff. "Ugh, my house is so empty and quiet, with only me rattling around. Almost makes me wish for a dog to have someone to greet me at the end of the day."

"See what I mean?" Amelia perked up. "You totally should get a pup, girl. Oh, and you could bring the dog to the shop with you, too!"

"Now that would be interesting." Ivy grinned at her friend's enthusiasm. "Though potty training a puppy while running the store sounds chaotic at best." She envisioned an energetic pup bouncing around the buckets filled with branches and twigs. It would be a mess, but a cute one.

"Owning a young dog is a big commitment." Amelia smiled. "But hey, you never know when the right guy comes along and—"

Ivy put up a hand. "I'm still recovering from my break-up with Will."

"That was a year ago, and Will Boyd was inconsiderate. Imagine just moving away without even telling you."

Memories of her relationship with Will and his declarations of love for her flooded Ivy's mind. "Yes, she replied. "So much for trust."

Could trust ever be fully mended, the way Amelia expertly arranged the flowers in a beautiful bouquet?

"All I'm saying is it's possible that this imaginary tall, dark, and handsome new guy is a dog lover too, and you can embark on an adventure together."

"Key word. Imaginary." Ivy smirked at the idea coming from her friend, always the romantic. "In the meantime, I'll live vicariously through your Bailey pictures. Who knows, maybe your dog can help me break my dating dry spell."

"I'm telling you, dogs are great icebreakers," Amelia teased. "You need to find a guy who can't resist those puppy eyes and warms up to you in the process."

"I'll keep your suggestions in mind."

An hour later, after they finished tidying and cleaning, watering the unsold plants, and conducting an inventory check, Ivy and Amelia huddled at the counter.

"I've been thinking about doing more for the auction." Ivy pictured a wreath with pine, holly, and white berries. "Let's design something unique."

"How about a huge vase arrangement, too? With some frosted branches and sparkly ornaments."

Ivy grabbed her sketchbook, mapping out evergreen boughs, woodsy stems, and metallic accents.

Amelia peeked at the drawings. "Awesome, girl! I can't wait to put it all together."

Ivy smiled, toning down her earlier elaborate vision to a more straightforward, stylish plan. With the design simplified, the winter plants could speak for themselves, unfettered by fancy embellishments.

As they admired her handiwork, the women grabbed their quilted coats and shrugged them on. Although Ivy owned a compact car, a small hatchback, she seldom used it to get around town, unless she was driving a longer distance.

Ivy turned to Amelia. "You mentioned Everett, the photographer who took pictures here? You said he owned the hardware store in town."

Amelia nodded. "Yep! Everett's Hardware."

"His photos in the *Gazette* were gorgeous. Didn't you mention he has a grandson who's a famous photographer?"

"Blake? He grew up here, but eventually relocated. Evergreen Valley isn't anywhere near as lucrative for a photographer as major cities."

Ivy arranged two empty flowerpots by the door, wondering if she'd bump into Everett's grandson around town someday. Being a world-traveling photographer sounded glamorous compared to her quiet life running a flower shop.

She smiled to herself, both appreciating the simplicity of her life, and secretly intrigued by the mystery of this local boy turned globetrotter.

Arm in arm, the women stepped outside, their giggles carrying into Township Avenue, the main street in town. Ivy's gaze inevitably drifted to the available storefront next to her shop.

She imagined quaint, overflowing window displays, shelves brimming with garden supplies, and a comfy corner where customers could sip tea while perusing flower books.

If only I had the resources to expand, she mused, her gaze lingering on the vacant space. *Perhaps one day, the stars will align.*

Across the square, vendors were setting up booths for the

Christmas market. Several women hung wreaths of foraged juniper, stacked wooden ornaments, and laid out glitter-dipped candles for sale. One booth sold mini cherry pies and mulled apple cider, the smell wafting across the square. Lively laughter resonated from a group of children, each clutching hot chocolate and candy canes.

As they walked, Ivy glanced at Amelia. Considering her tall frame and contagious enthusiasm, Amelia exuded a vibrant energy. Her passion for helping others was a quality that made her such a dear confidant and valued colleague.

Ivy, on the other hand, knew she didn't stand out, though she'd come to embrace her own unique qualities.

While Amelia's boisterous laughter drew people's attention, Ivy sought comfort in the quieter moments. It was okay to be petite in both stature and voice, because neither diminished her strength or impact.

Amelia's curly hair bounced with each step, eliciting a smile from Ivy. Their friendship was a tapestry of contrasts, and she was grateful that they shared this journey together, both in business and in life.

Christmas carolers passed around a sleigh bell wand for different singers to ring, their voices melding with the jingle of the bells.

"See you in the morning!" Ivy waved to Amelia as she headed toward her house, which was only two blocks farther.

"Bright and early!" Amelia walked in the opposite direction to her apartment on Cedar Street, about a fifteen-minute stroll. "It's a big day. Your Wishing Blooms always draw a huge crowd."

A few minutes later, as Ivy unlocked the door to her modest house, an unassuming Cape Cod on Winterberry Drive, a pang of loneliness hit her. The emptiness of the space was highlighted by the silence, with only her rattling around on the hardwood floors.

The home had an open floor plan with antique decor. While the living room fireplace provided a serene spot, she often wished she had a furry companion or potential partner to share the fire's warmth. An upstairs office allowed her space to work, but the absence of company became apparent as she evaluated customer orders during the wee hours or pored over feedback from lapsed accounts.

She had a Facebook page and Instagram account and posted photos a few times a month. However, social media was hardly worth the effort because she didn't get much of a response. Her business was local, and she rationalized that she didn't need to reach out to a far-flung audience.

If she hired a marketing manager, she would need an advertising budget.

But who had the money for an advertising budget?

She hung up her coat and set down her purse with a sigh. Another night alone in front of the TV or reading a book until she fell asleep. Ever since her breakup with Will, her personal life had stalled.

Certainly, she had her friends and flower shop to fill her time. But as she sank into the couch, she ached for someone to share this space with. Someone who would ask about her day and hold her when she was hurting.

She gazed at various photos and a framed inspirational quote on a side shelf and stepped over to it. There, she read the quote out loud, "Bloom where you are planted."

Such true words. She loved that quote.

Then, she lifted the framed photo behind it—a photo of herself and Will back when things were good. It served as a reminder of where she was and how far she had come.

They stood against the backdrop of the movie theater in town—arms linked and smiles wide. Him with his black hair neatly combed, and her blond hair catching a hint of sunlight.

Did she miss him or just the idea of not being alone? She had loved him once, before the arguments and distance grew. Ivy knew she deserved better than how he had treated her in the end. But part of her worried she'd never find that connection again.

Now in her thirties, she wondered if her chance at love and starting a family had passed her by. Maybe she was meant to be the single, career-focused woman who spent more time with her flowers than with people.

Ivy set the photo down. She wanted to believe there was still someone out there who would embrace both her independent spirit and her tender heart. Although on nights like these, it was hard not to lose hope.

Brushing away a tear, she pushed down the sadness. Someday, the right man would walk through that door and finally fill her house with laughter and love. She just had to be patient and ignore the creeping voice inside that whispered it was too late.

Before retiring, she mustered up the courage to reach out to the journalist. Steeling herself, she mentally prepared, and a glimmer of hope stirred. Perhaps Britney and her editor would be open to hearing Ivy's side, and they could find common ground.

She punched in Britney's number and left a considerate voice mail, aiming to address any misunderstandings. She politely requested a meeting to discuss the article in depth, seeking an opportunity to present her side of the story.

As she hung up the phone, Ivy's heart raced with uncertainty. The journalist's words caused Ivy to feel exposed and vulnerable, and she needed to set the record straight.

She turned off the lights and lay in bed, her mind filled with thoughts of what the meeting might bring. Sleep was elusive as she replayed the events of the day, her emotions tangled in a knot that refused to loosen.

Her phone pinged with a text. Ivy grabbed it, squinting at the bright screen. The message was from an unknown number.

It simply read: *Sweet dreams.*

Before Ivy could respond, another text appeared: *Tomorrow is a big day...*

Ivy's pulse quickened. Who was this? How did they know her name?

She hesitated, unsure whether to reply. The number provided no clues.

Tomorrow was the flower-wishing ceremony that most of the people in town attended. Although this text felt more sinister than a friendly reminder.

Ivy locked her phone, heart pounding as she huddled under the covers. The mystery texter's identity and motives remained unclear. But whoever it was, they knew too much.

As Ivy finally drifted off, she wondered what awaited her after sunrise.

CHAPTER 2

*A*n invigorating gust of wind filled Blake Shepherd's lungs as he stepped out of his Jeep Wrangler. The vintage jeep stood with a rugged charm, its exterior coat faded to a rustic red, rumbling the numerous rides on winding roads and open highways.

Blake's journey from Seattle, Washington, to Evergreen Valley, North Carolina, had taken forty-five hours. That amount of time didn't account for the rest breaks, meals, and three nights of lodging.

However, here he stood. Back in his hometown.

The nostalgic scent of cedar trees and pristine snow brought both comfort and an ache to his weary heart. He'd always considered Evergreen Valley his hometown, and now it was a refuge from the sadness of his colleague's tragic accident.

"Welcome home, Shutterbug. Ten Valley View Road hasn't changed a bit since you left." His grandfather, Everett Shepherd, appeared on the front porch. His hands, with visible veins and aged spots, cradled a mug of coffee, steam curling up into the chilly morning air.

Shutterbug.

When Blake was a boy, he explored with his camera, a simple point and shoot model with a built-in flash and took snapshots of everything and everyone. His grandfather started calling him Shutterbug, a name that stuck and became a cherished reminder of Blake's early artistic spirit.

"Thanks, Grandpa." Blake's breath misted in front of him as he spoke. "I could've stayed at the Evergreen Valley Inn."

"No need for that. You're always welcome here. Family's family, and that's what holds us together."

Blake surveyed the snow-covered landscape that encircled their ancestral home—a place where memories and history were woven into every creak of the floorboards. He glanced up as the whistling song of a male northern cardinal nestled in the fir trees.

"Come on in, I've got some breakfast ready for you." Everett ushered Blake inside, the familiarity of the house enveloping Blake as they stepped through the threshold.

Blake sniffed as he set his bags in the hallway. The irresistible scent of sizzling bacon wafted toward him.

As they settled around the kitchen table, plates heaped with fluffy scrambled eggs and crispy bacon, Blake marveled at how easily he slipped into the rhythm of this place. Every nook and cranny told a story, from the faded wallpaper adorned with delicate flowers to the worn leather armchair next to the fireplace. On rainy days, he would often lose himself in books, mostly kids' photography guides.

"Seems strange being back here," he admitted, glancing out the window at the snow-covered garden that had once been his playground. A mix of innocent laughter and carefree moments rushed in from his childhood. Memories from when he had a dear companion by his side. CooperCam, his loyal and loving black Labrador, who had shared countless adventures with him.

"Do you remember all the fun we had with our dog, Grandpa?" Blake asked, breaking the silence.

"Yep." Everett reached for a slice of toast and spread a thick layer of homemade strawberry jam on it. "Those were special times. CooperCam was your partner in crime."

Blake grinned. "Yeah. He was the best."

As the conversation progressed, Blake changed to a more subdued tone.

"I couldn't keep a dog in my Seattle penthouse. The landlord had a strict no-pet policy. Plus, with my frequent travels, it wouldn't be fair to the dog."

"That isn't why you broke your lease."

"No." Briefly, Blake shifted his gaze to his half-eaten breakfast. "I communicated my intent to leave and paid an exorbitant early termination fee."

"You were desperate."

"That's not the word I was looking for, though maybe it's the right one." A lump formed in Blake's throat. "Truth is, I missed home."

"Oh, my Shutterbug," Everett set down his toast and placed his hand on Blake's hand. "The pull of familiar streets and remembrances—it's a force that can't be denied."

"I couldn't agree more," Blake said.

In his quiet moments, he admitted the truth. No achievement would ever be enough to fill the vast hollowness inside.

Everett leaned back in his chair. "Big city life can be quite the whirlwind. I suppose it has its excitement, but it can also leave a person feeling disconnected. Here in this corner of the world, the pace is different. There's appeal in both, I reckon, but the choice is up to you."

Blake speared a forkful of eggs. The unpretentious breakfast was a stark contrast from Seattle—where he frequented trendy coffee shops and munched on slices of avocado toast. "This place is quite a change."

He was in his midthirties, yet he couldn't shake the guilt that he should have life figured out by now. Uncertainty tugged at him, wondering for the millionth time if returning home was a step backward or the possibility for charting a different course.

"Change is difficult." Everett took a slow sip of his coffee, his blue eyes mirroring Blake's own. "But sometimes it's exactly what we need."

His grandfather's words lingered, and Blake's mind retraced the path that had brought him back to town. The lifestyle he'd left behind in the city—the endless hustle, the constant noise and towering buildings, and the relentless pace that consumed him. A season of his life teeming with aspirations and ambitions, but also marked by heartache and mourning.

"Six months have passed since your colleague passed away." Everett's face bore the graceful marks of age. Faint lines etched near his eyes and mouth, hinting at a life rich with stories.

"I should've been there. Jason was my most trusted friend." Blake swallowed hard, forcing down the remorse that threatened to surface. "I was too absorbed in my work."

As photographers, Blake and Jason had supported each other through their college days, collaborating on assignments, attending exhibitions, and encouraging each other.

The memory of Jason's accident was an ever-present reminder of loss.

Blake's thoughts were overshadowed by regret. The guilt persisted, an unwelcome companion that seemed to grow stronger with each passing day.

"You traveled the world. Pay attention to all the recognition you gained," his grandfather was saying.

"But look what I lost."

"You didn't know there'd be an accident. You can't predict the future."

"Jason claimed it was a once-in-a-lifetime photo expedition in Switzerland." Blake's gaze drifted. Through the window, a solitary cardinal perched on a snow-covered branch. The sight brought a fleeting moment of wonder, a glimpse of nature and all he had missed. "We had discussed traveling to Switzerland all through college."

Over the last few years, Blake had been swept away in a tumultuous cyclone of success, leaving no time for the things that truly mattered. He neglected opportunities to collaborate with his friend, postponing their planned photography trips and forgoing their meetings.

Jason's trip to Switzerland was one of those times.

"I was committed to several high-profile assignments I couldn't get out of," Blake murmured. "A luxury car show and a handful of VIP parties. My buddy Rob was involved, too."

Rob was another colleague Blake had worked with. The man was on his way to becoming a resounding success—marketing, branding, and developing client relationships as if there were no limits to his future. Throughout their careers, the men maintained a cordial competition, a friendly rivalry, forever pushing each other.

Late at night, when Blake sat alone in his penthouse apartment, he wondered if this was all his life had become—a chase for some fulfillment that always danced just out of reach. Rob always seemed to be one step ahead of him.

With each sunrise, he buried the ache under crisp shirts and fake smiles, rushing once again towards the next fancy photography event, the next so-called win. His unshakable competitive spirit was a driving force in his life, and one that held him in its grip.

"I understand, and I well remember," his grandfather said,

pulling Blake out of his reverie. "There's no need to reiterate; I respect your feelings."

"I rationalized my decision and declined Jason's invitation." Blake fidgeted with his coffee mug, swirling the liquid distractedly. "I couldn't pass up another opportunity to elevate my career. I assumed we'd have another chance."

"Chance is an odd word. Options are not always definite or predictable. Some are unique and may never come around again."

"I was constantly stressed and adapting to my clients' demands," Blake continued. "It's an excuse, and it shouldn't be. I told myself that I embraced change—diverse job assignments—entertainment events and all that. Though I didn't. I prefer photographing riverbanks, sunrises, and sunsets."

He'd minored in environmental science at a prestigious university. During his education, he received a strong foundation in conservation, which he'd applied to his original profession as a wildlife photographer. How had he gotten so switched around?

"You're not alone," Everett replied. "Many people feel like you do. It seems more and more lately. Speaking of change, I've converted one of the rooms upstairs into a makeshift studio and moved my camera gear aside. You can set up all your equipment and continue your projects there. And your old bedroom is still waiting for you."

"Thanks. You mentioned that you've developed an interest in photography now that your hardware store is closed."

"A few freelance jobs keep my mind fresh." Everett patted at his lips with a napkin and stood. "Take the rest of the day to unpack. Most mornings, I'm out early, visiting a farmer's market or heading out of town for a doctor's appointment. Nothing as stunning and exciting as my famous grandson's life."

"Hardly." Blake pushed his half-eaten eggs aside. "You've always been my inspiration."

In this quaint town, Blake was back at his starting point. The place of his youth.

He'd resisted. He'd once considered Evergreen Valley too constricting. He'd been convinced that by going home, he was admitting defeat.

But here, he intended to immerse himself in his true passion—documenting the beauty of nature through his lens. Unfailingly, it brought joy, even in the darkest hours.

Jason's passing had been a turning point, prompting Blake to reevaluate his priorities. The idea of spending a holiday season in Seattle wandering Snowflake Lane by himself was unbearable.

"Your grandma was thrilled whenever you were here at Christmas," Everett said softly, his eyes glistening with unshed tears. "She always believed in you and your talents."

"After my parents passed away, you and Grandma raised me from when I was little. I can't tell you how much I appreciate all you did for me." Blake rose and faced his grandfather. "I promise I'll make her proud."

"You already have, Shutterbug. Just by being alive." Everett squeezed Blake's hand. "Your grandmother and your parents would be overjoyed to see the remarkable man you've become. They were gone too soon."

Blake was briefly rendered speechless by overwhelming gratitude. His grandfather's care and understanding were a balm to his bruised soul. He was grateful beyond words for the opportunity to heal and rediscover himself.

THE NEXT DAY, Blake woke to the amber light of sunrise filtering through the frayed plaid curtains. He laughed to himself as he stretched out on his boyhood bed, realizing how much smaller it seemed now compared to his six-foot, two-inch frame.

Transported back to the days of superhero capes and pillow fights with his friends, he felt like a time traveler. Tattered posters still hung on the walls, featuring his prized band obsessions—most notably The Rolling Stones, Queen, and Green Day—iconic legends and American punk rock.

He showered quickly and reflected on his appearance in the bathroom mirror. His light brown hair fell in an unkempt manner, and he ran his hand over his beard stubble. His associates often teased him, suggesting he "clean up" for special occasions. He'd assured them it wasn't an impressive display of facial hair by any means. His bristles resisted all his attempts at a smooth shave.

He pulled on an oversized cable-knit sweater in charcoal gray, paired with jeans, well-worn boots, and a faded leather jacket. His grandfather's note revealed that he would be gone for the day, but cinnamon rolls from the local bakery and a steaming pot of coffee sat on the stove.

Blake indulged in bite after bite of soft doughy layers, cinnamon sugar, and sweet icing. His eyes briefly closed in pleasure, and a contented hum escaped his lips.

After washing the dishes and placing them to dry by the sink, he grabbed his camera bag, slung a burgundy and gray tartan scarf around his neck, jammed fleece gloves into his pockets, and headed out. The snowflakes that had begun to fall during the previous night dusted the ground in a sparkling white blanket.

He snapped shots of frost-kissed branches and icicles hanging from eaves. His breath fogged up in the cold air as he lost himself in the art of finding the extraordinary in minute details.

As he roamed the familiar streets, memories washed over him like the gentle waves of the river that ran through town.

He pictured himself at nine-years-old, tromping through the forested trails that lined the riverbanks, his sturdy little boots splashing in the muddy shallows. Fear had welled up in his chest when he lost his footing on the slippery rocks and fell into the chilled water.

His bottom lip had quivered as he emerged, clothes dripping and tears springing to his eyes. But then his grandfather was there, wrapping him in his strong, comforting arms.

"It's alright, Shutterbug," his grandpa had said. "No reason to cry. What do you say we get you home to dry off?"

His cheeks sticky with tears, Blake had grabbed his grandfather's weathered hand and held tight. As they walked, his grandfather pointed out fiery red and burnt orange leaves drifting on the river's surface.

"See there? Looks like the trees are sending us their finest artwork," he remarked. "Bet we can find some nice ones to photograph later, hmm?"

Blake had smiled up at him. His grandfather invariably saw the bright side of any situation. With him, Blake was safe and cared for.

Back in the present, Blake sighed at the recollection. Even in difficult moments, his grandfather had known how to comfort him and kindle his artistic nature. Their bond had been a steady foundation throughout his childhood.

The nostalgic charm of the town square triggered another rush of sentimental emotions. The lampposts were wrapped in a string of shimmering lights, lush wreaths accented by bursts of red berries suspended from doors, and carefully curated holiday scenes transformed storefront windows into inviting displays. He stopped to take a photo of pre-school children playing in the snow, their flushed cheeks and bright smiles a testament to pure bliss.

He stood on the corner of Township Avenue and Breckenridge Road, briefly closing his eyes and inhaling deeply.

The sharp, earthy aromas of pine and cedar mingled with traces of cinnamon and baked bread floating from the cafés nearby. Evergreen Valley came alive through its smells.

He soaked in the jubilant tones of carolers singing on the street corner, blending with the merry jingling of store bells as customers entered and exited tiny boutiques. The town had its own soundtrack, its own rhythm. One he had missed during his years away.

As he resumed his walk, the packed snow snapped under his boots. He passed by the Evergreen Theater with its grand vintage marquee and the public library where he had spent endless winter days immersed in adventure stories as a child.

McKinley's Ice Cream Shop stood across the street, walls covered in memorabilia from his high school hockey team. Many winters, he'd celebrated victories with his teammates over hot fudge sundaes.

A father pulled his daughter on a wooden sled, her delightful squeals of laughter creating a heartwarming soundtrack. In the town park, toddlers waddled and tumbled into drifts, chubby legs churning as they created snow angels. Other children pushed each other into snowbanks, their grins extending from one ear to the other.

There was a liveliness here, a sense of community, that the coldness of Seattle had never allowed. This town was a part of him, as steadfast as the soaring evergreens, and he had been away for far too long.

As he continued, a recognizable voice called out, "Blake Shepherd?"

He turned. Mrs. Reynolds, his former third-grade art teacher, waved at him. Though her hair was frosted with white now, her eyes still radiated the same warm-heartedness.

"I can't believe it's you, all grown up and so accomplished." Along the lines of experience, her smile held the repeat of countless lessons. "Your work is being showcased in galleries everywhere! I especially liked your photograph of Lake Serenity at the foot of the Redwood Forest. I saw the photo online, and it truly moved me. I love keeping up with your career."

"How great to see you, Mrs. Reynolds." Blake grinned. He recalled those delightful days when the classroom buzzed with ingenuity, where paper and paint transformed into imaginative worlds, and popsicle sticks became bridges for endless creativity. "Those art projects were the best part of your class."

"I still have a few of your drawings framed in my home office," she said. "Even as a boy, I could tell you had talent. I'm retired now, but I sometimes substitute teach."

With a goodbye, Blake promised to visit his old school soon. This town was woven together by moments like this.

Just a week ago, he had been surrounded by the constant hustle of a sprawling city. Back in Evergreen Valley, he was struck by the slower tempo. No more honking horns or crowds jostling him on busy sidewalks. Instead, there was the quiet sigh of a soft wind and friendly nods from passing shopkeepers.

This place operated on its own timeline, a place guided more by seasons and community than formal schedules. In Seattle, he needed to rush to keep up. Here, he could finally breathe. Hours spent wandering and photographing were the norm, not a luxury.

He turned another corner, drawn to a quaint storefront adjacent to the bakery and cafe. The sign above a blue door read Ivy's Blooms in flowing calligraphy. A riot of flower colors and textures, as well as a lively crowd gathered outside the shop.

Nearby, a middle-aged woman wore a crimson coat decked with a faux fur collar. Not far off, an elderly couple strolled arm and arm. Their matching purple sweaters displayed whimsical patterns of reindeers and snowflakes.

A resplendent cart reminiscent of a fairy tale, with intricate carvings and delicate, lace-like patterns, stood outside the flower shop. Positioned above the cart sat an attractive sign with the words: "Make A Wish! Discover The Magic Of Christmas. Free Wishing Blooms For All" inscribed in hand-painted letters. The cart overflowed with translucent deep purple and lavender flowers that seemed to glow, as if lit from within.

A gentle breeze blew past him, seeming to whisper the cart's mysteries, carrying the essence of ancient secrets, and forgotten dreams.

Intrigued, he stepped closer and captured the moment with his camera. The sunlit morning cast a golden radiance on the dazzling blooms and brought a touch of magic to the setting.

Magic? And what on earth was a Wishing Bloom?

He lowered his camera and rubbed his eyes, trying to confirm if what he witnessed was real or a mirage.

As the enthusiastic crowd lined up to receive the mystical blooms, a nagging doubt crept in. This whole concept of wishing flowers granting people's deepest desires seemed too fanciful and unrealistic.

He tried to keep an open mind, though his natural skepticism made it difficult to accept such a whimsical premise at face value. As a photographer, he was wired to search for concrete evidence and confirmation.

Wandering nearer, Blake observed the blond-haired woman and her flower cart. He wanted to believe her motives were purely altruistic, though he couldn't help wondering if this was an elaborate event designed to take advantage of people. Perhaps she purchased inexpensive flowers and spun an enticing story around them to attract publicity and sales. After all, belief could be a persuasive force. He had seen it time and again.

For now, he told himself, he would try to remain balanced between openness and healthy uncertainty.

"What's going on?" He directed his attention to the elderly couple.

"Ivy Bennett's flower-wishing ceremony, and that's Ivy handing out her Wishing Blooms." The woman gestured to the blond-haired woman. "The flowers hold the power to grant wishes."

Clad in a vibrant red quilted coat that perfectly complemented her radiant blond hair, tied in a stylish bun, the petite woman stood beside the cart.

She was gorgeous.

Her face was framed by loose strands that accentuated her delicate features and fair complexion. Despite the cold, her demeanor was gracious and friendly, treating each customer as if they were cherished friends.

As Blake's gaze lingered on her, their eyes met, her hazel-eyed gaze locking to his. His heart skipped a beat, caught off guard by the unexpected connection.

Time slowed. The surrounding crowd vanished into the background. For a fleeting second, they were the only two people in the town.

Blake was struck by the genuine warmth emanating from Ivy's smile, an aura of kindness he seldom encountered.

A tall woman with curly auburn hair stood near Ivy, her attentive gaze focused on the display of flowers. Now and then, he caught her adjusting the arrangement to ensure the blossoms were presented artfully for the customers.

He advanced as an enthusiastic Ivy motioned to the cart. "A beacon of hope," she explained to the eager audience. "Each flower has a way of touching people's hearts."

He scanned his surroundings, a detached observer amid a

mass of believers. The ceremony seemed a heartwarming showcase of optimism and positivity, but his skeptic's mind searched for a different, more rational explanation.

Was this a charming spectacle, carefully orchestrated to evoke emotions? A clever marketing strategy? He expressed his thoughts out loud, and the elderly couple turned to him, exchanging a knowing smile.

"I've never seen anything quite like this before," Blake muttered. "How can she afford to give away flowers for free?"

"This is no gimmick," the woman replied. "Ivy's flower-wishing ceremony is a labor of love. She trusts in the potential of these blooms to spread happiness and hope."

"But still," Blake persisted. "Surely it must cost a fortune to donate all these flowers. What's the hidden catch?"

The elderly man laughed. "You're not alone in your doubt. People willingly contribute the money so that Ivy can purchase these flowers. This is a community effort."

Blake's lips formed a half-smile. "But what's in it for Ivy?"

"The delight she shares. Isn't that enough?"

Blake shook his head, dismissing the event as lovely but ordinary.

He focused on the middle-aged woman wearing a crimson coat who stood a few feet from him. She held a Wishing Bloom, its fine petals quivering in the slight breeze, and closed her eyes.

What deeply held wish had she entrusted to the fragile flower?

As a photographer, he was trained to observe people and details. Perhaps she wished for healing—for herself or a loved one. Or was she hoping for strength and comfort through a difficult loss?

Maybe she wished for reconciliation—the saving of a struggling relationship or marriage. Or something more profound, like searching for meaning amid life's unknowable mysteries.

Even the simplest wishes held power. Wishes for peace, purpose, or rejoicing.

As the woman clutched the flower to her chest, Blake was struck by how vulnerable and human her body language was.

Despite his reservations, he couldn't dispute the longing reflected in the woman's face. His natural curiosity compelled him to open his mind, even just for this moment, to the power of belief.

He focused his lens on her. The camera shutter clicked, freezing the image into a single frame, a fleeting instant of vulnerability, anticipation, and a hint of trepidation.

The ceremony concluded, and the woman traced a loving trail over the stem before walking away with the flower.

He didn't reject the appeal of holiday traditions, but a simple illusion influenced people's convictions. He'd witnessed enough shiny advertising campaigns covering significant Hollywood happenings to know that, and his training had ingrained in him a habit of considering every angle. Doubt was a lens he couldn't easily remove and extended to other aspects of his daily life.

The ceremony drew to a close, and Blake dawdled. The concept of wishing flowers sounded implausible when said aloud. But the anticipation and yearning etched on each person's face as they cradled their delicate blossoms was real.

Perhaps the actual magic was the spark of positivity the ceremony inspired, the childlike belief that sincere desires could become reality.

Life often didn't align with fantasies, yet Blake was moved by the sincerity of the participants. For a moment, he had seen past cynicism and doubt to something purer, a faith in possibilities. While he still sought tangible evidence for ideas, today he was reminded there were intangible wonders in the world off the measurable grid. Forces that, perhaps, science alone could not explain.

As he meandered farther into town, the beautiful Ivy and her Wishing Blooms occupied his thoughts, like an enigmatic puzzle begging to be deciphered. And her hazel eyes radiating with warmth and joy stayed imprinted in his mind.

CHAPTER 3

"*C*an you believe that it's eight o'clock already and two hours past closing?" Amelia nodded toward the antique clock on the back wall. "I'm thrilled that our Wishing Blooms ceremony was a grand success this morning."

Ivy looked up from arranging the spiky leaves on a bunch of sturdy holly branches. Beyond the wide front windows, darkness had fallen outside. The mellow gleam of the shop's pendant lights enveloped the interior, providing a relaxed sanctuary against the winter night.

"Time certainly got away from us," Ivy replied, setting the branches down. She removed the apron from her slender waist and breathed in the enchanting fragrance of roses and lilies. These flowers, roses in particular, reminded her of a summer garden, delicate and sweet.

"We both were caught up in the moment of endless work," Amelia chuckled, tending to a potted amaryllis plant. "As usual, I might add."

Ivy tidied the scattered ribbons and leaf trimmings.

"Everyone left with smiles on their faces this morning. That's a good sign."

"The best kind of sign, but I'm beat and headed home." Amelia slipped on her coat. "I can't believe Britney Knox hasn't returned your phone call. Notice that she didn't cover our Wishing Blooms event. We would've appreciated the positive publicity."

"Maybe she's out of town. I worried about our business suffering, but everything is holding up well for now."

Ivy refrained from mentioning the odd late-night text she'd received after phoning Britney. There was no need to worry her friend about what was most likely a prank message.

"Don't work too late," Amelia admonished.

"Me?" Ivy pointed to herself. "Never."

In between arranging flowers, Ivy spent the subsequent hour dusting and cleaning the shelves and display counter. By the time she stepped outside, the town's holiday lights had automatically shut off, and only the streetlamps emitted a faint amber glow.

Most of the shops were already closed for the evening, with only a few restaurants and the movie theater still lit.

As Ivy began her customary route home, the full moon provided only minimal light on the deserted sidewalks. The wind whistled as it wove through the bare branches of trees and sent stray newspapers skittering across the pavement. A chill seeped through Ivy's coat, and she shoved her hands in her pockets and quickened her pace.

She walked into the residential area after leaving the town square. Light gleamed from windows of welcoming homes. In her mind, families had shared chicken casseroles and hot cocoa while laughing together. At this hour, parents read bedtime stories to their children by lamplight, tucking young ones under snug, hand-stitched quilts.

Her boots lightly tapped on the wintry pavement, and her breath formed frosty puffs in the darkness.

Her ears perked up at the subtle rustling of movement, and she slowed her steps. In a dimly lit alleyway, a thin tabby cat crouched motionless beside a trash can. The cat's whiskers trembled, ever so slightly.

Ivy advanced, her footsteps slowing. The cat scrutinized her with wary eyes.

The lid of a trash can clattered as it hit the ground. The cat sprang back and disappeared into the alley.

Ivy jumped, then went to turn, but a flicker of movement followed by a faint whimpering made her pause.

Another motion.

She peered into the shadows, struggling to catch sight of whatever it was. Perhaps there was another creature who sought refuge or assistance.

The form moved again, and two sparkling eyes peered up at her.

As she crept closer, the shape revealed itself to be a puppy, and she glimpsed its fluffy body and wagging tail.

Her breath caught in her throat. The poor abandoned creature looked so small and helpless. How could someone leave this innocent puppy out here alone to freeze?

Kneeling on the cold ground, she spoke softly so as not to startle it.

"Everything is okay, little guy," she whispered.

The puppy flinched back.

She extended her hand, pale in the dim light.

The puppy hesitated, then inched forward to sniff her, its wet nose nudging her palm. Winter's chill left traces on its matted fur, and its protruding ribs were visible.

"There you go. I won't hurt you." She wanted to pick up the quivering animal and warm it but waited patiently for it to come closer.

She scratched behind its frostbitten ears, eliciting another tail wag. Her gaze darted about the alley, searching for any hint of an owner, but the surroundings remained silent and deserted.

She unbuttoned her coat and rose, lifting the puppy.

She was reminded of her own yearning for a puppy in her childhood days. She'd brought home stray dogs she found, begging her parents to let her keep them. Pleading her case, she promised to care for the puppy and assume full responsibility.

But her parents, worried about added expenses and chaos, always said no. "Perhaps when you're older," they told her, although that day never came.

An only child, Ivy keenly noticed the absence of a constant companion in those early years. She daydreamed about romping across grassy fields with her very own loyal dog at her side.

Now, decades later, Ivy held an orphaned pup that desperately needed her care. She cradled the puppy, feeling a deep sense of responsibility, and reversed her steps.

Her heart raced as a tall figure approached, casting a lengthy shadow in the alleyway. Squinting, she clutched the puppy tighter.

"Hey there. Is everything okay?" A man held up a gloved hand in a friendly wave. He wore a faded leather jacket and a tartan scarf.

"Oh, umm. I'm fine." She opened her coat just enough for the man to glimpse the puppy's face, and big brown eyes peered out at him.

"Cute! Poor little guy."

"The puppy isn't yours, by any chance?" She glanced at the stranger. "I think it was abandoned, and it's so cold out."

"Nope. Not mine." The man stepped closer. He had a strikingly attractive ruggedness, with defined features that suggested a life well-experienced. Strong jawline and dark, furrowed eyebrows, while his intense blue eyes bore traces of strength and kindness.

"Here." He slipped off his scarf, which was intricately woven in deep burgundy and grays. "Take this to keep the little guy warm. I'm Blake, by the way."

"Ivy. Ivy Bennett." She accepted the scarf, surprised at the pleasantly substantial texture. Quickly, the puppy snuggled into the luxurious fabric.

Blake smiled, genial and appealing, as if he and Ivy were long-lost friends. "You're the flower shop lady. We met this morning."

"We did?"

"Yes." His blue eyes glimmered with a touch of mischief. "I attended your Wishing Blooms ceremony."

"I...I remember. I'm grateful you came to the ceremony."

"I didn't intend to. I stumbled into it."

"Thanks a lot."

"No, that's not what I meant." He chuckled softly, his gloved hands adjusting the collar of his jacket against the chill. "To clarify, we didn't exactly meet, but I was there."

"Stumbled into it."

"Right. It's nice to formally meet you, Ivy."

"Likewise."

He hesitated. "Don't I get a polite Nice to meet you, Blake?"

"Alright." She offered a tentative smile. "Nice to meet you, Blake."

She recalled him more clearly with each word of their conversation. A tall man with a camera slung around his neck who had remained at the fringes of the crowd. She became aware of him watching her during the ceremony. When their eyes briefly met, she'd felt the faintest flutter in her heart.

Snowflakes floated down, leaving a fine white layer on their jackets.

Blake glanced up at the sky, as if contemplating an impending storm. "I'm available if you want me to walk with you."

"No, I—" She began lifting his scarf off the puppy, fully intending to give it back to him.

"Please keep the scarf. Consider it my gift to the puppy." He touched her hand, lightly, to slow her movements. "I recently returned to Evergreen Valley and moved into my grandfather's house at Ten Valley View Road."

She nodded. She knew where the road was.

"When did you return?" she asked.

"Yesterday." He laughed. "I'm a thirty-something guy in the middle of a career transition. At least, that's what I'm telling myself to feel better." He made no sudden moves, keeping a reasonable distance. His voice was calm, his hands visible and non-threatening. His laughter, presumably at himself, came readily and sincere.

Ivy smirked. "Welcome to the thirty-something club."

"I owned a black Labrador retriever once, a long time ago, and I still miss him. He had the goofiest antics, but I'm grateful for every minute we had together." Blake's tone faltered. "I hate the thought that this little buddy was out here alone."

The puppy peeked out of Ivy's coat and sniffed Blake's fingers.

Blake's thoughtful manner, his obvious love for animals, and the puppy's own instincts helped assure her he was on the level.

"Thank you." Ivy hugged the tiny dog closer as the wind picked up. "I appreciate the company."

She stole a sideways glimpse at him as they hurried along the snowy sidewalk. His wavy hair peeked out from under a knit cap. With his jacket hugging his broad shoulders and washed-out jeans accentuating his muscular legs, he cut a good-looking figure.

He cast her a quick, inquisitive glance. "Have you always lived in Evergreen Valley?"

She scanned the well-known scenery. The town exuded a quiet charm under the cover of night, its quaint buildings illuminated by scattered pockets of light, a subtle contrast against the dark backdrop.

"I grew up here." Her gaze briefly touched the old oak tree that stood sentinel at the crossroads. "After college, I relocated briefly to Pittsburgh to work in a flower shop."

"What made you return?" he asked.

"The slower pace, the sense of community, the changing seasons... This place aligns better with my soul," Ivy replied.

"I can relate. I lived in Seattle for several years." Blake kicked absently at a small mound of snow near the curb, sending a spray into the air. "A city of over seven hundred thousand people and noted for its iconic skylines."

"Impressive."

He shrugged. "Maybe for some people."

Ivy brushed a loose strand of hair behind her ear. "Are you here for the long term or visiting family for the holidays?"

"I'm not sure yet. I had sent a portfolio to a well-known gallery in New York City a while ago for a holiday exhibition." He slid his hands into his pockets and looked upwards. "It would've been a terrific chance to showcase my work, but I never heard back."

Ivy scratched the tiny puppy behind the ears, eliciting contented little grunts. "I'm sure the right opportunity will come along. In the meantime, taking time to reset might be exactly what you need."

"In Seattle, the constant hustle left me ungrounded."

Ungrounded. She pondered the word. How accurately it described her state of mind before she'd moved back to Evergreen Valley.

"You're seeking a simpler, more meaningful life," she said aloud.

Blake adjusted his knit hat, his lips parting as he exhaled. "Ah, you've managed to put my thoughts into words."

"Do you regularly wander the streets at night searching for abandoned puppies?"

"Not often. In fact, not ever," Blake chuckled, studying the little furball sleeping in Ivy's arms. "Ever since I owned CooperCam, I've loved dogs."

"CooperCam?"

"My black Labrador retriever I mentioned earlier."

"You named your black lab CooperCam?"

He smirked. "Yeah, it was a name with character."

"And then some. Were you preparing your dog for a future in photography?"

"Hey, he was a smart dog. He had a hidden talent for snapshots. Get the name?"

"Got it. Sounds like he was special." Ivy shifted the puppy onto one arm so she could adjust Blake's scarf with her free hand. "Are you sure you wouldn't be interested in a dog?"

"Good try, Ivy, but sadly, no." Blake shrugged. "I'm fairly certain my grandfather would banish me to the doghouse if I brought home a puppy right now."

"Your grandfather doesn't know what he's missing," she grinned down at the pup. "This little guy is irresistible."

"That he is," Blake agreed.

When they arrived at her home, she hesitated, toying with the fringe of the scarf.

"Thank you again for accompanying me," she said.

"Happy to help." Blake's gaze settled on her for a few

beats longer than necessary before he looked away. "Take good care of the little one."

"Of course." Her gaze flicked to her front door, and she considered, for a fleeting second if her house could accommodate more than herself and the puppy. Of course, it could. That wasn't an excuse. She hesitated. Should she ask Blake to come inside?

No. Certainly not. She scarcely knew him.

"Well, I should go. I would invite you in, but..."

"Please, I'm fine." Blake's smile took over his handsome face. "By the way, have you ever owned a dog before?"

She grinned. "I've never even owned a goldfish."

"I'm no expert, but what are you planning to feed the puppy tonight? I assume you have no puppy food lying about."

"Only a leftover tossed salad. Any suggestions?"

"Try plain white rice and bits of cooked chicken." Blake used his hands to show the portion size. "In the morning, a scrambled egg. And water to keep the puppy hydrated. Canned pumpkin is supposed to be good, though I've never tried it."

His advice eased her worries, and she nodded. "Okay, thanks. Tomorrow, I plan on visiting the vet, and then I'll try to locate the owners of this pup."

"Wishing you the best of luck." A sly smile crossed Blake's lips as he leaned in, as if sharing a secret. "By the way, challenge accepted."

"What challenge?"

He chuckled. "I'll see to it that our paths cross again."

"Oh, really. What do you have in store?"

He paused. "I know where you work. I'll show up at your flower shop and buy a bouquet of your finest blooms."

"For who?"

"For you."

"I'm already the owner. I don't need more flowers."

He grinned. "True."

"Are you in the market for flowers?"

"I've never bought them before."

She laughed and couldn't resist asking, "What about my Wishing Blooms?"

"Sorry, Ivy. When it comes to those flowers, there's not a chance."

"They're free."

"Free isn't the issue. Either way, I'll pass. I'll bring you a coffee, too."

"There is no comparison between my Wishing Blooms and a cup of coffee." Ivy adjusted the puppy in her arms. She found herself drawing nearer to Blake, the shared moment oddly intimate in the darkness. "Besides, I prefer tea."

"What kind of tea?"

"Peppermint." For some reason, her voice sounded as if it were a soft invitation.

"Peppermint tea it is." Blake's tone carried a subtle promise that caused her heart to quicken. "And trust me, Ivy Bennett. I have more to offer you than a cup of tea and pretty bouquets."

His comment ignited her curiosity, filling her with unexpected excitement.

"*My* bouquets," she reminded.

"Right." He winked.

She was flirting with a man, something she hadn't done in ages.

Blake turned, and Ivy watched him go. She gave a little wave as he glanced back at her when he neared the end of her walkway. Then she moved inside, the sleepy puppy nuzzling against her cheek.

She set the puppy on the floor and prepared the chicken

and rice as Blake had suggested. As the puppy ate, Ivy fingers gently explored the velvety fur.

"I don't know how much time we'll spend together," she said, "though I promise to make it as wonderful as possible."

After a warm impromptu bath in her kitchen sink, she wrapped the puppy in a fluffy towel, patting it dry with an attentive touch. The puppy's eyes blinked open, revealing a newfound calmness.

After drying off, the puppy slept soundly on Blake's scarf by the fireplace. She grinned down at the tiny belly rising and falling. Every so often, quiet cries pierced the silence when she tried to doze, tugging at her sleep and demanding attention.

She carried the puppy outside to go potty, staying close in the fenced backyard as the curious pup explored the grass.

Back inside, whenever it shivered, she cradled it closer. She knew the tiny creature's vulnerability, and her compassion expanded. Steadfast in her effort to protect, she layered on an extra blanket, creating a safe nest.

With each passing hour, she stayed fixated on the slight form, watching for any signs of discomfort. Each tiny whimper or movement sparked a quick response from her, adjusting the blankets or offering a gentle, reassuring pat.

The sun was barely up and filtering through the curtains as Ivy awoke to the puppy's energetic barks. Although she was reluctant to abandon the luxury of her comfortable plaid couch with the soft cushions, this fragile life depended on her.

She showered quickly, dressed in her usual attire of khaki pants and blouse, and pulled her hair up into a bun. Then she scrambled eggs for herself and the puppy and phoned the vet to schedule the earliest appointment.

Ivy set out for the vet's office as the sun rose over Evergreen Valley. Snuggling the puppy in Blake's scarf and an extra blanket, she walked into town.

The chill from the night before had lifted, and the air held the brisk freshness of early morning. Store owners were sweeping sidewalks outside their shops to get ready for the day. The rich aroma of roasted coffee beans wafted from one of several local cafés.

Ivy inhaled as she passed the bakery, the yeasty scent of fresh bread and cinnamon rolls drifting from within, creating an irresistible invitation to passersby. The movie theater was just putting out their signature spinning display of candy and popcorn.

Up ahead was the Evergreen Valley Inn with its old-fashioned veranda. The owner stepped outside to shovel the steps and waved cheerily to Ivy.

The sights, sounds, and smells of the neighborhood coming to life brought sentimental comfort. She was reminded of school days long ago when she walked this route to the bus stop, dreaming of the day ahead.

She greeted the early risers, meeting their interested smiles at the puppy with a brief nod, and entered the vet's office.

Dr. Emily Mitchell, the veterinarian, was a picture of confidence and compassion, and she examined the puppy as Ivy looked on anxiously.

"He's a boy. Overall, he seems healthy," Dr. Mitchell said. "A little underweight, but we can give him some nutritional supplements."

Ivy nodded, relief flooding through her.

As Dr. Mitchell administered the puppy's shots, then checked for a microchip, she glanced at Ivy. "You seem quite concerned. I can tell you two have bonded already."

"Last night, I found him abandoned and freezing. I want to make sure he's okay."

"Not everyone would have been so eager to rescue an orphaned animal." The vet smiled knowingly as Ivy's fingers explored the silky texture of the puppy's coat.

"He was just so cute and helpless. I couldn't leave him." Ivy lifted the puppy and cradled him. His little body tucked perfectly against her chest.

"Have you considered keeping him yourself?" Dr. Mitchell folded her hands. "I think he's already quite attached to you as well."

Ivy paused, surprised by the vet's words. Could she provide him with a forever home?

The puppy's big trusting eyes looked up at her, and a powerful ache rose within her. She wanted to be the person to give him the love he deserved.

"I don't know," Ivy said slowly.

"In any event, you have yourself a fine dog here." Dr. Mitchell's one hand stroked the puppy's back, while the other held a flashlight to examine its eyes, ears, and mouth.

Ivy's gaze connected with Dr. Mitchell's as she inquired, "What type of breed is he?"

"A Pomeranian, possibly a purebred, and I estimate him to be around fourteen weeks old. These dogs are a small breed, and an adult typically stands about six to seven inches tall and weighs around three to seven pounds. Today, he weighed in at over three pounds, and ten inches in length from the tip of his nose to the base of his tail." Dr. Mitchell rested her palms on the examination table. "A Pomeranian has a high energy level, and your dog will require lots of walks and play and frequent grooming. The good thing is he can comfortably fit into your hands."

"I don't have time for a dog." Ivy traced patterns on the sleeve of her quilted coat. "And, to clarify, he's not mine."

"He might be a stray, or lost, or a victim of neglect. Sadly, it happens often." Dr. Mitchell placed her hand on Ivy's arm.

"Some owners struggle to provide adequate care due to the associated costs."

"My heart breaks to think that someone could abandon such a precious animal."

"This is a heartbreaking reality, although I'm glad you brought him here." The vet nodded. "I have a certain protocol in place to deal with lost animals, including recommending temporary shelters or animal control. Do you plan on bringing him to an animal shelter if you can't find the owner or don't plan to keep him?"

Ivy pondered the question, her gaze drifting down to meet the puppy's chocolate-brown eyes, filled with innocence and trust.

"I'll house him until I locate his owners if that's okay?" She hugged the puppy, relishing the silky sensation of his fur against her palms.

"So, you'll provide temporary care?" the vet asked. "Then yes, I'm okay with that. This is a small town and I know you'll ensure his well-being."

A bulletin board held Ivy's attention as she exited the office. Jammed with photos of rescued pets and their forever homes, she paused, touched by the uplifting stories behind each happy ending.

As she made her way toward her shop, her quickening steps matched the increasing buzz of activity in town. Joggers were hitting the trails around the river. Families walked their dogs, the air resonating with the lively sounds of barking companions. School-age kids with backpacks hurried to classes.

A woman strolled past and fawned over the puppy. Ivy held her precious bundle tighter, a protective measure.

"How can I take him to a shelter?" she thought. "He needs me."

CHAPTER 4

*A*s Ivy entered her shop, she smiled at Amelia, who had her curly auburn hair fastened in a loose bun. She wore a plum-colored sweater with a floral apron tied around her generous waist. Her fingers, stacked with dainty gold rings, moved swiftly and skillfully as she wrapped a bouquet of white lilies in shimmering gold paper.

She greeted Ivy with a spirited tap on her watch and a hint of curiosity in her eyes. "What gives? You're never late."

Ivy laughed in response. "I had a good reason today. I stopped at the vet."

"Dr. Mitchell's office? Why?"

"Because of this little guy." Ivy held up the puppy.

"Wait, wait. You're kidding." Amelia raced over and caressed the puppy's fluffy fur. "Finally, you adopted a dog."

"Temporarily, and only until I find his owner, or the animal shelter finds him a forever home." Ivy was quickly becoming aware of the responsibility of caring for a pet. The practical voice in her head reminded her of the commitment required, but the pull of concern and the puppy's endearing presence tugged at her heartstrings.

"The most unexpected thing happened," she continued. "Last night, I was walking home after I left the store and heard this soft whimpering behind a trash can in an alleyway. There he stood, this little cuddle ball looking up at me with irresistible brown eyes."

"Oh, how cute!" Amelia lifted the puppy out of Ivy's arms, fussing and snuggling him.

"I couldn't just leave him there," Ivy said. "So, I scooped him up, and right at that moment, Blake appeared out of nowhere. He knew exactly what to do."

The memory of his unexpected arrival was vivid—his gentle demeanor, his willingness to assist, and the sense of comfort she felt in his presence.

While Amelia held the puppy, Ivy stepped behind the counter to ensure all the deliveries were on track. She'd hired a high school student who often rode a bike after school to deliver flower orders.

"Blake?" Amelia raised an eyebrow. "Who's that?"

"He's someone I met last night while I was with the puppy. He recently moved back to Evergreen Valley and gave me this scarf for the puppy." Ivy held up his scarf.

Amelia chuckled. "Lucky you, coming across a cute puppy and meeting a charming rescuer all in one evening."

"Please, it wasn't like that." Ivy fussed with Amelia's bouquet, her heart beating faster than normal. "But yes, he was kind enough to walk me home and even offered some good advice on puppy food. Turns out, he's had experience with dogs, and his help was invaluable."

Amelia leaned against the counter, her gaze probing with mischief. "And he gave you his scarf."

"He said it was a gift for the puppy to keep him warm."

"How thoughtful of him." Amelia examined the scarf. "An expensive tartan scarf. Sure."

Ivy laughed. Amelia read her like an open book. "You and your wild imagination. Seriously, he's a friend."

"A friend who makes you blush the way a teenager does with a secret crush." Amelia tilted her head. "Sometimes the most beautiful stories unfold in the most unexpected ways."

"Now you're a poet?" Ivy quipped.

"I'm a romantic. And that wasn't a poem. It was a declaration."

Ivy grinned at her friend's loveable quirkiness. Amelia had always been the one to nudge her toward different possibilities, even when Ivy showed reluctance to embrace them.

OVER THE COURSE of the morning, the puppy followed Ivy as she went about her work, snuggling at her feet and eagerly awaiting belly rubs.

"Come on, Ivy," Amelia urged. "You're such a loving person, and this little guy clearly needs someone like you. Just think about adopting him if the owner doesn't show up, okay?"

Ivy hesitated, torn between her desire to help the lost pup and the sobering reality of her already overwhelming work-load. She glanced down at the puppy, his big chocolate-colored eyes brimming with trust and hope. His plume-like tail wagged with unbridled enthusiasm, keeping time with the lively pace of her pulse.

"I'll finalize packing the flowers for delivery before the high schooler arrives." With care, Amelia gathered the pup in her arms. "And I'd love some assistance from our new best friend. I'll also run to the animal supply store with him. He needs food, water, and bowls, correct?"

"Blake advised me on food, though the puppy can't live on cooked chicken and scrambled eggs forever."

"We can set up quarters in the back room and ask the store to suggest the best nourishment for a little dog."

"Thank you. Excellent ideas." Ivy picked up the phone to review upcoming customers' orders, ensuring she had all the necessary details and materials.

As the jingling of the bell above the door announced the arrival of a customer, she looked up and extended a welcome. Blake sauntered in with an easy confidence, a foam cup in hand, his charm undeniable.

Her heart skipped several beats.

His wavy hair tousled just enough over his forehead to give him a laid-back appeal. His eyes, a magnetic shade of blue, held a secret sparkle. Tall and confident, wearing faded jeans and a tan leather jacket, he commanded attention without even trying.

Ivy set down the phone. "Well, well, if it isn't the puppy's rescuer!"

"That would be you, not me." Blake flashed a charismatic smile. "I gave in to the impulse and came to see the guardian angel and the adorable pup."

"You really think I'm an angel for rescuing a puppy?" The idea of being an angel was oddly gratifying, but she wanted to clarify the sincerity behind his words. "I'm really not."

"You really are," he said. "Rescuing that little guy was quite a heroic act."

The appreciation in his gaze was unexpected, and she found herself experiencing a curious blend of pride and humility.

She reached for a small decorative dish of polished stones on the counter, and began arranging the stones in intricate patterns. "He was a stray pup who needed assistance, and it's reassuring that he's safe."

"Not everyone would've taken the time to help. By the way, where is our rescued pup?"

"He's off on a shopping spree with my co-worker, getting all the treats he deserves," Ivy replied with a chuckle. "What brings you to my flower shop today?"

"I was curious about where you worked your floral magic. I saw the exterior, and I wanted to see the interior."

"Welcome to my kingdom of blooms." Her fingers still moved gracefully over the stones in the dish, the clinking providing a soothing rhythm to their conversation. "Do all my flowers pass the test?"

Blake feigned contemplation. He looked around, scanning the shelves of frosty white candles and arrangements of pink peonies. "Hmm, it's a tough one, but you definitely earned a coveted spot on my Floral Artist Wall of Fame." He exhaled a dramatic sigh. "Don't let it go to your head, though. The flower fashionistas are a jealous bunch."

Ivy placed a hand over her heart in mock astonishment. "Moi? Perish the thought!"

"Besides, I couldn't resist the temptation of seeing these enchanting flowers and the even more enchanting florist." Blake flashed a roguish grin.

"I try my best."

"And you succeeded."

Ivy's cheeks warmed. She picked up a vintage watering can behind the counter and sprayed a few imaginary drops in his direction. "You're quite the smooth talker."

"And you're incredibly talented."

As they traded quips, Ivy smiled, enjoying their relaxed rapport. "Although truly, what's your reason for stopping by today?"

"The flowers, naturally." He motioned to the mini-Christmas trees grouped by the window, glittering in tinsel and candy-colored baubles. "I thought I'd repay last night's angel with more flowers. Any recommendations?"

The word *angel* made Ivy laugh softly. "Flowers for an

angel, huh? Like I said last night, these are my flowers. Mine. So, you plan to gift them back to me?"

"That's the plan," Blake said. "You can call me a smooth operator, as well as a smooth talker."

His mischievous gaze prompted her smile to grow wider. "How about some red roses? They represent admiration and gratitude."

"A bouquet of red roses for my rescuer, then."

"Correction," she replied. "You mean the puppy's rescuer? I didn't rescue *you*."

He shrugged, that mischievous glint ever present in his gaze. "Perhaps you did."

His words seemed to carry a hidden meaning, and a delightful warmth spread through her.

He wandered around the shop while she arranged the bouquet, and she was grateful he didn't see her flustered fingers and flushed cheeks.

"All set." She lifted the flowers, then handed the bouquet to him as he approached the counter.

His gaze met hers, a silent connection. He accepted the bouquet and immediately handed it back to her. "These are for you, Ivy. What do I owe you?"

"Consider it a gift. I'll do my best to give *my* roses the care they deserve." She contained her laugh as she arranged the flowers in a vase, then went to the sink to fill the vase with water. "I must say, you're quite the gallant rescuer yourself."

"It's easy to be chivalrous when I'm near a captivating woman." He set the foam cup on the counter. "This tea is for you. I've been carrying it around, so it probably cooled off by now."

She gasped, taken by surprise. His thoughtfulness was unexpected, and she wasn't sure how to respond. A part of her melted at his sincerity, though another part held back, hesitant to let her guard down.

"Thank you," she replied, genuinely appreciative.

She lifted the lid, the cool minty scent of the tea soothing and revitalizing. "You didn't forget our conversation from last night."

He grinned, clearly pleased. "Of course not. I clung to it like it was my lifeline. It was the perfect excuse to spend more time with you."

Excuse? Time with her? Was he flirting or merely being friendly?

Stop, she told herself. You're overthinking things.

"You didn't have to go through the trouble," she said aloud.

"No trouble at all, I assure you." His smile spread to his ocean-blue eyes, coaxing a tender, softened look from them. "However, I forgot your tea preferences. Cream? Sugar?"

"I never said."

"I ordered plain tea." He patted his jacket pocket. "I brought packets of cream and sugar, just in case."

"Plain is fine." She sipped and let out a satisfied, "Mmm, it's perfect."

"Anything for a talented florist and a new friend. You are my friend, right?"

She smiled. "I am."

"Good." Casually, he touched her hand. The gesture was simple, though it had a surprising effect on her, leaving her slightly breathless.

Ivy took another sip, buying herself time to think. She glanced at Blake's handsome face and embraced the moment. "You're extremely kind. I appreciate your thoughtfulness more than you can imagine."

"No worries, Ivy. That's what friends do."

Friends. New friends. Ivy clung to the words, letting them temper the burst of emotions inside her. For now, friends were enough. She would simply enjoy getting to know this fascinating man.

"Hey, remember us?" Amelia emerged from the back room, cradling the puppy in her arms. "I got all the supplies, including a leash, and set up an area on the floor for him near all the seasonal stock. He's sure to get into mischief chewing up the Boston ferns."

"Let's hope not," Ivy replied, then hesitated. "Wait, is a Boston fern a pet-safe plant?"

Amelia laughed. "Yes. Just kidding. We don't need a floral disaster on our hands. So, I bought a bumpy teething ring and a bunch of cute stuffed toys—a cuddly lamb and a furry raccoon."

Blake joined in the laugher. "Hi there, little fella," he said, bending to scratch the puppy's head.

"He's a boy," Ivy clarified.

With a genial smile, Blake winked. "So, I assumed."

"Aren't you just full of assumptions?" Ivy smirked. "Dr. Mitchell said that he's a Pomeranian."

"This lady here saved you from a freezing and lonely evening in the cold," Blake whispered, speaking to the puppy.

"Forgive my rudeness." Ivy turned to Amelia. "This is Amelia, my best friend and co-owner of the shop, and this is Blake, the guy I was telling you about."

"Ah, the mysterious stranger from last night." Amelia nudged Ivy and gave a conspiratorial smile. "Nice to meet you, Blake."

He stood and held out his hand. "Likewise. I hope Ivy didn't bore you with the story about my dog."

"Nope. We hadn't gotten that far. She was sharing how you accompanied her home. Gotta say, wrapping the puppy in your designer scarf was a bold move. I hope you don't expect to get it back in one piece."

"Hey, that scarf was sacrificed for a worthy cause."

"Uh-huh. We all know you wanted an excuse to play the dashing hero." Amelia turned to Ivy. "Looks like he's taken a liking to you. Chances are you should keep him."

Was Amelia referring to Blake or the puppy?

"I'm sure he has someone waiting for him," Ivy replied, trying to sound nonchalant.

"He doesn't," Blake chimed in. "By the way, have you named him yet?"

Ivy shook her head. The weightiness of the decision was tangible. Naming the puppy would make it even harder to say goodbye when the time came.

Amelia, ever the decisive one, stepped in. "Let's think of one," she said, temporarily stepping away to attend to a customer's inquiries.

Blake leaned against the counter. "How about something classic, like Max or Charlie?"

Amelia returned, immediately adding her input. "Nice, but we need a more unique name. This is the Christmas season, after all."

Ivy nodded. The puppy deserved a distinctive title that suited his personality. She gazed down at the dozing bundle of fur.

"He's frisky, and definitely has a mischievous side," she said, her thoughts drifting to the puppy's bouncy antics.

The threesome observed the puppy as he slept at their feet.

"How about Cocoa?" Ivy broke the silence. "It's sweet, just like him, and fits those adorable eyes."

Blake raised an eyebrow. "Cocoa? Are you sure you're naming a puppy and not a dessert?"

Ivy feigned offense. "He's as irresistible as a warm cup of cocoa on a winter's day."

Amelia chuckled. "I like it."

"Cocoa it is, then," Blake said.

Ivy sighed and glanced down at the puppy. This small but meaningful act marked forging the connection between them. An unspoken understanding now existed. With a simple moniker, she had claimed a place in his world and him in hers. He was no longer a stray, but someone deserving of an identity. The choice of the name was straightforward, but the significance behind it was profound.

"Cocoa fits him perfectly," Ivy decided.

"I agree," Blake replied.

She offered him a smile. Being around Blake stirred feelings she had locked away after her breakup with Will. They'd dated for a while, but their relationship had crashed and burned when Will admitted he didn't share Ivy's vision for a future together. Furthermore, she discovered that Will had been secretly in contact with his ex-girlfriend, meeting her behind Ivy's back, and planned to relocate with her. This breach of trust created a lasting sense of doubt and insecurity.

She was devastated. She dove into her floral business, shielding her heart from any potential hurt. Currently, Cocoa's unconditional love and Blake's thoughtfulness were thawing her reservations.

"I realize it's silly, but I feel a bond with this little guy already," she said. "Letting Cocoa go when the time comes will be difficult."

"That type of connection is instinctive." Amelia extended an understanding smile. "He's won you over, hasn't he?"

"I know nothing about his background."

"Your heart doesn't care about details," Blake put in. "It knows a good fit when it sees one."

Ivy took another sip of tea. "He's such a sweetheart, and I can't deny how much I already care for him."

A subtle change in Blake's expression revealed his empathy. "Is it possible that Cocoa was meant to be in your life for a reason?"

Perhaps.

Yet hesitation tempered her attachment. She had no experience caring for a pet. What if she fell short in providing Cocoa what he needed? The fear of making mistakes was a heavy presence.

"I worry that I won't give him the time and attention he deserves," she admitted.

"Yesterday morning," Blake began, "I wandered into town and witnessed the Wishing Blooms ceremony. There you were, spreading goodwill with your free flowers."

Ivy's eyes widened. She hadn't expected him to bring up the event. However, he'd been quick to steer their conversation regarding adopting Cocoa to a different topic, and his insight into her feelings cheered her up.

"Hang on, Blake. I thought I recognized you." Amelia placed her hands on her hips. "You were the guy with the camera yesterday. Are you some sort of a photographer?"

"Some sort," he replied with a nonchalant shrug.

"A photographer." Amelia's raised eyebrow was hard to miss, as well as her quick, almost imperceptible glance toward Ivy. It was as if she sent a silent signal for Ivy to pay attention.

Ivy felt a faint flicker of suspicion. Amelia's glance was so subtle that it could easily be dismissed as a casual movement. The name Blake Shepherd had come up in their earlier conversation, and she couldn't shake the feeling that there was a connection.

She mulled over the possibility that he was the famous photographer but decided not to jump to conclusions or ask him outright. Instead, she'd piece together the puzzle if more clues emerged.

"The ceremony was charming, and I couldn't help myself," Blake was saying. "I captured the special moments."

"Did you make a wish?" Amelia pressed.

"With the Wishing Blooms?" There was more than a hint of disbelief in his tone. "That kind of stuff isn't for me."

"Please don't use any of your photos on social media." Amelia glanced at Ivy. "We've had enough bad publicity lately."

"Anything I can do to assist?" he asked.

"Long story." Ivy smiled gratefully. "We're set, at least for now."

"Well, it seems like fate is bringing you two together at Christmas time." Amelia clapped her hands. "I propose a toast to friendships and adorable puppies!" She grabbed three small vases and filled them with evergreens, then handed a vase to each of them.

As they raised their vases and clinked, Ivy couldn't help thinking that Amelia was right—perhaps this encounter with Blake and the puppy was more than a coincidence. Sometimes, the universe had a funny way of bringing people together.

Amelia picked up the puppy and led Blake into the storage room, inquiring if she had purchased the correct food for Cocoa.

Soon afterward, Ethan stepped into the shop.

"Hi, Ethan. I'm just about done." Ivy grabbed his order and weaved gold tinsel through the poinsettia leaves.

"Hi, Ivy. No rush." Ethan looked around, then approached the counter. "By the way, have you heard?"

"Heard what?" Ivy sprinkled faux snow on the arrangement to give it a wintery feel, then glanced up. She hoped he wasn't going to relate some bad news about the critique of her shop in the *Gazette*.

"There's another florist moving in," Ethan answered.

"Who?"

"It's a franchise called Garden Elegance. Have you heard of it?"

Of course she had. The franchise had locations all over the country. She'd heard rumors that another florist might be opening.

Ivy's heart dropped. Competition was the last thing she needed right now, with Britney Knox's scathing article casting a shadow over her shop's reputation.

"When are they supposed to move in?" She forced a smile, handing the arrangement over to him. She'd worked so hard to build her modest floral business. Could she weather both a PR crisis and a brand-new rival on the scene? Her perseverance had seen her through difficult times before, though this threat was daunting.

"Soon," Ethan replied. "Word is around Valentine's Day."

Blake strode from the storage room and hesitated, studying Ivy's face.

"Everything okay here?" he asked.

"It will be." Ivy exhaled slowly. "Somehow."

No matter what, she refused to give up without a fight, only now she didn't have one fight. She had two.

CHAPTER 5

*T*he following day, Blake sat at the polished kitchen table across from his grandfather. They had decided on an early lunch.

Late morning light filtered through the gingham curtains covering the window above the sink. The aroma of ripe tomatoes and crispy, golden-brown bread permeated the vintage 50s-style kitchen with checkerboard tile floors.

A bowl of steaming tomato soup and a grilled cheese sandwich lay before him, the gooey cheese still melting. His grandfather dunked a corner of his own sandwich into his soup and took a hearty bite.

Outside, snow drifted past the curtains as the two ate in companionable silence. Blake swirled another spoonful of soup, letting the comforting flavor warm him on this clear, chilly day.

His grandfather finished chewing and wiped his mouth with a napkin. "The *Evergreen Gazette* arrived the other morning, and I'm freelancing for them part-time. I left the magazine under a pile of newspapers somewhere. I'll check to see if they used any of my photographs. I shot a bunch a while ago." He shuffled into the living room and returned to his seat at the table.

"Well, will you take a look at this." His grandfather held up the magazine. "One of my photos is on the cover!"

Blake smiled indulgently. His grandfather loved when his work was published.

"And here we are again." He thumbed through the magazine, grilled cheese in hand. "They featured all my shots of Ivy Bennett's flower shop."

"Ivy Bennett?" Blake paused and set down his spoon. "Can I see the article?"

His grandfather passed Blake the magazine. "She's a sweet woman, and her shop is lovely. Have you met her?"

"As a matter of fact, I have." As soon as Blake read the accompanying article, his smile faded. While the photos were stunning, capturing the whimsy and vibrancy of Ivy's shop, the harsh words aimed at her business didn't match the images at all.

Blake's muscles tensed as he skimmed through the cruel critique. His jaw tightened. His hands clenched into fists around the magazine.

This was completely unfair. Ivy dedicated herself to her flower shop.

He recalled the discussion between Ivy and Amelia the previous day.

"Please don't use any of your photos on social media." Amelia had glanced at Ivy. *"We've had enough bad publicity lately."*

"Anything I can do to assist?" Blake had asked.

"Long story." Ivy smiled gratefully. *"We're set, at least for now."*

He'd wondered about the discussion, though he hadn't pressed for details.

So that's what it had been about.

"The portrayal is extremely unfair," Blake said, unable to keep the frustration out of his voice. "The tone of the article is off, Grandpa, despite your gorgeous photos. Ivy puts her whole heart into that shop, and she doesn't deserve to be criticized this way."

His appetite abandoned, Blake stood and placed his bowl in the sink. He snatched the magazine and his jacket, then yanked open the door.

"I'm going to Ivy's shop to show my support. Thanks for lunch, Grandpa. Is there anything you need while I'm out? I can pick up some groceries."

His grandfather's gaze dropped to Blake's half-eaten sandwich; the cheerful mood now fractured. "Not a thing," he murmured, the critical article about Ivy's Blooms settling between them like an unwelcome guest.

"I'll see you tonight, then," Blake replied.

A short while later, the bells on Ivy's florist shop made a tinkling sound as Blake entered.

The acoustic guitar strumming "Have Yourself a Merry Little Christmas," a nostalgic tune, complemented the seasonal interior. The windows were lined with animated blooms—amaryllis, cyclamen, and cheerful paperwhites. Slowly, he was learning the names of Ivy's precious flowers.

Several Christmas candles burned, and the surroundings were rich with the delightful scent of pine needles and spiced oranges.

He spotted Ivy behind her worktable, meticulously arranging peppermint-striped carnations into a cylinder vase. Her blond hair cascaded in loose waves around her shoulders, and a faint squint accompanied the determined set of her hazel eyes. A smattering of freckles graced her cheeks and the bridge of her small, turned-up nose, giving her a youthful and innocent allure.

Everything about her had an understated appeal that drew him in.

Nonetheless, her movements were rapid and tense.

Managing the puppy in addition to her business was clearly taking a toll.

Blake held back, not wanting to disrupt her creative process. There was something captivating about watching her craft floral arrangements. The way her elegant fingers skillfully transformed stems, flowers, and leaves into art.

After a final tweak to the bouquet, Ivy glanced up.

A radiant smile curved her lips, a vision that cast an undeniable brightness to the space. "Blake, you're here!" She circled the worktable to greet him. "How good to see you again."

"I had an urge to stop by." More than an urge, though that would do for now.

Casually, he folded the magazine and placed it in the inner pocket of his jacket. His hands itched to crumple those unjust pages.

She'd been functioning tirelessly. This conversation about the negative article was emotionally taxing, and he decided it was better to wait. Yet beneath his calm exterior, indignation churned.

He strode over to her, his thoughts a storm of contemplation. The desire to press a quick, friendly kiss on her cheek flickered through his mind, though he held back. Friends— that was the label they wore. But did it encompass all they were? The uncertainty persisted, a question he couldn't quite answer.

"I hoped for an update on how you and Cocoa are getting along," he said.

At the sound of his name, the puppy came bounding out from the back room. His little legs carried him enthusiastically over to Blake, tongue lolling in a doggie grin.

Ivy laughed, her cadence inviting and melodic. Her clear fondness for the dog awakened an emotion Blake couldn't quite label. Was it contentment? Affection? Or something deeper?

He squatted to give Cocoa's ears a friendly rub, earning a happy wag of the tail in response before the puppy scurried off.

Blake complimented her festive shop as he rose.

"I love this season." Ivy's eyes gleamed. "Everything is more magical in December."

"It's only December fourth. You have an entire month to celebrate."

"That's the beauty of it, Blake. With a whole month of magic ahead, there are countless opportunities for celebration."

He nodded, though he didn't fully understand. Christmas had lost its luster ever since Jason had passed away. Before that, even. Way before that. Nonetheless, seeing Ivy's enthusiasm made him wish he could recapture that childlike awe again.

"Is our favorite puppy being a good boy?" he inquired. A mischievous rustling drew his focus, and he chuckled as the furry culprit attempted to unravel a ribbon from a stack of gift boxes.

"That depends on your definition of good," Ivy said.

"Uh-oh."

"Cocoa is a handful." Her voice lacked the usual rise and fall, a monotone betraying her tiredness, though a fond smile creased her lips. "This morning, I caught him trying to sneak away with a pink feather from one of the displays. And then I rescued my prized garden gloves from his clutches. He's quite the curious explorer, though his boundless energy is undeniably appealing."

Blake smiled. "Undeniably, I'm sure."

His heart went out to her as he imagined the scene with a mixture of empathy and amusement. A frisky chaos, the tug-of-war over feathers and gloves, the inevitable mess that accompanied a feisty puppy.

Here, he witnessed her in a different perspective—not the composed florist. Instead, a woman who laughed in the face of unexpected antics, who embraced the whirlwind side of life with an open heart. His admiration for her patience and resilience grew, and he wanted to provide some relief for her.

"How did last night go?" he inquired.

"You mean, did I get any sleep?"

"Yeah."

"Umm. No. That tiny scamp kept me on my toes long after the shop closed. As soon as we arrived home, he started chewing on everything he could get his teeth on—my boots, the coffee table legs, you name it." Ivy shook her head. "I finally settled him with a toy Amelia purchased. He loves the furry raccoon."

"Where is Amelia, by the way?" Blake asked.

"She had a dentist appointment and should be back within the hour." Ivy turned to trim the stems of a bouquet, her attention divided between the flowers and Blake. "Anyway, I sat down to sketch a design for a sunroom display for a client, and Cocoa was off again, racing around my kitchen table."

"You dared to sit down?" Blake teased.

"I know. What was I thinking?" She rolled her eyes. "I puppy-proofed my living room by getting on the floor to see things from Cocoa's perspective. I tied up and hid cords and wires, anything temptingly chewable."

"Did it help?"

"Yes, although Cocoa tried to climb my Christmas tree. Luckily, I stopped him."

"Your tree is up already?"

"Next week is almost the middle of December, so yes, my

tree is up. A three-foot fir, nothing too fancy. I decorated it with mini white lights and red and gold bulbs. Oh, and I placed a few ornaments on it—a miniature snowman with a garland, a glittery pinecone, and a crimson bow." She laughed. "Needless to say, that tree is no longer on the floor. I set it on an end table. Thank goodness puppies don't fly."

"Most likely, your home mirrors your style," Blake acknowledged. The image she narrated took shape in his imagination, her living space radiating her personality.

"My home is an ideal fit for me." She smiled. "As I sat in my kitchen, I visualized where else I could add holiday flair —perhaps a tiny village with cotton-like snow on the mantel, or a vanilla-scented candle in a glass holder on the end table."

"Always the artist," he murmured.

"Nothing over the top." She kept her smile undisturbed, even as she noted the mess Cocoa had made with the ribbon. Excusing herself from their discussion, Ivy lifted the puppy before he created any more havoc.

"Cocoa, you little rascal." Her grip on him tightened as his tiny paws scrambled against her hold.

She came closer to Blake. "Do you mind holding him for a minute while I deal with this mess?"

"Sure." Blake grinned as Ivy handed him the wriggling bundle of fur.

As Blake steadied the pup, he felt the energetic vibrations coursing through Cocoa's tiny body. The puppy's inquisitive stare connected with his, and Blake found himself drawn into a moment of shared curiosity.

"When we turned in for the night, I hoped we'd both sleep soundly," Ivy continued, as she discarded the chewed ribbon in a trash can. "But no, Cocoa had other plans. Up every other minute, whining and licking my face. At dawn, I was zombie-like, barely able to drag myself out of bed." She sighed softly, her fatigue seeming to ease as she reminisced.

"I had to remake my bed three times while he destroyed another pair of my shoes. Though one look into those big brown eyes and I can't stay mad."

Blake chuckled. He inched closer to Ivy, and a meaningful smile passed between them—an unspoken understanding of the pup's lively nature. "You're doing an excellent job with him, Ivy."

"I've contacted my friends and some of my loyal customers, inquiring if they were interested in adopting Cocoa or knew someone who might be. The vet said it was okay to do so." She stepped back behind the worktable and selected eucalyptus leaves and juniper sprigs, crafting a fragrant Christmas wreath. "I also posted some flyers in town."

"I saw a couple on the park's notice board as I walked here."

"My goal is to find Cocoa a home." Her stance shifted slightly, as if torn between two choices—the urge to keep the pup and the practicality of letting him go.

Blake caught the emotional turmoil in Ivy's eyes, a flash of uncertainty that gave way to a guarded mask.

She had already bonded with the puppy. Losing him would shatter her heart.

"He sure is a cute little rascal," Blake said. "Reminds me of all the trouble my own pup, CooperCam, caused at that age. There was this one time when…"

Quickly, he steered the conversation to a funny memory, hoping to give Ivy a brief respite from her worries.

When she laughed, he asked, "Are you planning to purchase a Christmas tree for your shop?" As the little pup moved restlessly in his hold, he eased him onto the linoleum floor, and Cocoa promptly darted around the counter.

"I planned to pick out a tree with Amelia this upcoming weekend, though she volunteered to select the tree without me. I have plenty on my plate with keeping up with this puppy."

Ivy's description of trees and decorating stirred Blake's memories of the Christmas tree at his grandfather's house.

The tree was situated in the living room, a solid six-foot fir. When he was a child, it had been decked out with shimmering glass baubles, resin figurines, and piles of neatly folded gifts, every ribbon precisely curled.

Sadly, since his grandmother had passed, Blake had only returned to Evergreen Valley a couple of times and noticed that his grandfather's holiday decor was more understated. The tree was adorned with silver tinsel and a handful of heirloom enhancements—Blake's favorites being a vintage train carriage and antique miniature sleigh. No more massive piles of presents.

Still, the tree filled the room with the magical scent of pine. In the commotion of arriving, Blake hadn't commented on it.

He smiled to himself. Here, he had just teased Ivy for having her tree up already, and his grandfather's tree was up as well.

He made a mental note to accompany his grandfather to pick out a tree topper, because the shiny metallic star had broken some years back. A nostalgic ornament would keep the old traditions alive.

A FEW DAYS LATER, the sun hung low in a gray sky as Blake strolled toward the park with Ivy and Cocoa. A whisper-thin layer of snow covered the grass, with the air hanging motionless.

Ivy had agreed on taking the afternoon off while Amelia stayed at the shop with a couple of extra part-time workers.

Ivy had worked endless hours, and Blake convinced her that a break would do her good.

Ivy was bundled in dark jeans, tan boots, and her red quilted coat. Her blond hair spilled out from under a substantial ivory scarf. Her cheeks were tinged pink, whether from the chill or the laughter they shared, Blake couldn't tell.

He wore his favored brown leather jacket, the one Ivy said made him look like an old-time pilot. He hoped she meant it as a compliment. Beside him, Cocoa frolicked through the snowdrifts, his red sweater that Amelia had bought for him making him easy to spot.

Initially, Ivy had been hesitant to take Cocoa for a walk, but Blake reminded her how important exercise and socialization were for puppies. However, she pointed out potential dangers lurking around every corner. There were sharp objects on the ground, aggressive dogs, or getting lost in the snowy landscape.

"Stay close, Cocoa," she warned, maintaining a firm grip on his bright neon-green leash.

Their stroll continued, and Blake noted a sight that held a special place in the heart of the community—the Evergreen Chapel. Its walls were constructed from sturdy fieldstone, and a steeple rose majestically, crowned with a pristine white cross that seemed to reach for the heavens.

"Even when I was young, I admired the windows," he said. Adorned with intricate stained glass, the colors painted the ground with vivid hues of red, blue, and gold.

"Do you attend church often?" Ivy asked.

"When I was a kid, I went with my grandfather. Not so much anymore." He turned to her. "You?"

She smiled. "Every Sunday."

As they drew closer, the distant strains of a Christmas hymn, "Silent Night," sung by a choir, carried by on a light wind. The wooden doors were carved with meticulous detail, and a modest wreath of evergreen and holly graced the entrance.

They soon passed Nonna's Bistro, a much-loved spot for Blake. The restaurant was known for its unmatched Italian dishes, and the air carried subtle traces of melted mozzarella, garlic, and simmering tomatoes.

"I've traveled a fair amount, and I've never found food that compares to theirs," Blake said. "Especially their home-made fettuccini in a white Alfredo sauce."

"I'm with you on that, though it's a fancy place for Evergreen Valley."

"This town is fortunate to have a restaurant of this caliber," he said. He reminded himself to treat her to a meal there soon. Ivy's compassionate heart and caring spirit exuded more grace than any conventional socialite. "Although the company is what makes any meal truly special."

He gazed at Ivy, taken by her inner and outer beauty. She could wear a potato sack and still outshine anyone.

She blushed. "You certainly know how to make a woman feel special."

He smiled. "I just want you to know how special you are."

Children in fleece-lined coats squealed and lobbed snow-balls at a freshly minted snowman, and Ivy's face brightened. "Shall we build a snowman for Cocoa?"

"He'd love that. The park is safe, so let's unleash him for a few minutes." Blake smiled, delighted to see her excitement break through the cloud of exhaustion that had surrounded her.

Kneeling, Blake and Ivy packed icy handfuls of snow into a large round base. Cocoa darted around them, his tail reflecting his enthusiasm as he tried to catch the falling flakes.

"Ready for the snowman's head?" Ivy shaped a smaller

sphere, her slender fingers reddened by the cold. Blake confirmed and lifted the head onto the base with a dramatic grunt.

Ivy gathered sticks, breaking them to size for arms.

With tongue peeking out, Cocoa pressed his paws into the snowman's middle, molding imperfections.

"He's helping!" Ivy said. She found a discarded Santa hat on the ground, slightly worn. Carefully placing it on the snowman's head, the hat transformed the snowman into the beloved figure of Santa Claus.

At least, that was what she declared. Although Blake was inclined to disagree, he kept his opinion to himself.

The best part wasn't the snowman itself. The best part was the way Ivy's spirit had been reawakened. He kept that thought to himself, too.

He slung an arm around her shoulder, both admiring their creation—lumpy in spots, though Blake labeled it as enchanting.

"Not bad for amateurs," he said. "What do you think, Cocoa?"

Barking with enthusiasm, the pup leapt with surprising height, trying to nip at the snowman.

Afterward, Blake, Ivy, and Cocoa walked through town, the puppy secure again on his short leash—light and adjustable with a swivel clip.

"I'll hold his leash for a while," Blake volunteered. He soon realized that walking a puppy proved more challenging than he'd anticipated. Cocoa seemed to have a mind of his own, pulling at the leash and stopping every few feet to sniff something, most notably snow-covered rocks or puddles of melting snowflakes. Blake found himself constantly tugging Cocoa along, trying to establish some semblance of control.

Ivy released a sigh as they passed an empty storefront on Central Avenue, a couple of blocks from her shop. "This is where Garden Elegance is moving in. I can't compete with a franchise. They have brand recognition, support, and a business model."

Blake nodded, understanding the significance. "Hey, your shop is irreplaceable. Customers value a hometown business because you bring a personal touch."

"Sadly, it will be overshadowed by their marketing and advertising budget. And then, there's the issue of pricing. The store's buyers have the funds to purchase flowers in bulk and will potentially undercut my prices."

"You provide uniqueness and artistry. They don't."

"Still, customers might flock there seeking more affordable options."

"They won't. You'll see."

There was a hint of warmth in Ivy's smile, though the crease between her eyebrows told a different story—one of underlying apprehension.

Blake hesitated and handed Ivy back the leash, then pulled *The Evergreen Gazette* from his pocket. He might as well tackle another difficult subject. He'd been carrying the magazine around for days.

"Speaking of unique, my grandfather took some beautiful photographs of your Wishing Blooms. For a hobby photographer he's quite talented."

He opened to the article featuring the shop.

Ivy winced and held up a hand. "I've seen this. Thanks."

"My grandfather didn't realize—"

She blinked. Once. Twice. "So, it is true. Your grandfather is Everett Shepherd."

"Yes."

"And you're Blake. Blake Shepherd. I suspected but wasn't sure."

Blake nodded.

"Why didn't you come clean about this sooner?"

"I wasn't trying to hide anything. In any case, we're on your side." Blake paused and locked gazes with her, forcing her to stop walking. "As a professional photographer, I realize how special your shop is. Don't lose heart. This town needs your gifts."

"Hang on, Blake. Let's go backward for a minute." She shook her head, as if trying to clear it by stating his name. "Then you're Blake Shepherd?"

"Yes, we've established that."

"The photographer?"

"Yes. I told you I was a photographer. Remember? The night you found the puppy."

"No. You mentioned sending a portfolio to a well-known gallery in New York City for a holiday exhibition. I assumed you were an artist."

"I am. A photographer is considered an artist."

A stunned silence wedged its way between them, and she shook her head.

"I should've asked you outright," she replied. "In the flower shop, you mentioned you were sort of a photographer."

"No. I said some sort."

"That's even more vague. You were obviously evading the question. I wondered. I should have—" Sharply, she inhaled. "All these...disclosures...revelations...in one afternoon. What else are you hiding?"

"Ivy, there's nothing more to it. No hidden agendas, I promise."

They continued until Main Street intersected with Birch Avenue, and she settled onto a wooden bench outside of McKinley's Ice Cream Shop.

"Thanks for being honest with me, though this is a lot to absorb. And knowing your grandfather shot those photos for the article..." Ivy sighed, looking away. "Truthfully, it stings."

Blake scuffed his boot against a patch of ice. "I'm sorry. I should've been upfront. For what it's worth, my grandfather had no idea what would be written in the article. We both recognize your effort and how irrational those criticisms are."

"Is there anything else I should know?" Ivy managed a weak smile, but Blake knew the wounds ran deeper than his words could heal. Rebuilding trust took time.

"Do you want me to begin with my life story?" he half joked.

"We can start there."

He debated what details to share as he sat across from her. "My grandfather encouraged me to pursue photography at a young age. Over the years, I made a name for myself. I shot magazine covers for *National Geographic*, won some awards. Did a stint as a celebrity photographer in LA."

"Because you're Blake Shepherd."

"Nothing to brag about, I assure you." He rubbed the back of his neck. "The glitz and glam never suited me. I told you I returned here to regain my footing, and that's true. I want to discover the simple pleasure of taking photos of nature and people again, like my grandfather once inspired me to do."

Cautiously, he made eye contact with her. Would she treat him differently now? See him as some hotshot rather than Blake, the guy from a small town? The guy who shared that same small town with her.

Her hazel eyes, usually lively and expressive, held a muted wariness.

He cleared his throat and focused on the icicles dangling from the pine trees, refracting the sunlight into a spectrum of rainbow colors.

Neither he nor Ivy spoke.

With a friendly grin that tempered the lines in his face, Mr. McKinley, the owner, emerged from the entrance of his ice cream parlor, chalkboard menu in hand. The silver threads in his hair glinted in the flickering lights strung across the shop's window.

"Afternoon folks. What can I getcha? The usual, Ivy?" His apron showed a splash of shades reminiscent of his frozen dessert creations.

"A scoop of pistachio ice cream in a dish, please," Ivy said.

"And for the cute pup?"

She set the puppy on the ground, securing his leash to the table leg. "We'd better not. He's too young. He's only eating puppy food."

Mr. McKinley pivoted to Blake. "What will you have, sir?"

"Maple walnut ice cream. Two scoops in a dish," Blake replied.

When Mr. McKinley returned with their orders, he peered at Ivy over his spectacles. "Now don't you worry 'bout that fancy flower shop moving in on Central Avenue. Your Wishing Blooms are a town treasure."

Ivy managed a faint smile. "Thank you. You're very thoughtful."

"We small businesses must stick together." McKinley leaned in conspiratorially. "Though I hear the author of that nasty article, that Britney Knox, has reason to want your shop gone. Seems her boyfriend owns the new Garden Elegance place. He bought the franchise." He tapped his nose. "Mark my words, that's why she wrote such lies about you in the *Gazette*."

Ivy's lips slightly parted. "Do you really think so?"

"I surely do," Mr. McKinley said.

"We won't let her succeed." Blake set down his spoon. His fingers drummed a steady rhythm on the table, in sync with his resolve. "Your flower shop is too important to this community."

"You tell her, son," Mr. McKinley said, then turned to Ivy.

"I gave you an extra scoop of pistachio because you're one of my favorite customers. You've been coming here a long time."

Glistening tears gathered in her eyes. "Many, many thanks."

After Mr. McKinley stepped back inside, Ivy stopped talking for several minutes, vigorously stirring her ice cream to soften it.

Blake cherished their friendship. He cherished their companionship. Her quirky humor, compassion and gigantic fortitude proved extraordinary. He wanted to preserve their connection. That much was clear to him.

His relationship with Ivy was taking on a deeper significance, something that resonated on a level he hadn't anticipated. He couldn't deny the way his heart quickened whenever she looked at him.

"Ivy?" he asked.

"What is it?" Her hazel-colored eyes held a straightforward honesty.

"Am I forgiven?" His inquiry was soft, almost a whisper.

"Absolutely." Her expression radiated forgiveness, a clean slate awaiting new beginnings. "However successful you are, you're still the same thoughtful man who walked me and Cocoa home that first night. I've seen your photos, and your photography reflects your beautiful heart."

Blake let out a breath he hadn't realized he was holding.

Guided by an irresistible impulse, he leaned across the table, and his fingers gently lifted her chin. Their breaths mingled in the crisp, cold air. And then he kissed her.

Everything around them faded in the exquisite touch of their lips. The touch was electric, a silent confirmation of their attraction to each other. He felt the breath of her exhale, a shared moment suspended.

"Ivy," he murmured, his voice husky as he deepened the kiss.

A plump squirrel bolted down the sidewalk, just out of Cocoa's reach. The pup instinctively lunged after it, slipping out of his collar.

Their kiss was abruptly hijacked.

"No, Cocoa!" Ivy jumped to her feet. At his tiny size, the little dog was in grave danger against the snowy streets and traffic.

Blake threw some bills on the table and pushed back the bench.

In unspoken unity, Blake and Ivy rushed out into the falling dusk, frantically scanning for any sign of the runaway pup, who had quickly disappeared.

CHAPTER 6

*F*ear clutched Blake's heart. They had to find tiny Cocoa before the puppy strayed into traffic. And he was committed to setting things straight with Ivy. Their relationship was too important.

His breath came in panicked gasps as he sprinted down the sidewalk after Cocoa. The tiny pup was a blur of red knit disappearing into the snowy dusk.

"Cocoa!" Blake shouted, his voice bouncing off the deserted street. He cast a quick glance over his shoulder. Ivy was close behind him, her eyes widening in terror, mirroring his own apprehension.

Blake's protective instincts surged—for both the puppy and Ivy. He understood how devastated she would be if something happened to the puppy.

"That way!" Ivy cried, pointing as Cocoa's bright red sweater flashed under a streetlamp half a block away. Blake raced after him, his boots skidding on the frozen ground, momentarily throwing him off balance. As they drew closer, Cocoa stopped to sniff a snowbank, oblivious to the chaos he'd caused.

Blake slowed his pace and clicked his tongue, crouching down to appear less threatening. "Here boy," he cooed affectionately. "Come on back."

Cocoa's ears perked up. He bounded over to Blake, his tail in motion and his body ready to play. Blake swept him into his arms, both relieved and amazed that the wandering pup had made it this far without incident.

Ivy hurried over, breathless. "Oh, thank goodness! Don't you ever run off again, you silly pup," she scolded, grabbing Cocoa from Blake. The dog licked her nose affectionately.

Blake tousled Cocoa's fur, adrenaline fading as his heartbeat steadied. "He is definitely a pro at finding an adventure."

"He's going to be the death of me," Ivy said with a shaky laugh. "Blake, is it convenient for you to walk me home? It's not far from here."

"I know where you live, remember?" he joked.

Yet an undercurrent of awkwardness remained, the delightful memory of their kiss coloring the moment.

Blake was uncertain about what to say, so he opted for practical matters.

"Is the holiday toy drive scheduled to take place soon?" he asked.

The worry that had clouded her features lifted, replaced by an animated expression. "Oh yes! My flower shop is contributing a portion of our earnings from every sale. In addition, we're donating four large arrangements for the silent auction. The goal this year is to raise five thousand dollars. The kids adore picking out brand-new toys."

He smiled, picturing Ivy designing the flower displays. "Want me to go with you? I'm more than willing to lend a hand."

"Certainly," she said, meeting his gaze. "An extra set of hands is always welcome."

"I can provide professional portraits, a keepsake for the families after the children receive their toys."

"Excellent idea. I'm sure your skills will be well received."

He also decided to contribute a substantial sum of money to the event.

He hoped spending more time together would help smooth over any lingering unease.

Not to mention that interrupted kiss.

Which he was absolutely not thinking about right now.

They strolled at an easy pace, Cocoa on his leash, a cheerful link between them. Snowflakes drifted down lazily, providing a touch of winter enchantment. Shop windows illuminated the street, presenting an attractive backdrop to the darkening sky.

Cocoa kept stealing glances at Blake, his tail swaying in rhythm with his excitement.

"I think you have a secret admirer," Ivy teased as she nodded toward Cocoa, then back at Blake.

"What can I say?" He loved that they could tease each other in this way. "I have a gift for impressing women…like yourself."

Ivy raised a delicate eyebrow. "Oh, really? Is that so?"

Cocoa tried to wedge between them, and Blake laughed. "Although I might have some competition here." He stooped down to give the puppy an affectionate pat.

Cocoa was great, but Ivy was the one who truly held Blake's undivided attention.

They arrived at her Cape Cod-style house and stood on her front doorstep. She lifted the wriggling puppy, her cheeks pink from the chilly weather. She was gorgeous inside and out, and Blake counted himself lucky to have met her.

She shivered. "Would you care to come in for a bit? I can make us some hot chocolate."

He beamed at her invitation. "I'd love to."

Ivy shifted Cocoa to one arm as she unlocked the door. "You're welcome to make yourself comfortable," she said, stepping aside so Blake could enter.

He helped her off with her coat and scarf and stepped into the snug warmth of her home. After stamping off his boots on the doormat and sliding them off, he hung his jacket on a coat rack. The scent of vanilla and cloves welcomed him as he surveyed the living room.

Ivy placed Cocoa on the floor, and the puppy bounded over to sniff Blake's boots.

Blake chuckled. "Someone's curious about your unfamiliar guest."

"Cocoa definitely loves people," she replied. "You, particularly."

She removed her boots and slipped on a pair of snug slippers. She was so small, so petite. So lovely.

Positioned against the backdrop of her comfortable living room, her dainty frame brought a private glimpse into her world. He admired the charming decor—the couch's classic plaid pattern and fluffy earth-toned pillows. She'd decorated the room with merry touches of Christmas, from the pinecones scattered on the mantel to the two stockings hanging above the fireplace. One stocking had an elegant, traditional design with intricate patterns and shimmering gold accents. The other, slightly smaller, featured paw prints and a cute bone motif.

"One for me, and one for Cocoa," she explained before Blake could ask.

"Thank you for inviting me to come inside," he said again.

Her smile revealed a charming dimple. "I'm glad you accepted my invitation."

"Being with you feels…right." He tenderly brushed a wisp of hair from her face.

Her eyes flickered with a hint of surprise, and her lips curled into a faint, appreciative smile. "Would you mind lighting a fire in the fireplace while I tend to the dog?" she asked. "I love a fire on a freezing night, and everything you need should be there."

"Happily." He stepped to the hearth, surveying the firewood. He rolled a newspaper and ignited a fire starter among the kindling, and soon, the smoky fragrance spread through the air. Flames leapt to life, and the logs found their place, crackling with a warm radiance.

"Here, Cocoa," she called from the kitchen, offering him a miniature bowl of carefully portioned puppy food. "You must be starving after scaring us half to death."

Cocoa darted over, sniffing at the food before hungrily digging in.

Ivy sat on the floor next to him, tenderly running her fingers through his fur.

Blake stood by the doorway, absorbing it all and admiring her thoughtfulness.

"By the way, how is his potty training coming along?" he asked. "Good, I hope?"

"You're kidding, right? I'm trying to establish a routine with him and use positive reinforcement. As you might imagine, I'm not having much luck yet."

"Watch for signs," Blake said, as the puppy sniffed and circled the kitchen.

She glanced down at the puppy. "Like that, for instance?"

"I'll take him outside." Blake scooped up Cocoa. "Where is his leash?"

"On the counter. You're welcome to use the back door that leads to my fenced-in backyard." She motioned to a door in the kitchen. "My routine is leading him to the same spot by the oak tree. And hoping."

Blake laughed. When he returned a short while later, he declared the outing a success.

"Alright, since you've eaten and gone outside, how about some playtime?" Blake posed the question to the dog. He grabbed a rubber toy lying on the throw rug near the sink—a cherry-red squeaky ball decorated with green holly leaves. "Christmas-themed, and especially for you, courtesy of Amelia!"

Blake sent the toy sailing across the kitchen. The puppy darted after it, his fluffy tail a blur of excitement. Over the symphony of squeaks, Ivy's laughter joined in.

"Time to wind down, Cocoa." Her breathing steadied as she caught her breath. "A nap is certainly in order."

Cocoa trotted over, dropping the toy at her feet before curling up on the throw rug by the sink. His bright eyes half-closed, and a soft, relaxed breath escaped through his button-like nose.

"Odds are that you could use a nap, too," Blake teased her.

"I definitely could," she confirmed, "though I'm fine for now. Care for that mug of hot chocolate?"

"I'd never say no. Is there anything you need help with?"

"I'm set. This will only take a few minutes."

Blake sank into her plaid couch in the living room while Ivy prepared two mugs of rich hot chocolate, using milk steamed on the stove. Her method was simple, tablespoons of cocoa powder, sugar, and a pinch of salt and cinnamon, stirring the cocoa blend into the milk until it was creamy. She mixed in vanilla, and soon a delectable, chocolatey aroma saturated the little home.

Curiosity guiding his actions, Blake strode over to a side shelf to check out her various frames. One was an award she'd received for Florist of the Year. Another was an inspirational quote, followed by a candid shot of Ivy and Amelia, along with some seashells and trinkets.

His hands momentarily paused before he picked up another photo. A framed photo of Ivy with a guy.

"Who is he?" he asked, his tone measured as Ivy approached him, carrying two mugs of cocoa whimsically topped with whipped cream and sprinkles.

"That's Will," she replied, setting the mugs on a side table.

"Will," Blake repeated, his gaze briefly assessing the man. He couldn't overlook the distinct indifference in the man's posture, as though he always held the upper hand. "And who is he to you?"

Frustration tinged her hazel eyes, a brief glint of exasperation making its presence known. "He's an old friend, Blake. There's nothing more to explain."

He tilted his head. "Seems like there's a lot more history behind that photo."

"Our relationship has its own story, but it's in the past," she replied, her voice carrying a weight that spoke of closure. "We broke up."

"How old is this picture?"

"Over a year."

"And this guy's photo is still in your living room?" Blake's eyebrows drew together as his gaze lingered on the image. Will's sleek black hair was styled with calculated precision, and his smug expression exuded a self-assured arrogance that Blake found hard to ignore.

"Ours was a complicated split, but it's been a season of growth and learning for me."

"What did you learn?" Blake asked.

She released a contemplative breath. "I learned that guarding my heart is essential. People enter, people exit my life. I learned it's wiser not to get too attached."

He digested her words, touched by the melancholy that had slipped into the conversation.

"I'm not going anywhere," he said softly.

She shrugged. "Maybe. Maybe not."

"I'm having a hard time understanding why you'd choose to keep this photo."

"This is a memory, Blake." Her fingers traced the edges of the frame. "A part of my journey that has led me to this current moment with you."

He smiled. The heaviness that had settled on his chest lifted. "Can you describe this current moment?"

"I can. Like this." She stood on her tiptoes and kissed him on the cheek. "We all have our pasts, but our present is what truly matters."

He bent and kissed her, their breaths mingling.

"I'm sorry for overreacting," he said.

"Apology accepted. If anything, it's a bit of a compliment." She lifted the mugs from the table. "Now, can we enjoy our hot chocolate before it gets cold?"

A few moments later, they sat on the couch, her legs tucked beneath her. The fire blazed steadily, its heat gradually seeping into Blake's bones.

He draped his arm around her shoulders. "This hits the spot, thanks," he said after a few relaxing sips. "I thought they only sold hot chocolate in powdery packets at the grocery store. That's how I've always made it. Add some boiling water, and you're all set."

"Congratulations! You learned something new today. Homemade doesn't always require lots of extra time."

He pulled a crochet blanket over their laps. "Still concerned about the chain store?" he asked.

"More than I care to admit. I can't shake the feeling that it'll be impossible for Ivy's Blooms to compete. What if we lose all our customers? What if we're forced to close?"

He pressed a kiss on her hair, breathing in the floral scent of freshly bloomed roses. "That won't happen."

"I'm inclined to believe you're biased, despite my appreciation for your support."

"Admittedly, yes, I am." He set down his mug and gently tilted her chin up. He leaned in slowly, giving her time to pull away if she wanted.

But she didn't.

"And I don't regret it at all," he said.

Their lips met again in a gentle kiss that deepened naturally. Blake lost himself in the sweetness of her lips, the closeness of her body. This felt different from their impulsive kiss earlier today. This kiss was deeper, more intimate, with no reservations.

Time stood still as the flames of the fireplace flickered, casting a play of shadows on the walls. He couldn't imagine being anywhere else except here with Ivy, sharing this perfect unhurried moment. This was more than merely an attraction between them.

When the kiss ended, he caressed her cheek, deciding not to voice the words he was thinking.

She sat back. "I wish there was a surefire method to keep Ivy's Blooms afloat."

"Maybe, just maybe, there is."

She turned to face him. "What do you have in mind?"

"Your floral designs are outstanding." He tapped his fingers on his chin. "People need to see them, to be reminded of the elegance and artistry that your business brings to Evergreen Valley."

A blush crept up Ivy's cheeks as she took in his words. "How can I extend my reach? My advertising budget is nonexistent."

"Social media," he stated simply.

"I do social media."

"What do you do?"

She shrugged. "I post photos of my designs on Facebook and Instagram."

"That's not enough to compete nowadays," he replied. "I'll help showcase your designs on various platforms. We'll use hashtags and partner with influencers. We'll also include details about your Wishing Blooms to generate interest and curiosity. People are drawn to enchanting tales."

"Wishing Blooms are a lot more than enchanting tales," she said.

"The blooms have a special significance for those who believe in hope," he countered. "I'll give you that."

A subtle crease formed between her eyebrows. His statement had clearly touched a sensitive chord.

However, she listened intently, posing questions at the possibilities Blake presented.

"I've never considered social media seriously. I assumed it wouldn't make much of a difference in my type of small-town business. However, with your know-how and enthusiasm, it seems a viable option."

"It is possible. Very possible. Do you have a website?"

She shook her head. "No."

"A simple website is easy to set up."

"Can you help? You're busy enough with your own work."

"Of course," he responded immediately. "For the record, I'm not busy at the moment. I left everything behind in Seattle."

Almost everything.

On the outside, he represented success. The luxury high-rise apartment with sweeping city views, the platinum watch, the extravagant meals, had all the trappings of a man who had made it.

Inside, an unsatiable voice demanded more. No matter how many high-profile events he covered, that voice was never satisfied. He was successful, yes, but it wasn't enough. He always wanted to strive higher.

Months ago, he'd submitted photographs to the Catherine Eden Gallery in New York City for an upcoming multi-artist exhibition. He'd briefly mentioned it to Ivy.

This particular exhibition would be mounted before Christmas and run into January. Exhibitions often attracted the attention of art critics, journalists, and bloggers, as well as reviews in the press. Upon a successful exhibition, the gallery often agreed to represent and promote the photographer on an ongoing basis. It might also lead to a full-blown show for him.

Owned by a renowned art curator, Catherine's gallery was one of the most prestigious in the country. Blake had long dreamed of having his work displayed there.

The submission process for the gallery had been a deeply invested pursuit. First, he'd meticulously curated twenty of his most captivating photos, each a poignant message in its own right. Among them was a photograph that spoke of the urgency in protecting forests and preserving biodiversity: a lone tree stump defiantly standing alone in a cleared forest, its presence a powerful plea.

Then, there was his "Pollution Awareness" snapshot, a heart-wrenching capture of a seagull struggling to soar through a thick industrial haze—a stark reminder of the toll human activities took on precious air quality.

Titled "Urban Nature Resilience," another of his photographs showcased vibrant wildflowers and lush greenery thriving amid the concrete jungle of city life—a testament to the possibility of harmonious coexistence between nature and urbanity.

Then came hours of preparation—editing, framing, writing detailed captions. Finally, he'd packaged up the portfolio and sent it off to the gallery's review committee.

For weeks, he'd anxiously awaited their response. Catherine Eden was notoriously selective about the artists she showcased. Her gallery's standards were impossibly high. Still, he hoped his unique perspective might catch her discerning eye.

Eventually, the day came when all his colleagues mentioned that their submissions had been replied to. But no reply ever arrived for Blake. His couple of follow-up messages went unanswered.

It was a crushing blow, confirming his suspicion that his work wasn't good enough for the highest echelons of the art world. The photography industry could be viciously competitive. Talented artists were rejected. Others were chosen based on their connections or educational background and not on the quality of their work. Blake found it all increasingly demoralizing.

This was another reason he hoped a change of scenery would re-inspire his creativity. Nonetheless, the sting of rejection still persisted under the surface, fueling his doubts.

"Blake?" Ivy stared at him, pulling him out of his musings.

He blinked at her, then smiled. "I have faith in your abilities, and I want your business to thrive," he continued. "Besides, 'tis the season of generosity. Together, we'll help people rediscover the magic of Ivy's Blooms."

"I am grateful. Truly," Ivy began. "Though I admit, I'm concerned about the expenses of promoting on social media, and whether it'll truly be effective."

As they sat together on the sofa, Blake met her mesmerizing gaze. Her eyes were a stunning hazel, flecked with shades of emerald green and honey brown.

The fire in the fireplace popped, infusing the room with the earthy aroma of oak wood.

She angled her body toward him. The firelight played over her delicate features—her pixie nose, her rosy cheeks flushed from the heat. In this intimate moment, with the winter darkness held at bay outside, she was radiant.

How natural it was to be here with her. No pretense or false impressions, only her exceptional beauty shining through.

He gave silent thanks for whatever stroke of fate had brought this remarkable woman into his life. And he knew, as surely as the logs burned in the hearth, that his heart already belonged to her.

"Trust me, I understand your concerns," he replied. "Social media is cheaper than traditional advertising, especially if we create our own content. And it can be really powerful for small businesses such as yours."

Ivy chewed her bottom lip. "Do you honestly think so?"

"Without a doubt. Many bakeries, artists, and florists have found success and reached thousands of people. Plus, they build a loyal following. Your impressive arrangements deserve the same level of exposure."

"I've always taken pride in my designs," she whispered, half to herself. "Is social media actually capable of keeping my dream alive?"

"I have the photography equipment, so no extra expense on that front. And I'm more than happy to help as a friend." His lips found hers once more, the kiss a gentle affirmation of his feelings and commitment. As their lips parted, he murmured, "Though I'm thinking that I'm definitely more than a friend."

"You are." She smiled, sat back, and folded her hands. "Alright, shall we give social media a try? There's no doubt in my mind that Amelia will be on board."

Blake grinned. "Give it time and you'll see—the enchantment of your designs will win over Evergreen Valley and beyond."

"How can I ever repay you?"

"No repayment necessary," Blake said softly, his hand providing a consoling weight on her shoulder.

A while later, Blake walked down Ivy's front steps, zipping his jacket against the chill of the night air. He glanced back at the comforting sight of her well-lit house. The living room window framed Ivy's silhouette, moving with grace as she tidied up. She appeared deeply absorbed, her actions deliberate and pensive.

What was occupying her attention tonight? Was she pondering the hard path that lay ahead for her flower shop with the new competition in town? Or was her contemplation focused on the two of them and the potential that their budding relationship held?

Her silhouette faded as she ventured into another room. Reluctantly, Blake shifted his gaze and resumed his journey down the lamplit street, heading home. Yet his thoughts remained on her.

He drafted a social media post in his head about Ivy's shop and her amazing floral arrangements. First up, he'd set up a website for her.

Once he was back at his grandfather's house, Blake opened his laptop. He chose a domain name—IvysBlooms.com—selected and purchased a website hosting platform and picked a template. He customized a homepage, shared her services and products, and provided the shop's contact information—an email and business phone number for online orders.

Then his fingers flew across the keys as he composed a glowing review of Ivy's Blooms on Facebook and Instagram. He included a few photos of the Wishing Blooms ceremony for extra visual impact.

A definitive click marked the second his post went live. With a soft exhale, Blake eased back, his palms tapping lightly on the armrest of his chair. The screen's glow held the promise of unveiling Ivy's talent to the world, and he couldn't wait to see how people reacted. This beginning would breathe fresh life into her business, step by step, post by post.

Eventually, he surrendered into a restless sleep.

Tomorrow's conversation brewed in his mind. His purpose was steadfast, a silent vow to walk beside her on the path to success. The success she deserved. The kind that would light up her eyes, her qualms forgotten.

*N*utmeg, cloves, and narcissus scented the air inside Ivy's Blooms the following day as Blake and Ivy set to work preparing for Ivy's social media debut. Blake arranged his camera equipment and Ivy chose her finest bouquets.

He began by focusing his lens on her favorite Christmas arrangement—a vase overflowing with hypericum berries and frosted eucalyptus.

Meanwhile, Ivy arranged an assortment of seasonal flowers—fragrant gardenias, vibrant velvety-red poinsettias, and deep crimson amaryllis—inspecting each petal and leaf until perfect.

In the back room, Cocoa nibbled on a squeaky chew toy shaped like a gingerbread man, his tiny teeth biting on the red and green silicone.

Amelia prepared a Christmas centerpiece—fresh white lilies and artfully curled ribbons—while monitoring the energetic pet.

"Now I'll shoot your signature designs," Blake said to Ivy.

"We'll showcase what sets Ivy's Blooms apart from any chain store."

While Blake worked the camera, Ivy caught the intensity in his blue eyes. They held a quiet fervor, a deep connection to the scenes he was capturing. His gaze lingered on each detail, revealing a genuine affection for the beauty of the flowers.

He reminded her of her own enthusiasm for creating stunning floral displays, and another reason for her renewed hope.

Despite her doubts, the idea of collaborating with Blake seemed akin to an unexpected Christmas miracle. In the hush of a winter morning, she allowed herself to imagine her carefully crafted bouquets reaching people far and wide.

Her respect for Blake's support intensified as they delved deeper into his strategy. Her heart resonated with an unspoken gratitude for his constant presence by her side.

As she readied a bouquet of red and pink roses, thoughts of the future swirled like snowflakes. Certainty eluded her, but this season's gifts were clear. Blake's friendship kindled a spark inside her, thawing her doubts. His compassion nourished her creativity to blossom. And perhaps something more between them was blossoming, too.

Her gaze remained on him as he photographed the shop's festive interior. His wavy hair peeked out from under a navy beanie that matched his sweater. Relaxed in jeans, he peered through the camera lens with an artist's eye, seeing splendor in every corner. A week ago, he was a stranger. Now, her happiness surged like a fountain at the sight of his smile.

Of course, it was too soon for love. Wasn't it?

She tucked a red poinsettia blossom behind her ear and grinned at him. He grinned back.

"Okay, grab your jacket," he said. "Your arrangements will

look stunning against the backdrop of our Norman Rockwell town."

She bundled the flowers in her arms, and Blake opened the shop door, letting in a swirl of frost-nipped air.

His fingers traced the curve of her cheek. "The poinsettia is a perfect accent for you, love," he said.

Love. Ivy's heart skipped a beat at the affectionate name. When had he started calling her that? She couldn't recall. A few days ago, the endearment would have surprised her. Now it seemed natural.

"Let's take a selfie," he said.

"With your expensive camera?"

"Nope. I'll use this." He pulled his cellphone from his pocket, extending it at the perfect distance from their faces. "Say Wishing Blooms!" With a mischievous grin, he leaned in for an unexpected kiss, capturing her delightful surprise in a spontaneous photo.

"Now let's try this again," he said.

"Another selfie?"

He tucked his cellphone back in his pocket. "Something much better," Blake replied, his eyes holding a special gleam as he slowly lifted her chin. When his lips tenderly met hers, she melted into his kiss, overcome by the moment, drawn in by his warmth. As she returned his kiss, Ivy melted into his embrace. His woodsy scent, his fingers threading through her hair… Her heart opened to him in a way she'd never experienced.

Her doubts washed away. She cared for him, and knew those feelings were reciprocated. They parted breathless, foreheads touching.

A few minutes later, they reentered her shop to view the photos.

"Great job, Ivy, and you look gorgeous." Blake shared a sneak preview. "I'll print all the photos, including the selfie, so we both have copies." Some featured her in her red quilted coat and poinsettia bloom behind her ear. "I'll post these on Instagram and Facebook. I'll use some popular hashtags like #ChristmasFlowers, #WinterBlooms, and #EvergreenValley to increase your visibility."

The evening before, he'd set up a website for her shop, which had brought in a couple of inquiries and an online order. A response, albeit a small one, but still, in a single day. Social media was truly amazing.

A woman who had previously walked past Ivy's Blooms without a second glance stopped to peer through the window.

"I saw your arrangements on Instagram and came to look in person," the woman said. "They're stunning."

"Thank you so much," Ivy replied.

"Are you the artist behind this ornament?" a pair of visitors inquired, their hands linked as they admired a display near the entrance. Ivy had arranged dried lavender, crimson rose petals, and fragrant eucalyptus leaves to a tiny, rustic sled. "We're interested in purchasing it to hang on our Christmas tree."

Ivy assisted, chatting about holiday traditions and the pleasure of sharing this special season with loved ones. Moments like these reminded her why she had opened her shop in the first place—to create exceptional, meaningful connections through the art of floral design.

"Sales have increased a little, and it's not even the second week of December," she informed Blake over steaming mugs of eggnog latte later that day. They sat tucked in a corner café, away from the bustle of holiday shoppers, and sharing a slice of warm apple pie.

Normally, the café wasn't open later in the day and into the evening but varied their hours in December to accommodate shoppers during the holiday season.

"We'll continue to tweak your website and check content. A social media presence takes time." Blake tapped his phone, accessed his photos, and scrolled to a specific image. "I added one of my photos to the homepage banner of your website. I hope it's okay."

Her breath stilled. The photo captured a serene, sunlit meadow in full bloom. He'd framed the shot, showcasing a riot of colorful wildflowers, daisies, and tall stalks of lavender.

"Blake, this photo is beautiful." She took a bite of her pie; the sweet taste of cinnamon and sugar filled her mouth. "And it's more than okay. Your photo is exquisite."

"Thank you. At the end of the day, nature is my thing, you know?"

She nodded. She knew.

"I also meant to ask about the vacant retail space next to your shop," he continued.

"Eleanor Thornton was a long-time resident here and owned a toy shop for many years. Her health declined, and she retired and moved to the coast."

He folded his hands together. "Ivy, have you ever considered combining our talents?"

"How?" She set down her fork and cradled her latte mug in her hands. "I've thought about the empty storefront countless times."

"We could rent the space and open a joint gallery showcasing your floral designs and my nature photography."

"That takes more money and resources than I currently have."

He leaned in. "Fortunately, I have both."

"I'll run this past Amelia, though I'm sure she won't mind. She likes to travel to Indiana to see her folks and the dog every chance she gets, and another venture would only add more to her plate."

He smiled. "Got it."

She admired his windswept hair and the ever-present rough stubble on his chin. His gaze was attentive as she shared her vision and goals for the vacant store, nodding along in encouragement.

"What about the name Nature's Palette?" she asked. "That way my flowers and your photos will coexist."

"My lens is the palette." He grinned. "I like it. Nature's Palette it is. I'll see if I can contact the landlord, and we'll go from there."

He was becoming more special by the day; no longer relegated to the niche of a helpful new friend. He was becoming a business partner, too.

And the stars were aligning.

Cocoa sat on the floor of the café, secure on his leash. The café was dog-friendly, and the owners supplied the puppy with a bowl of water and a doggy biscuit.

"Once people witness your incredible talent, they won't be able to resist coming to Evergreen Valley to see for themselves or ordering online," Blake said.

"Britney's article in the *Gazette* doesn't seem to have affected business so far," Ivy replied, though unease tinged her voice. "But there's Garden Elegance…"

She studied Blake's face, trying to discern his reaction. His brows furrowed for a split-second before he smoothed them.

"I wouldn't worry," he said, though he looked worried to her. His fingers tapped his mug in restless beats. "I understand your concern, but your passion and artistry are miles ahead of a franchisor. Customers will see that."

"Will they? Clients who are loyal often switch to something flashier and newer."

"Maybe some," Blake conceded. "Though your devoted

regulars know the care you put into every bouquet. Nothing can replicate that personal touch."

Ivy nodded slowly, letting his reassuring words sink in. He made a fair point—she had a dependable following who appreciated the human element. "You're right. I shouldn't assume the worst."

"Exactly. Focus on sharing your talent and connecting with customers, old and new. The numbers and reviews will speak for themselves."

He certainly had a level-headed perspective, and her anxiety subsided. Still, her mind spun scenarios…

She wished she could read his thoughts. Had he heard rumors she hadn't and simply wanted to reassure her? She itched to press for more but held back. The holidays were stressful enough without borrowing trouble.

She reached for her latte, the sweet marshmallow foam suddenly cloying. No use speculating yet. For now, she would stay the course and focus on spreading seasonal cheer.

As she sipped, Blake grinned and gestured to her mouth. "You've got a little something… A dab of…eggnog."

"Oh!" Ivy grabbed a napkin, her cheeks growing warmer as she patted the foam.

"Allow me." He leaned across the table and gently wiped the corner of her mouth with his thumb. His touch lingered a moment longer, meeting her gaze.

Her blush deepened at his tenderness and the way his eyes, as blue as a sunlit ocean, seemed to see into her soul. "Thank you," she managed, her heart accelerating.

"Anytime, love," Blake replied with a wink that made Ivy weak in the knees. She playfully tossed her crumpled napkin at him, but his flirtatious glance hinted at their mutual attraction.

.   .   .

SEVERAL MORE DAYS PASSED, the middle of December arrived, and Ivy adapted to the challenges that came with caring for a puppy. She developed a routine that allowed her to balance her work at the flower shop and her time with Cocoa.

"Certainly, house training isn't as difficult as I feared," she admitted one evening to Cocoa. She'd gotten in the habit of talking with him.

She clasped a scalding mug of peppermint tea as she gazed out the window at the mesmerizing dance of snowflakes. "And I must say, you're quite the little gentleman now."

In response, his ears perked, and he tilted his head.

After the pup had eaten, he circled the kitchen, and she immediately stood at the ready, leash in hand. "Ready for a walk? It's time for more house training."

Once back inside, she realized that he'd tracked muddy footprints through the living room. Exhaling, she cleaned up after him. Yet another task added to her ever-growing list of responsibilities.

The reality of her business demands loomed large, and her heart ached with the realization that she couldn't keep him forever. She needed to find him a permanent home where he could grow and thrive.

She was making an altruistic decision, and one that held Cocoa's best interests at its center, she told herself.

That is, when she didn't glance down at his trusting eyes and wagging tail.

Or his unwavering devotion. Or their shared moments of joy.

Tears escaped as she crafted a social media ad and posted online: Give the Gift of Unconditional Devotion: Adopt an Abandoned Puppy this Christmas. Cocoa is a playful, loving, and intelligent four-month-old Pomeranian who deserves unconditional love. She added an adorable photo of him and her email for people to contact her directly.

"Remember, we're searching for a family who will care for you just like I do," she whispered to Cocoa the next day while scrolling through the responses on her phone. "You deserve nothing less."

Ivy returned home the following evening to find several promising messages from potential adopters. As she read them, she pictured Cocoa snuggled up with each household, romping through their yards, and showered with affection.

"Look, Cocoa, this family has two kids who would adore you. And this couple lives on a farm with lots of room to explore!" She shared the details of the prospective homes with him. "Nothing is definite, though. They're just inquiring."

As the evening wore on, Ivy contacted all the potential adopters, asking questions and discussing their plans for Cocoa. With each conversation, a tug-of-war between hope and heartache played out, a bittersweet reminder that soon, Cocoa would no longer be in her life.

"How about another cuddle?" She carefully enfolded the puppy in her arms and settled onto the couch. The living room glowed with strands of mini white lights draped over her compact Christmas tree and the red and gold ornaments shimmered. The miniature snowman, decorated in garland, was stationed in soundless merriment.

She hadn't bothered to light the fireplace, and it stood as a silent sentinel, waiting to enhance the room again with heat.

Her phone buzzed with a text message from Blake. He'd spent the past several days with his grandfather, looking through old family albums and reminiscing. They'd also tackled jigsaw puzzles, starting with an easy five-hundred-piece puzzle called "Colorful World Map," then moved on to a more challenging, one-thousand-piece puzzle, called "Venetian Canal Reflections."

Hi, love, Blake's text read, and her pulse sped up. *Since my grandfather and I share a passion for photography, we changed things up today. We watched a black and white 1929 silent film called "Man with a Movie Camera." Have you heard of it?*

No, can't say that I have, she typed back.

It's interesting to see how experimental and creative they were back then. Yesterday we saw "The Photographers," a National Geographic documentary that follows journalists on assignments worldwide.

She smiled as she read his informative texts. She was happy that he was having an incredible time with his grandfather, though she couldn't help missing him. Only a few days had slipped past, and her house seemed to sigh with loneliness. Vividly, she remembered his smile, and how his blue eyes crinkled when he laughed.

Enjoy every precious minute, she wrote.

Thanks. I miss you. A lot.

"I miss you, too," she whispered to the empty room, then typed her words to Blake.

Anyone respond to your online ad to adopt Cocoa? he asked. She'd told him and Amelia that she was placing the ad.

Several people have emailed me. I'm meeting with a couple of families tomorrow. They seem interested, though you never know.

You love Cocoa. Finding him a suitable home is selfless and brave, Blake continued. *And you can probably schedule puppy play dates, so it's not goodbye forever.*

Once more, his encouraging texts reminded her she wasn't alone.

Her phone buzzed with another incoming text from him: *What do you call an elf who just graduated from medical school?*

Ivy shook her head. Another one of his silly jokes, no doubt, designed to cheer her up. She texted back: *Alright, I'll* bite. What DO you call an elf who just graduated from medical school?

His reply came quick: *A DOC-tor! Get it?! Doc like doctor and doc like one of Santa's elves?!*

You mean "Doc" from Snow White?

Exactly. Doc, Grumpy, Happy, Sleepy, Bashful, Dopey and Sneezy.

I understand. She rolled her eyes and couldn't help laughing out loud. She typed: *Wow, that was truly awful. I think you're spending a little too much time with your grandfather's joke book.*

Blake responded: *And yet I still got you to smile, didn't I? Admit it, you miss my witty sense of humor.*

She tried not to grin. *You just keep telling yourself that. Cocoa is here and he keeps me smiling.*

Speaking of Cocoa, want to hear a funny story about a peanut? Blake texted next.

His unrelenting corniness made her groan out loud. She bantered back: *Do I have a choice? Lay it on me...*

After a few more quips, Ivy typed: *You always know exactly how to brighten my day.*

"And you make me happy, too," she told the puppy.

Cocoa licked Ivy's cheek, as if to say he understood and appreciated everything she had done for him. She cuddled with the sweet dog who had captured her heart, comforted by his love and warmth.

Thank you, Blake, she texted. *You've helped me be stronger and more optimistic.*

Hey, that's what I'm here for. And Ivy?

Yes?

I miss seeing your smile in person.

Blake, it's only been a few days. I miss your smile, too, and having someone like you around is truly a blessing. Grinning, she hit the send button.

I care about you. A lot. These days apart made me realize how much I appreciate you, he texted. *Pleasant dreams, love. I'll see you soon.*

Love. Pleasant dreams. Love.

They disconnected, and she hugged her knees to her chest. The anticipation of seeing him again held a new and deeper meaning.

She cared for Blake, that much was clear, though so many competing thoughts and emotions wrestled within her. The possibility of giving up Cocoa already shattered her heart. Could she handle another heartbreak if things didn't work out with Blake? And the genuine threat of losing her flower shop loomed large, even with their social media efforts.

Was now really the best time to explore a new romance? Her logical side hesitated. But when she reread Blake's texts, her heart fluttered with hope. She dreamed of snowy walks, cozy fireside nights, and exchanging gifts on Christmas morning.

A life with Blake seemed full of possibilities. Though it was also risky. If she shared her feelings, she feared they would be wounded like a delicate bird if things went wrong.

She stroked Cocoa's fur, taking consolation in his solid presence. For now, her focus had to remain on her business and doing right by Cocoa. Romance could wait...or could it? The resolution of the conflict between her heart and her head hinged solely on her decision.

She picked up her cup of tea and allowed the minty flavor to soothe her. She glanced around, the emptiness without Blake evident in her surroundings. She missed his presence —from his boots by the door to the empty spot beside her on the couch.

To cheer herself up, she decided to enjoy some girl time with the puppy. She snuggled next to Cocoa and flipped through the TV channels, settling on a holiday-themed Hallmark movie called *Mistletoe Magic*.

She perked up and took a silly selfie of her and the puppy curled up on the blankets. She sent it to Blake with the caption: *Someone looks pretty cozy without you here!* Adding a winky face emoji, she hit send, anticipating his reaction.

Blake's text response was immediate. *I've been replaced!* with a shocked emoji.

I wouldn't dream of it, she responded with a laugh.

After setting her phone down, she leaned back against the couch cushions, replaying her conversations with Blake in her mind. She cherished his easy-going wit and the way he could still make her blush, even from a distance.

Ivy closed her eyes, imagining his handsome face beaming down at her, remembering the feeling of his palm against her cheek, the sparkle in his crystal blue eyes when he gazed at her.

Though they had only known each other a short time, he already understood her in a way no one else did.

She shook her head. Much too soon for such romantic thoughts. Or was it? The line between friendship and romance felt blurred, and his absence left a distinct space in her heart.

In these reflective moments, Ivy also understood that taking care of Cocoa was more than a responsibility—it was a privilege. Despite the sleepless nights and endless cleanups, his unwavering love brought her true happiness.

Cocoa curled up in her lap. His compact body seemed to melt into the embrace of her wool sweater. She closed her eyes and breathed in. His sweet puppy scent mingled with the lingering taste of peppermint tea.

However, her fear of losing her business preyed at her, and a persistent doubt whispered that Garden Elegance would be the iceberg to sink her Titanic.

For several minutes, she kept her eyes closed and tried to rest, the drone of the television playing in the background.

A loud rapping at the front door snapped her to full alertness.

Her muscles tensed. Who in the heavens would stop by unannounced at this hour?

She lifted Cocoa from her lap and stood with him in her arms.

The knock came again, more insistent.

With unease coiling in the pit of her stomach, Ivy slowly approached the door. She peered through the peephole, though it was too dark outside to make out the visitor. Was it Blake deciding to visit her after all? Her pulse quickened as she unlocked the door.

Ivy shifted Cocoa's weight so she could grip the doorknob with her free hand.

When the door swung open, she stumbled back in shock. Standing on her porch was the last person she expected or wanted to see.

"Britney Knox," Ivy managed. "What are you doing here?"

*B*ritney stood outside, the wind lifting her ebony-black hair. She was dressed impeccably in a sleek royal-blue designer coat with shiny silver buttons and black stiletto boots. Behind her, pine trees creaked as an icy winter blast whipped through the snow-dusted branches. Frost clung to the ends of sagging boughs, sending pine needles skittering across the porch.

Ivy cuddled Cocoa in her arms. His small body quivered —whether from the cold or sensing her own unease, she wasn't sure. His big brown eyes peered up at Britney curiously.

Ivy inhaled and squared her shoulders. "Britney, what do you want?" she asked.

Britney's venomous article branding Ivy's flowers subpar still stung. Yet here she was, randomly showing up on Ivy's doorstep late at night.

How did she discover where I lived? Ivy wondered uneasily. She had never given Britney her home address.

Britney lifted her chin. "I presumed you'd want to know

that Garden Elegance is opening early. Like, the first week of January early."

Ivy's stomach dropped. That was less than a month away!

"What? I thought sometime in February..." Secretly Ivy had hoped that the store would miss their deadline and not launch until after Valentine's Day.

"Change of plans," Britney replied. "Andrew—he's my boyfriend and the owner—decided it made more sense to open at the beginning of a fresh year. Take advantage of all those New Year's resolutions to buy flowers more often."

Ivy's thoughts surged with lightning speed. She had been counting on many more days to boost her own business first.

Britney continued, "The holidays are one of your busiest seasons, so I'm giving you a heads-up. Consider it an early Christmas gift."

Gift? This "gift" could ruin everything.

"About your piece in the *Gazette*..." Ivy kept her expression neutral. "You never returned my phone call. My purpose was to discuss the article with you and your editor."

Britney waved her hand dismissively. "Ancient history. I'm over it."

"I'm not," Ivy replied. "And I received some strange texts one night. Was that you?"

"There's nothing wrong with wishing someone sweet dreams." Britney adjusted her stance, her boots making a firm impression on the snowy porch.

Ivy clutched Cocoa a little closer. "How did you know where to find me?"

"Since you didn't pick up when I called the shop, I asked around and got your home address."

"My shop is closed in the evening," Ivy said. The way Britney helped herself to Ivy's personal information irritated her. "For the record, I assure you that any insinuation about poor quality in my floral arrangements is untrue. My customers know better."

"Sure, sure. And those Wishing Blooms. Please." Britney shook her head. "Anyway, as I was saying…"

Britney launched back into delivering the "gift" of Garden Elegance's early opening.

"How thoughtful of you," Ivy replied. "Now, if you'll excuse me, I'll get back to work planning my own January promotions."

She started to close the door, but Britney wedged her foot inside. "Aren't you worried?" Britney glanced at the puppy curled in Ivy's arms. "Cute pup, by the way. What's his name?"

Ivy's defenses went up a notch. She bristled slightly, not particularly appreciating Britney's interest. "Cocoa," she said steadily.

Britney's lips curled into a sly smirk; her eyebrows arched a little too thin in amusement. "Precious."

Ivy met Britney's gaze head-on. "Happy holidays, Britney."

Britney's response was terse, a curt nod accompanied by a brief, forced smile. "You, too."

As Britney cautiously tiptoed down the frost-covered steps in her high-heeled boots, Ivy stifled a grin, finding a touch of irony in Britney's choice of footwear for a snowy evening.

She extended a hand. "Careful there, those steps can be quite slippery."

Britney, with a flippant laugh and a hint of condescension, retorted, "Ivy, it's adorable how you fuss over such little things. Snow or no snow, I always manage just fine."

"Alright." Ivy gently but firmly closed the door, unwilling to allow Britney's manipulative games to unravel her.

. . .

THE MORNING after Britney's unexpected visit, Ivy scheduled two interviews back-to-back with potential adopters interested in Cocoa. The first couple was Katie and Caleb, and the second was a woman named Janelle.

As Ivy tidied her home, she came across the old photo of her and Will, their smiling faces frozen in happier times. She paused, heart clenching.

They had history, yes. He'd been the first man she'd ever considered sharing a future with. But that naive dream died the day he broke her trust.

She gathered a deep, centering breath. That chapter was over. She was stronger and wiser, with her sights set on better dreams.

Blinking back sentimental tears, Ivy placed the photo in the trash. She had discovered something real with Blake, and it was time to close the door on the past. As she did, a symbolic weight lifted from her shoulders.

Wiping her eyes, Ivy continued straightening with a lighter heart, ready to embrace whatever lay ahead.

She'd already puppy-proofed the living room but blocked off access in case Cocoa decided to sneak behind the sofa. She also closed doors to the kitchen and hallway, so he could play safely during the meetings and not wander off unattended.

Meanwhile, Amelia watched the flower shop so Ivy could stay home. Unintentionally, Ivy had burdened her friend with the morning rush, but it was crucial to create a welcoming environment for Cocoa's potential adopters, plus a comfortable setting for Cocoa.

"Today you get to meet families who will love you as much as I do," she told him, scratching behind his velvety ears. Cocoa's rough tongue brushed against her hand in an enthusiastic, slobbery acknowledgment.

At 9:45 am, Ivy assembled a tray of sugar-dusted,

snowflake-shaped Christmas cookies and set a pot of fragrant spiced tea to steep on the stove. The first meeting was at ten o'clock with a youthful couple, Katie and Caleb, hailing from a neighboring town. Their enthusiasm had shown through during their phone conversation. But 10 o'clock passed without them showing up.

Ivy phoned, but her message went straight to voicemail. "Hi Katie, it's Ivy. Are you and Caleb planning to come and meet Cocoa today? Please give me a call when you can."

She hated the nervous edge in her own voice. Still, she held out hope that they were running late.

While waiting, Ivy phoned the flower shop. "Amelia, I'm so sorry, but the ten o'clock appointment didn't show. I'll hurry over after the second interview. How is it going there?"

"We're doing great!" Amelia assured. "This morning is quiet, and our part-time college students are readying our floral arrangements for the fire station's toy drive and auction tomorrow. And you had asked Mrs. Thompson to volunteer at the shop for a few hours a week."

"I hoped it would get her out of the house, and she could engage with customers."

"Good idea. She's assisting a customer as we speak, so we've got it covered. You focus on finding a good match for our little Cocoa. Take as long as you'd like. In fact, if you don't come into the store until later or even tonight, we'll be fine."

Ivy thanked Amelia profusely and hung up the phone.

She checked her watch, settled into a seat, and waited. Nearby, Cocoa wrestled with a squeaky plush reindeer, unaware of Ivy's mounting disappointment.

Next was Janelle, a single woman, scheduled for eleven o'clock.

By 11:30, after multiple calls to Janelle yielded no

response, Ivy came to the realization that no one was coming today. It simply wasn't in the cards.

Cocoa nestled his head in her lap, gazing up at her with comforting eyes.

"No problem, we'll keep trying," Ivy assured him half-heartedly. She noted the calendar. "After all, it's only December sixteenth."

Why hadn't anyone shown up? Was it a sign she should keep Cocoa as her own? Yet deep down, she understood that her hectic schedule wouldn't be fair to him.

DOWNTRODDEN AFTER THE NO-SHOWS, Ivy bundled Cocoa in a stylish deep-purple sweater, featuring a whimsical holly leaf design and headed downtown to the Christmas market. She loved that just about everything in town was within walking distance.

Robust fires crackled in iron grates, welcoming visitors. A medley of classic holiday tunes, "Jingle Bells" followed by "Frosty the Snowman," played through the overhead speakers. The air was tinged with the enticing scents of roasted chestnuts and the soothing hug of spiced apple cider.

The fragrance of fresh pine grew stronger as she approached, blending with the nutty aroma of gingerbread. In the distance, the faint jingle of bells chimed from horse-drawn wagons offering market-goers sleigh rides.

Cocoa's nose twitched, picking up each tempting whiff. His paws pressed through patches of snow, investigating the enticing traces of flavored treats, occasionally stopping to greet friendly strangers with a delighted and wiggling behind.

She cinched her oversized cable knit scarf snugly around her neck as the chill in the air deepened. She rubbed her mittens together. If only she had tucked hand warmers into her coat pockets.

Up ahead, the town's evergreen displayed golden lights. She wandered through the crowded stalls, taking in all the scents—the subtle sweetness of woody pine wreaths, cinnamon and sugar from the baked goods stand, and the spiced fragrance of mulled cider simmering in slow cookers.

Ropes of lights, artistically draped around each stall, threw a rainbow gleam that became more enchanting as dusk fell.

"Ivy! Over here!" a familiar man's voice called out.

She spotted Blake waving to her from a booth stocked with handcrafted ornaments. Beside him, his grandfather, Everett Shepherd, sat on a bench, bundled in a rustic brown plaid scarf that mirrored Blake's.

Ivy's mood lifted at the sight of Blake's smile, and she grinned. His smile was as infectious as ever. When she neared him, her burdens eased.

"Bailing out on the flower shop to hang out with me?" he asked good-naturedly, enveloping her in a hug.

"Amelia assured me that the shop is in good hands." Ivy laughed. "And I can't pass up quality time with my favorite guy."

Everett's gaze fixed on them, shining with affection. A flush crept up her neck, keenly aware of the public setting.

Sensing her self-consciousness, Blake met her eyes, his own glinting with humor. "No need to be shy on me now, love," he teased. "Any guy would be blessed to receive your megawatt smile."

Everett grinned fondly at the pair. "Don't you two make a fine sight." Getting up from the bench, he shuffled over, gray mittens outstretched for Cocoa to sniff. The puppy's little nose twitched as he stretched to lick at the fuzzy fabric, then spun in an exuberant circle.

"This must be wee Cocoa." Everett chuckled. "He's a cute rascal, and from what I hear, he's full of the holiday spirit."

"That he is," Ivy and Blake responded in unison.

"Good to see you again," Everett welcomed Ivy. "This shutterbug here never stops talking about you."

Ivy turned to Blake, a suppressed laugh in her voice. "Shutterbug?"

"What can I say?" Blake scratched his stubbled chin, mirth crinkling the corners of his deep-set eyes.

"That's my nickname for him since he was a little boy obsessed with his camera," Everett said. "Isn't that right, Blake?"

Blake cleared his throat, evading Ivy's questioning look. "Hot cider?" he asked, guiding her and Cocoa toward a nearby booth.

Ivy allowed herself to be led but slanted him an amused gaze. "You never answered your grandfather's remark."

"No comment," he replied.

She slid into the booth. "I think it's a charming nickname and perfectly suited to you."

"Can't argue with that logic." Blake signaled to a server for two piping mugs of cider. When Everett joined them, he opted for hot chocolate with a peppermint stick.

Hand in hand, Ivy and Blake continued through the market, sipping their drinks and weaving through the crowd. Ivy insisted on pausing to savor a slice of maple fudge, before treating herself to a scrumptious piece of cranberry bread.

"I love any dessert with cranberries!" she declared.

Cocoa bounded ahead, his leash pulling taut as he sniffed the toe of an interesting boot or a tantalizing scent of roasting nuts. Blake tightened his grip on the puppy's lead, guiding the pup back to heel.

Blake's grandfather walked behind them, occasionally stopping to chat with a neighbor or a friend.

Cocoa's leash strained again as he caught a whiff of sugar-dusted dog biscuits shaped like reindeer and Christmas trees. Ivy took the leash and steadied the eager pup while stealing a glance at Blake. "How are you enjoying your stay with your grandfather so far?"

"Every minute has been amazing," Blake said. "We've been reminiscing about holidays past. Snowball fights, chestnut roasting, caroling... Although I'm not a great singer, unless you count being selected to sing a bass solo in the high school chorus."

"Congratulations."

"Believe me, the chorus teacher was desperate for guy singers. I liked it, though." His eyes assumed a faraway look, as if he glimpsed a special memory.

Ivy's heart expanded, seeing the contentment etched on his handsome face. She realized how deeply Blake valued family traditions, especially at this sentimental time of year.

After a moment, his expression transformed, and he held her hand firmly. "In fact, it's got me thinking. I'm planning to buy a house of my own."

"Oh? And where might this house be?"

"Wherever you are."

Speech momentarily eluded her. As she read the sincerity in his gaze, her pulse skipped. No matter how often his romantic declarations caught her off guard, they never failed to make her feel cherished beyond measure.

As they continued browsing, one booth in particular beckoned. Garlands of pine boughs framed a display of antique Christmas ornaments. Each was a distinctive treasure, and Ivy stepped closer, imagining the stories behind each timeless heirloom.

"Aren't they beautiful?" she murmured, her fingers grazing a particularly lovely crystal bauble.

Blake nodded, admiring the wooden soldiers, carved

reindeers, and tiny angels painted in nostalgic Victorian hues. His grandfather, who had caught up to them, let out a low whistle and commented on the craftmanship.

Blake lifted a glass blown angel. "This would make a perfect tree topper now that your old metal star is broken, Grandpa."

Beside him, Everett's eyes roved over the glittering array of ornaments. His weathered fingers came to rest on a humble carved wooden star. He cradled it in his palm, tracing the nicks and cracks in the faded paint.

"This takes me back," he murmured. "Looks just like the star my father placed atop our tree when I was a boy." He smiled. "We always waited for him to put it on last, as the final Christmas touch."

Blake gave his grandfather's shoulder a firm pat. "Then it's decided. This year, that honor will be yours."

Everett's eyes misted over. He held the wooden star over his heart and gave a small nod. "I'd like that very much."

As they continued, Ivy admired several cozy hand knit woolens, picturing how a certain deep blue scarf would complement Blake's eyes perfectly. Besides, she owed him a scarf, as he had given up his tartan scarf for Cocoa.

She made a mental note to return and secretly select it as a gift for him.

She turned to Blake and inquired, just in case. "Will you still be in town come Christmas?"

He drew her close. "Where else would I go when everything I want is right here? We have a joint gallery to open. Remember?"

"You haven't mentioned anything since our discussion in the café."

"Doesn't mean I wasn't thinking about it."

"If we were to open a gallery, how could it be profitable?"

"We'll charge admission fees." He lifted five fingers to

emphasize the amount, then gestured to a souvenir stand. "We can also sell merchandise. Plus, consider renting the facility for private events—weddings, corporate gatherings, you name it."

"I'm impressed with you, Blake Shepherd. You are a visionary."

"Thank you. I'm impressed with you, Ivy Bennett. You are my inspiration." He punctuated his words with a kiss. "Now, I believe we were discussing Christmas. What are your plans?"

"On Christmas morning, I attend the service at Evergreen Chapel." Ivy hesitated. "Then I volunteer at a soup kitchen the church organizes. Would you like to join me?"

"I'd love to." His voice dropped to a teasing whisper. "As long as you'll do me the honor of coming back to my grandfather's house afterward for a proper dinner."

"Hmm. What's on the menu for this proper dinner?"

"Maple glazed ham, mashed potatoes, stuffing—the full spread," Blake said. "My grandfather is an excellent cook and Christmas dinner is a family tradition."

"What can I bring?"

"Whatever you want."

Ivy paused, her finger coming to rest at the corner of her mouth. "My orange-cranberry sauce is legendary. However, in exchange, I expect at least one slice of pie."

"What kind?"

"I love pumpkin pie."

"Store bought or homemade?"

"Either."

"Store bought it is." Blake laughed and drew her into a hug. "I'll reserve the entire pie just for you."

She grinned and nestled closer, beyond touched at being included in his family tradition.

Up ahead, a booth brimmed with poinsettias in every size and hue—classic red, pure white, and dusky pink.

Ivy glided her hands over the velvety petals, approving of their perfection. As she leaned in to inhale their faint peppery scent, she sensed Blake behind her, his warmth tingling against her back.

"They're gorgeous, aren't they?" she murmured.

"Not as gorgeous as you, love," he replied, his breath stirring her hair. A pleasurable shiver rippled through her at his closeness.

Turning, she said, "That reminds me—Amelia bought a miniature tree for the flower shop that desperately needs decorating."

"Say no more. I offer my services." Blake gave a slight bow, and Ivy felt herself falling deeper under the spell of the season…and of the man before her. Their first Christmas together would surely be like a fairy tale come to life.

Close by, Cocoa sniffed the base of an enormous evergreen tree. Clearly, he had detected an interesting scent and was trying to locate the source. The puppy let out a sharp "yip" as he discovered a dropped gingerbread cookie near the tree skirt. Before Ivy could stop him, he gobbled up the treat in a single bite.

"Uh-oh, busted!" Blake chuckled as they hurried over. "Good thing it wasn't chocolate." He scratched the satisfied pup behind the ears.

"I need to watch this little troublemaker even more closely." She took note to carry safe treats to distract Cocoa from any unsafe holiday snacks.

The marketplace quieted as closing time neared. Arms laden with gifts, Ivy, Blake, and Everett advanced toward Blake's Jeep, Cocoa trotting happily alongside them. After delivering Everett safely home, they headed to Ivy's Blooms to begin decorating.

When they arrived, the shop was dark and empty, Amelia having already closed up. Blake flicked on the lights while Ivy unearthed boxes of ornaments from the back room. Cocoa plopped down by the door, busily chewing on a puppy-safe gingerbread cookie from the market.

Together, Ivy and Blake set up the petite tree in the front window so its colorful lights would shine out onto the street. As they decorated, Ivy switched on the vintage radio, and the nostalgic notes of "Have Yourself a Merry Little Christmas" enveloped the shop, prompting her to hum along.

As she hung hand-painted glass bulbs on the tree branches, she said, "The strangest thing happened last night. Britney Knox showed up at my door out of nowhere."

Blake's brows tightened. "Britney Knox? What did she want?"

"She came to oh-so-sweetly inform me that the Garden Elegance grand opening got moved up to early January. So now I have even less time than ever before they become direct competitors."

"I don't appreciate that woman ambushing you at home and delivering news meant to intimidate you," he replied.

"You and me both," Ivy agreed. "She caught me completely off guard."

Blake turned Ivy to face him, his hands resting on her shoulders. "Try not to let Britney ruin things for you. She wants to get under your skin, but you're stronger than her petty games."

Ivy allowed Blake to draw her into his solid embrace. She focused on the strength of his arms and refused to give Britney's surprise visit any more thought. This moment belonged to her and Blake alone.

He stepped back. "Have you seen any more uptick in sales since we launched your website?"

"The orders are coming in slow but steady. I've seen a few

new reviews, some custom arrangements, and more Instagram followers daily."

"Focus on that progress. You've laid a solid foundation with loyal customers over the years. Consider this a fresh chapter."

As if on cue, the shop's phone rang. Ivy answered, taking down an order for a holiday centerpiece from an out-of-town customer. When she disconnected, Blake gave her a thumbs up. "See? The online community will soon realize the value you provide, while I continue to tweak your social media."

"Something else happened." She knelt to scratch the puppy behind his silky ears as he snoozed under the tree.

"Good or bad?"

"Disappointing. None of the people interested in adopting Cocoa showed up."

Blake crouched beside her. "I'm sorry. I intended to ask earlier how it went but got distracted at the market."

"Understandable." She managed a wan smile. "I'll repost the ad and keep trying. Except part of me wonders..." Her gaze shifted to Cocoa. "Part of me wonders if fate intended for me to keep Cocoa after all."

Tilting her chin up, Blake searched her eyes. "You have a sympathetic heart, Ivy. I know you'll do what's best for him."

As she met his stare, she found only kindness and support in their blue depths. He didn't judge, only seeking to understand her perspective.

Her smile eased. With Blake by her side, she could handle whatever came next, be it adoption or puppy parenthood. His unwavering presence gave her the strength to face each unfamiliar challenge.

After decorating the tree, Blake stepped to the café and brought back two mugs of caramel vanilla steamers. A café specialty. The steamers were made with steamed milk, caramel syrup, vanilla extract, and whipped cream.

As they sat in the back room, Ivy showed him a flyer for the toy drive and auction event at the local fire station.

He gave the pup's belly a rub. "I bet your floral arrangements will be a big hit."

She folded the flyer and set it down. "And your photo-op idea is—" Her train of thought was interrupted by her phone dinging with a new email. She picked it up, her gaze fixed on the screen as she scanned the message.

"That's strange," she murmured. "This email is from someone named Tonya Mills claiming that Cocoa is actually her dog who went missing over a month ago."

Blake leaned in close, peering over Ivy's shoulder. As he read, a crease formed on his forehead in a frown.

"Cocoa wasn't wearing a collar when I found him, and Dr. Michell confirmed that he didn't have a microchip," Ivy said. "He was in rough shape, and it seemed as if he'd been a stray for a while. You remember?"

"Of course." Blake nodded.

"She's insisting that Cocoa—she's calling him Luna—escaped from her backyard right before Thanksgiving during a bad storm. She included some photos." Ivy studied the pictures. "Blake, the puppy looks just like Cocoa."

"Something seems off, and Pomeranians are a popular breed. Why did she wait so long to contact you? Your flyers and online ad are everywhere." His gaze shifted between the photos and Ivy, doubt flickering in his eyes. "Maybe it's a mix-up?"

Or maybe not. Perhaps Tonya was Cocoa's true owner.

Ivy picked up the puppy and held him close to her chest. Cocoa peered up at her with guileless brown eyes, blissfully oblivious to her escalating concerns.

If this Tonya truly was Cocoa's original owner, the right

thing would be to return him. Though Ivy's heart clenched at the thought of losing the puppy she was growing so attached to.

"I'll reply and ask for more details," she determined, even though doubts spun.

"My instincts say to be extremely cautious," Blake said. "Don't accept any claims at face value."

Ivy had a disturbing sense this sudden email heralded trouble. Doubt and confusion crowded her mind.

She tried to stay hopeful and grasped Blake's hand for support. Surely, there was a reasonable explanation for the delay in Tonya's response to contact Ivy.

"Is this an occasion for one of your famous Wishing Blooms?" he asked. "I don't believe, but you do."

Regardless, he was aware of her conviction. She trusted in the potential of the blooms to spread happiness and hope.

"If only." Ivy gave a small, grateful smile, knowing that although Blake didn't put much stock in the bloom's powers, he always knew how to comfort her. "But I have a tradition."

"Which is?"

"Every year I save one of them. Just one."

"Why?" he asked. "Everyone seems to love them."

"It's a way for me to remember all the happiness the blooms have shared in our little town. And a reminder that even in the busiest or hardest times, there's still hope and happiness."

"Where do you keep the flower?"

"In a special place, in my home. I fertilize and water it, just like all the flowers in my shop."

"I know just the thing instead." He disappeared into the storage room and returned with a single vibrant red rose from the flower cooler. He trimmed the stem with care, then handed it to her.

"We'll share this one, love," he said softly. "A wish for faith that things will work out as they should."

Ivy accepted the rose, touched by his gesture. She inhaled the sweet perfume scent, then met Blake's optimistic gaze.

"Thank you," she whispered.

In any event, she expected to untangle the truth of Cocoa's past.

Until then, she cuddled the puppy, cherishing every second with him and Blake.

CHAPTER 9

The following morning, Ivy walked to a coffee shop on the edge of town. Through the window, she noticed an auburn-haired woman sitting alone and clutching a to-go cup. This woman had to be Tonya Mills.

After a tense email exchange, Ivy had reluctantly agreed to meet with Tonya to discuss Tonya's claims that Cocoa was her missing dog. Blake had offered to accompany her, but Ivy decided to handle the matter by herself.

The woman glanced up as Ivy entered, with Cocoa in tow. She immediately zeroed in on the puppy.

You must be Ivy," she trilled, though her smile didn't stretch to her watchful eyes. "And my precious Luna!"

Ivy tensed, brushing her fingers along Cocoa's back to soothe him as she sat across from the woman. Internally, she bristled at the name *Luna* rolling off Tonya's tongue.

She told herself to maintain a pleasant expression, to avoid any escalating tensions.

The woman leaned forward, her gold jewelry jangling on the table. "My adorable puppy," she fussed.

Cocoa recoiled, a low whine in his throat.

"Ivy, thanks to you, I'm so relieved." Tonya clasped her hands, focusing on tracking the puppy's movements. Her foot tapped a staccato beat on the wood floor.

Ivy distrusted the almost manic glint in Tonya's eyes. The name Luna didn't even cause Cocoa's ears to perk up in recognition.

"Cocoa was in poor shape when I rescued him. No collar, no microchip," Ivy said. "Please understand that I can't release him without substantial evidence."

"The storm probably ripped his collar off. However, it's definitely him!" She extended her arm to pat Cocoa, but Ivy subtly shifted. She tried to remain polite but firm.

"If he's your dog, provide something beyond the photos you texted me." Ivy studied Tonya's face for any sign of deception. "Do you have veterinary records, licensing paperwork, anything?"

"I'm way too disorganized for all that. But a mother knows her child." Tonya's gaze darted for a second before she reached into her bag. "See? Here's his favorite toy." She held up a battered stuffed bear, one that any puppy might have frolicked with.

Ivy held back her words. Every instinct screamed that things were off. Tonya seemed far more interested in Cocoa than discussing the proof he was hers.

"Where did...Luna come from?" Ivy asked.

"A shelter near where I live."

Ivy's guard went up even more. Why was Tonya so resistant to confirm Cocoa's identity? Could there be some ulterior purpose behind her reluctance?

Testing a theory, Ivy said, "I assume you spent a fortune on vet bills and supplies for little Luna in those initial months. Puppies are frequently accompanied by a significant expense."

"Expensive. No doubt about it." Tonya's fingers clenched

her cup as she redirected her attention to a sugar packet on the table.

"I want to make certain we're doing everything we can to authenticate this," Ivy said. "Can you give me specifics on when and where you got Luna?"

Tonya's gaze drifted, as if she were sifting through her thoughts. "About six weeks ago, I found him at a shelter in Waverly Falls."

"What about his medical history? Vet visits, vaccinations, anything like that?"

Tonya paused, tracing the rim of her unopened cup with her fingertips. "Buddy has been perfectly healthy. Never had any issues."

"I thought you said his name was Luna?"

Tonya blinked several times. "Luna, yes, that's what I meant."

"And the shelter where you found him?"

"I can't recall the name, though it was in Waverly Falls."

Ivy's eyes narrowed. Tonya spoke generally, not referencing any specific experiences one might expect from a dog owner. And the timeline didn't match. If Cocoa had truly been missing for over a month, as she claimed, shouldn't Tonya have been teeming with anxiety and desperation? Yet, her demeanor stayed strangely untroubled.

"You never came across my online ads and flyers posted in Evergreen Valley?" Ivy probed.

"No." Tonya adjusted the napkin next to her cup. "I don't mingle with folks often, and I rarely drive here. I live in a house the next town over."

"What's your address?" Ivy inquired. "You haven't given me that information."

Tonya's gaze flickered down to Cocoa, curled at their feet. "112 Elmwood Lane, Waverly Falls," she replied.

"Thank you." Ivy was courteous, although doubt bubbled.

"I'll bring him to the vet to scan for a microchip, even though it failed initially."

Tonya's smile faltered. "Naturally, whatever you require. I'm looking forward to bringing my sweet Luna home to spend the holidays with me."

Ivy lifted Cocoa and rose. "I'll connect with you later," she said. She exited before Tonya could object. Her heart pounded, feeling the woman's eyes boring into her back as she hurried to the door.

This was far from over. She didn't believe Tonya's stories for half a minute. There were too many discrepancies, too many odd behaviors.

Ivy stepped out into the frosty air. Somehow, she would need to sort this out.

AFTER THE MEETING WITH TONYA, Ivy stopped at the veterinarian's office. Another examination uncovered no microchip associated with Luna under Tonya's name. The puppy had no previous connection with Tonya, confirmed Dr. Mitchell.

Ivy then contacted the county clerk's office in Waverly Falls, where she found no documentation that Tonya owned the house at the address she had listed.

Exhausted from a long session of phone calls, Ivy arrived at her flower shop midafternoon with Cocoa in her arms. Blake and Amelia peered up from organizing last-minute details for the fire station's auction that evening. The part-time college students waved from behind the counter.

"I couldn't find any proof to corroborate Tonya's claims," Ivy reported to Blake and Amelia. "As far as I can tell, her stories don't add up."

Blake switched on his cellphone, typed into his search engine, then swiveled the screen to Ivy. "Exactly as I suspected," he said. "Tonya has attempted this pet adoption scam before."

Ivy scanned his research, anger and relief rising in her chest. This manipulative woman had tried, but fortunately, she had failed.

"You listened to your intuition, love." Blake drew Ivy close, and she relaxed into his embrace, the tension of the morning easing from her muscles. "Cocoa is here in the place he belongs."

Amelia clicked her tongue. "This Tonya woman is a horrible person. At last, we can stop worrying and concentrate on giving Cocoa his true forever home."

"Which is where?" Ivy asked, smiling over Cocoa's exuberant, unconcerned puppy kisses.

Blake and Amelia smirked in accord. "With you, of course!"

Armed with evidence, Ivy texted Tonya, stating that she knew her story was all lies and threatened to report her to the authorities. Tonya hurriedly dropped the act and blocked Ivy from texting her again.

With the Tonya drama behind her, Ivy refocused on the upcoming fire station benefit. She packed a bulky vase display that she and Amelia had created, which included evergreen branches and forested stems. Plus, four larger pieces—two Christmas themes and two winter mixes.

She also provided a certificate for a specially crafted bouquet to be auctioned off. In addition, she donated her services for any memorable occasion the recipient chose.

Blake loaded the arrangements, as well as his camera equipment, into his Jeep.

"Thank you, Blake," she said, handing him an extra vase, just in case one shattered during transport. "You're a great help."

"What can I say?" He beamed. "We're a team, Ivy."

She smiled. "Yes, we're a team."

"I'm so proud of you for how you handled Tonya."

Ivy fixed her gaze on the ground. "I can't understand why anybody would do such a terrible thing."

"Tonya saw the puppy as an asset and exploited your emotional attachment. I suspect that eventually, she might've suggested that you pay her to keep the puppy. That's how these cruel scams operate, taking advantage of people's care for lost pets."

Ivy shook her head, still struggling to comprehend such manipulation. "I find it hard to believe there are such callous people in this world."

Blake rested a comforting hand on her back. "Regrettably, the absence of brightness occurs even during the holidays. Nevertheless, knowing where to look can unveil far more light than darkness." He smiled tenderly. "And I know where to look, love."

A shadow lifted from Ivy's heart at his words. She nestled into his solid frame, allowing his strength to shore up her shaken faith.

Blake continued. "Are you bringing Cocoa to the auction tonight?"

"Never." She laughed. "He's far too energetic and might tear up all the gifts. Fortunately, one of my part-timers volunteered to watch him."

"A perfect plan." Blake smiled. "So, let's spread some holiday cheer. I'll drop you off at your place and pick you up in a couple of hours."

BACK AT HER HOUSE, Ivy twisted and pirouetted in front of the mirror, holding up an array of outfit options. Cocoa sat on the bedroom floor, gazing up at her while chewing on his current favorite, a rope toy.

Eventually, Ivy decided on a striking emerald-green cocktail dress that brought out the flecks of green in her hazel eyes. She smoothed the satin fabric over her hips, admiring the elegant drape.

Next, she perched at her vanity and artfully pinned back her long blond waves, leaving a few wavy tendrils to frame her face. A touch of mascara accentuated her black lashes, and she swiped on petal-pink lipstick.

Her employee turned pet-sitter arrived and leashed Cocoa for a walk.

Meanwhile, Ivy's stomach fluttered with eager anticipation as she spritzed on a hint of floral perfume. She did a final spin, breathing deep to settle the butterflies. An instant later, the doorbell rang, announcing Blake's arrival.

Her pulse quickened. It was time.

STRINGS OF LIGHTS bathed the firehouse hall, offset by oversized burlap wreaths accented with festive white bows. A majestic fir tree dominated the center of the hall, decorated with a carved wooden angel and popcorn garland.

The firefighters had stored their gear and trucks in apparatus bays at the rear of the station, allowing a wide, clear area for the event.

Toddlers sprinted about in oversized plastic helmets, cheeks flushed from exertion and sugary treats. Mothers and fathers chatted amiably, appreciating the brief respite.

A baby in his mother's arms stared curiously at the lights, chubby fingers reaching out to grasp at the shimmering colors. Close to the towering evergreen, a preschooler proudly displayed a candy cane with cherubic innocence.

Other children entertained themselves on the concrete floor, showing off their newfound treasures. A group of boys huddled together, intent on a remote-controlled race car's headlight as it zoomed past. A little chef-to-be brandished her play kitchen set, complete with pots, pans, and utensils.

Firefighters stood close by. Although several were young men with athletic builds, a few had graying hair and mustaches indicating their veteran experience. They sported standard T-shirts and bunker pants, and their welcoming smiles made them seem like father figures. The women wore station uniforms with the department's insignia, and several wore baseball caps with the fire station's logo.

A boy of about eight twirled a bright-colored pinwheel in his small hands, while his little sister hugged a fuzzy teddy bear nearly as big as herself. Two preteen girls marveled over a colossal Legos castle, exchanging ideas on what to build next—turrets or drawbridges.

On Blake's sturdy arm, Ivy smoothed the sumptuous fabric of her dress. She wanted to impress him with her appearance tonight.

Blake cut a dashing figure in a navy suit; his smile over-flowed with tenderness as he squeezed her hand.

"The bidding is really heating up!" Amelia informed Ivy. Amelia dazzled in a bold sequined evening gown, working the crowd with a natural charisma. "All those besotted suiters are vying for your attention."

Ivy laughed. "Yes, I'm fending off admirers left and right for flower arrangements."

"Can't say I blame them." Blake slid an arm around her waist. "Regrettably for those gentlemen, your dance card is completely full."

"You two are beyond precious," Amelia chuckled. "Quit sending heart eyes to each other and let's drum up more bids. I'll swing by the shop to notify the winners after the auction is over."

Blake and Ivy exchanged a smile at Amelia's good-natured teasing.

Weaving through the animated crowd, Ivy inspected the silent auction. Bids were indeed rolling in, and pride swelled inside her.

She noticed Blake had paused, his gaze focusing on a young girl in pigtails eyeing a shiny red bike that had been donated. The harried mother came over and pulled the girl away, saying the bike had already been claimed, and they couldn't afford the bid, anyway. The girl's smile faded as she cast one last, longing look at the bike before following her mother.

He immediately stepped over to a firefighter and spoke discreetly with him. He had a certain twinkle in his eye and a hint of a smile.

Soon afterward, Blake came up behind Ivy and brushed her hair lovingly behind her shoulder.

"Got any big plans for tonight?" she asked, suspecting he was up to something heartwarming.

"Just spreading some holiday cheer." He winked.

Ivy smiled, fairly sure she knew what that wink meant. He was too humble to make a show of his good deeds, but she sensed he had something special in store for that little girl.

"Have I mentioned how utterly stunning you are tonight, love?" He breathed into her ear and sent delightful shivers up her spine.

Ivy beamed at him. "Only a handful of times so far, but who's keeping score?"

"In that case, I better raise the bar." He chuckled. "That dress is exquisite on you. I'd compare you to an emerald suited for royalty."

"I must say, Mr. Shepherd, you are quite charming," Ivy said. "Careful, or I might get spoiled by all this flattery."

"I certainly hope so. Do you know why I call you *love*?"

She held her breath. "No, why?"

He kissed her, right there for all of Evergreen Valley to witness. "Because I am falling in love with you, Ivy Bennett."

He gazed at her as if she was the only woman in the hall, and the most beautiful version of herself.

Her heart hammered as he watched her. She ached to tell him how she felt, that she was falling for him, too, though a nagging inner voice warned her to be careful, to protect herself.

Was it too fast to feel this way about him? Her practical side said yes, but her heart pounded every time she looked at him.

Blake posed an understanding smile. He seemed to sense her hesitation, her inner conflict. Nonetheless, the cold fear of past heartbreak held her back.

Ivy closed her eyes briefly, willing herself to say it. *I love you.* It wasn't hard.

But the words froze on her lips. Not here, not now. Instead, she nestled closer to him as the children played. For tonight, this would have to do.

At the punch bowl table, a number of firefighters chatted with attendees while monitoring the children. The hall was transformed into a magical wonderland because of these selfless heroes and the generous community.

Within earshot, Blake's grandfather, Everett, engaged in a lively conversation with Mrs. Harriet Thompson. The gracefully aging woman exuded timeless elegance. Her dress, a delicate shade of blush pink, beautifully complemented her striking gray eyes and the shimmering silver waves of her hair.

In his well-chosen attire, Everett looked debonair. He'd chosen a tasteful deep-plum cardigan over a collared shirt and smartly tied necktie. His lady friend laughed at a humorous joke he made, and a twinkle of glee flickered in his eyes.

He beckoned Ivy and Blake over, extending a gracious hand of introduction, even though Ivy had shared many years of acquaintance with Mrs. Thompson.

Shortly afterward, Blake positioned his camera beside the Christmas village's Santa—a firefighter dressed in a complete set of gear, his helmet crowned by a bright red hat with a white pompom on the tip.

His hearty "Ho ho ho!" brought delight to everyone. Blake clicked away, capturing the pure elation sparkling in each child's eyes as they sat on Santa's lap and received their gifts. Ivy remained near, admiring Blake's skill and compassion.

She inhaled the sugary scent of gingerbread, allowing the familiar aroma of the season to wash over her. She stepped away and ladled two mugs with steaming cider and presented one to Blake, who smiled gratefully.

Parents whispered silly jokes, igniting giggles from their children exactly when the camera flashed.

"This is the best benefit auction ever," she said. "It's such fun to spread Christmas magic."

"All thanks to big-hearted folks like you." Blake gave her waist an affectionate squeeze. "Speaking of magic, want to assist Santa's photographer? I could use an elf helper."

Ivy nodded, donning a green elf hat with a jingling bell over her blond waves. She assisted in positioning enthusiastic children and families in front of the firefighter Santa, arranging their arms just so.

"Say pepperoni pizza!" she encouraged, eliciting a chorus of hilarity from the kids.

One sandy-haired boy stood for a photo with a plastic firefighter's axe, pretending to chop down an imaginary Christmas tree. "Timber!" he yelled.

"Careful where that tree lands!" she played along.

A cherubic six-year-old girl cradled her pristine teddy

bear, its plush warm-brown fur inviting cuddles. "Teddy wants to be an elf just like you!" she declared.

Ivy gave the bear a high five. "We're glad to have you on our team, Teddy!"

Laughter rang out as she shared witty remarks and acted out humorous scenes with the children, putting everyone at ease.

In the meantime, Blake's camera whirred, snapping shot after shot of heartening smiles. He slipped a gift card to McKinley's Ice Cream Shop and a candy cane to each child after their photo, though he never mentioned the gesture to anyone.

When a shy child around five years old seemed unsure about sitting on Santa's lap, Blake gently encouraged her and kneeled down to her level.

"I was scared to talk to Santa at your age, too," he said. "But you know what? He's actually really nice! Here, want to sit with him together?"

The girl nodded bravely. Blake held her hand, helping her whisper her Christmas list, as they sat side-by-side on Santa's lap.

"Looks like I have two special helpers this year," the Santa firefighter bellowed in good-natured humor. He jokingly pretended to strain under their combined weight, producing chortles from the little girl.

Blake smiled and gave them both a thumbs up.

Ivy's affection for Blake deepened, observing him with the children. Although his actions were understated, his generous spirit shone through. And it was in these quiet moments that she began to fall for him more and more.

After the auction wound down, Ivy bid Blake goodnight. He wasn't quite finished, because he had volunteered to stay late and help clean up the trash and decorations.

She decided to head home because she was anxious to see

Cocoa. As she walked, her boots left soft imprints on the pristine snow beneath her feet.

When she reached Central Avenue, a particular empty storefront caught her eye—the future site of Garden Elegance. The shapes of construction workers remodeling the space were distinguishable through the window.

The impending rival florist about to open in her small town twisted her stomach and dampened her holiday cheer.

The store's front door swung open with a creak, and Ivy stepped back, hoping whoever it was wouldn't notice her.

The figure emerged, and Ivy was quick to identify the woman with ebony-black hair swept into a stylish updo, winter coat cinched at the waist, and tall black boots clicking on the pavement.

Britney.

Ivy's unease curdled into irritation. Naturally, Britney would personally oversee the store's construction with her boyfriend, both keen to usurp Ivy's customers.

Ivy willed herself to stay optimistic. She would not allow Britney or Garden Elegance to ruin this special season.

She pulled her scarf tighter and strode briskly down the street. Despite the competition, she resolved to promote her shop with renewed dedication. With her loved ones' support, Ivy's Blooms would continue thriving.

After arriving home, Ivy's priority was to care for her beloved Cocoa after the pet-sitter left. The tiny furball had been impatiently awaiting her return, tail wagging and eyes brimming with elation. She knelt and was given an earnest reception as he nuzzled her.

"You're my little Cocoa Christmas love, you know that?" she whispered.

She tended to his needs and then focused on the business side by phoning Amelia to review the shop's bids post-auction. Tucked at her feet, Cocoa dozed.

"Good news first," Amelia said. "All those who won were notified, and balances paid. Plus, the event exceeded the five-thousand-dollar benchmark by an extra five thousand dollars. So, ten thousand dollars, total, was raised. The rumor is that an anonymous donor contributed a substantial sum of money."

"Any idea who it was?" Ivy asked.

"Blake Shepherd."

Blake? He'd never mentioned a word to her. He was generous, and humble, and considerate.

Another reason why she was falling in love with him, and there was no hope for it.

"On the flip side, a few red poinsettias are missing from our updated inventory," Amelia continued. "Only three or four, but they are definitely gone."

Ivy experienced a sudden plummeting sensation in her gut. "Are you certain, Amelia?" This was a setback the shop couldn't afford. "Perhaps the flowers were miscounted during delivery?"

"I suppose anything is possible," Amelia replied slowly. "I'll double check tomorrow morning when I open the shop."

"Please do," Ivy replied, her voice tight.

Something was amiss.

Britney appeared wherever Ivy turned, and now the possibility of missing inventory? An invisible storm seemed to be gathering, steadily intensifying in the quiet confines of her living room.

After disconnecting with Amelia, Ivy stood stock-still before her little Christmas tree, its mini white lights casting a muted glow. She fingered the garland on the tiny snowman, lost in troubled thought.

If the absent flowers weren't a counting mistake, then someone had intentionally removed them. Who, though? And why target her small shop?

She switched off the tree lights, then filled Cocoa's food and water bowls, ensuring his plush doggy bed was ready for a cozy night.

With Cocoa settled, she headed to bed.

Garden Elegance was on the horizon, and she had to consider everything carefully.

She was determined not to give up. It simply wasn't part of her story.

CHAPTER 10

*B*lake couldn't escape the shadow of worry that loomed in Ivy's eyes. She attempted to conceal her concerns with a placid smile, but he detected the uneasiness that simmered beneath her brave front.

To boost her morale, he suggested dining at his preferred Italian restaurant, Nonna's Bistro. At first, she refused. However, after some coaxing, and Amelia's volunteering to watch Cocoa, Ivy consented. In fact, Amelia agreed to the puppy sleeping overnight at her house.

"His first sleepover!" she had declared.

Blake picked Ivy up in his Jeep, and they arrived at the restaurant at seven o'clock.

At the entrance, a grand, sparkling snowflake-shaped chandelier hung from the ceiling, catching the light, and casting elaborate patterns on the walls. The dining tables were dressed in crimson tablecloths, each one featuring a centerpiece of evergreen boughs and pinecones. Tall, slender candles in antique brass holders added a flickering glow to the room.

As Blake and Ivy stepped inside, the mingling scents of

garlic, tomatoes, and fresh basil beckoned. The kitchen was noisy with dishes sizzling and silverware clattering, while a violinist's poignant notes floated above it all.

"*Buona sera!*" the host, wearing formal black attire, a crisp white shirt and plum-colored bowtie, welcomed them. They handed their coats to the attendant and proceeded to a small table near the back of the restaurant.

Flames leaped in a rustic stone fireplace, carrying a smoky-rich scent.

The host pulled out their chairs and seated them. A violinist perched on a vintage wooden chair played "White Christmas" with elegant precision. Her eyes were closed, absorbed in the music.

Ivy had chosen a midnight blue dress that hugged her slim curves and reflected the candlelight's subtle shimmer. She accessorized with a delicate silver necklace that accentuated her graceful neck.

Blake's breath stilled at the sight of her. Despite admiring her beauty many times, she never failed to move him.

"Ivy Bennett, you are absolutely stunning," he said, taking her hand and brushing a tender kiss on her knuckles.

Ivy smiled, a pretty blush enhancing her cheeks. "Why, thank you, kind sir. You clean up quite nicely yourself." She adjusted his silvery tie, an affectionate sparkle in her eyes.

Blake had chosen a charcoal-gray suit and lavender shirt, hoping to project sophistication. But standing beside Ivy, he was awestruck. Her inner radiance far outshone any of his outward elegance.

His gaze never shifted from her face. Her porcelain skin glowed in the soft, dancing light. The violinist launched into "It Came Upon the Midnight Clear," wrapping the restaurant in a warmhearted, intimate atmosphere.

"Have I mentioned how thrilled I am to share this night with you?" he asked.

"I'm truly delighted to be here. I feel the same way." Ivy's cheeks dimpled with a smile as she perused the menu. "And this is considerably better than another frozen pizza at home."

While they discussed the successful firehouse auction, their server arrived. Wearing a smart black vest and white dress shirt, he demonstrated an impressive memory of the evening's selections.

"May I interest you in our wine list?" he inquired, filling their water glasses with ice and a slice of lemon. "We have an exceptional selection to complement our menu."

Both Ivy and Blake refused with polite smiles.

"Appetizers?" the server inquired.

"No, we'll stick with the main course," Blake said.

"Certainly not a problem. If you change your mind, please don't hesitate to ask. I'll give you a few minutes to select your entrees."

When the server swerved to another table, Ivy leaned forward. "Blake, are you aware that the auction surpassed its goal by double the amount?" As she squeezed the lemon slice into her water, the scent of citrus mingled with the savory aromas around them. "Over ten thousand dollars was raised."

"That's incredible!" Blake grinned.

"A tiny bird told me that a certain mystery donor contributed five thousand dollars."

"Oh?" Blake feigned ignorance and added some lemon to his own water. "And who might this tiny gabby bird be?"

"A little Amelia bird," Ivy replied. "Did you think your donation would stay anonymous in a town this small?"

"I must confess, it was me. I didn't anticipate anyone finding out." Blake laughed and drank a refreshing sip of water.

"The toy drive reminded me of the power of teamwork,"

she continued. "The community joined forces, and it's remarkable what we accomplished together."

He recalled her jotting down her ideas for the flower arrangements she donated, her elegant cursive handwriting adding a touch of grace.

The server returned, producing a pocket-sized notebook and a pen. "What can I get the lovely signorina this evening?" he asked Ivy.

"I'll order the chicken marsala, and a green salad with olive oil and vinegar dressing," she replied.

"Excellent choice." The server turned to Blake. "And for you, signore?

Blake said, "Fettuccine Alfredo please. Been craving it!"

"Very good. *Molto bene.*" The waiter whisked up their menus and proceeded to the kitchen to place their orders.

"I can't wait to hear your thoughts on the marsala sauce," Blake said. His fingers laced with hers, forging a delicate link between them. "Now, please update me on what else is happening. You seem upset."

Ivy hesitated, then revealed her worries about the missing poinsettias. Blake listened, allowing her to vent her frustrations.

Their server approached with a basket of warm, crusty bread and placed it between them. Aromatic steam rose from the bread, along with faint whiffs of cedar from the fire.

"Ivy, I have great news for you," Blake said, offering the breadbasket to her first, then absently tearing off a small piece of bread for himself.

Her gaze fixed on him as she nibbled on the bread. "What is it?"

"Amelia sent me a text today. She couldn't solve what had happened with the poinsettias and was concerned. So, I investigated. Discreetly."

"And?" Ivy inquired. Their fingers brushed as they both reached for more bread.

"One of your suppliers inadvertently shipped a portion of your red poinsettias to a different town's flower shop." He gestured in the direction of the neighboring town with a nod. "They mistakenly took yours, but acknowledged the error and should be sending the flowers back to your shop soon."

Ivy lifted her water glass as a toast to him. "Fantastic. Thank you, Blake. When I spoke with Amelia, she said she was still working on the problem."

"Issue resolved. Amelia will text me when the poinsettias are delivered to your shop." He flashed Ivy a reassuring smile before placing his phone face down on the table. "So, let's enjoy tonight."

Regardless of the challenges, he wanted to keep the holiday bright for her. She deserved nothing less.

After concluding their meal, they selected a pot of chamomile tea to round off the meal.

Blake sank back into his chair with a contented sigh. "You know, I'm thinking of complimenting the chef on the excellent food."

"Right now?"

"Why not?" He laid his napkin on the table and stood. "I'll be back in a few minutes."

He had secretly asked for a decadent cranberry cheesecake for her, embellished with a cranberry drizzle, because she had expressed her fondness for any dessert with cranberries. He'd requested a romantic message on the side of the plate, scripted in rich chocolate sauce: "For Ivy, the woman I love."

He intended to double-check on his order to ensure the server hadn't forgotten.

Ivy regarded him with a curious smile as Blake excused

himself and disappeared into the kitchen. She tried to imagine what he had planned for her, because she'd detected an impish glimmer in his eyes.

The server arrived with an attractively organized silver tea tray. With a masterful touch, he arranged the dainty porcelain teacups and saucers, each accompanied by a gleaming silver spoon. The teapot, ornamented in sophisticated patterns, released a fragrant blend of jasmine and chamomile as he expertly poured her a cup of tea.

As Ivy savored her tea, Blake's cellphone chimed with a text.

"Blake?" She scanned the restaurant, though she didn't see him. "Blake? You got a text."

Assuming he wasn't within hearing distance, Ivy set down her teacup. The text was most likely from Amelia, relaying that the poinsettias had been delivered.

Hmm.

Ivy grappled with a momentary dilemma, debating the ethical implications. This was Blake's cellphone and reading his messages was an intrusion. On the other hand, her concern for Cocoa tugged at her heartstrings, and she would ask Amelia for reassurance that he was okay.

She clicked on the text, and a shiver ran down her spine as she read the first line: *Waiting for a reply regarding last week's email. Photography opportunity in New York City.*

Her breath hitched as she scanned the contents. Blake had received an offer to showcase his work in the Catherine Eden Art Gallery. This must be the well-known gallery he'd mentioned to her early on.

Her belly twisted. Why hadn't he shared this exciting news? How could he keep something so important from her?

She stared at the text again—such an incredible opportunity. She wanted to be happy for him, but somehow, all she felt was hurt.

Blinking back tears, she set his phone down with quivering fingers.

When Blake returned to the table, Ivy looked up with a start.

"You started to drink your tea without me," he teased, his voice light. He failed to notice the storm raging behind her eyes. "Sorry I took slightly longer than I expected. I couldn't find the chef." His voice sounded muffled, drowned out by the blood pulsing in her ears.

"Hey, Ivy, did you hear me?" Concern etched his brows. "What's wrong?"

His loving gaze had lost its ability to comfort her. The yawning space of the table between them was a vast, lonely chasm.

"Blake," she said, her voice quiet. "Why didn't you tell me about New York?"

"How did you know?" His reaction was immediate, a split-second falter in composure.

"I saw the text on your phone. I didn't mean to. I thought it was from Amelia."

He shifted. "Ivy, right, I should explain."

Her heart twinged, disappointment overshadowing all else. Transparency was obviously not in his vocabulary. Why would he conceal something of such significance?

"Look, I had no intention of upsetting you," Blake began, his tone careful and measured. He briefly averted his gaze before locking eyes with her once more. "Now that you're aware, it's important to know that I haven't decided if I will accept the invitation."

She tightly gripped her teacup. "What reason could you possibly have to assume that sharing this news would upset me?"

She wrestled with her disloyalty and chided herself,

struggling to reconcile the pain in her heart with the happiness she should feel for him.

Light snowflakes drifted outside the window. The murmurs of conversation and the clinking of cutlery provided a familiar backdrop, while the melancholic strains of the violinist's opening of "Silver Bells" added to Ivy's emotional battle.

Your photos capture the urgency of our environmental crisis like no other artist I've seen, the text to Blake had read, written by Catherine Eden herself.

"Don't you trust me enough to share big news?" Ivy asked.

He rubbed his temple. "Of course, I trust you. It's…complicated."

"What's so complicated?"

"This might lift my career to a whole new level."

Her fingertips tapped restlessly against her teacup. "You planned on making a choice without discussing it with me? Were you intending to say goodbye, or just leave town?"

He attempted to grab her hand, and she pulled away. "I was trying to figure out the best way to bring it up. It's important we hold on to this. Hold on to us."

"Important to who?" Her voice quivered, revealing the layers of hurt and confusion.

"To me. And to you, too, I hope."

"When is the exhibition?" she asked.

"A few days before Christmas."

"Will you be back here in time for Christmas?"

He lifted his shoulders. "I should be."

He'd invited her to his house to dine with him and his grandfather on Christmas Day. They were slated to serve at the soup kitchen in the morning. And she assumed he'd attend the church service with her.

She recalled their conversation at the Christmas market. She could recite it word for word.

"In fact, it's got me thinking," he said. *"I'm planning to buy a house of my own."*

"Oh?" she asked. *"And where might this house be?"*

"Wherever you are."

Well, she was right here in Evergreen Valley.

He seemed to struggle with his next words. "I didn't want to burden you, but the exhibition could lead to a full-time art grant and residency."

"In New York City?"

"Yes."

Her frustration mounted, her heart pounding against her ribs like a caged bird desperate for freedom. Why would he withhold such life-changing news from her?

"What about...what about the joint gallery we discussed opening?"

"Ivy, I've been looking into it. The space is unavailable because the owner is reviewing applications from multiple businesses."

"Oh." She frowned, disappointed. "What type of businesses?"

"The main contender is a pawn shop. They're willing to pay top dollar for the storefront."

A pawn shop, next door to her flower shop.

She dug her nails into her palms to distract from the tightness in her chest. She barely tasted her tea now, managing to force small sips while navigating her spinning emotions.

"If we intend to build a future together, Blake, we must be honest with each other." She attempted to conceal her inner turmoil with a weak smile, though her mind reeled. What else was he keeping from her? Their foundation of trust had been shattered, along with her dreams.

"Doesn't that include giving each other space to figure

things out?" he shot back. "I needed time to wrap my head around things before discussing everything with you."

"Time?" Her voice rose. "The text stated that the offer was sent last week, and you never brought it up? What does that say about us?"

"I didn't want you to think I was choosing my career over a life in Evergreen Valley with you." He averted his gaze, tugging at his shirt sleeve, wrinkling the fabric between his restless fingers.

"You spoke of buying a home here. Opening a gallery with me." She shook her head, her lips pursed. "By your silence, you lied by omission. That's not how a relationship works."

"Maybe I was afraid." He ran an anxious hand through his hair. "Afraid you might not understand or that you'd try to control how I handled the invitation."

That hurt. A sharp pang surged through her.

"Don't I deserve to be part of major decisions? Or am I merely an afterthought?" She gestured between them. "And when were you planning to tell me the news about our joint gallery?"

"Soon." He rubbed his jawline. "I just found out. I was waiting for an answer from the landlord."

"Soon." Ivy leaned back, letting out a long exhale as she stared up at the exquisitely ornate ceiling. Her pride was wounded, though there was more. He'd let her down, the man she trusted. The man she loved.

"Of course, you're not an afterthought," he insisted. But she detected the flicker of doubt in his eyes.

"Does your grandfather know?"

"Nope. No one until now."

"When would you leave?" A wave of nausea swept through her at the contemplation. "Christmas is in less than a week."

447

"I should've responded to the invitation already," he said. "If I accepted, I'd leave in a day or so. Maybe sooner."

A weighty hush settled over them like a thick blanket of snow on Evergreen Valley's rooftops. They remained sitting, their tea growing cold, neither one willing to make eye contact.

The once enchanting snowflake chandelier and the cheerful violinist failed to bring peace. Instead, the entire restaurant mocked the happiness that had slipped through Ivy's fingers, replaced by the bitter taste of unresolved conflict.

Ivy regarded the dancing flames in the fireplace, her thoughts a jumbled mess of sorrow and confusion. How had they reached this point? Where did they go from here? A single tear escaped and slid down her cheek, unnoticed by Blake, who seemed lost in his own musings. She imagined him reveling in this secret success, not considering how it would affect her.

I thought he loved me…

"Maybe we need some time apart," Ivy whispered.

"Maybe," Blake agreed.

The server bustled over, grinning widely. "A special dessert for the lovely lady from the handsome gentleman!" He positioned a creamy cranberry cheesecake in front of Ivy. Scripted in thick chocolate sauce, a note read: "For Ivy, the woman I love."

She stared at the plate, then back at Blake, an unspoken ache for clarity she couldn't express.

"I had requested this dessert before…everything." Blake couldn't seem to find a comfortable position in his seat. "The plan was for the cheesecake to be a surprise."

The server glanced between them, apparently realizing his interruption had been poorly timed. "I'll just give you two a moment," he said, backing away.

"Thank you, Blake, but I can't do this now." Her voice strained. Grabbing her purse, she rushed to retrieve her coat and exited the restaurant. The grinning server and extravagant dessert faded far into the background.

Winter air stung her tear-soaked cheeks as she hurried down a shoveled path. Blake's thoughtful gesture had only made things more complicated. Distance was necessary to steady her shaken heart. Distance was her lifeline, a desperate escape from the turmoil inside her.

As she crossed the street, her phone buzzed. It was Blake. She hesitated but didn't answer. The seconds ticked by, and she grappled with the unspoken truth. Only time alone could save her.

Suddenly, strong hands grasped her arms, stopping her, turning her to face him.

"Let me drive you home," Blake said, his breath turning to mist in the chilly night air, "We can talk, sort this out."

She didn't respond.

The dimly lit streets, cloaked in the silence of the late hour, were hauntingly empty. The storefronts were veiled in darkness, their usual daytime charm hidden under the obscurity of nightfall. Across the way, the restaurant's exterior, with its ivy-covered walls and the mellow glow of candlelight flickering from windows, stood in stark contrast to her turbulence.

"Ivy, please. I made a mistake, but it changes nothing between us. You're still the most important person in my life."

Shivering, she held her arms close to her body. "I wish I believed that."

"We can make this right." He tried to bring her nearer. She stiffened. "I love you. We'll get through this."

She met his gaze steadily. "No, I need to walk home. Without you."

"Give me a chance to fix everything."

Her lips trembled. "Allow me some time alone." She turned and started walking again.

Her fragmented heart pleaded: turn around, quick, turn around.

Her feet carried her forward. She heard his defeated sigh, though she didn't allow herself to look back.

She wandered aimlessly, allowing tears to escape freely down her cheeks. She advanced one step at a time, praying that the night air would clear the fog of bewilderment and hurt.

CHAPTER 11

Standing on Ivy's doorstep the following day, Blake drew in a bracing breath and knocked. Her eyes were red-rimmed and guarded as she opened the door. The evidence of a long sleepless night. He recognized it. Her struggle mirrored his own.

"Good morning," he said.

"Good morning."

"May I come in?" He motioned toward her open doorway, a wordless suggestion that he shouldn't stand outside in the brisk air.

She faltered for a second but relented, the unresolved tension from their argument hovering between them.

"Only for a minute. I'll be leaving for work soon." She ushered him into the hallway.

Her blond hair nested on her head in a disheveled bun. Despite her pale complexion, her finely sculpted features and high cheekbones, her delicate loveliness, was undeniable.

"This won't take long." Blake studied her, knowing he had caused this rift between them. He shoved his hands into the pockets of his well-worn leather jacket, which was unnecessary, because they were now indoors.

He peered around the living room. "Where's the puppy?"

"He had a sleepover at Amelia's, remember? She's bringing him straight from her place to the flower shop. She bragged about how he was the best boy." Ivy shrugged. "Whatever that means."

"It means that he refrained from chewing every pair of shoes she owns."

Ivy gave a brief smile. "I didn't expect to see you again."

"I texted you several times last night. I called, too."

She nodded. "I know."

"You never answered, you never responded."

"I know.

He placed a hand on her arm. For the first time since they'd met, he wasn't sure how to begin. Ultimately, he led with an apology.

What he really wanted to say was, "Marry me before I leave for New York."

He gazed down at her bent head and uttered the only words that truly mattered. "I love you."

She went rigid, then lifted her head.

"I'm not the least bit surprised," she said, her tone airy. "Everyone wants my flowers this season, especially tall men." She tilted her head thoughtfully. "I suppose my petite stature has them bending over—"

"What?" He tried to steer the conversation back to his original purpose. "I came here for…" He trailed off, unable to find the appropriate words.

He gazed at her strained expression and wondered how his talk about love had turned into a discussion of flowers and height.

She glanced at her watch. "Don't stop now, Blake."

He stepped closer, arms partially outstretched. "I've been

mentally kicking myself. You expect truthfulness and I respect that. I've undermined your trust."

Her arms tightened around herself like a shield. "I don't even know what trust means anymore."

He winced at the pain in her voice and cleared his throat. He might as well get on with it. "I wanted to give you advance notice. I accepted the invitation from Catherine Eden and will fly to New York City."

"When?"

"Soon."

Ivy inhaled a sharp gulp of air. Her hands trembled before she clasped them together.

"This is an exhibition, only an exhibition." He rushed to clarify, his gestures mirroring his haste. "I'll arrive for the grand opening gala, so I can meet the attendees and they can meet me."

"How long is the exhibition running for?"

His fingers tapped nervously on his leg. "Through the holidays and into January."

"I assume this will open many, many doors for your career."

He tried to catch her down-turned eyes. "If my work aligns with the theme and style Catherine is looking for, I might receive a proposal for commissioned assignments and projects."

Ivy mustered a smile, though it stayed just shy of her lips. "In New York City?"

"Yes." He rubbed his unshaven jaw. "They assured me I'll be back here in time for Christmas." As he spoke, he drew an imaginary calendar in the air, marking the days until their reunion.

Ivy stood silent, processing.

He shifted his weight, eager to comfort her, although unsure if she'd accept it.

This opportunity held the promise of an extraordinary future far beyond anything he had ever imagined. Except he couldn't shake the persistent question. What sacrifices would it demand if this truly came to pass? And what about the gallery he and Ivy planned to open?

He imagined the festive days leading up to Christmas without Ivy. Her smile lighting up a room, her kindheartedness and sweet personality. Evergreen Valley was home to him, not some bustling metropolis.

He took her hands, ignoring her flinch. "Please, if this is too much, just say the word. I'll decline and stay." He searched her face, deciding to lay his feelings outright. "You're what matters most to me. The rest is nothing more than background noise."

Tears shimmered in her magnificent hazel eyes. With a wavering breath, she whispered, "Go. Enjoy New York. I'll never stop you from your dream."

"You don't think I'm coming back?"

"Are you?"

"Absolutely." Blake drew her near, relief and sorrow mingling. Regardless of where this opportunity led, he wouldn't lose sight of what actually made his life worth living. Ivy was his compass, his guide.

"You realize this might change everything between us?" Her fingers twisted the silver necklace she still wore around her neck. She stood barefoot, dressed in her trademark work clothes, a taupe-colored blouse and khaki pants. Wrinkles were visible down the legs of her normally crisp pants, and she had unevenly pushed up her sleeves.

Blake glanced down at himself. Rumpled jeans and a wool sweater stained with coffee. Remnants of snow clinging to his boots.

"I told you. This separation won't change anything." He

rubbed his thumb over her knuckles reassuringly. "We may not be physically close, but we'll still be together."

She pulled her hand back and crossed her arms. "You're talking as if you've already accepted a permanent residency."

"I never said that." He tried to meet her gaze, though she refused to look up. "I haven't received any type of long-term offer yet."

"Long-distance relationships are hard, Blake. What if we grow distant or you realize you prefer a glamorous life without me?"

"Ivy, I'm right here, standing in front of you. You're speculating about a future that hasn't even happened." Using a single finger, he tilted her face toward his. "I believe in us, and I need you to believe, too. We can make anything work, no matter how far apart we are."

He wrapped his arms around her, stroking her hair. "Please trust me. Have faith."

She stepped back, putting distance between them. Her gaze locked on the flicker of a vanilla-scented candle on her end table, avoiding his eyes. "I'll miss the gala opening. I would've liked to see it."

"I would love for you to attend," he replied. "Maybe you could get your part-timers to cover the shop for a couple of days."

Her eyes were still focused on the candle's flame. "December is one of the busiest seasons for a florist. Plus, with the additional online orders, there's no way I could take off all that time."

"Then this will have to do for now." He opened his phone and showed her photos of the gallery. The large glass windows displayed a curated collection of paintings and sculptures, each piece more captivating than the last. A small plaque beside the entrance read: "Catherine Eden Gallery: Showcasing Exceptional Talent Since 1985."

"I'll video chat with you during the event," he said. "How's that? I'll give you a virtual tour, introduce you to people. It'll be like you're right there with me."

She nodded slowly, her gaze finally meeting his.

"Can you imagine?" He tucked a strand of hair behind her ear. "My photographs are displayed there, with some of the most talented artists of our time."

Her lips turned up into a soft, bittersweet smile. "I'm so proud of you, Blake. I realize how hard you must've prepared for this."

He held her close, breathing in her floral scent. After a few moments, he pulled back reluctantly. "I should go so I can pack. I'll probably leave tonight. We'll make this work, Ivy. I promise."

"I want to believe you."

"I'll phone you when I arrive. I'm driving to the airport in Roanoke, Virginia, parking my Jeep there, then catching a flight to New York City. I could drive the entire way, but it would take ten hours. Considering the Blue Ridge Mountains and some of those hairpin turns, I'm better off flying much of the route." His thumb wiped away a tear that had escaped and was running down her cheek. His fingers lingered on her soft skin. "I'm booked at the Astoria Royale."

"Sounds posh."

"Definitely from the photos. A grand old hotel, though not nearly as charming as the woman before me." He gave her hands a final, affectionate squeeze. "We'll talk every day."

"Okay. I'm holding you to that."

With one last kiss, Blake withdrew. "I'll be back on Christmas Eve, love."

She soldiered onto the porch and waved as he walked down the steps to his Jeep. As he climbed inside and cranked the engine, his cellphone rang. He glanced at the screen in surprise—it was his friend Rob.

"Hey Rob, what's up?" Blake answered. In the rearview mirror, he glimpsed Ivy standing small and alone. He gave her one last smile before shifting the Jeep into drive, and she soon disappeared from his view.

"Blake, my man!" Rob's enthusiastic voice came through the speaker. "I saw you got invited to the Catherine Eden exhibition, too. Congrats!"

"Thanks."

"Where are you staying in New York City? They put me up at the Astoria Royale. Plush carpets, velvet draperies...I'm in."

"That's where I'm staying," Blake replied, his fingers drumming lightly on the steering wheel as he put more distance between Ivy's house. "Congratulations to you, too."

"Are you in Seattle?" Rob asked.

"Evergreen Falls," Blake replied, his voice conveying a touch of pride.

A momentary pause was punctuated by the hum of the engine.

"Where in the blazes is that?" Rob asked.

"My hometown in the Carolinas, near the Blue Ridge Mountains," Blake began, glancing briefly out the window. "I met a woman here."

"Women get in the way," Rob responded casually.

"Not this woman," he replied firmly.

Rob laughed. "Don't let some small town chick distract you from making it big."

Blake shook his head even though Rob couldn't see him. "It's not like that. Ivy is... She's everything I never knew I needed. My priorities have changed since meeting her."

Rob scoffed. "Have they? We're both competing for the same residency."

Good old Rob, Blake thought, always ready with a verbal jab.

But was Rob right? Did Blake's hunger for success still eclipse all else?

"I titled my photographs Ethereal Dreamscape," Rob continued, a smug tone seeping into his voice. "Abstract photography, an otherworldly realm where imagination and reality blur."

"Sounds interesting," Blake said neutrally.

"Sure hope Catherine Eden thinks so. What did you submit?" Rob asked.

"My photographs reflect environmental concerns."

"Uh-huh," Rob said, clearly not impressed. "Just don't lose focus, alright? This is our big shot. Or I should say, please lose focus, so I can win because my photos are fabulous."

"I won't lose," Blake assured. He tuned out Rob's bragging. Part of him thrilled at the chance to compete with his old rival again. To beat out Rob and prove he was the superior photographer. That hungry ambition still hummed inside him.

But ambition warred with different desires now—of shared holidays and home-cooked dinners with Ivy, long walks with her and Cocoa through sleepy Evergreen Falls, a future built together.

He switched the phone to mute, staring pensively out the windshield as Rob droned on.

His gaze drifted to the envelope containing his prints resting on the passenger seat, IVY written across the front in his bold script. Each photograph captured her essence—her almond-shaped hazel eyes, her sweet smile, the way the sunlight caught the blond highlights in her hair. She was his inspiration, not national acclaim, and he planned to bring the photos with him to keep him rooted.

He'd captured the images outside her shop to help boost her social media presence. She'd sported a whimsical flower tucked behind one ear.

He had also photographed her unique Wishing Blooms ceremony. Much as he had been hesitant to admit it, the beauty and symbolism moved him. As he observed her gifting free flowers during the Christmas season, he couldn't help but recognize her extraordinary kindness.

Blake ran his fingers over the envelope, over her name, as he drove farther away from her. The physical distance didn't matter. She traveled with him in spirit and through his photos of her.

She was the purpose behind his creative renewal. His muse, his inspiration, and his driving force. If the vacant storefront wasn't available, there would be others. They had time.

Yet when he least expected, he could practically taste the heady cocktail of fame and prestige that New York promised.

He switched his phone off mute as Rob launched into speculation about the other exhibiting artists. Blake half listened, his thoughts returning to the woman who had stolen his heart.

As he turned onto the road leading to his grandfather's house, only a few stray snowflakes lazily swirled around the tall pines. Most melted instantly when they landed on the still-warm asphalt bathed in sunlight.

He flipped on the radio, catching the weather report. "Winter storm warning in effect starting Thursday," the meteorologist announced. "Expect heavy snowfall accumulating up to a foot in the higher elevations."

Blake frowned slightly. The flakes were sparse now. Just a whisper of the storm brewing ahead.

CHAPTER 12

On December 22, Ivy took a bite of her sandwich, the closest she could come to a lunch break between fulfilling orders. Then, she said goodbye to Amelia, who was flying to Indiana for the holiday.

Cocoa snuggled on Blake's scarf on the floor behind the counter. Cocoa preferred staying near Ivy, and she had relented. The customers didn't seem to mind.

She sniffed the intoxicating scents of blossoms and greenery as she worked on the afternoon's deliveries, but thoughts of Blake kept tugging at her focus. Since he'd left, she'd kept the shop open until late, and started early each morning, so that she and her employees could keep up with customers' last-minute demands.

When her cellphone rang, her heart leaped. Blake was phoning. She missed him desperately and had hardly heard from him. Once, when he arrived in New York, and then intermittently.

He'd promised to video chat and show her his exhibit while mingling with attendees. However, she was too busy with rushed flower orders and couldn't answer when he called. Later, she'd sent him an apologetic text, only to receive a disheartened emoji in response.

"Hey, you," she answered, unable to hide her elation.

"Ivy, love, I apologize for not connecting sooner. Life is nonstop here, and I keep losing track of time. Sometimes I look at my watch and realize I've stayed longer at an event than I intended."

"You must have such a hectic schedule. I hope you're not too overwhelmed." She tracked her finger along a floral order pad, wishing he was with her instead of miles away. Freezing rain pattered against the window, mirroring the storm of emotions inside her.

She glanced at her shop's walls, one side decked out with the photographs he had captured for her website. A few featured her sporting a bright red poinsettia nestled charmingly behind her ear.

Her absolute favorite photograph was the candid selfie of the two of them. Her spontaneous reaction, frozen by his unexpected kiss, was forever celebrated with a joyful, ever-present smile on her face.

He had created three sets of prints, ensuring she had duplicates for her shop and home, while keeping an additional copy for himself.

"The gala was quite formal," he said. "Luckily, I was able to rent a tuxedo."

"Wow, fancy you!" she chided.

"Catherine Eden wanted to chat with you." His voice had a slightly lower tone than usual, somewhat deflated. "Regretfully, you missed her."

"Sorry." Ivy absently adjusted a cluster of holly branches as she absorbed the news.

"Some celebrities and models attended, too. I bet if I told you their names, you'd recognize them."

"I bet I would." She tried to keep her tone friendly but

expressed no further interest. Deep down, uncertainty flickered. Would the allure of New York and its glamorous scene change him, drawing him away from her?

"How's the weather there?" he asked.

"Freezing temperatures. We expected a snowstorm, but thankfully, it bypassed us. You?"

"Blizzard conditions, but it's not supposed to hit until Christmas Day, and I'll be gone by then."

"I hope so. Holiday travels can be a nightmare."

"Not for me, love. I'm booked and ready to fly."

She smiled. Her heart lightened. "How was the exhibition?"

As he described the opening, his words quickened, conveying an infectious energy that painted vivid images. She was proud of him and told him so.

"Thank you," he said. "That means a lot."

The phone fell silent for a beat.

"Ivy...they offered me the residency. I won first place," Blake said. "I wanted you to be the first to know." Presumably, he was holding his acceptance letter, as paper rustled on his end.

"Oh." In an effort to calm her racing heart, she pressed a hand to her chest. Adrenaline flooded her veins, causing her limbs to shake. "Are you intending to say yes?"

He released a heavy sigh. "The entire program is an incredible opportunity. However, it means being apart from you. Not permanently. A short period of months."

"Definitely, you should accept," she said.

"Are you certain? I don't want to lose you."

His tenderness calmed her. The image of his earnest blue eyes and dark, furrowed eyebrows blurred everything else.

"You won't lose me," she whispered.

"I'm grateful for you. I'm grateful for your understanding." His tone took on a respectful, reverent quality. "This is a major step for my career."

"I know. I know. So, you'll be living in New York?" She knew how significant this honor was and aimed to be supportive.

Still, the concept of all that distance between them burdened her heart.

"Yes," he replied. "I booked an afternoon flight on Christmas Eve, so I'll see you by nightfall. We'll have time to discuss things."

She clutched the phone tighter, wishing she could feel his embrace. "The church service at Evergreen Chapel is at nine o'clock on Christmas morning."

"I remember. I'll be there. I received an invitation from Catherine to a formal holiday luncheon on the Eve, but the flight is only two hours from New York, then an hour's drive from there, barring bad weather. Don't forget, my grandfather is planning a Christmas dinner, and of course, you'll bring Cocoa. Plus, I have a special surprise."

"What kind of surprise?"

"It wouldn't be a surprise if I told you, now, would it?"

She laughed. "I'm looking forward to a wonderful holiday. I bought the ingredients for my orange-cranberry sauce."

"Legendary, right?"

"Definitely." She grinned. "Sounds like you've mapped everything out."

"I try. Once I've officially moved to New York, I'll fly to Evergreen Valley at least once a month. More often if my calendar allows."

"How many months will you be away?" she asked.

"Six, although there's talk of an extensive project which might detain me a little longer. Some type of collaboration, so they may prolong my stay."

Collaboration. Nature's Palette, the vacant store, was supposed to be a collaboration. Had he forgotten everything they had planned together?

Her thoughts ran rampant, her lip caught in a tight grip. She imagined attending Amelia's birthday party in January by herself, and small-town gatherings without Blake accompanying her. She visualized countless lonely nights, memories of him everywhere, missing his warmth in the lengthy, cold months ahead.

"What if we drift apart?" she asked, expressing her deepest fear aloud. "What if we suddenly wake up and discover we've become strangers?"

"We can exchange photos, videos, messages. When I'm in town, we'll discuss the logistics."

"Will you be here long?" she inquired.

"Unfortunately, only a handful of days. Catherine wants me back in New York for a New Year's Eve gala."

Ivy briefly shut her eyes, imagining their new reality: the physical space separating them, the sporadic phone calls, the bittersweet reunions. It was a far cry from the few weeks they had shared but love sometimes demanded change and compromise.

The celebration of his achievements became a painful reminder of their once unbreakable bond.

"How is our little Cocoa?" Blake asked.

"He's fine, and up to his usual mischief." She stepped over to a bouquet of white roses in a porcelain vase, distractedly pruning the flowers as she spoke.

"Nobody else has surfaced to claim him?"

"No." Ivy set down the pruning shears and brushed her hands on her apron.

"Has your shop been busy?"

Her gaze swept across the stack of orders resting on a shelf. "We've been swamped, even with the college students pulling extra hours. My online presence is having a real impact."

"Mark my words. Garden Elegance won't take an iota of business away from you."

"I'm starting to believe you're right." She nodded before realizing he couldn't see her.

She stole a quick peek at the Christmas tree. She and Blake had spent a lively evening decorating it together, the hours overflowing with laughter and stolen kisses. Currently, its beauty only magnified his absence.

"Blake." A woman shouted his name from the background. "Reservations are in fifteen minutes at The Crystal Chateau. We'll be late if we don't leave now." Her tone was commanding and bore a flirtatious undercurrent.

He muffled the phone. "I'm coming."

"Who is that?" Ivy asked.

"Catherine Eden. She arranged for several of the photographers to dine at some ultra-exclusive restaurant. My buddy Rob is joining us."

"Who is Rob?"

"He's a photographer friend from Seattle. The guy snagged the runner-up position, and he's clinging to Catherine like she's the winning lottery ticket." Blake laughed. "I swear, he's probably praying for me to disappear so he can swoop into first place."

"Blake?" the woman called out again.

"I'm coming," he repeated.

"Where are you?" While handling a rose, Ivy accidentally pricked herself on a thorn. As a tiny drop of blood welled up, she continued conversing while grabbing a tissue.

"I'm leaning against a stately column in the lobby of the Astoria Royale. It's quite a tall sight that rises from the floor to the ceiling." His resonant voice flowed, causing Ivy to dig deeper into her emotions—longing, doubt, and a touch of insecurity. She clenched the phone, trying to anchor herself to the conversation.

"A bunch of exhibitors are staying here," he continued. "You would enjoy it. Maybe someday, right?"

"Yeah, sure." Her attention wandered before fixing again on the pristine white roses in the vase. "Maybe someday."

"Ivy, never forget." He spoke more gently, as if he detected the vulnerability in her voice. "I love you."

She closed her eyes for a brief second, finding her equilibrium as she reined in her emotions. Hints of honey and spice, the delicate fragrance of roses, surrounded her. "I...I love you, too," she murmured.

She clicked off, already missing his voice. Until then, she'd measure the hours until she saw him again. Two days. Surely, nothing could happen in two days.

She peered out the window at the dreary weather. Somehow, she would find the courage to endure this season of separation.

Prior to shutting the shop down for the night, Ivy phoned the vet's office to set up an appointment for Cocoa's follow-up exam and booster shot. The receptionist informed her that Dr. Mitchell had an available appointment the next morning. Ivy confirmed before hanging up.

"Cocoa, you're all set for your visit tomorrow." Ivy settled into a chair in the back room, and the puppy curled contentedly in her lap. Affectionately scratching behind his ears, she pushed aside any concerns about Blake.

He loved her. He'd told her as much. And she loved him.

For now, her top priority was to complete Cocoa's records.

Ivy arrived at the veterinarian's office with time to spare. She'd escalated her part-time workers to full-time, and they arrived at her shop early to begin fulfilling orders for the day.

The vet's waiting room was hushed, with the mild hum of fluorescent lights overhead and the subtle odor of antiseptic in the air.

As she sat down, Dr. Mitchell entered, bearing Cocoa's medical file. "As I discussed with you, Cocoa is probably a purebred Pomeranian, based on his physical characteristics and temperament." She pointed to the fluffy, energetic puppy on Ivy's lap.

"You suspected as much," Ivy replied, caressing Cocoa's fur. "Now I'd like to learn how he came to be abandoned."

"The number of Pomeranian breeders in the area is quite limited in this region, but I can give you contacts for a few of them." Dr. Mitchell jotted down a list of names and numbers and handed the information to Ivy.

"Thank you." Ivy accepted the paper, tucking it carefully inside her handbag. "I'm committed to finding out the truth about how he came to be shivering behind a trash can on a cold night."

Within an hour, after several phone calls and digging through online resources, she unearthed a disturbing story. Cocoa was from a notorious pet store that acquired puppies illegally before they were old enough to leave their mothers. The store was in a semirural area, outside the immediate vicinity of Evergreen Falls.

Instead of bearing the costs for veterinary expenses, the pet store had abandoned Cocoa when he fell ill. The discovery left her both saddened and more determined than ever to provide the finest possible care for him.

She should've investigated his background earlier, although her initial goal when she first found him was to reunite him with his previous owners. Then she had focused on finding him a nurturing household.

When she returned to the vet to go over the information, Dr. Mitchell assured her that Ivy could assume ownership, and there was no need for a formal adoption. She provided Ivy a collar and a tag for Cocoa and suggested implanting a microchip when the puppy was neutered.

"Congratulations!" Dr. Mitchell said. "What can be better than adopting a sweet puppy during the holidays? I hope that Cocoa is your Christmas love."

COCOA IN TOW, Ivy walked through the front door of her home and set her key on the kitchen table. The place felt too tidy, too hushed without Blake. She studied the solitary mug sitting neatly in the drying rack—her morning coffee had been a solo affair.

Her miniature Christmas tree sparkled merrily, its lights contrasting her nostalgic state. The bright bulbs strung over her mantel enlivened the living room, though not enough.

Shaking off her loneliness, she immediately phoned Blake.

"I have fantastic news," she said. But his phone directed her to voicemail, and she didn't leave a message.

She disconnected, her excitement fading. She had hoped to share Cocoa's origins with him. Nonetheless, she understood he was busy with gallery events.

She took a quick look around her home and blinked back the onset of tears. The only sound was the soft clacking of puppy paws on the floor as he darted over to her, his plumed tail swaying with excitement.

"Hey there, little guy." Ivy bent down to stroke behind his velvety ears. "Looks like you're 100 percent Pomeranian, after all. We figured out where you came from."

Cocoa yipped and licked her hand.

"How about some dinner?" she asked, heading to the

pantry. Cocoa followed closely at her heels, nuzzling her leg. At least she had some company.

Ivy loaded his bowl and watched as he noisily crunched his food. She prepared herself an egg salad sandwich, but the creamy flavors of the eggs and whole-grain bread tasted bland. Her eyes stung as she thought about sharing her recent update over a celebratory supper with Blake tonight—if only he were here.

She peered through the frosted window above the sink. Night had fallen, cloaking the backyard in inky darkness. The tree's bare branches swayed in the biting wind and rattled the panes. The previous flurries and ice had coated the ground in a dusting of shiny, powdery white.

They'd only been separated a few days. Imagine when they were apart for months. She missed his tender hugs and the impact of his smile. Her home was hollow without him.

She reached up to a shelf above a cabinet, where she had placed Blake's Christmas gift for safekeeping. The woolen scarf, in a deep blue, matched his eyes. She'd hurried to the market during a lunch break, anticipating he'd be pleased with her choice.

She phoned him again. As before, the call went straight to voicemail.

Uncertainty crept in. Was he avoiding her? Caught up with his dynamic new life in the glittering "Big Apple"?

Her eyes darted to her silent phone, willing him to call her.

Cocoa pattered over, his tiny frame quivering with boundless enthusiasm. He stared up at her, expecting her undivided focus.

While brewing a cup of chamomile tea before bed, she switched on the radio. Reports blared of an impending blizzard sweeping the coast and heading for New York City.

Her breath hitched, fears spiraling.

Snowed in. Power out. Blake unreachable. He needed to get out of New York sooner rather than later.

She tried once more to contact him, worry rising when she couldn't reach him.

Leaving another voicemail, Ivy speculated—was his schedule truly that hectic? Or was there a different reason he was unavailable? Cocoa's wet nose nudged her leg, jolting her from her anxious thoughts.

She contemplated calling his grandfather to find out if Everett had received any word from Blake but decided not to alarm him.

Her mind flashed to Catherine Eden, recalling how Blake had muffled the phone when she'd spoken. Ivy shook her head, struggling to shake off her suspicions.

"You're overreacting," she scolded herself.

Her mind conjured up an image of him in her comfortable living room, both sipping hot cocoa after he'd shoveled her front walk. Yet all that surrounded her was the mournful sounds of the chilling wind.

She peeked out her front window. The freezing rain had subsided, leaving trees heavy with frost and a shrouded, frozen landscape.

She blinked and turned away. Some things remained elusive on this never-ending frigid night. Blake's disappearance was one of them.

CHAPTER 13

On Christmas morning at nine o'clock, Ivy sat in Evergreen Chapel. Alone.

Today was a special day. Today was Christmas.

She'd chosen a knee-length sweater dress in a deep, jewel-toned orchid, and a pair of silver stud earrings. She'd combed her hair slightly off center and left it loose, securing it with a whimsical poinsettia hairpin to keep it out of her face. A hint of blush and a classic red lipstick completed her outfit, along with a white woolen coat she reserved for church and special occasions.

She'd left Cocoa at home, his first time unattended, assuring him she wouldn't be gone for more than a couple of hours. She limited his reach to any dangerous items and made sure he had access to food, water, and his favorite toys.

"Happy Holidays," she said, and gave him his plush raccoon toy. A bonus, it squeaked, which made the toy even more exciting.

Hollowness swelled within her as the service began. Blake promised he'd be home for Christmas, yet his place on the hard wooden pew beside her remained empty. She shifted, her shoulders slumping. The brief, vague text from him the evening before, that he was stuck on the airport tarmac on the last flight out of New York City, only heightened her unease. The chill from the frosty morning seeped through the fabric of her dress, and she pulled her wool coat tighter.

The choir's harmonized hymns resonated, though to Ivy, the joyous notes sounded muffled and distant. She could hardly focus on the lyrics, promising solace when her thoughts remained fixed on Blake's empty seat beside her.

Where was he? She held back tears and avoided the sympathetic glances from nearby neighbors and friends who were celebrating Christmas with their happy families. Today was supposed to be special, even enchanting, but she had never felt more alone.

She peered around. Members of the congregation had fashioned evergreen wreaths for every window using pinecones, red ribbons, and holly leaves.

The wooden beams that crisscrossed the ceiling, showing signs of age and history, enhanced the church's character. She'd sat in this church for decades, bearing witness to countless Sunday sermons, weddings, and baptisms.

The choir of townsfolk—men and women dressed in simple robes—stood with their hymnbooks in hand. A member played an old upright piano, her fingers gliding over the keys with practiced ease, accompanying their voices.

The choir sang a harmonized rendition of "O Come, All Ye Faithful," inviting all believers to adore the newborn King. Friends shared heartfelt greetings with radiant smiles. Sitting alone, Ivy couldn't escape the overwhelming void of Blake's absence.

In her mind she saw him, charming the crowd at the luncheon, devastatingly handsome in a black tuxedo, mingling with celebrities and models. He'd mentioned he often lost track of time at events, staying later than intended.

Ivy fought to restrain her tears as the pastor began his sermon, his deep voice booming through the chapel. He spoke of nurturing relationships, showing love to one another, and coming together during the Christmas season. She turned more than once to the back of the church but saw only families seated in solidarity.

Where was Blake?

She longed to have him by her side, to embrace him on this holy day.

Doubts crept in. Was he truly committed to their relationship? She had cleared her schedule and she and her assistants had delivered all the flower orders. Her shop was closed for the following few days, and she'd anticipated spending every waking minute with him.

Meanwhile, he'd chosen a fancy luncheon over her. The blizzard seemed like a convenient excuse for his delayed arrival.

At the end of the sermon, Ivy bowed her head and prayed. She wanted to believe the best in Blake, yet these past couple of days were difficult to ignore. The pastor's message about love inspired her to talk openly with Blake about their relationship when she saw him again.

If she saw him again.

Ivy stepped outside the church after the final hymn faded. She peered up the path, hoping to see Blake rushing toward her, full of apologies and explanations for why he hadn't contacted her. But he wasn't there.

With a resigned exhale, she walked home to retrieve Cocoa before volunteering at the soup kitchen in the church's fellowship hall.

An hour later, as she plated roast turkey, gravy, and green

beans to the grateful patrons, she continued thinking about Blake. Where was he? Her initial frustration at not hearing from him had shifted to real concern.

She anxiously checked her phone, but only received a message from Amelia wishing her a Merry Christmas and a cute photo of her golden retriever.

Blake's text had stated he was aboard the last flight before the blizzard completely battered the Northeast.

That text was over twelve hours ago. If the airline canceled, why hadn't he called? Was he stranded alone on Christmas Day? She steadied herself, her cheerful façade masking the turmoil within.

He was supposed to be here with her right now.

She surveyed the hall, decorated with red and green tablecloths by the congregation volunteers also serving the holiday meal.

Cocoa darted between people's legs, creating a comical dance as they tried to avoid stepping on him. His frisky antics helped lift her mood, at least temporarily.

Shortly afterward, Ivy returned home and phoned Everett, confirming their dinner plans. "Have you heard from Blake?" she asked hopefully. "I texted him several times, and called, too. All my messages went to voicemail."

Everett's silence gave her the answer.

Ivy secured Cocoa in his crate with a seat belt in the back seat of her hatchback and drove to Everett's house. She had wrapped the hand-knit blue scarf as a gift for Blake, hoping, somehow, that he would arrive to open it.

She also brought something else. Something special. Her last Wishing Bloom.

Inside Everett's home, the kitchen table overflowed with slices of maple glazed ham, mashed potatoes, stuffing, and a pumpkin pie for dessert. Ivy had prepared an orange-cran-berry sauce per their plans.

"Merry Christmas," she said, handing Everett the Wishing Bloom in a slender green vase.

Her precious bloom, the symbol of hope. The petals quivered, displaying a translucent quality with shades of lavender that seemed to shimmer.

"Thank you." The meaning wasn't lost on him. In his aged blue eyes, she glimpsed a reflection of the endless skies that had watched over his many years. "I didn't get you anything, Ivy, and this is—"

"Precious. We need hope now, like we've never needed it before," she said. "We're here, together. Celebrating Christmas, and that's a blessing."

He centered the bloom on the table. "You are my grandson's true blessing. Meeting you is the best thing that ever happened to him."

Ivy followed Everett into the living room. Under the Christmas tree, she set Blake's wrapped gift and placed a wriggling Cocoa on the floor.

"I baked a tasty reward for our puppy here." Everett dipped his hand into a jar on a bookshelf, retrieving a cookie.

"Is it safe for Cocoa?" she asked.

"Totally. I shaped it like a dog bone." Everett presented the treat to Cocoa, who snatched it with gleaming eyes. He scampered off with the cookie in his mouth and settled between the brightly wrapped gifts under the tree.

She stepped back to admire the hand-carved tree-topper. "Blake told me he didn't want you standing on a ladder, so he placed the star up there for you. It's beautiful."

"I agree." Everett sank into an armchair and gestured for Ivy to sit across from him.

"My grandson is a special guy." A genuine fondness colored Everett's tone. "Even from when he was a boy, he had a huge, generous heart." Everett squinted, as though he viewed the world through a gentle, nostalgic filter. "His

475

parents passed when he was a child, but he persevered bravely."

Ivy clasped her hands in her lap. "Please tell me a little about his childhood. He mentioned you and your wife raised him from an early age."

"Oh, I have lots of tales." Everett chuckled. "Here's a favorite. One Christmas when Blake was eight years old, a few months after losing his parents, he asked me if we could leave an extra plate of sugar cookies out for Santa accompanied by a note saying that people cared about Santa, too. When I asked why, he said it must get lonely traveling all over the world with nobody to keep you company. He wanted Santa to know there were folks thinking of him too."

Ivy pictured a young, innocent Blake, striking blue eyes, brown hair soft and tousled. She empathized with the burdens he had carried because of his losses.

Everett paused, taking a shaky breath as he dabbed at the corner of his eyes with a handkerchief. "When I pressed for more, Blake said..." Everett grew quiet for a moment. "He said, 'Because I don't want anyone to feel as lonely as I do without Mom and Dad.' That made me cry. That's just the thoughtful guy he is. My Shutterbug."

Ivy wiped the tears from her own eyes and reached out to squeeze his hand. "Blake was on that last flight. I checked, and it never took off. However, he hasn't contacted either of us since. Should we alert the authorities?" She hesitated, almost afraid to ask the haunting question. "Where is he?"

"He'll find his way back home," Everett looked down at his hands, his voice cracking. "I reckon all we can do is wait and pray. I'm certain he's safe. I feel it in my bones."

Ivy's thoughts drifted to Catherine Eden, a name that intruded on her mind uninvited. Jealousy surfaced, an unexpected emotion that threatened to overshadow her concern for Blake.

No. Impossible. Not Blake. Ivy silently protested the idea that he might be safe with someone else, but she couldn't ignore the flood of resentment.

Hearing a car pull up, her pulse quickened. But it was Mrs. Harriet Thompson, wearing her bright canary-yellow coat. She stood at the door with a delightful assortment of buttery shortbread cookies in hand. As Everett greeted her, inquiring about her plans for dinner, she grinned and graciously accepted his invitation to join them.

BLAKE MISSED the Christmas Eve flight he'd booked from New York City to Roanoke, Virginia, by mere minutes. Frantically, he dashed to the airline counter, desperate to exchange his ticket for the final departure of the evening. After receiving a lecture from the attendant that it wasn't easy to change a flight on a holiday, she found a cancellation and issued him a ticket.

Thirty minutes later, he stepped aboard the plane, and breathed a faint sigh of relief.

As the snowstorm loomed, the plane sat on the tarmac. Inside the cabin, Blake grappled with spotty cellphone service, each attempt to phone Ivy tense with frustration. He left a message, though he feared the transmission was uncertain.

Eventually, even that fight was cancelled, with no seats available until Christmas Day. His luggage had vanished into the holiday abyss.

Blake declined the airline's voucher for a free hotel room and meal and decided to wait at the airport for the first flight to Roanoke in the morning.

There, he questioned his choices.

Why did he dawdle at Catherine's lavish luncheon, chatting with influential photographers and critics? He justified it as the pursuit of career advancement, the belief that networking was the key to success.

As the terminal lights dimmed and the snowstorm raged on, his patience wore thin. He stared outside, hostage to the whims of the unforgiving weather. He checked his cellphone, noticing the battery nearly drained. In his haste, he'd forgotten to stow a charger in his carry-on bag.

With an irritated grimace at his oversight, he decided that staying cooped up in the departure lounge was no longer viable.

He approached the customer service desk just in case there had been a change. The agent, trying to manage the chaos caused by the weather, provided him with somber news—there was nothing available now until well after Christmas.

Okay, that settled it. He had no other option but to take matters into his own hands. He requested a refund for his canceled flight, which was promised at a later time, and made his way to the only rental car counter that remained open.

There, Blake exchanged words with the attendant. He intended to drive the SUV to Roanoke, and then take his Jeep on to Evergreen Valley.

The attendant handed Blake the keys to the last vehicle available, an SUV, instructing Blake to take an airport bus to the parking lot that had the rental cars.

Blake stepped from the bus a few minutes later and eyed the vehicle skeptically. Its tired tires bore the marks of wear and tear, looking ill-prepared for the persistent snowfall.

Taking a calming breath, he settled into the driver's seat, the rusty frame and faint sputtering of the engine increasing his unease. The clock on the dashboard displayed a time that taunted him, ticking away the precious minutes leading into Christmas Day.

As he merged onto the snow-covered highway, the city lights slowly receded in his rearview mirror. Flakes the size of cotton balls swirled in the headlights' feeble glow, creating an eerie, otherworldly landscape beyond the windshield. The wipers struggled to keep pace, their erratic thumping echoing the fitful beat of his heart.

His breath formed frosty patterns on the windows, a testament to the bitter cold that seeped into the SUV, despite the feeble attempts of the heater.

The snowfall intensified.

His hands clenched the cold steering wheel. Arctic air sank into his bones, fueling his desperation. The radio, his sole companion, crackled intermittently with static, and the soothing tunes of Christmas carols were drowned out by the wind.

Once he arrived at the Roanoke Airport, he left the SUV behind at the designated rental car return area and released the keys in the company's drop box. After locating his Jeep, he tried the ignition. A few tense moments, and the engine roared to life.

Navigating through the treacherous mountains was daunting, causing him to fear that he wasn't up to the task. His gaze darted between the dimly lit road and the GPS screen, where the estimated arrival to Evergreen Valley seemed to recede like a mirage.

He glanced at the photographs of Ivy he had set on the seat beside him. He always carried them with him. She was the reason he was determined to make this journey, to overcome the odds stacked against him.

Mile after endless mile, hazy headlights approached through the storm before disappearing. Blake squinted into the sea of white, every muscle tense.

Only a few hours. Please let my trusty Jeep make it.

His mind wandered to his recent conversation with Rob

at the luncheon. They had discussed their achievements, laughingly trying to one-up each other.

Rob had nursed a tumbler of whiskey, its amber hue catching the light as he swirled it. Blake held a flute of sparkling water, the condensation chilling his fingers. As the discussion progressed, Rob became increasingly vocal, his gestures interspersed by the clink of ice in his glass.

As Blake replayed their chat, he recalled Rob's words, which had initially sounded like humorous banter. Rob had chuckled and said, "You got me today, Blake, but next time, I'll take that top spot."

Rob's competitive spirit was unwavering and pursuing victory was ingrained in his nature.

In a moment of reflection, Blake paused.

Rob's words, though couched in rivalry, helped him understand the stark contrast in their priorities. While Blake strived for recognition, Rob's commitment to competition served as a reminder that success, although satisfying, was not the most important thing in life.

While fulfilling, winning wasn't as meaningful as the love Blake shared with Ivy. He imagined her alone by the fireplace with an expectant yet troubled look in her eyes.

His phone, still clutching to the faintest glimmer of a signal, allowed him a brief call. The spotty connection was a link, a fragile thread connecting their hearts across the miles.

"Ivy." He spoke her name softly. "I'm on my way. I promise I'll make it up to you."

He only hoped that his message had gone through.

With those words, the road stretched before him. Every mile drew him closer to Ivy, to Cocoa, and to their shared love.

In Everett's homey kitchen, Ivy picked at her slice of pumpkin pie with her fork. Even the taste of Mrs. Thompson's butter cookies dusted with powdered sugar, so delicious that they crumbled in her mouth, failed to stir her appetite.

Laughter echoed around the table as Everett and Mrs. Thompson shared stories and inside jokes, then walked into the living room to sit by the fire with Cocoa close behind. Ivy managed a wan smile and cleared the dishes, while her thoughts stayed anchored on Blake.

She checked her watch. Almost four o'clock and still no word from him.

She shut her eyes against the sting of tears, and a cold nose nudged her feet under the table. Ivy glanced down to see Cocoa.

"Don't worry, boy, I'm sure he's trying," Ivy whispered to the puppy, wishing she believed it, before Cocoa bounded back to the living room.

The rumble of a familiar Jeep's engine jolted her heart. She rushed to the front window, pulse racing. Could it be…?

There, in the waning light of late afternoon, Blake climbed out of his snow-covered Jeep and reached into the back seat for his carry-on bag. His height and strong build were commanding. His tousled brown hair and the shadow of a dark beard gave an appealing touch of ruggedness that nearly brought her to her knees.

As she continued to stare out the window, an undeniable warmth spread through her, a moment that seemed suspended in time.

"He's here!" Slipping into her boots, Ivy burst out the front door into the biting December wind.

He was here, he was really here.

"Blake!" She blurted out his name. In seconds she was flying down the steps, the frozen air burning her throat.

He swiveled, his face breaking into a relieved grin. He opened his arms just as Ivy crashed into his chest.

"Ivy, I'm so sorr—"

"I was beyond worried. Are you alright?" Her words tumbled out in a rush.

"Nothing could have kept me from you, love."

Her happiness became tears of elation as they held each other close. Blake's jacket was cold against her flushed cheeks, but his embrace was reassuring and steadfast. Ivy breathed him in, the familiar leather and pine scent.

Overwhelmed, Ivy sought his lips in a kiss that radiated longing, forgiveness, and the simple bliss of reunion. The world around them faded away. In this perfect moment, there was only Blake and Ivy united at last.

"Even a blizzard couldn't stop me," he murmured, his warm breath tickling her ear. He cradled her face in his gloved hands and kissed her again. "Especially on our first Christmas as a couple."

He deepened the kiss, releasing every ounce of her longing.

Finally, they drew apart, breathless. Blake rested his forehead against hers, his thumb caressing her cheek.

"The airline cancelled all the flights because of the blizzard, so I drove over ten straight hours." His breath clouded the crisp air. He described the wait in the airport, on the tarmac, and the hazardous conditions.

Ivy searched his face, seeing only earnest love in his exhausted blue eyes. Slowly she smiled, the hollowness within her beginning to thaw.

They entered the house, stamping snow from their boots, then removing them. Blake set his jacket and gloves by the entryway.

In the snug kitchen, the lone Wishing Bloom sat in the center of the table, its delicate petals glowing under the lights.

Blake stared at it and grinned. "Isn't this bloom your last one?" he asked.

"Yes. While you were gone, we needed a little hope to wish on. What would be better than a Wishing Bloom?"

"Nothing at all." Blake's grin widened as Everett and Mrs. Thompson peered at him from the doorway of the living room. Mrs. Thompson held Cocoa in her arms.

"Welcome home, Shutterbug," Everett said.

"Thanks, Grandpa." Blake stepped forward and hugged his grandfather. "I'm sorry I'm late."

"No need for apologies. We hold each other up in the hard times and celebrate in the good times. That's what brings us together and keeps us strong." Everett returned Blake's hug with a heartfelt squeeze. "So, how did you find the big city experience? Again."

Blake's gaze drifted away momentarily, taking in the humble kitchen. "Stressful. I'm done with it—all of it. I feared I wouldn't have another chance—to make things right with Ivy." He took her hand in his.

"Sometimes life presents opportunities that only come around once." Everett stroked the puppy's ears and received an enthusiastic lick to his gray-bearded chin as a reward. "If other opportunities arise, ones we mistakenly believe to be more significant than they truly are, it's possible for second chances to slip right through our fingers."

Ivy's eyes filled with tears. She knew Everett was referring to her and Blake.

"You're absolutely right, Grandpa, but not this time," Blake replied. "I don't intend to waste another chance."

"Good. We should never assume or underestimate our blessings." Everett placed a hand on Blake's shoulder. "Now, let's get you something to eat. We've got a Christmas dinner waiting."

As Everett and Mrs. Thompson marched into the kitchen with Cocoa, Blake kissed Ivy again. "Well, Ivy Bennett, I guess your Wishing Blooms have some real magic after all. Maybe they do help wishes to come true."

Ivy chuckled. "Indeed, Blake Shepherd. Seeing is believing, but sometimes believing is what makes you see."

Later, after Blake had refreshed with a shower and donned a clean outfit, they all gathered while he enjoyed dessert. Ivy waited patiently, overflowing with anticipation. As he finished, she finally handed him her gift, and he carefully unwrapped it to reveal a deep-blue scarf that complemented the shade of his eyes.

"Thank you," Blake murmured, kissing her. "I also have a holiday surprise for you."

Intrigued, Ivy glanced around, but no physical gift was in sight.

"It's not here," he confirmed, taking her hand.

They bundled up against the winter chill, Cocoa prancing on his leash as they walked downtown.

Ivy gazed at Blake, searching for some clue in his expression, as he led her to the empty storefront neighboring her flower shop.

She looked up and drew in a small, sharp gasp. There, where the faded wooden sign for Eleanor's Toy Emporium had hung crookedly, was something else. A pristine sign declaring Nature's Palette in bold green lettering.

He hadn't forgotten. This thoughtful man—so often lost in his work—had remembered the quiet ambition they had shared. A fanciful notion that they might run a gallery together, filled with light and creativity.

He met her gaze, a hint of boyish shyness in his smile. Blake hadn't just remembered. Carefully, he had brought her wisp of a dream to life, crafting something real and lasting.

"You did this for us?" she managed to ask.

Blake traced a path along her cheek, his touch tender. "For you, love. Our new beginning. I texted Catherine Eden and declined the offer." He chuckled. "I'm sure I've made my friend Rob a very happy guy tonight."

Ivy threw her arms around his neck, laughing and crying all at once. Blake's embrace held a thousand unspoken promises. Of roots put down, of a shared future nourished by patience, compassion, and unwavering devotion.

The sign represented everything she loved in the handsome man before her—creativity, mindfulness, and an endless capacity for trust.

"But I thought you told me this place was rented," she said.

"It certainly was. While I was in New York, I phoned the owner and presented him with a proposal he simply couldn't resist. The logistics of leasing this storefront and creating the sign has been a few trying days in the works." Blake wrapped an arm around Ivy's shoulders. "I want to live our life together, right here in Evergreen Valley. This is where I belong."

"Then you're staying?"

He nodded. "I'm staying."

Ivy's vision swam, tears gathering on her lashes. After their time apart, his gesture rooted their love firmly in this place, their home.

She turned to him, words escaping her. To create something permanent for their mutual dreams was the most thoughtful gift he could ever give.

"Nature's Palette is the perfect next chapter for us." Her voice was thick with giddy tears.

"Our planet's beauty is fragile. I intend to share my environmental concerns through my photographs." He pulled her closer. "We'll inspire each other."

Ivy looked up at the sign, a future hand-painted just for them.

Later, Ivy and Blake relaxed by the fireplace in Ivy's

home, mugs of hot cider in hand. Cocoa snoozed on Blake's lap.

"To Cocoa," Blake said. "The unexpected Christmas gift who brought us together."

Ivy smiled at the slumbering dog. "Our tiny yuletide matchmaker."

Cocoa blinked awake and snuggled deeper into Blake's lap, tail wagging.

Ivy chuckled. "Someone's getting extra belly rubs tonight!"

"Me?" Blake teased.

"No." She jokingly swatted his arm.

Cocoa rolled over, his little paws kicking in contentment.

Blake pulled Ivy to his chest and kissed her temple. "To imagine that you and I both lived in this same small town all along and never crossed paths."

"You're a couple of years my senior. Our lives might have intersected at some point. Who's to say what destiny had in mind?"

"To destiny," he proclaimed. "And to Cocoa, whose Christmas love story brought two lonely hearts together.

Ivy snuggled into his side. "To Cocoa's Christmas love. Who knew that a chance encounter in an alleyway would change our lives forever?"

Blake grinned, glancing down at the puppy. "If you hadn't found him shivering behind that trash can, I never would've met either of you. My two Christmas angels, bringing light into my lonely world."

Her heart brimmed with gratitude—both for Blake's love, and for the adorable homeless pup who had unexpectedly given them a treasure.

Blake leaned in for a tender kiss. Cocoa turned back on his stomach and dozed, oblivious to his role as the conductor of their holiday romance.

Thanks to one fateful December night, two strangers had found an unexpected gift.

Their own endearing tale of Cocoa's Christmas Love.

THE END

EVERETT'S HOMEMADE DOG-FRIENDLY GINGERBREAD COOKIES

These treats are not only festive but also safe and enjoyable for your furry friend. Here's a simple description of how to make them.

Ingredients:
- 2 cups whole wheat flour
- 1 cup oats
- ½ cup unsweetened applesauce

For the gingerbread flavor, include a pinch of ground cinnamon and a touch of powdered ginger. These spices will give the cookies that classic holiday aroma.

Roll out the dough on a floured surface and use cookie

cutters to create holiday shapes like bones, stars, or Christmas trees. Remember to adjust the size and shape according to your dog's preference and size.

Place them on a baking sheet lined with parchment paper.

Bake the cookies at 350 degrees Fahrenheit, or 175 degrees Celsius, for 20-25 minutes or until they are golden brown and firm. After baking, allow them to cool completely before serving them to your pup.

Your dog will be overjoyed!

A NOTE FROM JOSIE

Dear Reader,

Thank you for reading my sweet holiday romance, *Cocoa's Christmas Love.* I hope you enjoyed this heartwarming story featuring Blake, Ivy, and an adorable puppy named Cocoa.

If you loved this story as much as I loved writing it, please help other people find it by posting your review.

Cocoa's Christmas Love is available in ebook, paperback, Large Print paperback, audiobook, and Hardcover.

I'd love to meet you in person someday, but in the meantime, all I can offer is a sincere and grateful thank you. Without your support, my books would not be possible.

As I write my next sweet or inspirational romance, remember this: Have you ever tried something you were afraid to try because it mattered so much to you? I did, when I started writing. Take the chance, and just do something you love.

With sincere appreciation,
Josie Riviera

Love music?

My Spotify Playlist for Cocoa's Christmas Love is here.

ABOUT THE AUTHOR

Josie Riviera is a *USA TODAY* bestselling author of contemporary, inspirational, and historical sweet romances that read like Hallmark movies. She lives in the Charlotte, NC, area with her wonderfully supportive husband. They share their home with an adorable shih tzu, who constantly needs grooming, and live in an old house forever needing renovations.

To receive my Newsletter and your free sweet romance novella ebook as a thank you gift, sign up HERE.

Become a member of my Read and Review VIP Facebook group for exclusive giveaways and ARCs.

ALSO BY JOSIE RIVIERA

Seeking Patience

Seeking Catherine (always Free!)

Seeking Fortune

Seeking Charity

Seeking Rachel

The Seeking Series

Oh Danny Boy

I Love You More

A Snowy White Christmas

A Portuguese Christmas

Holiday Hearts Book Bundle Volume One

Holiday Hearts Book Bundle Volume Two

Holiday Hearts Book Bundle Volume Three

Holiday Hearts Book Bundle Volume Four

Holiday Hearts Book Bundle Volume Five

Candleglow and Mistletoe

Maeve (Perfect Match)

A Christmas To Cherish

A Love Song To Cherish

A Valentine To Cherish

A Christmas Puppy To Cherish

A Homecoming To Cherish

Romance Stories To Cherish

Aloha to Love

Sweet Peppermint Kisses

Valentine Hearts Boxed Set

1-800-CUPID

1-800-CHRISTMAS

1-800-IRELAND

1-800-SUMMER

1-800-NEW YEAR

The 1-800-Series Sweet Contemporary Romance Bundle

Irish Hearts Sweet Romance Bundle

Holly's Gift

A Chocolate-Box Valentine

A Chocolate-Box Christmas

A Chocolate-Box New Years

A Chocolate-Box Summer Breeze

A Chocolate-Box Christmas Wish

A Chocolate-Box Irish Wedding

Chocolate-Box Hearts

Chocolate-Box Hearts Volume Two

Chocolate-Box Double Hearts

Recipes from the Heart

Leading Hearts

New Year Hearts

SENIOR HEARTS

A Summer To Cherish

Summer Hearts

Romance Stories To Cherish Volume Two

Cherished Hearts

Christmas in the Air

A Very Christian Christmas

The 1-800-Series Volume Two

The 1-800-Series Complete

Christmas Tails of the Heart

Cocoa's Christmas Love

Pawfect Christmas Hearts

Most books are available in ebook, audiobook, paperback, Large Print paperback and Hardcover.

Many are FREE on Kindle Unlimited!